CHRIS BOHJALIAN

•

Water Witches

Chris Bohjalian is the author of twenty-two books, including *The Red Lotus*; *The Guest Room*; *Close Your Eyes, Hold Hands*; *The Sandcastle Girls*; *Skeletons at the Feast*; *The Double Bind*; and *Midwives*, which was a number one *New York Times* bestseller and a selection of Oprah's Book Club. His novels *Secrets of Eden*, *Midwives*, and *Past the Bleachers* were made into movies, and *The Flight Attendant* is now a limited television series on HBO Max starring Kaley Cuoco. His work has been translated into more than thirty languages. He is also a playwright (*Wingspan* and *Midwives*). He lives in Vermont and can be found at www.chrisbohjalian.com or on Facebook, Instagram, Twitter, Litsy, and Goodreads.

NOVELS BY CHRIS BOHJALIAN

The Red Lotus
The Flight Attendant
The Sleepwalker
The Guest Room
Close Your Eyes, Hold Hands
The Light in the Ruins
The Sandcastle Girls
The Night Strangers
Secrets of Eden
Skeletons at the Feast
The Double Bind
Before You Know Kindness
The Buffalo Soldier
Trans-Sister Radio
The Law of Similars
Midwives
Water Witches
Past the Bleachers
Hangman
A Killing in the Real World

ESSAY COLLECTION

Idyll Banter

PLAYS

Midwives
Wingspan

Water Witches

WATER WITCHES

CHRIS BOHJALIAN

Vintage Contemporaries
VINTAGE BOOKS
A DIVISION OF PENGUIN RANDOM HOUSE LLC
NEW YORK

FIRST VINTAGE CONTEMPORARIES EDITION, JUNE 2020

Originally published in hardcover in the United States by University Press of New England, Hanover, New Hampshire, in 1995.

The Cataloging-in-Publication Data is on file at the Library of Congress.

Vintage Contemporaries Trade Paperback ISBN: 978-0-593-08178-5
eBook ISBN: 978-0-593-08179-2

Book design by Mary A. Wirth

www.vintagebooks.com

Printed in the United States of America
10 9 8 7 6 5 4 3 2 1

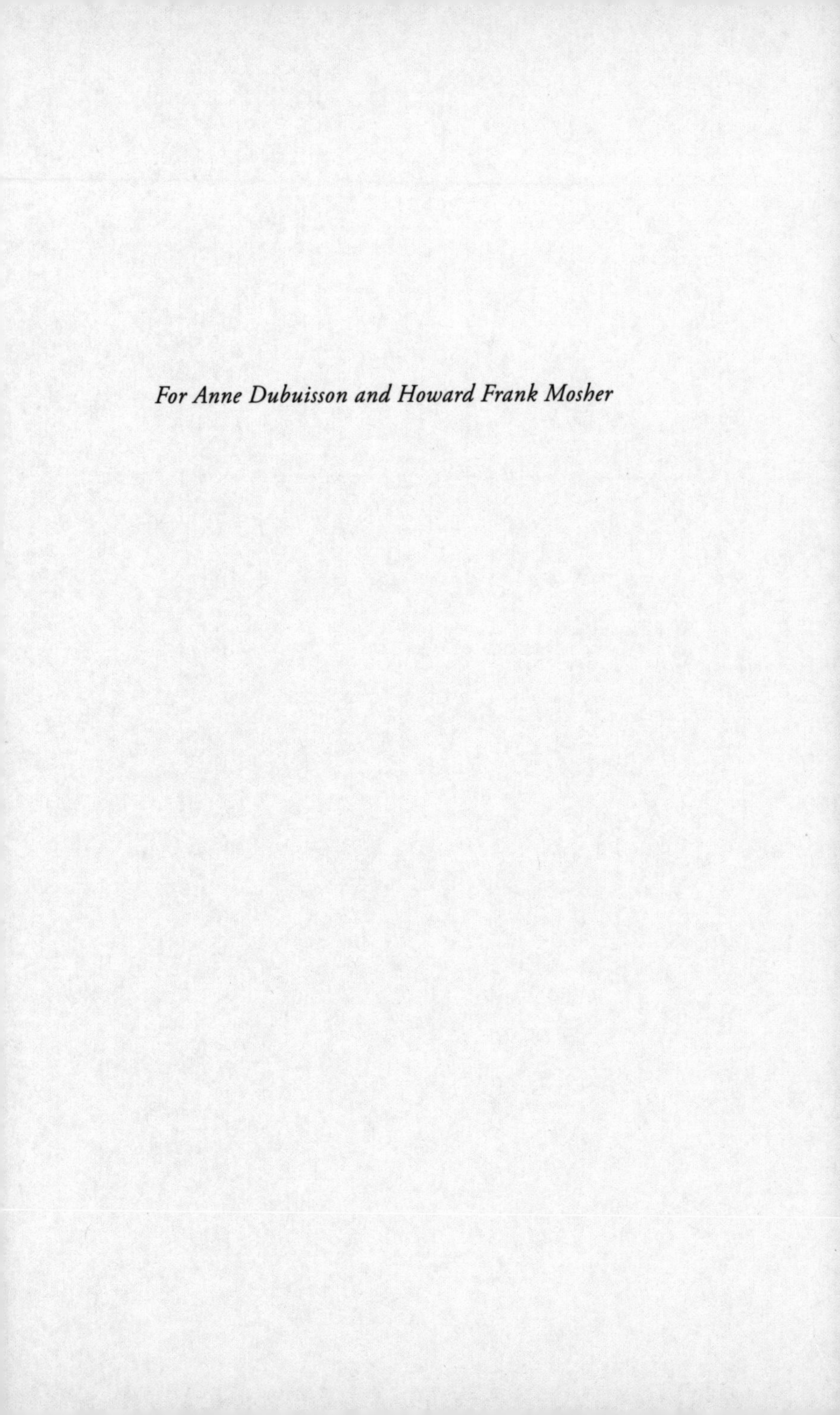

For Anne Dubuisson and Howard Frank Mosher

And Moses lifted up his hand and struck the rock with his rod twice; and water came forth abundantly, and the congregation drank, and their cattle.

—NUMBERS 20:11

Kilimanjaro is a snow-covered mountain 19,710 feet high, and it is said to be the highest mountain in Africa. Its western summit is called the Masai "Ngaje Ngai," the House of God. Close to the western summit there is the dried and frozen carcass of a leopard. No one has explained what the leopard was seeking at that altitude.

—ERNEST HEMINGWAY

ACKNOWLEDGMENTS

I could not have written this book if a great many lawyers, lobbyists, legislators, journalists, meteorologists, naturalists, and (of course) dowsers had not been enormously kind with their knowledge and their time—especially James E. Bressor, environmental policy analyst for Governor Howard Dean of Vermont. I thank you all.

I am also grateful to everyone in the ski industry who explained to me (slowly, patiently, carefully) what it takes to manage a mountain. I thank you too.

Finally, I want to thank Mike Lowenthal, an editor whose ideas are thoughtful and his suggestions precise.

AUTHOR'S NOTE

for the
Twenty-Fifth-Anniversary Edition

When I began writing *Water Witches,* I didn't own a cell phone. I had no idea that a thing called the Internet was about to change everything except, perhaps, how we grill a cheese sandwich. Vermont had daily morning newspapers (note the plural) with dozens of reporters and editors working into the evening at each newsroom. My daughter, Grace Experience, who is now an adult, hadn't been conceived.

And yet when I reread the novel because this twenty-fifth-anniversary edition was in production (thank you, Vintage and Anchor Books!), I was struck by how eerily timely it is. It's not that I am so prescient or insightful, but I was writing about Vermont in a moment when the small state was a microcosm for and an augur of change.

The novel had its origins one day when I read two newspaper articles. The first was a (forgive the pun) rather dry story about a Vermont ski resort's upcoming water-withdrawal permit hearing before a local environmental board—a hearing that clearly was going to be contentious as environmentalists and developers did battle. The second, beneath a photo of a magisterial woman with a magnificent mane of long gray hair, was about the upcoming meeting of the American Society of Dowsers—or "water witches," people who find water using divining rods or pendulums—held annually in Vermont's remote Northeast Kingdom.

Wouldn't the world be a better place if we could simply marry the two articles? I thought glibly to myself.

And the novel, in that moment, was born. On the surface, *Water Witches* is about a ski resort that, in the midst of a cataclysmic drought, wants to savage a mountain's rivers and forests in a massive expansion and the new age dowsers and environmentalists who want to prevent the development. But John Gardner wrote eloquently about how the two points on a compass that matter most in fiction are conflict and human transformation. In *Water Witches,* whether some characters were going to prove capable of transformation was going to be as important to me as the more obvious conflict.

Despite the lack of cell phones, social networks, or Wi-Fi in *Water Witches,* there are two currents in the novel that feel as if they could be memes in today's world. The first is how the novel addresses climate change and global warming in a book that is set in the mid-1990s. Among the sentences that haunted me when I reread the story was the moment when lobbyist Scottie Winston is watching his nine-year-old daughter sob and is unable to comfort her: "It is not solely for Elias that my daughter is crying, these are not tears spilled only for a once-ancient dowser. These are, I believe, tears shed also for trees now gone, for land that is scorched, and for rivers and brooks and streams that are dry. They are tears brought on by the drought, tears from a fear . . . that nature somehow is changing." The references to holes in the ozone, the inexorable rise in Earth's temperature, and the way that the weather and the environment have become dangerous suggest that even when I was writing the novel, these issues were beginning to alarm us.

The second of the themes that struck me as contemporary are the observations from so many of the women about toxic masculinity. Narrator Scottie Winston reveals early on, "Patience told me two things when Laura, my wife, introduced us almost twenty years ago. She told me that as a dowser she is in touch with the earth. And she told me that as a man I have great potential to become grotesque." I'm not sure I have written anything truer.

I love the character of Patience and how she constantly calls out Scottie and his male peers for the myriad ways that men have "unfairly co-opted power from women." When I saw her discussing "the ritualized subjugation of women," I felt her pain and frustration as acutely now as I did when I wrote those words for her.

Water Witches is the earliest of my novels that I allow to remain in print. It was my fourth published novel (and the sixth I had written) and preceded *Midwives* by two years. It is less about dread than everything that would come after, novels such as *The Double Bind*, *The Guest Room,* and *The Flight Attendant.* It was before I had started to write historical fiction, such as *Skeletons at the Feast, The Light in the Ruins,* and *The Sandcastle Girls.*

It was born in a period when all my books were set in Vermont or (in one case) Vermont and New Hampshire. Everything I wrote between 1995 and 2007 was set in northern New England. I think, at the time, I thought that would always be the case.

And *Water Witches* is far and away the closest I have ever come to writing a novel with jokes. I'm not sure I can call it a gently comic novel because the stakes are too high, but I found myself smiling at Scottie Winston's take on his neighbors and the utter absurdity of what he does for a living as a lobbyist for big business, such as it is, in Vermont.

Finally, this is the only book I ever wrote with touches of magical realism. And that, too, made me happy.

I mention happiness here because while my work continued to evolve over the last twenty-five years, rereading this early novel made me smile. It wasn't simply the text; it was those Proustian madeleines of where I was at that point in my life. I remember how much fun I had researching and writing the tale, especially the days I spent with water witches outside and lobbyists inside.

And I remember imagining fatherhood and wondering what it would be like. There is a moment when Scottie is watching his young daughter, Miranda, dancing alone in the family backyard one summer night amid the fireflies, and he thinks to himself, "Miranda is grace." My daughter was at least a year from being born when I wrote that passage, but my wife and I named her Grace when she arrived. And while I hadn't yet discovered first-hand how much I would love being a parent, it's clear even from the text that parenthood would be among the two favorite roles I have gotten to play in this world. (The other is being a husband, a role that Scottie also cherishes.)

Water Witches will always exist for me in that liminal period just before I would become a father and just before the Internet would change the world—and as, quite literally, I was finally understanding how to write a novel. It was a gift for me to rediscover this story.

Happy reading. Fingers crossed my work never disappoints you.

—Chris Bohjalian

Part One

1

•

Some people say that my wife's sister is a witch. My father, for one. My brother, for another. And while I will not dispute their use of the term when they are merely alluding to her somewhat contrary nature, I do take issue with them when they use the word to malign what she believes is her calling.

After all, it is a calling that to a lesser extent my wife hears as well.

No, my sister-in-law is no witch, at least not literally. She, along with my wife and my mother-in-law, is simply a dowser. She is capable of finding underground water with a stick. She is capable of *divining* underground water with a stick. And unlike my wife and my mother-in-law, she is an active dowser. She does not merely have the power, she uses it.

And she uses it profitably. Patience is a well-paid dowser.

On a regular basis Patience finds for people the underground springs that for generations will feed their wells. She finds water. She finds the water for drinking that will flow cold from kitchen taps, and the water for bathing and shaving and splashing that will gush (or trickle) warm from bathroom faucets. She finds the water that will rain down from hoses and sprinkler systems onto a state that is full of back-door gardens, and rich in cornfields and dairy farms. And while water has rarely been the precious commodity here in Vermont that it is in other parts of the world, the difference between finding it twenty yards belowground and two hundred yards belowground is often a matter of feet. Sometimes inches. Drill sixteen feet east of that maple, and you'll find a spring at forty feet; drill a dozen feet south of that same tree, and you'll have to pound your way through eight hundred feet of granite. Vermont granite.

According to her logbook and diary, Patience has now dowsed 1,812 wells, of which about 1,500 were in Vermont. Most of the others were in New England, although my sister-in-law has indeed used maps to find water for clients in Texas, Colorado, and throughout the Southwest.

Moreover, Patience has dowsed in her life for far more than just water. She has been paid handsomely for finding oil, gold, and natural gas. She has found well over a dozen missing children and injured hikers for the Vermont and New Hampshire state police, and thousands upon thousands of dollars' worth of jewelry and money and antiques that had been lost. She has even helped solve crimes as far south as Boston and as far north as Montreal, although to this day the authorities who called her in will deny her involvement. ("But it's me who keeps my participation in those sorts of investigations hush-hush," Patience has told me, "not the police. A dowser like me must always fear reprisals.")

Patience has a track record of professional achievement that spans almost two decades now, and it is only a matter of time before the American Society of Dowsers—seventy-six dedicated chapters and five thousand divining members strong these days—starts a dowsing hall of fame in her honor, or finds a public relations firm to publicize her success.

. . .

PATIENCE TOLD ME two things when Laura, my wife, introduced us almost twenty years ago. She told me that as a dowser she is in touch with the earth. And she told me that as a man I have great potential to become grotesque.

We were sitting in the farmhouse in Landaff in which Patience and Laura grew up, in the kitchen that—like in many farmhouses in Vermont—was the soul and center of the structure. The Avery family did not just cook in that kitchen or eat in that kitchen, they lived in that kitchen, savoring the warmth that came from the woodstove they kept burning eight months of the year. The kitchen table, a pumpkin pine monster longer and wider than a Ping-Pong table, was the desk on which Laura did her homework every school night for twelve years; it was the cutting board on which the girls' mother chopped vegetables, rolled dough, sliced bacon; and when that table wasn't covered with papers of algebra problems or the remnants of a pie crust, it served also as the conference table around which the Avery family would gather whenever there was a decision of any magnitude that had to be made.

And so when Laura brought me home to meet her family the spring of our senior year at college, it was only natural that she would sit me down at the pumpkin pine heart of the Avery homestead.

Laura had warned me about Patience, telling me flat out that Patience would probably try and scare me away for no other reason than the thrill of the hunt, but I was twenty-one and unconvinced (or unaware) of my God-given inability to win this sort of fight. So I asked Patience what she meant about men being grotesque, challenging her, and she asked me in return with a flatness to her voice that in tone alone conveyed oceans of disgust, "Are you stupid or curious?"

Patience has since mellowed, becoming in her own way at

least a tad more pacific. She has even married twice, although neither marriage was able to survive the spring construction season in Vermont, when Patience's services as a dowser are most in demand.

As I have gotten to know Patience (as much by necessity as by choice), I have been able to glean from her only small hints as to why some men become grotesque. But I have learned from her a great deal about dowsing. "Dowsing is a prelinguistic sensory perception," she has explained to me on occasion, "that's all it is." "Dowsing is an incantation of the mind," she has said at other times, "it's a means of accessing our spiritual and visceral links with nature—nothing fancy." Unlike most dowsers who believe that with proper mental conditioning anyone in the world can dowse, Patience insists that only select people have the power. People like her. And while she will acknowledge that many famous dowsers—"master dowsers"—do indeed happen to be male, she insists that most male dowsers are charlatans.

"A man could no sooner find water with a divining rod than he could breastfeed a baby," she has pronounced on occasion—usually an occasion like Thanksgiving or Christmas. "Dowsing is all about fluid, and a woman's life revolves around fluid a hell of a lot more significantly than a man's."

Patience is very fond of great pronouncements, especially if it is Thanksgiving or Christmas, and my family is present.

"After all, no one talks about earth *fathers*, do they?" Patience will often add from her spot at the head of the table, raising an eyebrow.

This belief is, of course, a major philosophical break with the opinion of the American Society of Dowsers: Officially, dowsing is not a gender-specific talent. Consequently, my wife and my mother-in-law, who have attended the annual dowsing convention with Patience many times in the past, say that Patience is uncharacteristically quiet at these annual meetings, and lets her accomplishments speak for her.

• • •

HOW DOES MY sister-in-law know that men have great potential to become grotesque—other, of course, than what we read in the news? Patience has consistently refused to elaborate. But Laura thinks the opinion grew from the same seed that spawned her sister's dogmatic bias that only women can dowse. Laura and Patience come from a family of women.

Or, as my brother says, a coven.

As far as we know, there are no other fathers, sons, uncles, brothers, male cousins, or male pets with the Avery name. At least in this area. The Avery clan today is a clan wholly of women.

I imagine an extended family of women is rare anywhere, but it has always seemed to me especially unlikely in a small Vermont village such as Landaff. Landaff sits on a ridge off the Green Mountains, in a no-man's-land (I use that term figuratively) between the Vermont state capital of Montpelier, and the maple syrup capital of St. Johnsbury. It is the sort of town where everyone is indeed related to everyone, and the town meeting that occurs on the first Tuesday in March is as much a family reunion as it is an exercise in legislative self-determination.

Laura and Patience's father, at least in photographs a lion of a man, lasted the longest of any male who has come in contact with the group in recent memory (except for me). He came to Vermont to marry my mother-in-law forty-plus years ago, and stayed long enough to father Patience one year and Laura three years later. He then died all alone in a hunting accident.

It was a tragedy. He fell on his gun the first day of deer season, when he slipped on wet leaves at the start of a snowstorm. Patience, four years old at the time, used a hickory stick to find the body, buried by then by a good three feet of snow in the gore.

My mother-in-law is the oldest of three sisters, all of whom still live in Landaff. She never remarried, simply—she says—because she never found the right man. And just as Patience gave marriage a shot (two, actually), each of her aunts experimented with what one aunt refers to around me as the ritualized subjugation of women. Between Patience's two ex-husbands, and the three ex-husbands that the aunts have collected, there are five men who at one point married into Landaff's family of women, and have now moved far south, far west, and far north.

It is worth noting that none of these men came from Vermont, including me. They all came from big cities like Philadelphia and Boston and New York, and then, after the marriages went bad, they returned to cities like Atlanta, Vancouver, and San Francisco. Cities chosen because they are far, far from Vermont. Cities chosen, perhaps as well, because to get to them one need never traverse what Steinbeck referred to as "the mother road," Route 66.

No, of all the men who have come in contact with the current crop of Averys, only I have stayed, because only I was fortunate enough to find amid the human maelstrom of Averys a soft and gentle tide pool named Laura. And only we—Laura and I—were fortunate enough to be blessed with a child, a little girl whom we named Miranda.

Part Two

2

•

I sit on the front steps of the courthouse one Tuesday afternoon, my tie loosened and the top button of my shirt undone, and I stare up through closed eyes at the afternoon sun. Even in Montpelier the sun is warm by the end of May, but I have never before felt it this strong this early. It is almost warm enough that if I breathe slowly and deeply and think only about the heat that pours through my eyelids, I know I will soon feel the sun in Key West: the hot tropical sun that burns thousands of miles south of here, a sun of enervation, relaxation, and—for Laura and me, as often as we can get there—a sun of dehydrated slow-motion lust.

"I never trust people who daydream at the courthouse," a voice behind me warns. "Especially lawyers."

I turn away from the sun and look back over my shoulder into the belly of Roger Noonan, an impressive awning that blocks the man's chest and face from this angle and—were Roger standing before me instead of behind me—might block out the sun.

"Rather prejudiced of you, don't you think?" I ask.

Roger sits beside me on the steps, spreading his legs to allow his stomach room to droop, and loosens his own tie as well.

"Yup. But that's me: Prejudiced. Prejudiced, provincial, and completely uninformed. And goddamn proud of it."

"What brings you by the courthouse, Roger? Contesting a speeding ticket? Trying to cut your alimony payments once again?"

Roger smiles. "Clara does okay by me. She has no beef that I know of. No, I'm just here to see you."

Across the street from us, two professors in saris and sandals from the Green Mountain School of Earth Science sit by the curb eating ice cream: carob-coated pops called Peacesicles.

Normally when Roger Noonan says that he wants to talk to me, air raid sirens explode in my brain. The man is convinced that I have secret and profound connections with the state legislature, the judicial system, and big business (such as it is) that exists in Vermont, and that I can be an important source to him on every story that his newspaper prints. Roger is wrong. But he grounds his faith on the fact that over the years I have indeed lobbied for a variety of Vermont's larger corporations, and that as an attorney I have been involved with some relatively visible legal proceedings—always, of course, as the proverbial black hat. I'm usually that fellow on the evening news explaining the need for a fourteen percent rate hike for the local utility.

Today, however, the sun has made me drowsy. It has dulled me just enough that I really don't care what Roger wants to ask.

"Just here to see me, eh? Well, I'm flattered," I answer.

"You want to join me for a bite to eat? No sense in bakin' out here in the sun."

"Sorry." I shrug. "I've already eaten."

He wipes sweat off his forehead with a handkerchief the color of dirty footprints. "Do you think this heat's ever going to break? Lately it's felt more like Mobile, Alabama, than Montpelier, Vermont. I'm sweatin' like a fat man."

"You are a fat man, Roger."

"I'm only makin' a point."

"Sure, I'll join you for lunch," I tell the editor of the illustrious Montpelier daily, the *Sentinel*, as I stand up and stretch. "But I'll stick to iced coffee."

Roger gets to his feet as well. "Well, the coffee will be my treat. I have some questions I want to ask you."

"Imagine that."

"I want to talk a bit about that mountain of yours."

"Far as I know, I don't own any mountain."

"You know what I mean, Scottie. Powder Peak. The ski resort you're representing."

"There's nothing to talk about. There's nothing you don't know, nothing you haven't already published."

"I hear they're about one creditor away from bankruptcy."

"The entire ski industry is about one creditor away from bankruptcy. It didn't snow a whole lot this winter, remember?"

He shakes his head. "It's more than weather. Your boys have snow guns that make Mother Nature look like a weakling."

"I wouldn't undermine Mother Nature around me," I tease Roger. "I have connections, you know."

"I'm serious! Powder Peak makes snow on forty-eight of seventy-one trails. How can you folks blame a bad year on bad weather?"

"No matter how many snow guns you have," I explain, "they don't work if the temperature doesn't remain below freezing."

I follow Roger as we turn onto Elm Street, watching as the back of his shirt grows wet.

• • •

AFTER WORK, I change in my office from gray flannel to gray fleece, and try to find meaning in the world with a divining rod of my own. A Hillerich & Bradsby softball bat, wooden and chipped and old. It is a piece of wood with which I will never find water, although I do now and then find a hole in the infield or a gap in the outfield.

I swing the bat at the high school field that evening, our last practice before the season begins, an old man in a fast-pitch softball league. I really am a dinosaur of sorts, as antiquated as my wooden bat. When I turn forty this fall, I will be able to look back on sixteen seasons in this league, all with the East Barre Quarry Men. Today I am no longer able to turn ground balls to third into singles the way I could fifteen years ago, but I still get my share of base hits.

"Quick bat, Scottie, quick bat!" a fellow not quite eligible for the team yells from a perch by first base. He is not quite eligible for the team because he will not turn twenty-one for another two weeks. But he practices with us, and as soon as June fifteenth—his birthday—is behind him, he will take over first base. He is still wearing the red and blue baseball cap he wore when he pitched the local high school team into the state championship three years ago.

"Wait for your pitch, Scottie, wait for your pitch!" he continues, after I chop a ground ball into the dirt. I look over at the lad and smile. I will never understand why people who barely know me insist on calling me Scottie. Especially people half my age.

But for all of my life I have been Scottie. It seemed appropriate when I was seven, and it will probably seem appropriate again if I reach seventy. But now, somewhere in between, it seems to me odd.

"It'll rain," someone is saying near the backstop behind me. "There's a front in Chicago movin' this way. It'll be raining this time tomorrow," he says confidently.

The infield tonight is as hard as asphalt, and the grass is as brown as tobacco. Ground balls skid over the dirt like bullets, setting off small firecracker puffs of smoke wherever they skim the earth.

When I leave the batter's box, I start toward the pile of gloves in which mine is now resting. And then I stop. For a long moment I stare at the small drops of condensation that run slowly down the plastic water jug that sits on the bench, and I realize just how thirsty I have become.

. . .

WHEN I GET home that night, a little past seven thirty, Miranda is in the kitchen with Laura. The pair are hunched over the kitchen table, mother helping daughter with her fourth-grade geography. Spread out on the table between them is a colorful map of South America.

I leave my sneakers by the coatrack just inside the front door, and toss my glove and baseball bat in the hall closet. After I kiss Miranda on the forehead and Laura on the lips, my daughter says to me, "I'll bet you don't know the capital of Paraguay!"

I think for a moment. She's correct, I haven't a clue. "I'll bet you're right."

"Asunción," she tells me. "What about Uruguay?"

"Nope. No idea."

"Daddy! It's Montevideo!" she says, folding her arms across her chest. "Do you know any of the capitals?"

"In South America?"

"Uh-huh."

I think for a moment. "I know a few."

"Name one."

Behind her, Laura is smiling. She is clearly relieved that I have replaced her in the hot seat. "I know the capital of Argentina. Buenos Aires."

"That's an easy one," Miranda says.

"Hey, I named one."

"Mom at least knew Quito," she mumbles in disgust, standing up and folding the map in half. "I'm never going to need to know this stuff after tomorrow's quiz, am I?"

The question is not directed at Laura or me specifically, but Laura answers quickly, "That all depends, sweetheart. It all depends upon what you want to be when you grow up. It all depends upon what you want to do."

Miranda places the map in her notebook, and starts toward her room. "Well, unless I want to be a teacher and torture nine-year-olds with the capitals of South America, I probably won't need it."

She stops by the hall closet, and pauses for a moment in thought. "Daddy, did you put your bat in there?"

"Sure did."

She rolls her eyes in frustration. "I've told you, you can't put it there if you ever want to get any hits! There are noxious rays under there!" she says, pronouncing the word *noxious* exactly the way her aunt Patience has taught her, stretching out the *N* into one long, almost independent word. She then opens the door, reaches inside for the bat, and leans it beside the coatrack nearby.

3

Once, when Patience was Miranda's age, a fellow moved to Landaff from Concord, New Hampshire, and took over the small farm three and a half miles up the road from the Averys. The farm received water from a well atop the foothill behind the silo, with gravity feeds descending into the barn as well as the house. The well was sourced from a spring about fifteen feet belowground, and pumped a good five gallons of water per minute—enough to support a family, a couple of horses, and at least a half-dozen dairy cows.

Unfortunately, the Concord farmer wanted more than a half-dozen dairy cows. He believed he had the land to manage ten times that number.

Consequently, he retained an engineer from Boston to help him determine where he should dig a second well, one that might be able to offer ten-plus gallons per minute. The engineer surveyed the land, and concluded that if the farmer dug a second well at the base of the foothill, he would only have to tunnel somewhere around five hundred feet belowground before he found a spring with the kind of power he needed. At that time, most well companies charged about six dollars per drilled foot, meaning—the engineer said—it would only cost the farmer a little over three thousand dollars to dig his new well. *Only.*

The farmer groaned, paid the engineer his fee, and then added the three thousand dollars to the figure he had told the bank he would need to start his dairy farm. The loan officer, a local boy from Landaff, listened calmly when the farmer said he planned on digging a good five hundred feet underground, and then shook his head. In and of itself, the officer said, another three thousand dollars wouldn't kill the deal. But three thousand dollars for a five-hundred-foot well might. That seemed a mite excessive, and showed pretty piss-poor judgment. He told the fellow that before he did another thing, he should call up Mrs. Anna Avery, and ask her if she would mind bringing her nine-year-old daughter Patience by the farm.

Patience, the banker said, could probably find a spring a hell of a lot closer to the surface than five hundred feet belowground.

The farmer was skeptical, but he also was desperate. He wanted his money. So passersby the next day could see from the road a little girl with dark eyes and deep brown hair that hung to her waist, holding a Y rod in her hands. The child was walking from the spot the engineer had marked, across the yard to the house. About halfway to the house she stopped, nodded at the farmer and at her mother beside him, and then said simply, "Here."

The farmer brought in a backhoe, and they began to dig. They stopped at exactly twelve feet. By nightfall, the twelve-foot hole was filled with six feet of water. And the farmer had a spring that could pump six hundred gallons an hour.

. . .

WHEN I COME home from work Wednesday night, the yard smells of verbena—soft and sweet and just a bit like talcum powder. The Scutter twins, two of Laura's pieceworkers, are still hard at work in the shed, rolling the beeswax candles that my wife wants to ship the day after tomorrow. I park the truck by the barn and wander over to the pair, hunched over the long cafeteria table Laura purchased from the elementary school last fall.

"Evening, Gertrude. Evening, Jeanette." I have no idea which older woman is which and direct my greetings at the thin air between them.

"You got no business bein' out here 'n those noice shoes," the woman on the left says, chastening me, as she places a wick in a thin strip of beeswax.

"Shoes aren't much good if you can't walk from your truck to your shed in them," I answer.

"Then those ones ain't worth old pudding!" her sister says, looking up at me and squinting. The sun is over my shoulder, just about to fall behind Camel's Hump for the night. When the woman squints, the thousands of lines on her face crack like dried mud, moving away from her eyes like the ribs of a fan. The Vermont climate has never been particularly kind to a person's skin, and the sixty-five-plus winters the Scutter twins have spent before their family woodstove have finished the job the state's natural cold and wind started: Their skin might be parchment—withered and shriveled and mummified. What is most astounding to me about the Scutter twins, however, is the fact that as they have aged, they have somehow remained identical. All of the changes that nature has wrought on the pair, it has wrought with an exact and indistinguishable care.

"You two are working late," I tell the sister on my right, trying to change the subject from my shoes.

The sister smiles. "Your wife may be pretty, but she's tough."

. . .

"YOU KEPT THE Scutters here pretty late tonight," I tell Laura, as I dump the pasta into the colander in the sink, watching the water rush through the drain like a whirlpool.

Beside me Laura is grating Parmesan cheese, the block disappearing bit by bit between her long, soft fingers. "Oh, they wanted to stay. They're afraid the spring that feeds their well is going to dry up, so they're trying to earn some extra money to drill a new well someplace else."

"I can't believe they have anything to worry about. The Scutters have been on that land longer than Vermont has been a state."

"Well, Jeanette's worried."

"I didn't hear the weather on the way home. Isn't it supposed to rain tomorrow?"

"It was. But it looks like that front will end up going south of us. Some towns down around Bennington and the Massachusetts border might get some rain. But that's about it."

She tosses the fettuccine noodles back into the pot.

"Who's the order for?" I ask, referring to the candles the Scutters were producing.

"Some lingerie stores in California and the Southwest. A chain. I don't know much about the stores, but the company looked fine on the credit check. Seventeen shops, mostly in Los Angeles and San Diego."

"How did they hear about you?"

"The gift show in New York last February. They came by the booth, and liked the line. They said they remembered the name of the company," she adds, punching me lightly in the ribs because I have always teased her about the name. The Divine Lights of Vermont. It has always sounded too spiritual to me, too much like a new age religion.

"They would," I tell her. "They're from Southern California."

In the bedroom above us I hear Miranda rearranging her

furniture, pushing her bed or her nightstand or her toy chest a few feet to the right or the left. Miranda rearranges her furniture fairly often, usually in response to evil emanations from the earth. Sometimes she uses a pair of her angle rods to disperse the emanations, but sometimes she decides it's easier to push her bed eighteen inches further from (or closer to) the window.

Often, I've noticed, she determines there are evil emanations rising up through the earth on the nights before or after a school quiz.

"How did Miranda do on her geography test?" I ask.

"She thinks she did fine. Which means she probably got a hundred."

I nod, and smile with pride. Miranda has not just been blessed with her mother's beauty—with goldenrod hair and bewitching blue eyes—she has as well her mother's brains.

. . .

SOME SAY SENATOR Reedy McClure is an environmentalist. I think he just likes to see dead birds. Reedy is one of the two state senators from our county, a native—like the Avery clan—of the town of Landaff. When the Vermont legislature is not in session, from May through December, he will often volunteer his time to travel around the world to the site of the latest, greatest, most ecologically devastating oil spill he can find (usually there are a half-dozen spills from which he can choose, a half-dozen bodies of water he can see in despair). And then he goes there at his own expense to scrub rocks and birds and plants. In his forty-two years, he has cleaned crude oil off sea otters, cormorants, penguins, a baby walrus, dozens of seals, and perhaps hundreds and hundreds of seagulls. With his brushes and lotions and cleansers, he has visited the Persian Gulf, the Gulf of Mexico, California and Baja California, Alaska and Alabama and the coasts of Venezuela.

He has photographs of almost every animal he has saved.

And when Reedy is home in Vermont, he spends his nights sleeping with my sister-in-law Patience, and his days tormenting me. He has told me many times in the hallways of the capitol building and as we have ridden the chairlifts together at Powder Peak's mountains, that he and Patience really have only one thing in common: the rich, enveloping happiness they receive from seeing me squirm. But they have dated for close to four years now, since about the time that Miranda started school. They keep separate houses, but it is commonly understood around town that most nights they are in one bed.

Most of the legislature believes that Reedy and I dislike each other, but nothing could be further from the truth. We actually like each other a good deal. And we respect each other. If Laura and I had stronger stomachs, perhaps, or the kind of money that lurks in Reedy's family trust funds, it is possible that we would follow him on his periodic trips into the environmental nightmares in which he revels.

The fact is, I like to ski with Reedy, I like to drink with Reedy, I like simply to sit and talk with Reedy. Perhaps the one issue on which we fundamentally cannot agree is his choice in women. But I too view myself as an environmentalist, I too am a democrat with a large and a small *d*. The difference between Reedy and me is one of degrees: I am a reasonable man and Reedy McClure is a fanatic.

As a result of these degrees, however, Reedy and I will almost always wind up on the opposite sides of Vermont's more public debates. In the last year alone, we have fought over the construction of new condominiums near the Powder Peak Ski Resort; the expansion of a computer company in Burlington; and the addition to a small factory in St. Albans that makes colorful little statues of the Virgin Mary. I am confident that if Reedy and I were to look back over the last five or six years' worth of legislation, the last five or six years' worth of state changes, we would find that each of us has won about equally often.

Moreover, when—as Laura's mother would say—the sap is finally boiled down to something like syrup, most people would probably see that I am not the ogre of expansion as I am sometimes portrayed, and Reedy is not the mindless but dangerous tree hugger my clients have feared.

When I arrive at my office Thursday morning, Reedy is already waiting for me on the couch in the small reception room that looks out over the capitol building parking lot. He is reading the business section (business page, actually) of the *Montpelier Sentinel*, his mass of curly brown hair still wild with sleep. Our firm has a temporary receptionist this week, a young woman named Peg who happens to be the daughter of one of my two partners, Duane Hurley, and she is eyeing Reedy suspiciously. It may be that she knows who Reedy is, and fears an enemy infiltration of sorts; or it may simply be the dirt that Reedy has left on the new carpet, perfect brown footprints that match the soles of his hiking boots.

He stands to face me, frowning, and directs my attention to a story in Roger Noonan's newspaper.

"This is a joke, right?" he asks, referring to something on the business page.

"The *Sentinel*? Well, yes. But I wouldn't tell Roger that."

"I don't mean the newspaper!"

I take the paper from Reedy and skim one of the top articles, a continuation from the main section's front page. As I had expected, someone in the state's Agency of Natural Resources told the newspaper about the permits Powder Peak officially requested yesterday morning.

"Want to go into my office?" I suggest.

"I would rather drown on sick animal vomit. But since I want to hear how in the name of God you think you're going to pull this off, I'd love to."

"Coffee?"

"That would be great. You want some?"

I nod that I do. Peg starts to stand to get us our coffee, but Reedy motions for her to sit down. "You, relax," he says, smiling. "I know where it is."

. . .

REEDY STRETCHES HIS legs on the rug in my office to torment me. My carpet is clean, his shoes aren't, and he understands me well enough to know that the footprints he leaves will annoy me until I break down and vacuum them up myself.

"It's a simple equation," I hear myself saying, my voice friendly and calm. "We can't compete with the West if we don't have snow. And we can't have snow these days unless we make it. And we can't make snow without water."

"You already make snow on fifty trails!"

"Forty-eight."

He snorts. "So how big is the expansion? Really?"

I sip the last of my coffee, watching the sunlight from the window reflect off the bottom of my mug. "It's not all that big," I tell him, unsure whether I have said this sarcastically or in a halfhearted attempt to downplay the project. It was probably a little of both. "Fifteen million dollars. The plan is to add snow-making to the existing trails on the southwest side of Mount Republic, construct a few new trails there, and then add some connecting paths between Republic and Moosehead. That's it, essentially."

"Connecting paths . . ." he says, raising an eyebrow doubtfully. It is one thing for a ski resort to clear a small path to link existing ski trails; it is another thing to mow down enough trees between the top and the bottom of a mountain to create a whole new trail.

"Yup. Connecting paths."

"Wide enough, maybe, to be considered ski trails?"

"Perhaps a couple."

"How many new condos?"

"Zero."

"Are the plans drawn up yet?"

"Sure are."

"Can I see them?"

"Sure can. Just go by the Agency of Natural Resources. They're a matter of public record now."

"Oh, for God's sake, Scottie, you must have a set right here in your office."

"Of course I do. We're professionals here. We make copies of everything."

"You won't save me the trouble of getting a set myself?"

"Nope. I tend to think Powder Peak might frown a bit if you were to get your copies of the plans right here. Don't you agree?"

He shuffles his feet on the carpet, leaving a brown skid on the rug the length of his shin. "So how many trails will get snow?"

"Probably another eleven," I tell him.

"And of course you're going to need more power."

"Of course."

"How many poles?"

"Enough to power the snow guns. And the new lift on Moosehead."

"You son of a bitch, you're putting in a new lift?"

"You're going to love it. It's a high-speed gondola that will get you and me to the top of the mountain faster than you ever thought possible. Ten-passenger cars, twelve hundred feet per minute. Reedy, you won't have time on the ride to take off your goggles."

He shakes his head, furious. Evidently, the newspaper reporter had either missed the detail about the new gondola or failed to report it in the story. "Patience is right. You really can be an asshole."

"Patience never calls me an asshole, Reedy, you know that. She calls me a prick. In her eyes, that's much, much worse."

"I just can't believe you waited until the legislature had recessed to put in your permits."

"Gee, we tried to get them in last month. We tried so hard . . ."

"I'll bet. Where do you plan on getting the water to make your snow?"

"The Chittenden River."

"You can't do that, Scottie, that's a wildlife habitat."

"Only in West Gardner and East Montpelier. Not in Bartlett."

"You want to tell me how the mountain is going to get fifteen million dollars to pay for all of this? You told Roger just the other day that Powder Peak was on the verge of bankruptcy."

"No, I don't think I did. I think I told Roger that the entire ski industry was on the verge of bankruptcy. There's a difference."

"I hope you don't plan on pulling all of this off for this season."

"No, of course not. Only the gondola. The plan is to open the gondola in time for Christmas this year, and the new trails and new snowmaking system next year."

He shakes his head. "New snowmaking system. Have any of your fat cat friends from down country looked at the Chittenden River lately?"

"Yup."

"Any of them comment on the fact it's about twenty percent below normal for this time of year?"

"Yup."

"And they think they're going to get away with draining it to make snow?"

"No one's going to drain the Chittenden River, Reedy. You know that as well as I do."

"Damn right I do," he says, sitting forward in his chair and leaning across my desk. "Because I'm going to stop them."

4

Patience was eleven years old when the governor's son and his best friend disappeared. It was early March, when the weather in Vermont can be both unpredictable and unforgiving: The temperature might climb into the forties one day, and then plunge to near zero the next. Snowstorms and squalls will appear out of nowhere, abruptly blocking out the sun and the sky, and dropping more snow on the ground in an hour than the ski industry's snow guns can make in a night.

The governor's son was an excellent recreational pilot, and he and a friend were flying from Montpelier to Plattsburgh, a small upstate city on the New York side of Lake Champlain. Both men were in their early thirties, and both worked for Vermont: The governor's son was a sergeant in the state police, and his friend was the Washington County state attorney.

When the pair left the ground in Montpelier one Saturday, the skies were partly cloudy, but visibility was excellent. The governor's son's single-engine Piper climbed quickly to four thousand feet, veered northwest, and then continued upward through five and then six thousand feet. At six thousand feet they hit turbulence, and the pilot asked air traffic control for permission to climb through a cloud to eight thousand feet. Air traffic control said fine.

As the plane powered through the cloud, the wings iced up. Almost instantly, the wings, the propeller, and the cabin were completely covered with ice. It happened within seconds, the sort of abrupt and dangerous dousing for which Vermont squalls are well known and rightly feared.

The pilot immediately asked for permission to fly to ten thousand feet, but by then it was too late. The pilot saw the plane's automatic free-fall gear drop, and the plane lost all thrust and lift. Air traffic control asked the governor's son if he wanted to turn back to Montpelier, or whether he wanted to try and coax the aircraft to Burlington. He never bothered to answer. The air speed indicator had dropped to zero, the controls were mush, and the plane was falling at a rate of five thousand feet per minute.

It crashed somewhere near Mount Ira Allen, but no one was quite sure where. The Vermont Civil Air Patrol flew over the mountain until dark Saturday afternoon, and at one point there were six planes in the air, circling the mountaintop like osprey, and terrifying the skiers on Spruce Peak. But they never saw any sign of the crash. The search was scheduled to resume at sunrise Sunday morning, but overnight a cold front moved in, and with it a layer of thick clouds at about two thousand feet. Air reconnaissance was impossible.

The families of the two men were desperate. In addition to clouds, the cold front had brought with it temperatures well below freezing, and a very good chance of snow. Especially at the higher elevations. No one was exactly sure what either man was wearing when they took off, but the pilot's wife was fairly confident that the jackets they wore were no heavier than windbreakers. After all, it was forty-five degrees when they left Montpelier, and they had planned to return to Vermont that night.

Even if the pair had managed to survive the crash, if they weren't found soon they would probably die of exposure.

The governor had never met Patience Avery of Landaff, but he had heard stories about her prowess. The little girl dowser. The little girl who could not just find water, she could determine its depth; she could tell you whether it was potable or poisonous, whether it was from a spring that could be diverted. The little girl who had tracked down her own father, dead, one fall, but who had also found a small boy, alive, one spring.

He wondered aloud to his press secretary whether it was possible the little girl could find for them his son and his friend.

The press secretary shrugged, but said that he knew the little girl's mother, Anna, from high school. He said he would be happy to call her.

The governor knew little about the art of dowsing itself, but by then it was almost noon on Sunday morning, and the planes were still grounded. The search parties on foot were moving over the mountain very, very slowly. And the front wasn't due to break for at least another day. At least. Moreover, the weather service had upgraded the chance of snow from fifty percent to seventy-five percent, and thought that it might start well before sunset. And so the governor told his press secretary to call Anna Avery of Landaff, and ask her if her daughter could . . . if her daughter would help them.

The press secretary thought Anna sounded reluctant when he first spoke to her, and attributed that hesitation to money. He hadn't thought to offer any, and he decided he should have.

He was wrong. Money wasn't the problem at all. Anna Avery wasn't the type to charge for her services, or those of her daughter. She and her daughter—dear God, especially her daughter—had a rare and special gift, and it was a gift they were meant to share, not sell.

No, Anna's hesitation stemmed from the simple fact that it was twenty-five degrees outside, it looked like it might snow, and the last thing she wanted was her eleven-year-old daughter running around Mount Ira Allen in a blizzard.

Patience and Laura were with their mother when the governor's press secretary called. Patience had heard about the plane crash on the public radio news that morning, so she understood exactly what the press secretary wanted. He wanted her. He wanted her to find the people who had crashed somewhere near Mount Ira Allen.

"I'm sorry," Patience heard her mother saying, "I don't want my daughter up on that mountain today, not with a storm coming in. She's only eleven years old!"

Patience climbed out of her chair and went to her mother. She tugged on the sleeve of her mother's blouse, and insisted, "I can do it."

Anna Avery put her hand over the mouthpiece of the telephone, and said quietly, "I know you can, sweetheart. But I don't want you to climb—"

"No," Patience continued, shaking her head, "I can do it from here."

Anna continued to hold her hand over the mouthpiece, trying to digest her daughter's confidence. She realized she was experiencing something very much like skepticism, and tried to push the thought from her mind. She of all people shouldn't be skeptical, she of all people mustn't doubt her daughter. She herself was a dowser.

The press secretary continued to plead with Anna Avery, and from the governor's office in the capital he thought he was wearing her down. He thought by her silence that she was about to give in, and any minute he would be offering to send a police cruiser to Landaff to pick the girl up. He was truly shocked when Anna finally interrupted him, saying, "Why don't you send someone up here with some maps of the mountain? Good, up-to-date maps of the terrain up there?"

The press secretary was unfamiliar with map dowsing, and couldn't figure out why in the name of God the woman wanted "good, up-to-date maps." He tried to recall what the woman had been like in high school, whether there was anything about her that had struck him at the time as patently insane, but he could not remember anything specific.

He could certainly not remember the woman having any interest in voodoo, witchcraft, or the supernatural. He started to remind her how little time there was, but she cut him off, and explained to him patiently how Patience might be of service.

The press secretary listened. Perhaps it was because he feared time was running out; perhaps it was because Anna Avery was always extremely eloquent when it came to dowsing; and perhaps it was because he believed that once the cruiser arrived in Landaff, common sense would prevail and the mother would bundle her daughter up and pile her into the car with the state police; but the press secretary listened to Anna Avery, and when he got off the phone with her, he sent a pair of troopers to Landaff with the latest topographic maps of Mount Ira Allen.

While the officers and Anna and young Laura Avery watched, eleven-year-old Patience unfolded the maps on the kitchen table, and knelt over them on a chair. She held in her hand a thin metal chain, the sort that is used often to hold keys. Dangling from one end of the chain was a shard of blue glass—thick, opaque, and filed to a smooth finish. It was shaped roughly like a long and flat triangle, although no two sides were the same length.

She grasped the chain between her thumb and forefinger, draping the end without the weight over her wrist and the back of her hand, and dangled the small glass dagger over the maps spread out before her. She rested her elbow on an edge of the table for stability, so her arm became a fulcrum, and then mouthed to herself a variety of questions, some of which her audience could read from her lips. Did the plane crash here? Or here? Was it higher? Higher? Higher?

The glass pendulum swung fore and aft in her hand, sometimes rolling clockwise, sometimes counterclockwise, sometimes following the wavy red ripples that comprised Mount Ira Allen. She passed numbers reading 2100, 2600, 3300, and skirted ponds with names like Goshen and Vengeance and Peacham. The little girl dowser periodically raised and lowered her arm, occasionally moving her elbow around the edge of the table.

And over her shoulder, the state troopers would glance up periodically at the clock on the shelf by the door.

Abruptly she looked up at the two men, and pushed her index finger into the map. "They're right here," she said, resting her pendulum beside the spot. "They're right beside their airplane."

"They couldn't be there," one of the troopers said reflexively, looking at the map. "That's the west side of the mountain." Given the plane's speed of descent, the Civil Air Patrol had focused their search on the eastern side of the mountain. It didn't seem possible that the governor's son could have brought the plane over the top of Mount Ira Allen.

"I'm telling you, they're right here," she said, her voice growing petulant. She turned her head to read the words and numbers by her finger: The elevation was 3,800 feet, not far from the summit, and the pair were just off of something called Deer Leap, a hiking trail open only in the summer.

Anna Avery stood by her daughter, and told the troopers that Patience was correct. They had to have faith, they had to look for the pair beside Deer Leap. At this point, what could they lose? Reluctantly, the troopers radioed the information to the state police barracks in Montpelier, and to the Civil Air Patrol. A search party was dispatched to the area, but principally to appease the families of the two victims. No official in the state capital held out any serious hope that the plane would be where the little girl from Landaff claimed that it was. If she had picked a spot on the eastern side of the mountain, maybe . . .

The governor's son and his friend were found just before sunset, when the first heavy flakes of snow were beginning to fall upon Deer Leap. Although the governor's son had a broken ankle and his friend had what would prove to be second- and third-degree burns over much of his upper body, both men had survived the crash. They were cold, they were miserable, they were hungry. But they were very much alive.

And they were exactly where Patience Avery had said they would be.

• • •

IN SHAPE, IN size, in sheer accessibility, there may be no more perfect mountain in this world than Mount Republic. It is not tall, although it is one of the higher mountains in Vermont, but its slopes rise to the sky on all sides with a symmetry that is astonishing. Its mold was a giant teacup, pressed firmly into the molten mud that was once this planet, and then removed when the mud had cooled and the mountain was made. Its shape has allowed trees to grow along its sides in lush tiered rows that in the fall look like the bright red and yellow stripes of a rainbow. In the winter, when the mountain is white, it becomes albino white, a white more ghostly and sublime than the chain of towers to the east that have commandeered that word for their name. Its summit is almost flat. Its peak is one grown man taller than four thousand feet. It is the highest of the cluster of mountains that comprise the Powder Peak Ski Resort.

On a magnificent summer day like today, I still get a little boy's pleasure from riding the chairlift, even if the purpose of the ride—like today—is all business. We need to get to the top of the mountain.

Riding the chairlift now is very different from riding it in the winter. In the winter, the chairlift seems clunky, slow, and—despite its eerie quiet—almost primitive. But it is the pace that is most frustrating, especially to a skier, whose body has been conditioned that morning or afternoon to moving rapidly down hills. Not at a snail's pace up them. Besides, time is money at a ski resort, and the more time one spends on the chairlift, the less time one spends actually skiing.

In the summer, however, the chairlift's leisurely pace is a delight, a Ferris wheel that seems to go up forever. The slopes that comprise Mount Republic spread out below the lift in luxuriant green blankets, and in the stillness that overtakes the resort this time of year, one can hear the sound of the Chittenden and Deering Rivers as they rush through the valleys at the base of the mountain. At the top of the lift—at the top of virtually every lift in the Powder Peak network—are views of the Green Mountains to the north and south that cause even the most jaded tourist and neon-clad skier to sigh. In early May and October, the top of Mount Mansfield—a mountain sharper, higher, and colder than Republic—is often capped by a white halo, a reminder in the spring of what is behind us, and a reminder in autumn of what is ahead.

There isn't a cloud in the sky Friday afternoon, but there's just enough wind to buffer the worst heat from the sun. The group of us riding the chairlift today, surveyors and engineers and the senior executives from Powder Peak, ride the Mount Republic lift largely in silence, savoring the sun after winter.

Beside me on the lift is Goddard Healy, president of Schuss Limited, the corporation that owns Powder Peak in the East, and two ski resorts in the West: one in Northern California and one in British Columbia. Healy flew in from the Schuss offices in San Francisco yesterday to see firsthand the Powder Peak expansion plans he has studied on paper for weeks.

"Know anyone who's ever seen a catamount around here?" he asks me out of the blue as we approach the summit and prepare to jump off the lift.

"No. I doubt anyone's seen a catamount in Vermont in fifty years. At least with a camera," I tell him. And then, correcting myself, I add, "I doubt anyone has been able to prove they've seen a catamount in fifty years. A couple people claim to see one every year."

Healy must be twenty years older than me, but I can see by the size of his arms and his chest that he could probably wrestle one of those wildcats to the ground if he had to. He was a member of the Canadian Olympic Ski Team thirty-five, maybe forty years ago, and finished as high as fifth one year. He has always struck me as the sort of manager capable of inspiring great loyalty from the people who work for him, and tremendous disgust from his opponents. People such as Reedy McClure. Reedy contends that Healy would cut down half the national forest in Vermont if he could, drive whatever animals remain into zoos, and build ski resorts and golf courses and vacation homes.

Reedy is wrong. Goddard Healy hates golf.

I don't particularly like Healy, but I don't mind working for the people who work for him. There are sufficient roadblocks and restrictions in Vermont's development laws to prevent a developer like Healy from turning the state into Ski World.

"Actually, it was more like a hundred years," Healy says. "Not fifty. No one has been able to photograph a catamount in these parts since the end of the last century. There was an article about them in a local magazine I saw at the hotel last night. Prettiest cat I've ever seen. How much do you suppose they weigh?"

The fellow running the lift at the top of the mountain slows it to a crawl so Goddard and I can hop out of our seats and rush to the side, ducking the chairs right behind us.

"I'm not going to answer that question, Goddard," I say, when we're safely off to the side. "That article probably told you exactly how much a catamount is supposed to weigh."

He smiles. "About seventy-five to a hundred pounds. But it's a mean hundred pounds, Scottie."

Behind us the rest of the group jumps off the lift in pairs, until there are eight of us assembled at the top of the mountain. It's an odd group. Goddard and I and Ian Rawls, the managing director of Powder Peak, are wearing neckties and blazers, while the rest of the group are clad in blue jeans and sport shirts. These are the engineers and builders who will drop pylons from helicopters for the new high-speed gondola this fall, and then sweep clear wide swaths of evergreens next spring.

"The primary trail will run about two and a quarter miles from this spot," Ian Rawls tells Goddard, wiping a strand of blond hair from his forehead, and then pointing down toward the base lodge. "Right now, it will be intermediate to advanced. A few moguls."

One of the engineers, Gertrude and Jeanette Scutter's nephew, unrolls a geographic footprint of this side of the mountain, indicating with a series of dots and dashes where the proposed trails will be. The dots and dashes cut through some of the thickest forests that remain on the mountain. Healy glances briefly at the map, and then walks toward the top of one of Powder Peak's most popular trails, a wide and gentle descent that goes on for three miles. I wander beside him, and watch as he stares pensively into the valley.

"You got yourself a pretty mountain here, Scottie. It's not like the towers in the West that'll sometimes take my breath away. But it's a pretty place to be. Calming."

"These days, it's even quieter than usual."

"How so?"

I put my finger to my lips. "Listen carefully."

Together we stand at the top of the mountain, ignoring the occasional snippets of conversation that drift our way from the small group still standing back by the top of the chairlift.

"Hear anything?" I ask.

"Nope. Just the wind."

"Right. See where the trail cuts to the left," I begin, pointing at the first curve. "Straight past that turn, about a hundred yards below it, there's a pretty good-sized tributary to the Chittenden River. Normally you can hear it on the top of the mountain."

"Why can't we hear it right now?"

"Might be as simple as a beaver dam. Might be the fact that all the rivers and streams around here are well below where they should be this time of year. At the base of the mountain, the Chittenden's running about twenty percent below normal, and the water flow's way down."

"The drought?"

"The drought now. The lack of snow this winter."

Healy thinks for a moment. "What are you suggesting, Scottie? A drought is a short-term problem. The sort of thing that comes, brings a little inconvenience, and then goes. I certainly don't see it interfering with long-range expansion plans."

"Maybe not. But the water in the Chittenden is the water you need to make snow here. It's possible the water flow could fall far enough this summer that you won't receive the permits to tap it for quite some time."

"The Chittenden River is not going to dry up."

"Doesn't have to. There are trout in the Chittenden, which means we can't touch it if the water flow falls below a certain speed. You should also know that there's a little pond back there. About a half mile off the trail. Come every spring, a fair number of bears come out of hibernation and spend their summer there."

"And you're about to tell me that the pond is part of the proposed water system."

"I had planned to, yes."

Healy sighs, and rubs his eyes in frustration. "Shit."

"I must confess, Goddard, I'm thrilled with this new environmental sensitivity of yours. But clearly there's something behind it. This just isn't you."

He reaches into the breast pocket of his blazer, and removes his wallet. He flips it open to a small plastic sleeve in which there is a photograph of a young woman half his age, with raven's black hair and misty green eyes.

"Her name is Tanya. I met her in British Columbia."

I bite my tongue and try not to laugh. "Environmental Defense Fund?"

"Greenpeace."

"Well. Guess that explains it . . ."

"Nope. Best piece of ass I've ever had. *That* explains it."

. . .

ARCHER MOODY STANDS up at church Sunday morning, a thin man in his thirties with great bags under his eyes. Sitting in the pew beside him is his wife, Sally, and their little boys, one about six and one about seven. All eyes in the congregation turn toward him, wondering what this normally reticent, shy farmer is going to share with us. It can't possibly be good news: Nothing good ever happens to the Moodys.

"It's gotta be cancer," Gertrude Scutter whispers to Laura, turning around in her pew to face us. "Moodys all get it, you know."

Archer coughs once, nervously, before speaking, and then asks the congregation to pray for rain. "First cutting is still weeks away," he explains, referring to the hay in his southern fields. "And at this pace, we might not get a second. And I'm worried about the corn. We all are. So please ask the Lord for a couple days of good, gentle rain."

Amid the chorus of amens from the farmers scattered throughout the church, I can overhear Jeanette Scutter tell her sister, Gertrude, "Idiot. Man's an idiot. You ever hear of a bad, gentle rain?"

5

I do not come from a family of men the way that Laura comes from a family of women. I grew up with a mother, and was surrounded at holidays by what I assumed was a fairly normal complement of grandmothers and aunts and cousins who happened to be female.

But I have no sisters, and so when my mother died soon after I left home for college in Massachusetts, I was left with an immediate family of men. A father and a brother. My father has not remarried, and now, at seventy-one, I doubt that he will. My brother, four years my junior, is a high school principal. He is married to an English teacher at the rival high school, a conflict of little consequence since neither school fields football or field hockey teams of any merit. He and his wife have three children, two boys and a girl, and they live in the same suburb of New York City in which my brother and I grew up. They live in a colonial with gray shingles exactly one-point-seven miles from the colonial with beige shingles in which we lived as boys, and my father lives still. Our parents purchased that house thirty-five years ago, just after my brother was born, and my father shows no signs of leaving it now that my brother has moved his family nearby.

My brother tries hard to entice Laura, Miranda, and me south from Vermont for as many holidays as he possibly can, using our father's proximity as his rationale. I know, however, that there is more to it than that: His own wife has told me on at least two occasions that she and my brother believe all the Avery women are strange, and Patience is an absolute lunatic. "Don't you think that six hours is a long time for our family to drive," she has said, "just to watch you and my husband be castrated?"

. . .

WHEN I RETURN home from work one Friday evening, Laura and Miranda are hard at work in the garden. Miranda is in charge of the day's harvest: the early asparagus from a bed Laura has meticulously maintained for almost a decade now, and a variety of different kinds of leaves. Lettuce that is almost lime green, and lettuce that is a dark ruby red. Spinach that grows in rich bouquets, with leaves on some plants as wide as Ping-Pong paddles. And while Miranda gently tears off the lettuce leaves and pulls up the spinach plants, placing them in a small wicker basket, Laura is thinning the long rows of carrots and beets she has planted this spring.

Laura's garden—and it truly is Laura's garden, despite my assistance weeding and watering a few days each week—reflects much of Laura herself: It is a serene place that is endlessly giving, despite a climate that is harsh, unpredictable, and often unkind. It forgives the early frosts, prospers in the rockiest of soils. Every plant in it is less fragile than it looks.

"The paintbrushes are up!" Miranda yells to me, referring to the asparagus her mother has allowed her to harvest, as she hops over the mounds for our golden girl and aristocrat squash.

Behind her Laura waves, and then tosses a handful of carrot

plants she has thinned into the grass bordering the garden. I kneel to kiss Miranda, and coo over the asparagus in her basket.

"Are those for dinner tonight?"

"You bet!" Miranda says proudly. "Come look at the lettuce, it's everywhere!" She takes my hand and leads me to the side of the garden in which her mother is working. Indeed, despite all that Miranda has taken in this evening, she has made barely a dent into the row of Black Seeded Simpson threatening now to overrun a row of Swiss chard beside it.

"Hi, sweetie," Laura says, wiping her hands on her jeans.

"You've made a lot of progress," I tell her, pointing at the substantial pile of carrot and beet plants she has thinned.

"Sophie's Choice," she says, shaking her head. "I hate this."

She steps carefully over the rows of carrots and beets and lettuce between us, and joins me on the grass. "Do you mind if Patience comes by for dinner? She'll probably spend the night."

"No, of course not. Anything special?"

"She didn't say, but you never know with Patience. Of course, she might just be bored. Reedy's giving his slide show about the Caracas oil spill at the town hall tonight, and Patience might not want to sit through it one more time."

"I can't say I blame her."

Miranda races across the yard to the back porch, and trades her basket of vegetables for our huge metal watering can. By the way that she hoists it with both hands, and limps back to us under its weight, I can tell that the can is completely full. When she gets to the edge of the garden, she starts to pour some of the water on the first row of peas, and then stops. She looks concerned.

"Miranda? Did you hurt yourself?" her mother asks, afraid that the can may have been too heavy for the child.

"No," she says, shaking her head almost violently back and forth.

Together Laura and I walk to her.

"Then what?" Laura asks. "Is something the matter?"

She looks up at us sadly, and for a moment I am afraid she is about to cry. "There used to be an underground spring right below here," she says, her voice cracking. "And now it's all gone!"

. . .

"I DOWSED A house today," Patience says after dinner, sipping the last of her wine. She puts her feet up on the ottoman she has kicked with her foot into the kitchen, and watches me while I clean up the dishes.

Patience likes nothing more than to watch me do dishes.

Upstairs, Laura is putting Miranda to bed.

"Anyone I know?" I ask.

"Hope not. They're all going to die. It's going to be nasty."

Patience might be tipsy from the wine that she, Laura, and I have polished off tonight, but it's hard to tell for sure. Patience says things cold sober that most people don't think when they're drunk.

"Noxious rays?"

"Don't be sarcastic, Scottie."

She sounds almost hurt, so I look over my shoulder at her and frown, trying to convince her that I was completely serious. "Noxious rays are a deadly business," I add, trying to sound sincere. "I would never be sarcastic about them."

"Oh, no, never," she says, shaking her head emphatically when she says the word *never*. "Never."

Age has been kind to Patience, as it has to all the Avery women. Evidently, Mother Nature looks out for her own. She is forty-two now, but a stranger to the community would guess she was much younger. Thirty-five, maybe. There is not a strand of gray in the bay mane that frames her face and falls down her back, and her skin has survived four decades of winters before a woodstove with extraordinary resilience. With her pronouncements, assurance, and occasional orneriness, she carries herself like a woman considerably taller than in fact she is.

"I'm serious," I continue, shutting the door of the dishwasher. Part of me wants desperately to turn the machine on and drown out this conversation, but Patience would see through my dishwasher ruse in a second. "I want to know about the noxious rays."

"For your information, it wasn't noxious rays. Not in this case." She sounds almost petulant. "It was electromagnetic radiation."

"So where was this?"

"Near Sugarbush. Down on Route 100, in one of those new condos that went up two or three years ago by the ski resort."

"A second home?"

"Yup. In a complex called the Fortress. Or the Bastille, maybe."

"You're thinking of the Armory."

"It's called some such nonsense. Some completely moronic, militaristic male name. A family from Connecticut bought one of the places. Two-bedroom condo they're going to use as a weekend house."

"And they asked you to dowse it?"

"The woman's father did. Old guy from Bennington I know through the American Society of Dowsers."

"Any special reason he didn't dowse it for them himself?" I ask, knowing full well the answer to this question.

"He wanted the best for his family."

"And you found electromagnetic radiation in the place?"

"I found four separate hot spots. One in each bedroom, and two in the kitchen. I used both a Y rod and my L rods. The chrome ones, not the brass."

"And you couldn't divert them?"

"Not unless I could convince New England Power to move about a dozen transformers and utility poles."

I don't worry a whole lot about noxious rays, but I do about electromagnetic radiation. It doesn't, after all, take a dowser to find the presence of electromagnetic radiation. Even a scientist can do that.

"What did the family say when you told them?" I ask Patience.

"They didn't believe me."

"Even the woman's father? The dowser?"

"He believed me. But his daughter didn't, and neither did her husband. The only reason they even let me into their house was to pacify her dad."

"So they're just going to stay there . . ."

"Yup. I'd guess it'll be leukemia that gets them. Maybe prostate cancer in the husband."

Laura returns to the kitchen, and pours herself the last of the coffee.

"So, did you and the world's greatest niece solve the problems of the world?" Patience asks her sister.

"No. But we figured out why Seth Reston is so quiet around her in school, and so outgoing when he comes over here to play."

"Because he has a crush on her?" I venture.

"Because he has a penis," Patience offers. "Explains most every bit of lunacy, misbehavior, and unhappiness in this world."

"Yes, Seth has a crush on Miranda," Laura says, ignoring her sister.

"Well, I think Miranda likes Seth. He's a good kid. I watched him play a few games of Little League last year."

Patience rolls her eyes. "I hope you make sure my niece keeps a cool head when it comes to men. Cooler than her aunt, anyway."

"I think you're pretty cool when it comes to men, Patience," I tell her.

"Usually. Not now," she says, taking her feet off the stool and sitting forward in her chair. She brings her empty wineglass to her lips, looks at it with disgust, and then continues, "The reason I wanted to come here tonight is that I have some news. It may surprise you, it may not. But here goes: Reedy McClure asked me to marry him today."

"That's wonderful!" Laura says, reflexively going to her older sister and wrapping an arm around her shoulder. "I'm so happy for you! You said yes, didn't you?"

"Not exactly."

Laura removes her arm from her sister, and looks at her with concern. Laura shares my affection for Reedy, and would be thrilled to see him as a brother-in-law. "What did you say to him?"

"I said I had to think about it."

"Did you hurt his feelings?"

"What do you think I am, some callous idiot? Of course I didn't!"

"What did you say, Patience?" Laura asks again.

"I said I didn't know if I wanted to spend the rest of my life with him."

"And what did he say?"

"He said he understood. But you know what's the damnedest thing? I think I'm going to say yes. Can't you just see it?" she asks, raising her eyebrows in wonderment. "Patience Avery, a possible three-time loser."

. . .

LAURA AND I awaken Saturday morning to the sound of Miranda and Patience in the yard by the garden. Laughter and an occasional sentence filter up through the crisp spring air.

I can tell that today—like almost every day in recent memory—there is not a cloud in the sky.

"Don't you daydream, Miranda Avery-Winston," Patience is saying. "Don't you let your mind wander . . ."

Sometime in the middle of the night, either Laura or I kicked off the last blanket that had remained on the bed since winter. It's nice to wake up underneath only a sheet.

"Visualize . . . visualize what the water looks like . . ."

My hands roam underneath Laura's nightgown, and I begin to rub the small of her back and her tummy, pulling her gently across the bed to me.

"Dowsing school," Laura murmurs lightly, her back to me. "Hear it?"

"I do." I start to pull her nightgown up over her head, and still half-asleep she raises her arms to help me.

". . . what a vein looks like. Maybe it's trickling. Maybe it's pouring. But you need to picture it . . ."

Laura's neck and hair still smell of black currant, the scent from our bubble bath last night. She presses her bottom against me, as I kiss the side of her neck, her ear, then her lips.

"Patience has never had a protégé like Miranda," Laura says softly, after we kiss.

I lean on my elbow and smile. The black currant is sweet, fruity. It almost reminds me of Kool-Aid. "No, I don't think she has. Maybe you, once."

Laura shakes her head. "Not really. I don't have anything like Miranda's . . . aptitude. I wish I did."

"It's a trickle," Miranda says. "That's what I'm thinking."

"Good. Now concentrate . . ."

Laura rolls onto her back and looks up at me. She looks pensive. I start to kiss her again but she turns her face away, giving me only her cheek. "Sometimes," she says, "it makes me jealous."

"Miranda's aptitude?"

"No. Patience's. Sometimes I wish Patience would leave Miranda alone. At least when it comes to dowsing."

I stretch my legs. I could suggest to Laura that she talk to her sister. But I know that she won't. Not about this.

"How deep is the vein?" Patience is asking.

"They spend so much time together," Laura continues, folding her arms across her chest.

"Don't be jealous," I murmur. "It gives them something to share."

Laura turns to face me again. "Don't try to reason with me," she says, a touch of anger in her voice. "It sounds condescending."

"I'm not trying to reason with you. Honest. I'm just trying to seduce you."

"You sounded condescending."

"I didn't mean to."

"Condescension is a lousy way to seduce someone."

I fall back into my pillow. I try to keep exasperation from creeping into my voice. "I'm sorry. But I figured your sister and Miranda were going to be out there awhile, and we may as well take advantage of the time."

Laura sighs. "They will be out there awhile, won't they?"

"Sure will."

"That is a bright side."

"I hope so."

Her voice lightens. "Sometimes, you're such a baby."

"It's true. I am."

"Shut the window so we don't have to hear them," she says. "And when you get back in bed, you better be naked."

6

Patience was twelve years old when she discovered that she was not merely capable of finding underground water, she was able to divert it as well. And while it is not uncommon today to find dowsers who take great pride in their ability to move underground springs, when Patience was a child, diversion was viewed by the dowsing community as barely a step beyond sorcery. And the last thing that any responsible dowser wanted was for the uninitiated to take the expression "water witching" too literally.

As with many great discoveries, Patience realized that a vein could be diverted by accident. The Avery basement was flooding after a spring thaw, and Patience was watching the plumber try and install a sump pump in one of the corners. She was playing with her Y rod, watching it react to the streams trickling into the basement from different parts of the foundation. The plumber, standing in perhaps a half inch of water, was hammering clips around the electrical wiring that would attach the pump to an outlet high up on the wall. The power was off in the house, and so the plumber was working by the light from two lanterns.

As the plumber slammed the clips into the thick wooden

beams in the basement, Patience felt the Y rod twitch in her hands, and begin to suggest that one of the underground streams was moving. She began following the vein with her divining rod, walking slowly away from the plumber, watching it react as she moved further and further away from the man. It was as if the reverberations from the hammer were pressing the vein inch by inch in the opposite direction.

"It's all about sonic forces at work," Patience says today when she explains the process of diversion. "Just as sonic booms will smash glass, a good bang on a crowbar in the right spot will divert an underground vein." Consequently, Patience is now one of perhaps two dozen members of the American Society of Dowsers across the country who believe they can marry two veins together (often doubling the water flow), or divert an "offensive" vein away from a building or house.

"And unlike most of the plumbers I know," Patience boasts proudly, "I don't get mud all over the kitchen floor when I'm done."

. . .

THE FACT THAT there are indeed more male dowsers in the country than there are females means nothing to Patience. She remains wary. Nor do the facts that there are almost twice as many men as there are women on the Board of Trustees of the American Society of Dowsers and among the group's sixteen officers carry much weight. Patience says these are merely additional examples of how men have unfairly co-opted power from women, how they have invidiously usurped control of yet one more God-given female talent.

"Rectal womb implants for men. It's only a matter of time," she has said to my father and brother on at least a half-dozen Easters, shaking her head in frustration.

Both Laura and the two sisters' mother, Anna Avery, fear

that one day Patience is going to open her mouth at a dowsing conference, and utter the worst sort of blasphemy. Whether she would begin with her belief that only women can dowse (and that all men should be heaved from the temple), or her belief that only select people—people like her—have the true calling is hard to say. But it is entirely possible that one day, Patience Avery is going to stand up at the annual meeting of the American Society of Dowsers, and preach to the thousand-plus dowsers who descend each year upon such small Vermont villages as Danville or Lyndonville that men can no sooner dowse than menstruate.

What has kept her in line so far? Laura contends it is not so much a what as a who. And that who is Elias Gray: the oldest practicing dowser in Vermont, a tall, thin farmer now in his nineties. Elias has lived all of his life in Landaff, and Patience believes that if God gave the power to dowse to any one man, it was to Elias.

"Look at his hands," she explains. "They're long and sleek like a woman's."

Elias is also a vegetarian, and in the fun house mirror through which Patience Avery interprets the world, this is a further indication that the man is sufficiently sensitive to dowse. He has never even been deer hunting.

Like Patience, Elias is a dues-paying member of the American Society of Dowsers who looks upon the organization itself with some skepticism. After all, with the exception of Patience, no one in the group has anywhere near his ability or his accomplishments, and it is possible that he views many of his fellow members as mere dilettantes.

Elias, however, has never kept a log of his work the way that Patience has, and he has never dowsed outside of New England. But most people believe that it is impossible to drive down almost any Vermont or New Hampshire road north of Concord without passing at least one well that Elias has dowsed. If Patience has found eighteen hundred wells, then Elias has probably found eighteen thousand.

Moreover, although Elias charges a fee for his services, he has never earned a dime in his life from dowsing. "If you don't charge 'em something, they won't think you're worth a damn," he told me once. "So I charge 'em whatever they want to pay, and then donate the money wherever in Landaff I damn well please." Consequently, from 1936, when Elias began to dowse seriously, through 1977, when Elias began to slow down, the Landaff Volunteer Fire Company never asked the town for a penny, and the Rescue Squad held not a single fund-raising picnic.

"The Lord gave me a talent," he says, "and I share it the way I'm supposed to. If I were meant to be rich, the Lord wouldn't have made me a farmer."

After Patience and Laura's father died, Elias looked out for the Averys. He would help repair the clapboards on the house after a particularly bitter winter, he would make sure the family always had plenty of wood come fall, and he would fix the screens on the windows each spring. His wife visited the Averys much less often than old Elias, but she too would do what she could, sending the Averys' way her Christmas pickles, and tremendous baskets of vegetables from her garden.

At both of Patience's previous weddings, it was Elias the dowser who gave her away. And while I have always thought it rather odd that Patience of all people insisted on having a man "give" her away at her weddings, Laura wasn't surprised.

"Sexism is one thing," she told me about her sister. "Ritual is another. Patience loves ritual."

If Patience should decide to marry Reedy McClure, Laura and I have every faith that she will ask the old man to escort her down the aisle once again. She probably loves Elias Gray as much as she loves my wife and my daughter, and views him on some level as kin—a man not related to her by blood but by water, a bond that may in fact be much stronger in the eyes of a dowser like Patience.

Consequently, Laura and I tend to think that as long as Elias Gray is alive, Patience Avery will keep her dowsing beliefs to herself.

. . .

"I GOT THESE charts and graphs from a meteorologist up in Burlington," the editor of the *Montpelier Sentinel* tells me on a Monday evening in the middle of June. "John Dexter with the TV station—WCAX."

I hang my tie and jacket on the hook behind the door in my office, and pull on a red and neon yellow shirt with the words "Quarry Men" sewn across the chest, and the seams from a softball sewn through the "Q."

"Dexter took the information he gets every day from the National Weather Service, and combined it with their long-range forecasts," Roger Noonan continues. "Then he plugged it all into a computer, and the computer generated these graphics for television."

Some of the charts are maps of the United States, and some are maps of Vermont. All of them are rich in blues and greens and yellows.

"They must have looked very impressive," I tell him, trying to reflect his enthusiasm, but it's difficult. I've never been especially enamored with graphs and maps and charts.

"They *will* look very impressive. They won't be on television until the six o'clock news broadcast tonight. Almost another hour."

"Guess I'm going to miss them, in that case. We should be well into the second inning by then."

Warren Birch, the more senior of my two partners in the firm, leans into my office, his sports jacket draped over his shoulder.

"I'm out of here," he says to me. "You'll lock up?"

I nod, and a moment later the front door to our office falls shut.

"They'll be on again at eleven," Roger continues, referring to the maps as if we were never interrupted. "But you can really take your time with them tomorrow morning. I have permission from the television station to run them in tomorrow morning's edition."

I throw my cleats and glove and antique Hillerich & Bradsby into a gym bag, allowing the bat handle to protrude through the top.

"Well, I'll look forward to it."

He rests his arms atop his stomach. "Damn it, Scottie, you didn't even glance at these for five lousy seconds!"

"Was I supposed to?"

He looks hurt. "Might have been nice, yes."

"I'm sorry, Roger. I just don't get excited about maps."

"Do you have any idea how serious this drought could be?"

I sigh, and put down the gym bag. Roger Noonan would not be standing in my office at five in the afternoon unless he had something important to discuss. "Aren't you supposed to be in an editorial meeting or something? Shouldn't you be in your newsroom?"

"Of course I should!"

I wander back to my desk, and together we stare down once again at the maps spread out on the blotter. He points at the first map with his index finger.

"Precipitation is almost sixty percent below normal for the first five months of the year in Vermont," he begins. "New Hampshire is about forty-five percent below normal, and upstate New York is about twenty percent behind where it should be by Memorial Day. They'll both feel a little pressure this summer, but nothing like Vermont."

"Any special reason why Vermont is so bad off?"

"According to Dexter, northern Vermont gets a fair amount of rain because we're lodged between the White Mountains to the east and the Adirondacks to the west. Clouds sit between the ridges, and give the state a good dousing. This year, the mountains on either side of us are keeping the clouds away, instead of keeping them here. Burlington is the cloudiest city in New England, you know. The city averages one hundred and ninety-nine cloudy days a year," he continues.

"I'm not surprised," I mumble, trying to concentrate on the chart showing the long-range weather forecasts. "Am I reading this correctly?" I ask nervously.

"It depends on what you're getting out of it. But judging by the altogether pathetic way your voice just cracked, I have a feeling you are."

"According to this chart, we're only going to get two or three inches of rain—two or three inches, tops—over the next ninety days . . ."

"Bingo."

". . . when we should be getting ten or eleven."

I have lived in Vermont almost twenty years now, and I have seen at least two droughts that I can recall, summers that seemed to last forever without any rain. I try not to let this particular drought alarm me, but for some reason it does. Perhaps it's the expected severity.

"Look at the projected temperatures," Noonan adds, motioning toward a line of two-digit numbers across July and August, all of which begin with an eight or a nine. "It's going to be one hell of a hot summer. The temperature is going to be a good five or six degrees higher than usual this year."

"And all of this is going to be on the weather report on tonight's news?"

"Weather report, my ass! This is their lead story, Scottie!

Don't you get it? This is the number one, lead fucking story in Vermont!"

. . .

FIFTEEN MILES TO the north, two magnificent white clouds of cotton rest for a moment on the long, flat summit of Mount Republic. Then they move on, one lone pair, flying into the clear night skies to the east.

"Tag up on any fly ball to right or center," Clinton Willey is saying to me from the coaching box, as I stand on third base. I turn from the mountain to him. He continues, "It's going to have to be hit deep if it's hit to left. That guy out there has a cannon for an arm."

Gulping in great swallows of air, I mumble, "I'm too old for this, Clinton. Never again am I stretching a double into a triple."

Clinton, an elementary school teacher perhaps twenty-five, shakes his head. "That was a single with a two-base error, Scottie. Sorry."

In the bleachers behind Clinton, Reedy McClure wanders down from his perch in the top row of seats, and starts to hover beside the Quarry Men bench.

Our next batter is Ian Rawls, the managing director of Powder Peak.

"Let's go, Ian, little bingo, little bingo!" Clinton says, clapping.

Ian lets two pitches fly past him for balls, then strokes a ground ball through the infield for a base hit. With Clinton screaming his lungs out behind me, I jog home with the run, touch the plate, and then veer toward Reedy McClure.

"I believe some congratulations are in order," I begin, taking his hand and shaking it.

"Well, I thank you. There are many today who offered me their condolences instead."

"You know what you're doing. You know Patience as well as I do. Probably better."

"I know I love her," Reedy says, handing me a paper cup full of water.

I nod my head apprehensively. But I am able to remain silent.

"I do, you know. You only see one part of Patience. You only see her when she has her guard up. With me, that guard comes down."

"Sounds like a reason for marriage to me."

"You don't see her when it's just the two of us, Scottie. Or the two of us and her dogs. She can be very sweet. Very giving. Very kind."

I swallow the water he has offered me. I smile. "You sound like a man trying to convince himself he hasn't struck a bad bargain."

"Not at all. I was only nervous when I thought she might say no."

"Oh, there was never a chance of that. I knew Patience would say yes the moment she told me you asked her. I think she only took the weekend to think about it because her first two marriages failed."

He nods, then motions out toward the diamond. "You guys are embarrassing them," he says, referring to the team now in the field.

Clark Rawls, Ian's younger brother, hits a fly ball over the left fielder's head. While the fellow chases the ball into the high grass behind him, Ian races all the way home from first base, and Clark doesn't stop until he is standing where I was only a few moments ago on third.

"Let's face it," Reedy continues, "nobody stands a prayer against you boys from Powder Peak. You guys are animals."

"Now, Reedy, only a few of us have anything at all to do with the resort. As far as I can tell, it's just me and the two Rawls brothers."

"And Hugo Scutter."

"Scutter is an engineer."

"He's working with you on the expansion."

"Have you and Patience set a date?" I ask, grinning as I change the subject.

"No. But we'll figure that out this week. Patience thinks she wants a summer wedding."

"Patience has always liked the summer."

Reedy shakes his head. "It's not the season. It's Elias. She wants him there, and doesn't figure she should press her luck and wait too long."

"No, probably not."

"Of course, she also said she may want to wait until the second week of September—which really isn't all that far away—but only if she's pretty sure Elias will hang in there."

"The annual dowsing convention?"

"Yup. She thinks it would be great to get married with a bunch of dowsers."

"What do you think?"

He shrugs. "Wouldn't make any difference to me."

Behind us we hear the peculiar plink of an aluminum softball bat making contact with the ball. Another of the Quarry Men has hit a solid line drive to left field. This one, however, is hit right at the fielder. He catches it and fires a bullet to home plate, holding Clark Rawls at third.

"I was briefed on your permit applications," Reedy says when the crowd has quieted down once again. "I don't think you're going to be able to pull this one off."

"Oh, God, Reedy, do we have to talk about this now?"

"No, of course we don't. But I just think you should know:

There is no way you can withdraw three hundred and seventy-five million gallons of water from the Chittenden River a season. You'll kill it. You'll kill the river."

I watch Hugo Scutter swing at the first pitch, and hit a sharp grounder to second base. The infielder scoops it up, and throws out Gertrude and Jeanette's nephew by a half-dozen strides. I punch Reedy lightly on the arm, and then reach down for my glove.

"Just guess I've got to run," I tell the state senator. "Just guess I was saved by the third out."

. . .

MOST DOWSERS ARE evangelists. Most dowsers love to proselytize.

They believe that virtually anyone can dowse, and they're always looking for new converts, new believers, new blood. When the founding members of the American Society of Dowsers wrote a charter for their group in 1961, one of their five primary objectives was "to disseminate knowledge and information about dowsing to as large a group as possible." Today, the group's literature boasts that "everyone is born with the capability," and refers to dowsing as a "birthright talent."

Sometimes the American Society of Dowsers even holds membership drives, and existing members are offered "bounties" of sorts, for signing up new members. Things like a year's free membership. Once, the Society even gave what amounts to its "dowser of the year" award to a fellow solely for his success in one particular membership drive: This individual started a new chapter and signed up an impressive twenty-nine members, an especially eye-opening number since he lived in a town in South Dakota with a total population under two hundred.

Patience, of course, takes objection to the idea that dowsing is a birthright talent. And while she keeps her doubts to herself when she is among most other dowsers, she makes no secret of her frustration with her family. Just as she believes that virtually no men can dowse (except Elias), she is convinced that the few chosen women in this world with the calling should keep the secrets to themselves.

"There is just nothing I hate more than seeing some idiot with a Y rod tramping through some idiot farmer's land," she has said to me many times, "except, maybe, some idiot with a Y rod trying to teach someone to dowse."

Her one exception to this belief is when Patience herself is the idiot with the Y rod, and my daughter Miranda is the pupil. Patience is positive that with proper training and practice and mental conditioning, there are no limits to what my daughter may someday accomplish ("Your daughter's gift makes mine look like a dime-store ruby," she confessed to Laura in what must have been a particularly touching moment of sisterly camaraderie).

When I return home from the ball game, I find myself smiling as my truck coasts to a stop at the end of our driveway. Miranda is at that very moment practicing what her aunt must have been teaching her Saturday morning. She is walking in slow motion from the barn toward a small cluster of blue spruce trees Laura and I planted just before she was born, walking with her two L rods before her. She is moving slowly, haltingly, trying her best to allow the rod in each hand to point wherever it chooses.

Occasionally her lips move as she asks herself a question, trying to be as specific and focused as possible. In theory, when the rods open so that they are pointing in opposite directions, she will be receiving a "yes" response to her question—whatever that question is.

I watch for perhaps a full minute, the time it takes her to reach the blue spruce trees. When she gets there she stops, and

I finally climb out of the truck. She turns to me, frowning. The two L rods are still pointing straight ahead, indicating that she never received a positive answer to her question.

"No luck, huh?" I ask, kissing the top of her head and guiding her with me toward the house. It's almost eight thirty.

"Nope." She sounds very disappointed.

"What were you asking?"

"I was looking for water."

"Practice?"

She stops dead in her tracks, and folds her arms across her chest. "No, I'm not practicing," she says, her voice quivering.

I stop with her and kneel beside her, a father's protective antennae at attention. Something has frightened my daughter. "Then what, sweetheart? Are you still worried about the vein you think went dry under the garden?"

"Yes! I've got to find us some new ones!"

"Oh, don't worry about that one. Really, you don't have to worry about that at all. We have a well, and it's just fine. Just fine. We have plenty of water, sweetheart, all that we need."

"It's not just that the other vein disappeared!" she continues, raising her voice nervously. Over Miranda's shoulder I see her mother wandering out the back door to see what's the matter.

"Then what?" I ask. "You can tell me."

"It's what Mom and I saw on the news tonight! We watched the news tonight after the Scutters went home, and they said . . ." She stops speaking and looks down at her feet, and for a brief moment I am afraid she is crying. But with her mother now beside her she abruptly looks up and continues, "And they said it's not going to rain at all for the rest of the summer, and all of the corn might die!"

7

Patience was nineteen years old when she dowsed a half-dozen fraternity houses at Amherst College. A pair of supermarket tabloids ran short stories about the "mystic sorceress" who used "magic" to find missing objects of value, and the *New York Post* published a blurb on its society page implying that the princess of Monaco lived at Smith College with a practicing witch.

In actuality, it was all rather harmless, and had it not involved the princess of Monaco, no one outside of western Massachusetts would ever have heard about it. But it did involve the princess of Monaco, a beautiful young woman who spent as much time with aging rock stars in Manhattan nightclubs as she did with her sophomore-year roommate at Smith, one Patience Avery of Vermont.

It is also worth noting that what happened then could not happen now, at least not with quite such a sexually suggestive and newsworthy hook for the tabloids: Smith has remained a women's college, but Amherst is now coeducational, and the fraternities have become great brick Georgian dormitories. Amherst and Smith are still separated by only eight miles of state highway, but in all other ways they have grown thousands upon thousands of miles apart.

Then, however, the two schools were inextricably linked by hormones.

And with the princess of Monaco in residence at Smith College, it was only natural that the capture of her lingerie—a bra, panties, perhaps a single silk stocking—would become a part of the annual spring hazing ritual for the freshman pledges at Amherst's fraternities. And so one evening in April, while the princess was somewhere in Manhattan and Patience was at the college science library, Smith security officers apprehended fifteen young men—boys, really—trying to sneak into the large single room the princess and Patience shared on the college campus. Some boys were caught shinnying up the ivory trellis outside the pair's room; others were found drunk on the house's sharply pitched roof.

By the time Patience returned late that night, the dean of students at Smith was confident that his security people had repulsed the final invasion from the fraternities eight miles away. He was incorrect.

The moment she entered the room Patience sensed that something was missing, something was different, something was . . . wrong. She tried to convince herself that it was merely paranoia brought on by the stories she had been told about the Amherst students caught sneaking around the house, but when the princess returned from New York the next day, her suspicions were confirmed.

Her normally serene, husky voice raised in panic, the princess told Patience that a monogrammed silk bag with her stockings and panty hose was gone. It had sat in the top drawer of her bureau, buried beneath nightgowns. And while the princess didn't give a damn about the stockings, she had to get the bag itself back. The tears flowing freely now down what gossip columnists usually portrayed as an astonishingly poised face, the princess explained through sobs that the inside wall of the lingerie bag had a secret lining, and in that lining were a variety of explicit, no-holds-barred love letters from two different lovers.

Patience had heard of both men. She knew that one was a married novelist who had recently won some sort of award, and one was a rock star who had recently been featured on the cover of *Rolling Stone*, naked from the waist up, with a huge tattoo of a tongue on his chest. Patience and the princess discussed the idea of approaching the police or college security, but the last thing the princess wanted was publicity. "Lives," she said, her voice a quavering mixture of melodrama and desperation, "would be ruined!"

Besides, she added pragmatically, "My father would freak if he ever saw those letters."

And so during dinner that evening, when almost all of Amherst College converged on the dining commons, Patience Avery began dowsing the fraternities in search of the lingerie bag. She and the princess were hoping that whoever had discovered the bag was so busy showing off its more obvious contents to his fraternity brothers that he had not yet found the secret lining.

Using her Y rod, Patience began walking slowly up fraternity row, the princess behind her in tow. And while the princess tried to conceal herself with a scarf and black sunglasses, onlookers knew who she was.

Moreover, while most students were indeed at that moment at dinner, many were not. Patience and the princess passed a group of young men lightly tossing a baseball in the front yard of Theta Delta. They waved—by necessity—at a cluster of men and women drinking keg beer on the front porch of Psi Upsilon.

As six thirty approached, and the upraised Y rod had shown no inclination to move in Patience's fingers, the princess began to panic. It wasn't merely that they had now walked past five fraternity houses, it was the fact that they had begun to generate a crowd. Four or five men and two or three women had started to trail the pair, always a good thirty yards behind them, but always there.

It was at quarter to seven, while Patience and the princess were standing in front of the tremendous white columns surrounding the front porch of Phi Gamma Chi, that Patience's Y rod abruptly pointed straight into the ground.

"It's in that building," Patience told the princess solemnly, and she led her roommate inside.

The group of students hovered at the end of the driveway, and then followed them.

Pointing her Y rod again toward the sky, Patience strolled through Phi Gamma Chi's wide front doors, and into the majestic entry hall. She continued to mumble to herself as they walked through the house, asking whether the lingerie bag was in this room or that, whether it was behind this dresser or in that drawer. Finally, at the entrance to a room on the second floor of the fraternity, Patience looked at the princess and murmured, "Bingo."

The princess saw that the Y rod was pointing straight into the carpet.

From the stairs at the end of the hallway they heard the whispering and soft footsteps of the students who had followed them. Suddenly one voice rose above the others, a young man's.

"Hey, that's my room!"

A decent-looking fellow in a crew neck sweater who would prove to be the fraternity president raced into the room, and he confronted the two women.

"What the hell do you think you're doing?" he asked, his hands on his hips.

"You're talking to the princess," a male voice whispered quickly in a hushed tone from behind him. "Don't be an idiot."

The fellow looked at Patience and the odd stick by her thigh, and then at the woman behind her. He bit his lip and began to nod. "Well. Welcome to Phi Gamma Chi," he said, spreading his arms expansively. "I'm Robert Oates. Can I get you two a . . . a beer?"

"No, I don't think so," Patience said, shaking her head in disgust. "We're not here for your well-known hospitality."

"Then what can I . . . what can we . . . do for you two?"

Patience felt the tip of one of the princess's long fingernails dig into the small of her back. "You know why we're here."

The fraternity president extended his hand to Patience. "I'm sorry," he said, stalling. "I think I missed your name."

Patience refused to take his hand. "I didn't give it."

Oates sighed. "Look, I don't know what the deal is here," he said. "I don't understand all this hostility. All I know is I came back from dinner, and there were a half-dozen people I hardly knew walking inside the fraternity. Now I find two women I've never met poking around my room with a . . . a weird-looking stick—"

"Make it easy on yourself," Patience said. "Return what you took."

The fraternity president shook his head. "I don't have the slightest idea what you're talking about."

Patience walked behind him. "Sorry, folks," she said to the small group in the doorway, "but I'm about to be real rude." She then pushed the door shut.

"We're here for one reason," she said to Oates, her tone even but angry. "You took something that doesn't belong to you. You stole something."

"I didn't steal anything," he said, smiling broadly.

Patience watched him and paused. At first she was surprised, because something in that smile convinced her that Oates was telling the truth. She could tell that he really hadn't stolen anything. But she knew also that the lingerie bag was somewhere in this room. Hadn't her Y rod said so?

"Of course you didn't steal anything," she said, softening her voice. "I'm sorry I accused you wrongly of that."

"Apology accepted."

"Some freshman brought it to you like a trophy, and you've simply hidden the item in this room."

Oates was silent for a long, quiet moment, and Patience took the offensive once and for all.

"We're here to recover some stolen merchandise. A little bag of stockings. Now you can either hand it to me right this very second, or I'll find it myself. Just as surely as I figured out where the bag was on this whole stupid campus, I'll find the drawer in which you hid it."

"I wish I could help you, but I just don't know what you're talking about," Oates said again, but his voice was weak and unsure.

"Fine," Patience said. She raised the Y rod before her, and turned away from Oates and the princess. She asked if the silk bag was buried in the dresser, stowed in the closet, stored in the loft. She asked if it was hidden in the wastebasket, placed neatly in the desk, and—finally—tucked inside the small refrigerator in the corner.

It was then that the Y rod responded.

"An ice-cold stocking is not very appealing," the princess said as she watched the Y rod react, her first words since they had entered the bedroom of the president of Phi Gamma Chi. It was clear that she was appalled.

"Want to open that up?" Patience asked, referring to the refrigerator.

The fraternity president thought for a moment, wrestling with his options. Finally he opened the door, reached inside, and from the bottom of a tub of Milky Way chocolate bars removed a paisley lingerie bag about the size of a purse.

"We had every intention of returning it," he said softly, tossing the bag to Patience. "Everything should still be there."

The princess grabbed the bag and immediately glanced inside. Patience could tell by the almost orgasmic sigh of relief that escaped from the princess's lips that the secret lining was undisturbed, and the letters were still there.

"We really were going to return it," Oates continued to babble from his spot on the floor, as the two women left his room, smiling, unconcerned by the fraternity brother with a camera who snapped picture after picture after picture.

. . .

I TRY NOT to listen to the sound of running water in the small sink in the next room. Our receptionist is cleaning the coffee cups and saucers that were used in a client meeting earlier this afternoon, and suddenly the urgent rush of water from the tap to the sink to the drain unnerves me. I felt this way when I was shaving this morning.

Ian Rawls has come into Montpelier from the ski resort just outside of town, to join me for a conference call with Goddard Healy in San Francisco. While gallons of water douse a few small coffee cups in the room beside us, Ian and I stare at a speakerphone in the middle of the round conference table between us.

"When you use the word *protest*," Goddard is asking, his voice strangely tired, "do you mean a thousand people with television cameras, or a couple of idiots in flannel shirts with a handwritten banner?"

"I expect this will be an extremely well-organized event," Ian tells him. "I don't know if they'll actually get a thousand people, but I wouldn't be surprised if they were able to round up four or five hundred. Counting the children."

"Counting the children . . ." Goddard repeats.

I reach behind me and gently push the door shut, shielding myself from the sound of the running water.

"And I'm sure the CBS affiliate up in Burlington will send down a crew. So might the NBC station out of Plattsburgh."

"Who's behind the rally? Locals or professionals?"

Ian looks at me, not understanding Goddard's question, and then motions with his finger that I should answer this one.

"We don't believe there are any outside activists or organizers," I explain, recalling the photograph Goddard showed me of his new girlfriend. "No one from Greenpeace, no one from Earth First. At least we haven't heard of anyone. But the group is being led by a very savvy, very smart local politician: a state senator named Reedy McClure."

"Is the group protesting the whole expansion, or just some part of it? Like that river we're tapping?"

"Well, the Chittenden River is a big part of their concern. Especially with this drought—"

"Droughts come and go! I keep telling you that!"

"I understand that, Goddard. But the fact remains, it's exacerbating the situation. It's making everything seem more dire than it really is."

"So is the Chittenden their focus?"

"Yes. But they're not real wild about the trees we plan to cut down on Mount Republic either."

Goddard snorts. "Give me the date for the rally again. It's a week from today—"

"It's a week from yesterday. It's Monday, June twentieth."

"They're smart. Monday is usually a slow news day. They'll have a better chance of television coverage."

"Reedy McClure is very smart," I add. "He's putting together a coalition of mothers, fathers, fishermen, hunters, environmentalists—it's quite a group."

"Either of you boys know anyone with any sway over him?"

"He's about to become Scottie's brother-in-law," Ian says, grinning at me.

I mouth the words *thank you* to Ian, smile back, and then extend toward the ceiling the middle finger of my right hand.

"He's what?" Goddard asks, and I envision the man sitting forward in his desk chair a continent away, sitting up in disbelief. It's sometimes difficult for anyone who doesn't live in Vermont to comprehend just how small this state is, and—because of that size—how incestuous politics have become.

"He's marrying my wife's older sister," I explain, keeping my voice even. "I probably have as much sway over Reedy McClure as anyone in Vermont, and that's not very much."

"What's the name of this . . . coalition?"

"It's called the Copper Project."

"I suppose Copper is an acronym."

"Correct."

"Okay: The two *P*s come from Powder Peak. What's the rest?"

"Citizens Opposed to the Powder Peak Environmental Rape."

"Good God, isn't that a little melodramatic?"

"Not for Reedy McClure."

The speakerphone goes silent for a long moment. I am about to ask Goddard if he is still there when his voice returns. "Scottie, no offense here, but you know what I hope?" he asks, his voice low with exhaustion, frustration, and disgust.

"What?"

Speaking as slowly as I have ever heard him, Goddard says, "I hope some goddamn squirrel bites his goddamn tongue off, so he has to keep his goddamn mouth shut."

. . .

WHEN I WENT to law school, I never said to myself, "I hope someday I get to represent ski resorts." I never set out to help developers build condominiums and vacation homes in Vermont's older mill towns, or to assist the state's Agency of Economic Development recruit new factories, new plants, new manufacturers. It just worked out that way.

I grew up as something native Vermonters refer to as a flatlander, a person from New York or New Jersey who visits the state to ski, to hike, to watch the leaves turn in the fall. And then goes home. It never occurred to me when I was twenty-four that a ski resort could cause conflict, that a housing development could trigger debate. Perhaps I was naive. Perhaps things changed.

But when Laura and I decided that we would build our lives in Vermont, I chose simply to work for the law firm that made me the most lucrative offer. It was not, to my mind, a political decision. Laura, an economics major at college, had already begun work as a commercial loan officer in a Vermont bank, a job she would hold until Miranda was born.

In any case, three months after I started practicing law, I was defending the tax-exempt status of Vermont's largest hospital before Burlington's revenue-hungry mayor and city council, while justifying the hospital's profits.

It all just happened, I tell myself now. It all just happened.

8

Elias Gray still drives. He drives badly (although probably no worse than he did fifty years ago), creeping along Vermont's two-lane highways at a top speed of perhaps twenty-five miles per hour. He drives an ancient blue pickup with rounded wheel covers and rust along the doors that everyone in Landaff can recognize at a very great distance.

There is a bumper sticker on the back of the truck that reads *Indago Felix*, an expression Elias roughly translates to mean "Fruitful Search."

Indago Felix is the motto of the American Society of Dowsers, and is often a part of their logo.

Saturday morning, Miranda and I find ourselves trapped in our own truck behind Elias, as he twists his way west down Route 2 toward Montpelier.

"Has Aunt Patience told him she's getting married again?" Miranda asks, looking straight ahead at Elias's truck.

"I don't think so. I think she and Mr. McClure are going to visit him this afternoon. I think they're going to tell him together."

"How come?"

We approach the long winding descent into East Montpelier, and I begin to brake, anticipating the fact that Elias will drive this part of the road at about ten miles an hour. Between the grocery shopping, a trip to the hardware store for me, and a trip to the bookstore for Miranda, I figure we have about an hour and a half's worth of chores before us.

"Because it's nicer that way. That way, Elias can see how much Aunt Patience and Mr. McClure love each other."

"Do they really?"

Above us roll blankets of gray and black clouds, part of a low-pressure system that has been crossing Vermont for two days, but has left behind not a single drop of rain. The only comfort the clouds have brought us is a short break in the eighty-five- and ninety-degree temperatures that have haunted us since almost mid-May. Today it will probably not break seventy.

"I don't believe they'd get married if they didn't love each other," I tell my daughter, aware that my answer is vague and evasive. She wanted a categorical, unambiguous yes.

"Do you want me to start calling Mr. McClure 'Uncle Reedy'?"

"Only in my worst nightmares . . ."

Miranda looks at me, confused.

"No," I explain, "I don't think you should. If you were a very little girl, maybe . . . but not now. I don't think Patience would want you to."

"Well, I don't think Patience even wants to get married," she says, folding her small arms in front of her chest.

"You don't?" I raise my voice slightly, trying to sound surprised.

"Nope."

"Did she tell you that?"

"Nope. I just think it."

A drop of rain falls on our windshield, then a second and a

third. As I reach reflexively for the handle by the steering wheel that will turn on the wipers, Miranda says quickly, "No, Daddy, don't! Let them stay!"

• • •

WE PARK BESIDE Elias in Montpelier, in the parking lot around the corner from the state capitol. Elias emerges slowly from his truck, stepping down onto the asphalt like a man made of balsa, and wiping his forehead with a handkerchief when he is back on the ground.

"Good morning," he says to us, waving, as he pushes his handkerchief into his pants pocket.

"Morning, Elias," I say, taking his hand briefly.

He bends over as much as his ancient back will allow, his hands cupping his knees, to speak to Miranda. "Broken any hearts lately? Or just an old man's leg?" he asks her, smiling, a reference to the fact that Elias broke his leg two years ago playing croquet with my daughter and Patience.

"Your leg feel okay today, Mr. Gray?" Miranda asks, looking at the spot on the old man's shin that was once cracked by an errant croquet ball.

"My leg's fine. It's as good as any ninety-three-year-old leg," he says, adding as he straightens his back, "which means it ain't any good at all."

"How is Giannine doing?" I ask, referring to his wife. "Is she over her summer cold yet?"

"Yup. She's feeling fine, thank you." He looks up at the sky, shaking his head. "I thought for a moment we were going to get some rain," he says. "Back in East Montpelier."

"I thought so too."

"This dry spell ain't so bad for an old fellow like me who don't farm no more, but it's causing fits for the younger fellows."

"It sure is," I agree. Beside me I can almost feel Miranda

grow tense at the thought of the drought. "I hear you're building a new sugarhouse," I tell Elias quickly, trying to change the subject.

"Yup. Course, I'm not buildin' it myself. I'm just the old cuss watching. Supervising."

"That's not what I hear. I hear they're your plans, your design."

"It's for my grandson. Anson."

"Yup, that's the rumor. But the whole rig sounds wonderful, Elias. The talk I hear is that you just purchased some monster evaporator—four by sixteen feet, someone told me."

He smiles. "They told you wrong. Try six by eighteen."

"Wow. You'll boil away half the sap in Vermont in something like that," I tell him, recalling the dozens of March afternoons that Laura and Miranda and I have stood in Elias's sugarhouse, watching vats of sap from sugar maples roll and gurgle and thicken. When the sugar first runs in March, it might be forty degrees outside, but inside Elias's sugarhouse the air feels like a sauna and the room smells like heaven.

It smells like it's misting maple syrup.

"I won't. But someday, Anson will."

"Oh, you will too, Elias. You know it's not sugaring season in Landaff without Elias Gray. The sap just won't run if you're not there."

He sighs, and then smiles down at my daughter. When he looks back at me he says, "I'm enough of an optimist to build the thing, Scottie. But I'm not stupid enough to ever expect to use it."

• • •

AS MIRANDA AND I walk down Main Street in Montpelier, Miranda sometimes skipping a few feet ahead, we pass by store after store with the same small sign in the window:

STOP POWDER PEAK!

Help prevent the destruction of acres of
forest on Mount Republic!
Help preserve one of Vermont's great wildlife habitats!
Help save the Chittenden River!
Show your opposition to the expansion of the
Powder Peak Ski Resort!
Rally on the Capitol Steps
Monday, June 20, Noon to One thirty

SPONSORED BY THE COPPER PROJECT:
CITIZENS OPPOSED TO THE POWDER PEAK ENVIRONMENTAL RAPE

"Did Mr. McClure do that?" Miranda asks, when she sees me staring at one of the signs.

"Yup."

It is clear that the poster was designed by some professional graphic designer, probably some friend of Reedy's from Burlington or Boston. There is a silhouette of the magnificent, hemispheric curve that is Mount Republic along the bottom of the poster, and the Powder Peak Ski Resort logo in the upper right-hand corner.

The logo sits in the middle of a circle with a wide red line slashed diagonally across the center. No Powder Peak, the slash says.

Miranda continues, "Is that why you don't want me to call him 'Uncle'?"

Beside the poster announcing the Copper Project rally is one promoting the Barre Town Volunteer Fire Company's annual Fourth of July picnic and dance. The fire company poster has letters written by hand in about five different shades of Magic Marker.

I kneel in front of Miranda, and put my hands on her shoulders: "Sweetie, if you want to call Mr. McClure 'Uncle Reedy' when the time comes, I won't mind at all."

. . .

I SIT ON the porch after church Sunday afternoon with Laura and Patience and their mother, reading thick piles of newspapers. Sometimes we look up to watch Miranda and two of her friends from Brownies play croquet.

Miranda is actually an extremely accomplished croquet player, capable of far more than merely cracking a ninety-plus-year-old shin, and she makes short work of her friends in game after game. Occasionally, she will race onto our porch and grab a handful of strawberries from the bowl on the wrought iron table.

"Elias asked Reedy if he was going to start staying home more, once he becomes a married man," Patience says, referring to the day before when she and Reedy visited the old dowser.

"Is he?" Anna Avery asks, a trace of concern in her voice. My mother-in-law, now close to seventy, worries about her older daughter. Although she has spent almost all of her adult life as a widow, she always had Patience and Laura for company. Patience, in her mother's eyes, lives alone in an old village house with neither husband nor children for comfort.

Patience shakes her head no. "Not a prayer."

"Well then, you'll just have to go with him," Anna says. "Personally, I'd love to visit half the places he goes to."

"We'll see. I think Reedy would like having me with him. But . . ."

"But . . ."

"But I don't have any great desire to see a lot of dead cormorants. You know I can't bear to see a sick animal."

Anna smooths a wrinkle in her slacks. I'm not sure when my

mother-in-law stopped wearing skirts to church and started to wear pants. Laura and I both have noticed that in the last four or five years she has become less fastidious about her clothing.

I close the newspaper's Sunday magazine, and turn to my sister-in-law. "Is Reedy around this afternoon? I didn't see him in church this morning."

"Yup, he's around. He has a meeting up at his place with some of the people who are helping out at tomorrow's rally. Of course you'll be there, right, Scottie?"

I grimace. "Gee, Patience, I just have a terrible feeling that my calendar's all booked tomorrow afternoon."

"But you wish you could be there . . ."

"I think I'll watch from a distance, thank you very much."

Over my shoulder I hear the sound of little-girl giggles, as wood hits wood and someone's croquet ball winds up in the middle of the pumpkin patch.

Anna waves at her granddaughter, and then cleans the frames of her tortoiseshell eyeglasses. "They all have so much energy, don't they?" she says.

"Sometimes they have too much energy," Laura tells her.

"What time do you think Reedy's meeting will be over?" I ask Patience. "By dinner?"

"Oh, I sure hope so. We're having dinner together tonight, and I don't really feel like talking about your stupid ski resort all night long."

"Think Reedy would mind if I stopped by?"

"Why, Scottie," Patience says, her voice a mask of mock sincerity, "I don't think there is anything that Reedy McClure and I would like more than the pleasure of your company."

. . .

"I DON'T EXPECT you to call off the rally," I hear myself saying, as if I were listening to my voice play back on a tape recorder.

It sounds strained, frustrated, more than a little bit irritated. "I understand that's impossible."

"Darn right," Reedy says.

From some other room in the McClure homestead the phone rings. I pause, waiting for Reedy or Patience to leave me to answer it, but the two of them remain with me in Reedy's den. Patience looks up once from her magazine, but neither she nor Reedy moves.

"Do you want to get that?" I ask both of them.

"No, the answering machine is on," Reedy says.

"Are you expecting Laura to call?" Patience asks me.

"No."

Abruptly the machine comes on, interrupting the fourth ring.

"So what do you want?" Reedy continues.

"Well, for starters, I want you to keep the melodrama down to a minimum."

He spreads his arms, palms up. "Consider it done."

"I mean it. I think that poster of yours is a little overwrought. I think those ads you have on the radio station are downright nuts."

"I think you and I have a different definition of melodrama. Personally, I don't think there's anything melodramatic on that poster or in our ads."

Reflexively I roll my eyes. "No one's destroying a forest. No one's destroying a wildlife habitat."

"That's debatable."

"And the name of your group—that's just plain inflammatory."

"It's an acronym, that's all. A grassroots group needs an acronym."

"Not with the word *rape* in it."

Patience turns to Reedy and shakes her head, agreeing with

me for one of the only times in her entire life. If I kept a diary, this would be a seminal entry. "He's right, you know. You shouldn't have used the word *rape*."

"Isn't that what they're doing?" he says to her. "Raping the entire side of a mountain? Raping what's left of the Chittenden River?"

"That's exactly what I mean!" I tell Reedy. "Listen to yourself: 'What's left of the Chittenden River.' You make it sound like the Chittenden's a sick river, and the resort's expansion project is going to kill it."

"It would kill it! Three weeks ago the river was twenty percent below normal. By Friday it had fallen to about twenty-five percent."

"That has nothing to do with Powder Peak."

"Of course it doesn't. All I'm saying is that this drought proves the river can't support snowmaking."

I sigh. "What exactly are you hoping to accomplish tomorrow? Are you just trying to scare a few people? Or is there more to it than that?"

"I'm not trying to scare anybody. I just want the folks who are reviewing your permit applications to understand that the people who live in this area are opposed to the expansion. They're opposed to draining a river, they're opposed to expanding a parking lot into wetlands, they're opposed to—"

"Reedy, relax," I say, cutting him off. "The extra parking spaces will be nowhere near the wetlands."

"You want them east of the base lodge, don't you?"

"Yes."

He pauses. "I was told that your plans—"

"They're not my plans," I remind him.

"The resort's plans," he says, correcting himself, "proposed adding two hundred and seventy-five parking spaces in the wetlands area east of the base lodge."

"Look at the plans yourself, Reedy. Whoever briefed you screwed up. Yes, the parking spaces will be east of the base lodge, but they'll run parallel to the access road. They won't touch the wetlands. I promise."

"You didn't change the plans?"

"Oh for God's sake, of course we didn't!"

He looks at me, and I can see in his eyes that he is disgusted with himself for not reviewing the plans himself. He rubs his temples.

Sensing his frustration, Patience finds an excuse to leave us. "I'll go see who called," she says, squeezing Reedy's shoulder as she passes by.

I consider for a moment trying to be kind to Reedy, and telling him that he has a lot to do, and he can't be expected to read every land-use permit that's submitted to the Agency of Natural Resources. But then I choose not to, deciding instead to allow Reedy to wriggle and twist for a moment.

From the kitchen I hear the voice of either Gertrude or Jeanette Scutter on the answering machine, but I cannot quite make out what the woman is saying.

"Hell, everything else that's pissing you off is true," I finally tell him, shrugging. My tone is soothing, but I know that my words will disturb him. "The resort really does plan on using the Chittenden to make snow. It really does plan on cutting down a couple of trees."

Out the west window there is a thin strip of pink left in the sky, the last moments of daylight.

"A couple," he says, his voice still depressed.

"A couple." I wink. "A little firewood."

He allows himself a small groan, and then looks up when Patience returns from the kitchen. She stands in the doorway, her arms crossed before her chest, and looks concerned.

"Who was it?" Reedy asks her.

"Gertrude Scutter."

"I should probably call her back right now," he says, standing. "I doubt I'll have time tomorrow."

"Don't bother," my sister-in-law says. "She was looking for me."

"Why?"

After pushing her tongue into her cheek she says, "Poor things, their well went dry. Bone, desert, burnt-toast dry. So they want me to find them a new spring."

9

Exactly why does dowsing work? I'm not sure. I know only that it has never worked for me.

Over the years, I have tried to dowse many times. Sometimes I have been alone, sometimes Laura and Miranda have been with me. It hasn't made a difference. I have tried dowsing with brass L rods with copper sleeves, and with steel L rods with plastic sleeves. I have used my wife's L rods, hoping that somehow her "residual aura" would help me. I have toyed with the Y rod that hangs on a peg inside our pantry door, and I have spun Laura's quartz and crystal pendulums around my fingers for hours, twirling the chains as if they were rosary beads.

But, for me, dowsing has never succeeded. I have stood for what might have been hours at a time directly over our well and felt not the slightest tug in the Y rod. I have stood on top of our septic tank, forced myself to see and smell and hear the fluids roiling below me, and felt absolutely nothing course through my fingers.

"You're not concentrating," Laura told me.

"You're not taking this seriously," Miranda said.

Either reason may account for my continual failures. When I

walk around with a Y-shaped stick in my hands, or a pair of coat hangers bent into Ls, it is indeed difficult for me to take dowsing very seriously.

When that Y rod or those L rods are in the hands of an experienced dowser such as my wife or my sister-in-law, however, then I am capable of taking dowsing completely seriously. Then I am able to believe that it works.

But I still cannot explain it.

I have heard all the explanations, some more rational than others. Few dowsers, after all, agree with Patience Avery that successful dowsing results from a link that a few specially chosen women have with the fluids surrounding them in nature.

Many dowsers—including most of those who believe that virtually anyone in this world can dowse—contend that dowsing is a physical process: When water flows underground, they say, it emits an impulse that causes an involuntary muscular contraction. That contraction, in turn, causes the rods to move.

Others view dowsing as a natural instinct, an innate survival mechanism that exists in almost all animals—including humans. "Elephants in the middle of the desert will find water," a past president of the American Society of Dowsers once told a local newspaper.

This, of course, doesn't begin to explain map dowsing, or the sort of witchery that makes dowsers such as Patience Avery very rich. Finding gold. Lost objects. Missing persons. It doesn't explain how Patience once found a downed pilot and his friend on Mount Ira Allen, or a lingerie bag with secret letters in a fraternity house at Amherst College. It doesn't explain the obstacle course of oil rigs off the coast of Santa Barbara and in the dry soil south of Redding, Oklahoma—testimony to my sister-in-law's prowess when she was in her twenties, and married to an executive with one of the larger oil companies.

Consequently, some people insist that dowsing can only be

explained by the presence of a sixth sense, by extrasensory perception. Some would say that this sixth sense is in many of us, and some—such as my sister-in-law—would say it is in only those small, select few.

Personally, I could not begin to guess how many people in this world can actually dowse. But I do believe that whatever it is that gives them the power is stronger in some families than in others, and that lurking somewhere among the basic physical units of heredity, among the linear sequences of nucleotides that determine whether we'll have black or blond hair, whether our eyes will be green or blue or brown, whether we'll be poets or potters or lawyers for ski resorts, is an honest-to-God, carefully coded, RNA-ready dowsing gene.

• • •

MEN WITH BEARDS and women in peasant skirts, little girls whose hair needs to be brushed, crowd the front steps of the capitol building, clapping and chanting and singing and—whenever Reedy McClure opens his mouth from the top of the steps—listening with rapt attention. Almost as one, somewhere between six hundred and one thousand people move or stand still, sway back and forth or dance in one place. There is the smell of hot June sweat in the air, and the ground seems to move when Reedy stamps his feet and six hundred to one thousand pairs of sandals and work boots and sneakers stamp in response. Or respect. Or adulation.

The Copper Project, this afternoon at least, is one unified, focused, unquestioning phalanx against development. It is a living buffer against change, a breathing stream of hate against Powder Peak.

And providing the single-minded animus is the voice of the man who will soon be my brother-in-law, echoing over loudspeakers, reverberating throughout Montpelier. Videotape cameras bob up and down before him, boom mikes hover around his face like butterflies, the sun bounces off the glass of his wristwatch whenever he raises his arm to the sky in disgust.

"He's going to single us out," Ian Rawls murmurs to me. "He's going to single us out, and the whole mob is going to hang us."

We lean against parking meters across the street from the wide lawns of the capitol building. "I wouldn't worry," I tell Ian. "Reedy promised me last night that he'd keep the melodrama down to a minimum."

His voice is robust, but he has indeed toned down his melodrama. I have not once heard words like *rape* and *slaughter* and *crush*. Nevertheless, I know that in spite of the measured tones of his delivery, his relatively evenhanded choice of words, he is filling the heads of the tie-dyed, blue-jeaned, overalled crowd before him with an apocalyptic vision of treeless mountains and dead rivers, of bears and moose and deer that must move north to Quebec to survive.

"I just don't understand what they expect to accomplish," Ian says. "Don't they have jobs they're supposed to be at?"

There are still more people arriving, strolling, sauntering, skipping in the case of the children, into the back of the mass held in thrall by Reedy McClure. Some of them come merely to gawk, drawn to the scene as much by the presence of the cameras and lights as they are by the crowd itself; others were perhaps vaguely aware all along that there was some sort of rally today, and now gravitate to the mass with interest.

And towering over them all is the dome of the state capitol building, its gold leaf reflecting the searing afternoon sun. It is a luminescent beacon inviting the opponents of the Powder Peak Ski Resort to come together and protest, to come and gather and fight, to do all that they can to oppose a couple new ski trails on the side of a mountain.

. . .

"DOES THIS SORT of rally influence your thinking?" Roger Noonan's reporter asks Ian, while over her shoulder the crowd on the capitol lawn slowly disperses. Some of Reedy's apostles stand around to watch the senator forty yards behind us, as he is interviewed by the television stations.

"It certainly does. The resort lives in this community," he says, answering with words he rehearsed with our firm, but delivering them in so clipped a fashion that he sounds almost angry.

"Then how will you respond?"

The reporter, a young woman with shoes too stylish for Montpelier, is new to Roger's newspaper and new to the area. She has introduced herself as Rosamond Donahue, and made it clear that she is never—ever—called Rosie. She has a slight Southern accent, and will probably last about six months at the *Sentinel* before being stolen away by a better paper in a bigger city.

Ian is supposed to answer here by citing the permits we have submitted to the state and federal governments: environmental impact statements, building permits, expansion permits. I can almost see the filing cards flashing on the gray matter screen behind Ian's eyes, as he tries desperately to remember his lines.

"How we will respond," he says slowly, groping, "will depend on a variety of issues."

"Such as?"

He opens his eyes wide, having found his mental crib notes, and begins to stammer a response. "We have no intention of building anything that will . . . undermine the environment. Of course. We are . . . we are now awaiting an environmental impact statement on the effect our expansion will have on the Chittenden River . . . and on the mountain itself. Obviously, if that statement suggests our plans will have a negative impact, we'll . . . we'll revise our thinking."

"And amend your plans?"

There is a moment of silence that is probably only seconds, but feels to us all like minutes. Hours.

"We would have to," I add finally. "That's the law."

Rosamond turns her small recorder in my direction. "I assume you expect the government to rule in your favor?"

I nod. "Yes. The resort does. But it's not as if Powder Peak views it as an 'our favor/your favor' issue, Rosamond, it's not as if the resort views it as an 'us against them' issue. The fact remains, this expansion is in the best interest of this entire area."

"Now, why is that?"

"There are enormous economic benefits to expansion," I begin. I hadn't planned on jumping in like this, but Ian is clearly relieved that I have. Sweat is running down the sides of his face, triggered more by Roger's new reporter than by the overhead sun.

Continuing, I tell the writer, "The expansion would create construction jobs throughout this year and next. But that's only a small part of the story, a short-term benefit. In the long run, it would create hundreds of permanent jobs in the lodging and hospitality industries in this area. Jobs in restaurants, in gas stations, in welcome areas. I think it's also worth noting, Rosamond, that these are environmentally 'clean' jobs."

"Do you have exact figures?"

"Sure do. In the resort's economic studies and forecasts."

"May I see them?"

"I can drop them off at the *Sentinel* on my way home tonight. My office is just around the corner from the paper."

"What time do you leave?"

"I can have them on your desk by five thirty."

"That would be great," she says, smiling for the first time since we've met. "That would be very helpful."

"It's no problem," I say, hating for a moment the sound of my voice: It sounds cloying, ingratiating, and slick. Unstoppable at this point, however, I continue, "What I think it's important to understand"—and I repeat her name yet again—"Rosamond, is that the people who work at Powder Peak are environmentalists too. They really are. That's why they work there. They love the outdoors. They don't merely love to ski, they love to fish. Their children don't simply love to snowboard, they love to camp. They love to hike. No one up there wants to hurt the river or hurt the mountain. That's the bottom line."

Behind her the television cameras are approaching, led by the eleven o'clock anchorman. Rosamond Donahue and the *Montpelier Sentinel* have been a first-rate dress rehearsal for opening night on the news.

. . .

AFTER SUCCESSFULLY DEFENDING a utility company's request for a rate hike before the state power commission . . .

After convincing the socialist mayor of Burlington to give a ski boot manufacturer huge tax incentives to build a plant on the outskirts of the city . . .

And, again, after helping a real estate developer get all the state and federal permits he needed to build a forty-unit luxury condominium complex at the edge of the national forest . . .

Patience told me I was so slick I should never clear the table after dinner: She was afraid that the plates would slip right through my hands.

These memories come back to me as I watch myself on the television news that night at eleven, telling Vermonters that the executives who run Powder Peak are environmentalists, that their expansion will create hundreds of new jobs.

Every time that I incorporate the name of the television anchorman who is interviewing me into my response, Laura pokes me in the ribs ("I think he knows his name," Laura says). Every time I refer to the resort in the third person, Laura rolls her eyes and pretends to wash her hands ("Me, work for the resort? Nah. I don't have anything to do with them," she says, clicking her tongue against her teeth).

When the news is over, Laura turns off the television, and then sits on the ottoman beside the couch in the den.

"You know something, sweetheart?" she says.

I sit back in the couch and wait. I know exactly what's coming, I know exactly what Laura is thinking.

"It's a good thing I already know you and love you," she begins, "because if I only saw you on television, I'd think you were the fastest, sleaziest thing on two legs in this state."

. . .

PATIENCE WALKS THROUGH the weeds that once, when the Scutter twins were many years younger, were the backyard of the Scutter family homestead. She walks with her L rods before her, her eyes half-shut, her feet barely leaving the ground with each step. She is almost shuffling.

If she were not wearing a white polo shirt and crisp new blue jeans, strangers to town might mistake her for a witch, for someone possessed, for a glazed-eyed sleepwalker. Instead, she looks merely like some nut from a local country club.

"I got a hunch she'll hit us a water dome," Jeanette Scutter tells Gertrude. I know which woman is which at the moment because Laura is with me and has called each twin by her name.

"Well, if she does," Gertrude says, "I hope it's not closer to China than Landaff."

A water dome occurs when underground water flowing upward hits a layer of porous materials: Often, instead of flowing straight through that material, the water will form a dome and begin to spread horizontally in veins.

"It'll be within one hundred feet of the surface, and it will give you five or ten gallons per minute," Laura says, trying to cheer up the Scutters. "You know that better than I do." She reaches down and runs her fingers along Cocoa's black fur, reminding the animal that it should stay here beside us. A jet-black Lab, Cocoa is one of three dogs Patience has rescued over the last decade from the Humane Society in Montpelier. She is the most demanding of the animals, the most dependent upon my sister-in-law for attention; if it were possible, she would never leave Patience's sight. If Laura had not been petting her every few moments, I imagine by now she would be racing beside Patience.

"A hundred feet?" Gertrude says. "This summer, that'd sure be nice."

When the L-shaped rods in Patience's hands open—when they begin to point in opposite directions—then Patience will be receiving a positive response to her questions. Is there water here? A spring? How deep? Is the water potable? Always the questions will demand a simple yes or no answer.

"If she is thinking about a water dome," Laura continues, "she's envisioning one of our mother's light blue mixing bowls. Upside down, of course."

"Of course," Jeanette says.

"Once, when she was thirteen or fourteen years old, Patience took a half-dozen of those blue bowls, and set them all around the side yard like an obstacle course. They looked like some kind of lawn game."

Occasionally Patience's lips move, as she tries to focus on the ground below her, and she asks herself questions. Sometimes, Patience says, she will not simply phrase her questions to elicit a general yes or no answer, but what she calls a "personal" yes or no response. Is there water here for the Scutters? Is it water the Scutters can drink?

"What was she doing with 'em?" Gertrude asks, referring to the blue mixing bowls.

"She was trying to divert the springs that fed our well."

"What for?" Jeanette asks, incredulous. "Why would she go and do a fool thing like that?"

The two rods in Patience's hand quiver just the tiniest bit, barely enough for the four of us watching to notice. Reflexively the Scutters and I look to Laura for confirmation, but she shakes her head no. This is merely a false alarm.

"The spring that fed our well also fed our neighbor's well," Laura answers. "The Mahlers. You remember them, don't you?"

Patience turns and begins to walk away from us, and we can no longer watch the L rods. Cocoa sits up and cries once, and Laura quickly loops two fingers underneath the dog's collar. Gently she scratches the top of the animal's head.

"Of course," Gertrude says. "He died, and she moved to . . ."

"She moved to St. Johnsbury. Her son now lives in Boston. Ethan. Anyway," she says, "there was some sort of dance at the school, a real big deal. Patience wanted to go to that dance very, very much. Unfortunately, every boy in the school was already scared to death of her. Even at thirteen, she had a pretty sharp tongue."

Patience stops walking, and stands perfectly still. She is probably thirty yards from the house.

"None of the boys in the school asked Patience to the dance. Not a single one. So Patience decided to take matters into her own hands. One afternoon she marched over to Ethan Mahler's house, knocked on the back door, and asked him to take her to the dance. I think she said she'd give him the money for the tickets, and for soda."

"I don't see it," Gertrude says, "I just don't see Ethan Mahler goin' anyplace with your sister. It doesn't seem like a real good fit."

"Well, Ethan didn't think so either. As I recall, he did say yes to Patience that afternoon, but only because he was afraid to say no. The day of the dance, he came down with the sort of life-threatening cold that prevented a boy like Ethan from going to the dance that evening, but not playing baseball all afternoon."

"Poor Ethan. I always knew that child was born without a spine," Jeanette tells us, shaking her head.

"You can imagine how angry Patience became. She had a classic Patience Avery meltdown. And she directed every bit of that rage at our mother and me, and said some really hurtful things. At least she hoped they'd be hurtful. I remember her storming through the kitchen, telling Mother that she had been an abused and neglected child. Telling me that I was so ugly I was scary. Telling us both how ashamed of us she was, and how she hated going out with us in public because we were such an abnormal, repulsive family.

"Well, Mother finally got her to stop talking long enough to listen to a sentence or two. And she told Patience that it was okay to be hurt and it was okay to be sad, but she shouldn't be taking it all out on her sister and her mother. This wasn't the first time in her life she had been hurt, and it probably wouldn't be the last. Whatever Mother said, it seemed to be registering. She quieted down, she agreed to behave. I think Mother then promised Patience and me that we would all go to the new ice cream parlor in Montpelier the next day, and we assumed Patience was pacified.

"We were, of course, wrong. That evening Patience took a half-dozen of those blue mixing bowls, and proceeded to try and divert the spring that fed the Mahlers' well so the well would dry up and the family would lose their water."

"My heavens, did she do it?" Gertrude asks.

"Dry up the Mahlers' well? No, thank heavens. Our mother saw what Patience was up to, and brought her inside. I think she grounded Patience for about a month after that."

Abruptly Laura starts toward her sister, walking through the brown, dry grass.

"I think she has found it," Laura says, as the Scutters and Cocoa and I start to follow.

. . .

THE L RODS point away from each other, open, signaling yes to the last question Patience has asked.

"Is this the spot?" Gertrude asks, smiling, her old, hoarse voice filled with excitement and hope.

"It's a spot," Patience answers, shaking her head. Laura and I steal a glance at each other: Something has upset Patience.

"What do you mean? Is there a better spot?"

Patience drops her L rods to her sides, and allows herself one long sigh. Cocoa nuzzles her leg, trying to get her head between the palm of Patience's hand and her thigh.

"No," she says finally, "my recommendation is that we drill here. My recommendation is that we tap into the vein right here."

"Is it a dome?" Jeanette asks, but with little enthusiasm. She too can tell that something has disturbed Patience.

"No. There's no water dome here. Over there, by those mountain ash," she says, pointing at a pair of the trees, "there was a water dome once. But not anymore. It's all . . . it's gone."

"So what do we got?" Gertrude asks nervously.

Patience runs her arm across her forehead, and gathers herself. I imagine the last thing she wanted to do was frighten the Scutters.

"It's going to be fine," she says, forcing a smile. "There's a perfectly good vein here, one that should last a good long time. It will give the two of you lots of crisp, fresh, drinkable water."

With her pinky Jeanette pokes at something deep inside her ear. "But it's deep, ain't it?"

"It could be worse. It could be a lot worse."

"Two hundred feet, ain't it? We're going to have to drill two hundred feet," Jeanette says, calculating in her mind how many thousands of dollars that will cost. She sounds almost angry.

"Maybe. But I believe it's deeper than that."

Gertrude gasps. "Deeper than two hundred feet?"

"I'm sorry, Gertrude," Patience says. "But yes, you should expect to drill deeper than two hundred feet. The water table is low, you know that. A lot of springs have just disappeared, like the one that's been feeding your well for years."

"How bad, Patience?" Gertrude asks. "How bad is it?"

"Right where we're standing there's a vein that pokes up a bit toward the surface. A bit. My feeling is that if you drill here—and here is your best bet, by far—you should expect to drill somewhere between four hundred and four hundred and twenty-five feet."

Jeanette covers her eyes with her hands, as Gertrude taps her gently on the shoulder.

"We'll have to go to the bank and cash in the CD," Jeanette groans. "And they'll make us pay penalties . . ."

"You don't know that for sure, Jeanette," I tell the woman. "You really don't know for sure how much it will cost. Let me talk to Michael Terry."

Gertrude lets her hand rest on Jeanette, and says, "That Terry's a pirate. He's got the only drill for thirty miles. Don't waste your breath."

"Terry Drilling is hoping to get some work up at the ski resort," Laura explains. "A lot of work, actually. Scottie might be able to help."

Patience looks away. She hates this kind of political back-scratching, even if in this case it might help the Scutters.

"You're sure there ain't a better spot?" Gertrude asks Patience. "Maybe over by those sugar maples?"

Patience clears her throat. "I'm sure," she says.

"Well, that's that," Gertrude says. "Let me go get the checkbook."

Laura looks quickly over at her own sister, and stares intensely at Patience. Patience meets Laura's eyes for the briefest of seconds, and then tells Gertrude, "Don't bother. This one was on me." She nods at Laura, a slight motion that I believe neither of the Scutters noticed.

"A person's time is worth something, Patience, especially yours," Gertrude says.

"Maybe. But that doesn't matter. This one was on me."

"Patience—"

"Look, if you hit water above two or three hundred feet, you owe me some jam, okay? Some of your blueberry jam. And I don't mean one small tin, I mean a couple good size jars. Okay? Enough to get me through the winter."

"I just can't believe we'll have to go to the bank and ask 'em for our CD back," Jeanette says, and I realize she hasn't heard a word that we've said.

10

When I come home from work, Laura is seated along one of the long sides of the kitchen table, surrounded by piles of invoices and receipts and small ledger books.

"This looks ominous," I tease her, gesturing toward all the pieces of paper with numbers. "What's up?"

She sits back in her chair. "I got two really monster orders today."

"Well, that's good news."

She shakes her head. "No, I mean really monster. They're from catalog companies. One wants the candles shipped within ten days."

I put my attaché case down by the closet, and then, remembering Miranda's insistent warnings about noxious rays, kick it halfway across the hallway. "Not possible, huh?"

"Nope."

"You'd need more help?"

"Yup. I'd also need to buy lots more materials—including packaging. I'd need more of those little brochures we put in each box."

I sit down in the chair beside hers. "Someday, you'll outgrow the barn. Someday, you'll have to move into town."

"No. I will never, ever outgrow the barn. If the Divine Lights of Vermont ever got that big," she says, flipping her pencil onto the table and smiling, "I'd sell it to somebody like Hallmark, and we'd live forever like royalty. But, no: As long as I own this company, it never outgrows the barn."

Outgrowing the barn is no small issue for Laura. Running her business from our home has always meant that she was available for Miranda. It has meant that she was there when Miranda returned home from school, and that she could help our daughter with homework, she could teach her to ski, she could watch her play on the porch. It has meant that she could take time out from candles to weed the garden when she wanted to, that she could take the time to plant bulbs, or wallpaper a guest bedroom, or simply bake a pie with the blueberries that grow along the south edge of our driveway.

It has meant, essentially, that she could always view candles as more of a hobby than a business. A relatively lucrative hobby, but a hobby nonetheless.

And while it is at least remotely possible that we could convince the local board of selectmen to give us the building permits we would need to expand the company right here on our property, Laura and I have discussed that eventuality perhaps a half-dozen times as well, always coming to the same conclusion. If the company were to get larger, we would no longer want it at our home.

"Where's Miranda?"

"She's playing with the Woolfs," Laura says. "Cynthia said she'd drive her home a little before seven, on her way to choir practice."

She begins to gather the papers she has been examining on

the table. “Patience called today. She and Reedy have begun to finalize the wedding plans.”

“A September wedding?”

“Yup. Saturday, September ninth, one o’clock sharp. It’s going to occur during the annual convention.”

“Oh, God. Poor Reedy. Getting married before a thousand dowsers.”

“Not true. They’re getting married at the Congregational church here in town, and there will be invitations, just like a . . .”

“A normal wedding.”

“Right. Just like a normal wedding.”

“Trust me. The idea that the world’s greatest dowser is getting married will draw a crowd.”

“Nope. She and Reedy chose one p.m. because that’s when the convention’s ‘Earth Energies/Earth Mysteries’ field trip to a sacred site is scheduled,” Laura says, only half-serious. “The only dowsers who will be at the ceremony are the dowsers that she and Reedy invite.”

“Will it be a big wedding?”

Laura smiles. “Well, yes. After all, Patience knows a lot of dowsers.”

. . .

ARCHER MOODY’S CORN has begun to poke its way through arid beaches of sand—small withered plants with sickly parchment-like leaves. His fields, which never get all the moisture they should, are long plains as dry as dust, the ground thirsty, scorched, baked to a hungry, cracked moonscape. In a good year, the corn is supposed to be knee-high by the Fourth of July. That isn’t likely this summer.

Archer Moody will be lucky if his corn is even alive on the Fourth of July.

I find myself adapting to the heat wave in small ways, even as I drive past the Moodys' farm each morning on my way to work in Montpelier. I no longer wear my sports jacket or suit coat in the truck, tossing it instead onto the passenger seat beside me. I have purchased a half-dozen short-sleeve dress shirts, although I am confident that *Gentlemen's Quarterly* would not approve. And I have begun to drive with the front window all the way down, despite the fact this makes it harder to hear the radio, and I dangle my left arm in the breeze.

And as I drive, I try to concentrate solely on the road before me, so I do not have to see yard after yard that is burned short and brown, I do not have to see toasted corn plants with shriveling leaves.

Even our little garden, despite the love and ministrations of Laura and Miranda, has begun to look droopy. Not exactly ill, at least not yet. But the flowers forming on the peas and the pumpkins look dry, and the mounds for the squash and zucchini and the cucumbers look parched. And everything looks a little bit sunburned.

And still there is little—if any—rain in the forecast.

• • •

I GATHER BEFORE me on my desk all the newspaper stories from the past two days about Reedy McClure's rally at the statehouse, and survey the damage. Roger's *Sentinel* gave the event front-page coverage, but most of the newspapers relegated the story to their local news sections.

The Vermont wire reporter filed a tiny, four- or five-inch story that was buried in the back pages of *The Boston Globe* and *The New York Times*.

In the story in the *Sentinel*, the story that shared the front page with news from Moscow and Washington and a volcano in South America, is the one piece of information that I find disconcerting, the one piece of information that surprised me when I first read the news Tuesday morning.

The chairperson for Vermont's District Five Environmental Commission, Liza Eastwick, told *Sentinel* reporter Rosamond Donahue that she was moving the public hearing on the resort's requests for building and land-use permits from the community meetinghouse in Bartlett to the Hammond Auditorium in Montpelier. The meetinghouse seats about forty people; the auditorium seats close to four hundred.

I went to college with Eastwick, and I know she is about as open-minded as anyone who sits on a state environmental commission; I find it disconcerting that she has decided our hearing might draw that large a crowd.

I look for the calendar on my desk, buried under three or four of the newspaper clippings. The hearing is set for Thursday, a week from today.

. . .

SOMETIMES ROGER NOONAN is right about me: Sometimes I do have profound connections with the powers that move and shape Vermont.

I run into Peter DuBois, the governor's administration secretary, at the variety store around the corner from the statehouse, while buying felt for Miranda.

Peter too is buying felt. His daughter and Miranda are in the same Brownie troop. "I have a terrible feeling this has something to do with butterflies," Peter says apprehensively, holding in his hands a large swatch of blue. Peter has been a fixture in state government for over a decade, as a legislator, a lobbyist, and now as Governor Florence Webster's right-hand man.

"It does. It has everything to do with butterflies."

"I have a terrible feeling this beautiful piece of felt is going to be covered with butterfly goo. They're going to mount the little critters on this stuff all summer long, aren't they?"

I shake my head no. "I think they're going to cut the felt into the shape of butterflies."

"This isn't for a biology badge or something?"

"Nope. Just arts and crafts. I think it has to do with their float in the Fourth of July parade."

"I'm relieved."

"You look relieved."

"I didn't want butterfly goo all over the kitchen table." He takes a large square of black from the shelf. "Think they have orange?"

"Somewhere." I nod, envisioning the monarch butterflies that descend every year onto the milkweed that grows along one side of our garden.

"I thought you handled that rally thing very well on the news," he says, reaching across me. "The governor did too."

"Thank you. Thank her," I add, referring to the governor.

"She was relieved to see someone talking about jobs."

"It's important."

He jumps away from the shelves of felt, as if burned. Eyes wide, he says quickly, "Don't tell Reedy I said that. Governor Webster has purposely kept a low profile on the expansion."

"I understand."

"She only said she was glad to see the employment issue raised. She wants to see the environmental impact statement before making up her mind."

"That's fair."

"So you won't tell Reedy?"

"I won't tell Reedy."

He sighs. "Thank you."

"No problem."

"I probably seem a little jumpy."

"No more than usual. You always seem a little jumpy."

"There's going to be a press conference tomorrow. I hate press conferences."

"What's on the governor's mind?"

He looks around him, as if we were standing in the middle of Red Square in 1965, trading secrets about nuclear weapons. He folds the felt in his hands into small, crinkled squares. "I shouldn't tell you."

"Does it have to do with the ski industry?"

"Nope."

"The environment?"

"You can keep a secret, right?"

"Of course I can."

He sighs. "It's about the drought. And we won't know for sure until this afternoon. But we're expecting a call from the White House, or from Senator Lurie. Lurie is ninety-nine percent sure that the governor and he have convinced the president to declare Vermont a disaster area. A drought disaster area. And that means we'll be eligible for millions of dollars in aid. Millions!"

"Millions of dollars" still means a lot in Vermont, a state with an annual budget that has never exceeded seven hundred million dollars.

"You're going to make a lot of farmers happy," I tell him.

"Damn right," he says.

"Of course, that won't bring back the corn. Or give them a second cutting of hay."

"No, but it will keep them in business for another year. And it seems to me, that's a major victory in this environment," he says, shaking his head, and I can tell that he chose each of his words with care.

11

Aunt Patience is taking me to see the sugarhouse Mr. Gray is building today," Miranda tells me over breakfast Friday morning.

"Don't you have to work on your float for the parade?" I ask her. "How did you escape butterfly duty?"

"I didn't. We have a meeting this afternoon."

"Well, when you go by the sugarhouse, say hi to Elias for me."

"Yup." She jumps up from the table and races to the pantry, and takes down from an inside peg on the door her mother's Y rod.

"Aunt Patience dowsed the spot to build the sugarhouse, but I get to find the place for the holding tanks."

"That's a lot of pressure."

"Yup." She sits down in her seat, holding the forked stick in her hands so that it points upward. "Know what?"

"What?"

"When I was playing with the Woolfs the other day, I heard Mrs. Woolf tell someone on the telephone that the forests are so dry right now they might all burn up." I know by the way

Miranda is scrupulously avoiding eye contact with me that this idea petrifies her, and she is trying to downplay her fears. I'm sure the fact that it was Mrs. Woolf who made this remark, the woman who is married to the chief of the Landaff Volunteer Fire Company, made it seem especially ominous to Miranda.

"I wouldn't worry too much about our forests. Want to know why?"

She nods, staring up at the divining rod.

"A hundred years ago—even more than a hundred years ago, right after the Civil War—Vermont had very few trees left. The forests had been almost completely cleared for sheep farms and dairy farms. Only a little bit of the whole state was forest. But now, so many trees have grown back that it's the other way around. Only a very little bit of the state is clear, and we have plenty of trees."

"But that doesn't mean they can't all burn down," she says, finally looking at me.

Gently I push the tip of the divining rod down with my fingers, and then lift my daughter onto my lap. "We'll lose some trees to forest fires this summer, sweetheart, just as we do every summer," I tell her softly, almost murmuring. "That's part of nature. Maybe because of the drought we'll even lose a few more trees than usual. But I promise, we won't lose very many."

"What about what Mrs. Woolf said?"

"I don't think Mrs. Woolf thinks we're going to lose all our trees either. She's concerned, as we all should be. But no, she doesn't think our forests are going to disappear either."

Miranda sighs. "Well. I just wish it would rain."

"Me too."

We hear Laura returning from the barn, where she was setting up the Scutters' work for the day, and Miranda slides off my lap and starts toward the front door.

"You know what I wish?" Miranda asks.

"What?"

"I wish Mom and Aunt Patience and Mr. Gray could find water in the sky. I wish they could find water in the sky as easily as they find it underground."

. . .

GOVERNOR FLORENCE WEBSTER reminds me of Laura and Patience's mother, when she was fifteen or twenty years younger. She moves with the same, almost confident carelessness I will always associate with the Anna Avery I met when I was twenty-one years old: a Vermont earth mother's faith that her movements cut a literal swath through the world, her belief that perfect poise is presumptuous. Her gestures are wide, her mannerisms extravagant, her smiles are broad.

I cannot imagine the woman's hair as anything but gray, just as I cannot envision most bald men with hair. And like Anna Avery twenty years ago, Governor Webster is a large woman: tall, assured, and—as Roger Noonan wrote once in an editorial—"of considerable presence."

The American Society of Dowsers has been known to claim that Florence Webster is one of them—a dowser—but she laughs the suggestion off and, essentially, denies it.

"We have been told by the White House that the emergency money will be available to the state immediately," the governor says to a reporter from the *Burlington Free Press*. "And we will, of course, follow up on that."

"Has the National Weather Service given you any sense that there's rain on the way anytime soon?" Rosamond Donahue of the *Sentinel* asks.

The governor picks her glasses up off the table. She takes a deep breath as if she has a long answer, and then says simply, "No."

The *Sentinel* reporter tries to clarify the governor's response.

"No, they haven't given you a forecast, or no, there's no rain in the future?" she asks.

"As far as they know, it's not going to rain. At least soon." Quickly Governor Webster smiles, and adds, "But who ever trusts a weather forecast?" She looks at John Dexter, the meteorologist from the CBS station in Burlington in attendance, and says, "Isn't that right, John?"

He smiles good-naturedly and looks down at his shoes.

"It'll rain a week from Monday. It'll pour," Peter DuBois, the administration secretary, whispers to me, his voice a soft whine. "After all, it's the Fourth of July, the one day each year when we all have to stand outside and watch our children march in parades."

. . .

ON SATURDAY AFTERNOON Laura, Miranda, and I bump over the aging, rickety wooden bridge that leads to the hundreds of acres Elias Gray owns. I bring our truck to a stop when the bridge is behind us, and look up at the thin dirt road. Once, when the bridge was new and capable of supporting heavier loads, the road was an active logging highway. But that was years ago; Elias hasn't had loggers on this land in over forty years.

"One of these days, that bridge is going to fall into the river," Laura says, although these days there isn't much river left. "Didn't there used to be some sort of sign warning against heavy loads?"

"Yup. Anson Gray took it down two weeks ago, when the evaporator for the sugarhouse was being delivered. He didn't want to scare the delivery truck away."

Laura nods. "Oh, good. Very responsible."

Miranda sits between Laura and me in the long couch of the pickup, occasionally staring through the front windshield at the high, hot overhead sun.

"Ready?" I ask the pair, before shifting the truck to bounce up the old dirt logging highway.

"Ready," they say in unison, and as three jerking, shaking, shuddering pistons we jostle our way up the mountain.

. . .

"ALL I GOT to do is sit here and look ornery, and those boys keep up the pace," Elias says, smiling, from his perch on one of the thick tree stumps bordering the clearing for the sugarhouse.

Those "boys"—his thirty-year-old grandson Anson, and two of Anson's friends—are in the midst of hanging one of the two wide front doors. Even in the shade this deep in the woods, the ninety-degree heat is inescapable, and the shirts of the three men are soaked through with their sweat.

But the work is worth that sweat. The sugarhouse is clean and new and almost finished. It's magnificent. The wooden shed rises two stories into the forest, with a metal chimney poking through the highest point of the roof. Inside, there is enough room for the six-by-eighteen-foot evaporator Elias has purchased for his grandson, perhaps a half-dozen cords of wood to stoke the evaporator fire, and plenty of "extra" room to can and store the syrup.

The whole area now has the wonderful smell of sawdust, and the wood and timbers are so fresh that they're almost pale yellow in color.

Miranda rushes to a cleared spot about a dozen feet higher than the sugarhouse, and about fifteen yards away.

"This is where I said the holding tanks should be!" she boasts to Laura and me. "This is just the spot!"

Eventually, two monstrous vats will be placed where Miranda is standing. Anson may hook buckets to a few maple trees next March, but the days when sap is collected in individual buckets are largely gone. Instead, Anson and his two friends will attach miles—literally, three or four miles—of plastic tubing to sugar maples throughout the forest, an interconnected spider's web that will collect the sap from the trees, and draw it eventually into the vats where Miranda is standing.

When there's a good run next March, the vats will have well over two thousand gallons of sap in them, waiting to be transferred into the evaporator in the sugarhouse and boiled down into syrup.

"Yes, indeed," Elias agrees with Miranda. "That's just the spot. Good deal." He turns to my wife and says, "She takes after your sister—your sister and you. She dowsed that spot yesterday in minutes."

Laura shakes her head that he's wrong. "Patience has the real talent," she says, her voice almost wistful. "You know that. If she takes after anyone, she takes after her aunt."

"Well, maybe when it comes to dowsing. But in a lot of other things, I'm glad she takes after you. You got a very sweet little girl on your hands."

Laura nods, trying to accept the compliment with grace. But I know that it's hard for her, I know that it's frustrating. All her life she has been the "sweet" sister, the "normal" sister, the "traditional" one. Meanwhile, it has always been Patience who has been the center of attention. Sometimes it's because of her dowsing achievements, other times it's because of her tantrums; sometimes it's the simple result of the daily lunacy that Patience Avery has always mistaken for conventional behavior; but, for a variety of reasons, Patience has always seemed to find a way to commandeer the spotlight. Sometimes this makes Laura jealous, and sometimes it makes her angry. Sometimes, it makes her both.

"Thank you, Elias," she finally says to the old dowser.

"Welcome."

Miranda walks over to the men hanging the door, and

watches cautiously from a few feet away. With his one free hand, Anson gives her a small salute.

"Patience seemed pretty happy when she was here yesterday," Elias continues. "Happy for her, anyway. Is it Reedy?"

Laura shrugs. "I don't know. I hope so. But I agree, she has seemed a little more serene than usual."

"I sometimes wonder if I'm bad luck givin' her away. A jinx."

"I doubt that," Laura reassures him. "Whatever problems Patience had with her first two marriages had nothing to do with you."

He pushes down on the stump with his hand, and rises slowly to his feet. "I told her Reedy was a good man," he says. "I never said that about the first two."

"Did she agree?" I ask.

There is a chorus of grunts and groans behind us as the three men try to line up the hinges on the door with the hinges screwed into the frame, while trying to steady the door less than a quarter of an inch above the ground.

"About as much as Patience will agree with anything," Elias says. "So I kicked up my feet a bit. I warned her that it was about time she grew up, and lived up to that name of hers. I reminded her that men had a history of leaving her. And if any man was willing to just pick up and go somewhere, it was Reedy McClure."

I find myself laughing, and from the corner of my eye watch Laura try hard not to smile. "You said all that to Patience?"

Elias nods. "Sure did. Old man like me? Hell, I can say anything I damn well please and get away with it."

12

•

Patience calls me at my office Tuesday afternoon. Although she says she is standing in Gertrude and Jeanette Scutter's kitchen, a good thirty-plus yards from the spot where a well is at that moment being drilled, I can hear clearly the sound of Michael Terry's four-story drill. It is not noise in the background, it is noise on the line beside Patience: an earsplitting, teeth-shaking, window-rattling, headache-inducing hammering.

"If I bring Terry in here, will you talk to that idiot?" Patience shouts over the banging, the sound of a hundred-pound hammer slamming its way through Vermont rock, a thousand—perhaps more—crashes per minute.

"What for?" I yell back, wondering if my sister-in-law can hear me. A young associate, a woman from Vermont Law School who graduated only last month, stands in the hall, watching me shout.

"That idiot brought his pounder!"

"So?"

"I asked him to bring his rotary drill!"

"What difference does it make?"

The sound is reminiscent of a jackhammer, but louder: machine-gun-like bursts of blasting that fill the air, eventually deafening perhaps everyone who ever drills wells for a living.

"It makes all the difference in the world! Some fat cat up in Stowe is getting his rotary drill, and your neighbors right here are getting the pounder!"

"Both cut through the rock! Both will find a vein!" The associate in my doorway is joined by Warren Birch, the two of them wondering why I'm yelling. I point the phone's receiver in their direction so they too can appreciate Michael Terry's pounder. I smile.

"You're all idiots!" I hear Patience shout, and I can almost see her shaking her head in disgust. "The pounder might divert the vein! It's shaking up so much stuff down there, it might move the goddamn water vein!"

I rub my eyes. "But a rotary drill wouldn't?"

"Less likely!"

"So what do you want me to do, Patience?"

"Talk to him, for God's sake! Tell him to stop using his goddamn pounder, and get his rotary drill up here this goddamn minute! It's a fragile vein they're about to tap, and I don't want them to divert it!"

"Patience, I'm not going to do that!" I insist over the booming behind her. "Terry is already doing me a big favor! He's only charging the Scutters for the well casing and expenses! That will save them a couple thousand dollars!"

"But he might move the vein—and miss it!"

I try a different tactic: "I doubt that! Patience Avery doesn't find movable veins—"

"Don't you dare put the onus on me, you smug little prick!" she hisses, and a split second later she slams down the phone and the line goes dead.

. . .

I WAS LUCKY, Michael Terry was lucky.

The Scutters were very lucky.

And Patience Avery's perfect record remained intact.

Evidently, Michael Terry's pounder did not divert the vein Patience had dowsed. It hit a healthy vein of potable water at four hundred and two feet—exactly where Patience had said it would.

. . .

FOR EVERY MEMBER of the Copper Project in attendance, there is an employee of Powder Peak, or one of the restaurants and motels and clothing stores that ring the resort, and depend upon it for much of their business. For every person that Reedy McClure has convinced to take a seat tonight in Montpelier's Hammond Auditorium, there is one that Ian Rawls and I have had the local Chamber of Commerce coax there as well.

All told, there may be as many as four hundred and fifty people at the hearing this evening, given the fact the auditorium seats four hundred, and there are a couple dozen people standing along the edges of the stage. And every single one of them is hot, ill-tempered, and sweating profusely. There is no air-conditioning in the auditorium, there are not even any fans. The air sits upon us like quilts, clothing sticks to us all as if held there by rubber cement.

Sitting on the stage at the front of the room, behind a line of wobbly card tables, is the District Five Environmental Commission, three individuals chosen by the governor and charged with giving and withholding land-use and building permits for projects that might affect the environment.

Projects such as Powder Peak's. Projects that tap rivers for water, or cut down trees for trails. Projects that—based on the testimony of one professor from the University of Vermont—can adversely affect more than just our small corner of Vermont.

"That means," says the young professor in hiking boots and a blue blazer, a mugwump who has somehow managed to dress like me from the waist up and Reedy McClure from the waist down, "that the ozone layer is at least four or five percent gone over North America and Europe. It's disappearing much faster than we ever thought, faster than we even thought possible."

I can't tell how much of his testimony Liza Eastwick, the Commission chairperson, believes, but I can see that the men sitting on either side of her buy every word of it.

"Trees," the professor says, "are our future."

"And our friends," Ian Rawls whispers sarcastically beside me. "Trees are our friends. Don't you just hate this sort of Arbor Day fanaticism?"

I nod politely in agreement, although my feelings are far more mixed tonight than I can admit to the man who represents my client. Lately, the drought and the heat and the way my wife's and my daughter's vegetable garden is shriveling have begun to unnerve me. I tell myself that there is nothing wrong with cutting down a few trees on Mount Republic—a few miles of trees, if I am truly honest with myself—and tapping a river for snow, and in my head I still have no trouble believing this.

But on some other level I find words like *global warming* frightening. Or *ozone depletion. Greenhouse gases. Wetlands. Trout. Evergreens. Bears*, *moose*, and *deer*.

The evening becomes a battle of rhetoric and statistics.

Ian Rawls cites the average annual snowfall in Burlington over the past few years, stammering out a staggering series of numbers: ninety-one inches of snow three winters back; sixty-eight inches two winters ago; and only forty-one inches this past winter. He tells the Commission that fewer people are skiing in

Vermont every year, a result, he says, of increasingly poor snowfall.

"The fact is," Ian concludes, "if we can't make more snow, we can't stay in business."

"And do you know why it doesn't snow here the way it once did?" an angry, middle-aged woman with a Copper Project button says, standing. "Because developers like Schuss Limited are destroying the atmosphere!"

An expert I found from the National Weather Service testifies that the change in Vermont's climate has nothing to do with global warming.

"It's a temporary aberration in the jet stream," she says. "The jet stream has moved about three hundred miles north of us. In time, the jet stream will move back south."

Liza Eastwick asks Ian Rawls how many people Powder Peak currently employs.

"About fifty people year-round, and about three hundred from November fifteenth through April fifteenth," he says.

"There are also another five hundred jobs in related service industries that depend upon Powder Peak," I add.

Liza looks down at her notes, and pulls the tortoiseshell barrette out of her hair. The woman has waist-length red hair, and there is something oddly provocative about the movement, something inappropriate and disarming.

"Scottie," she says, looking up at me, "you have gone on record as saying the expansion would result in six hundred new jobs next year. Could you break that figure out?"

I repeat the numbers I have mouthed over and over for weeks now: "In the short-term, the expansion will result in about two hundred construction jobs—some this fall when the gondola is built, some next year when the new trails and the new snowmaking system are brought online. In the long run, however, the resort believes it will create anywhere between three hundred and five hundred jobs in the tourism industry. Motels. Restaurants. Bars. A lot will depend upon the overall economy, but the resort believes that three hundred is an absolute minimum."

Sherman Teeter, a bearded state senator from Burlington, raises his hand and says, "I don't think the people of this state want another three hundred to five hundred opportunities to clean toilets for minimum wage. I'm all for creating jobs, but not this low-end, dead-end, service industry slop."

Before I can respond to Teeter, Reedy jumps to his feet from his seat about six rows ahead of me and a dozen seats to my left.

"Scottie," he begins, "even if these jobs had any value, do you really believe the expansion will result in three to five hundred of them? You keep saying the resort believes this. The resort believes that. What do you personally believe?"

I fold my arms across my chest and smile, stalling, preparing my answer. Before I have to swallow my soul and respond, however, Reedy is undone by his own followers. In the pause that occurs as I stand naked before the hearing, the Copper Project swells into life.

"Cop-per, Cop-per, Cop-per!" a small group begins to chant, as others quickly, almost instantaneously join in, "Cop-per, Cop-per, Cop-per!"

A ski instructor begins to respond, pounding his hand into his fist as he yells, "Pow-der, Pow-der, Pow-der!" The resort's groundskeepers, the seasonal men and women who run lift lines and fit ski boots, the family that runs the series of concession stands in the base lodge, join the instructor.

"Pow-der! Pow-der! Pow-der!"

The assembled groups stand, facing off against each other, trying to drown each other out. Someone begins to shout, "Jobs! Jobs! Jobs!" and someone else shouts back something about "Rape!" but the rest of his chant is lost in the chaos of hurrahs, huzzahs, and howls.

Somewhere very far away Liza Eastwick is hitting the card table with a book, trying to regain a semblance of order, while beside her the two men yell something about quieting down or settling down, but none of them have a prayer of getting through.

And still standing in front of me and to my left is Reedy McClure, staring at me with a smile on his face that says more than all the voices around us. You lucky bastard, his smile is saying. You lucky bastard.

• • •

FIRST COME THE fire trucks, new ones polished to a red brighter than ripe tomatoes, and old ones that are smaller, perhaps a bit tired-looking, but with a clunky, antique charm of their own. There are in this year's parade fire trucks from the nearby villages in the county, including Danville and Plainfield and Cabot, and a contingent of fire and rescue vehicles from the state capital: huge sausage-shaped silver pumpers, jeeps, vans, ambulances, and the sort of honest-to-God, almost urban fire engines with hose lines preconnected to the trucks themselves.

Landaff may be small, but it is well situated for a first-rate parade: It is right in the center of the county, and fairly close to Montpelier, the state capital.

From the high front seats of the fire trucks, volunteer firefighters throw handfuls of candy to the small children lining Landaff's Main (only, really) Street.

Peter DuBois was wrong at the governor's press conference: It will not rain on our parade. It hasn't rained this morning, and it won't rain this afternoon. And the sun is as hot as ever. For better or worse, the Fourth of July is another hot sunny day in Vermont, in a summer in which day after day is bright and clear and dry.

"How many butterflies will there be?" I ask Laura, trying to see down the road past the marching band from the high school, and the fellow leading a llama on a leash.

"Many. It's a downright migration."

As late as yesterday afternoon, Sunday, Laura was assisting the Brownie troop leader and the dozen or so little girls in her troop to sew and stitch and glue felt butterflies together.

"But," she continues, "I was made an honorary troop leader for my service."

"I'm impressed."

The llama stops dead in his tracks in the middle of Main Street, causing the rest of the parade to come to a halt as well. The llama's owner, a tall man with a beard who I believe works for Michael Terry's well crew, tries to yank the animal forward, but he won't budge. And then, with an audience of hundreds and hundreds of spectators on both sides of the road, the llama begins to pee. With something that I assume is the equivalent of a llama smile on its face, the animal begins to empty what must be a bladder the size of a small automobile.

"They're going to be there a while," Laura says, as the yellow stream begins to run down Main Street, down the slight incline toward the float with a half-dozen cows and a milking machine built by the Landaff Historical Society ("We Love Our Dairy Farms: Let's Milk the Past for Our Future!").

Seconds pass, and grow into minutes. We crane our necks to see past the floats from the Historical Society and the Humane Society, and there, perhaps twenty-five yards away, is the vanguard of three troops of Brownies. Little girls in shiny brown shoes. Waiting. Like a radioactive cloud the urine approaches, winding its way slowly toward them. They know it is coming, and they know there is nothing they can do.

When it arrives, however, when the llama urine becomes more than warning and stench, when it becomes a tangible river of pee bisecting their two lines of marchers, they begin to squeal.

And while Cynthia Woolf is able to rally her troops and prevent a full-scale retreat, for one long moment the little girls fall out of formation, dancing and jumping and oohing and laughing and pointing their fingers at the stream, as they try and avoid what they are probably calling the single most gross thing they've ever seen in a parade.

• • •

BUT THE LITTLE girls regroup and they rally. When the llama is finished it agrees to move on, and the parade resumes.

The Brownies, some on foot and some in a hay wagon pulled by two majestic Vermont Morgans, are surrounded by their arts and crafts butterflies. There are hundreds of them, some with wingspans as small as inches, some that are as wide as a yard. There are yellow ones and blue ones and orange and black ones; there are ones with psychedelic colors that I cannot imagine have ever been found in nature; some of the butterflies have safety-pin wings that move and flutter, while others are glued to coat-hanger stanchions and fly over the hay wagon like medieval pennants.

The little girls wave, some continue to giggle, and some stand at the sides of the hay wagon, fanning the air with purple and green butterflies the size of throw rugs.

Miranda, along with two other little girls at the front of the wagon, is not wearing her Brownie uniform. She is dressed instead as a human-sized butterfly, with a black leotard, wide pink wings made of gauze, and felt antennae that bob and twist as she ripples her wings in slow motion.

"Why butterflies?" a woman beside Laura asks, as the little girls begin to pass by.

"Watch," Laura says, motioning toward the banner on the side of the wagon.

"Brownies," the banner reads, "Ready to Shed Our Cocoons and Fly!"

. . .

WE SIT ON our porch the day after the parade, and watch what's left of the sun fall behind Camel's Hump and Mount Mansfield. Even this summer—a summer of ninety-degree days and a sun that won't cease to shine—it cools off a bit in the evening. Tonight, it will probably fall into the high sixties.

Laura puts her feet up on the porch railing, her white sneakers brown with dry dirt from her garden.

It's no longer a garden of mud, even after watering it again today with the hose. It's a garden of dry dirt. The corn is sick, the peas are lame, the tomato plants are tiny.

"The wedding will look pretty weird without any groomsmen," Patience says, standing by the screen door, aimlessly picking at the flecks of white paint on the porch table. "Can't you talk some sense into Reedy?"

I swirl the ice cubes in my coffee. "You sound like Goddard Healy," I tell her. "You both think I have some control over the man. I don't."

"I just can't believe he's being so stubborn!"

The clouds in the valley over Montpelier are almost pink now, each one ringed by red along the bottom edges.

"You're both pretty stubborn," Laura reminds her sister.

"Because I want bridesmaids and Reedy refuses to have groomsmen?"

"That's only one small example."

"How many bridesmaids are you having?" I ask Patience. "Including Laura and Miranda."

"Six."

My wife and my daughter do not share an equal enthusiasm for the actual, planned wedding ceremony of Patience Avery and Reedy McClure. Laura, who is matron of honor, is appalled that at the age of thirty-nine she will be dressed as a bridesmaid, one of a half-dozen essentially identically clad women. Miranda, on the other hand, is absolutely thrilled with the whole idea of being one of her aunt's bridesmaids, and genuinely flattered. This is extremely grown-up stuff to our nine-year-old: a fine gown, flowers in her hair, marching up the aisle of the church, for one brief moment the center of attention.

Miranda is many things, but she isn't shy.

"I'll be honest with you, Patience," I say, "even if I thought for one moment that Reedy would listen to me, I probably wouldn't tell him to go find some groomsmen. Personally, I think he's right. He is too old for groomsmen."

"Are you suggesting that I'm too old for bridesmaids?"

Laura rolls her eyes. "It's not an issue of age," she says, jumping in. "It's the fact that this is your third marriage. Think about it: Don't you believe six bridesmaids is a little inappropriate for a third wedding?"

"It's an important part of the ritual," Patience says, as her nails scratch against the tabletop. She actually sounds more hurt than angry. "The bridesmaids and groomsmen support the couple getting married. Look at where they stand in the ceremony. They provide a literal phalanx against cynicism and doubters, they—"

"Who are the other bridesmaids?" I ask.

A pair of bats streak past the barn, darting by the front doors, and then fly up and over the weather vane at the peak.

"The core group," she answers, irritated with me for interrupting her. "Same women as last time. Except, of course, Miranda's joining us."

"The core group," I say, repeating the words as images of the women flash through my mind. I recall them from Patience's second wedding, some from both Patience's first and second go-rounds.

All these women are, of course, dowsers, and all of them have dowsing specialties. Sas Santoli is a psychic healer, with her own radio program in Pittsburgh. She says that she dowses human energy fields to find what she calls "the sickly imbalance."

Carpe Tiller is a graduate of the University of Metaphysics in Los Angeles who works now with her father as a private detective in Las Vegas. She finds runaways, stolen goods, adulterous husbands, wives, and lovers.

One bridesmaid is a physician, a graduate of Harvard Medical School, who specializes in dowsing her patients' gene maps. Dr. Katherine Whiting practices in Montpelier, so that she is able to teach two days a week at the Green Mountain School of Earth Science.

And another bridesmaid, a virtual neighbor who lives up in Danville, is currently obsessed with dowsing labyrinths to find a new world order. The woman, who at some point in her life changed her name from JoAnn Pomerleau Brandy to Angel Source Brandy, told me at the rehearsal dinner before Patience's second wedding that she once dowsed a dog to discover its past lives.

Each of these women—each in her own way a self-proclaimed feminist, hypnotist, spiritualist, cosmologist, astrologist, psychotherapist, each in her own way a student of esoteric science, a believer in sacred spaces, in wholeness, in apartness, in auras, in anything mythic, lithic, and runic—makes Patience appear stable, serene, and steadfastly normal.

"Yup, all of your favorite women will be there, Scottie," Patience says sarcastically, as a smile begins to form on her face. "Maybe if you behave yourself at the wedding and treat Dr. Whiting real nice, she'll be willing to dowse your genes and tell you exactly what illnesses and infirmities you can look forward to as you grow old."

. . .

ON WEDNESDAY NIGHT Ian Rawls sits beside me on the Quarry Men bench, after grounding out to second base. He wipes his forehead with a terry cloth towel.

"When's your 'secret' lunch with Liza?" he asks after catching his breath, referring to the chairperson of the local environmental commission.

"They're voting Tuesday night. So I'm seeing her on Monday."

"Want me to join you?"

I don't, but I also can't offend Ian. "You're more than welcome. But I don't think it's smart. Ethically, she shouldn't even be seeing me. The only reason she agreed to is because we went to college together. But in theory, we won't even discuss Powder Peak."

"But of course you will . . ."

"I assume so."

"In that case, I probably won't join you. It doesn't sound like you need me to bring it up."

One of the younger men on the team smashes a line drive just over the third baseman's head and down the left field line. Reflexively we both stand and cheer, as Clinton Willey, the elementary school teacher on our team, races all the way home from first base.

"Joel will start running one of the lifts this season," Ian tells me, pointing at the fellow who hit the line drive, standing now on second base.

"I thought he had a year-round job at a ski company. Down in Montpelier."

"He got laid off," Ian says, as we sit back down.

"Joel Stebbins? I didn't know he was part of that group."

"Yup. Thirty-six employees. Out of a workforce in the neighborhood of ninety-five people. Just over a third of the factory was let go."

After slapping a variety of palms, shoulders, and bottoms, Clinton Willey joins us on the bench.

"A two-base knock does the soul good. Joel really needed that."

"I was sorry to hear he got laid off," I tell Clinton. "Ian just mentioned to me what happened."

Clinton, who lives in the same part of Barre as Joel, shakes his head. "Yup. He was pretty depressed. He's not even sure where to begin to look for work. He says nobody's hiring in the ski industry."

Ian frowns. "Well, nobody is on the manufacturing side. But he's joining us up on the mountain from November to April. He'll be running a chairlift."

Hugo Scutter lofts a shallow fly ball just over the shortstop's head that drops in for a single, giving us runners on first and third.

"That was pathetic," Ian says, referring to the droopy base hit.

"Is the ski industry really as deep in the toilet as the newspapers say it is?" Clinton asks.

Outside of softball, I do not know Clinton Willey. I do not know the name of his wife, I do not know if he has or wants any children. I don't even know what grade he teaches in elementary school. Consequently, my immediate reaction is to give Clinton some sort of polite but evasive answer, to tell him that things aren't terrific, but they're not all that bad either.

Perhaps because I am sitting beside Ian Rawls, however, a client and the managing director of one of the state's largest ski resorts, I take a deep breath and begin to proselytize.

"Yup. It's pretty deep in the toilet," I tell the young teacher. "There were eighty-one different ski resorts in Vermont in 1971. How many do you think there are in existence right now?"

He rubs his chin. "I'm guessing."

"Of course you are."

"Fifty."

"Wrong. Try nineteen."

"Nineteen?"

"Nineteen."

"Where the hell do sixty ski resorts go in a couple of decades?"

"Out of business," I tell him. "Insurance has gotten too expensive. And the resorts have gotten too little snow."

"And they have to battle too many regulations," Ian adds, disgusted. "Too many environmental regulations, and a permit process that must have been designed by the devil himself."

Clark Rawls hits a ground ball to third, and the inning looks as if it will come to an end. But the third baseman throws the ball high over the first baseman's head, and Clark winds up on base.

"And it's not just the resorts that are in trouble," I tell Clinton, almost relishing the opportunity I have taken to speak freely in public about the woes of the industry. "About one out of every six ski retailers declared bankruptcy or closed its doors for good between January first and May thirty-first. And of those retailers still in business, probably a quarter will go belly-up this season if we don't get a ton of white stuff dropped on us."

Clinton looks past me at Ian, and then back at me. "Is there anything you guys can do about all that?" he asks.

"Like maybe make snow?" Ian asks in response.

"Sure. Like that."

Ian looks at me, waiting for me to jump in once again.

"Write the governor," I tell him. "Write the District Five Environmental Commission. Write your state senators and representatives. Tell them how much this state needs a healthy ski industry."

One of the few actual men from the Barre quarries on our

team hits the next pitch to deep center field, but the outfielder runs the ball down to finally end the inning.

As the three of us reach for our baseball gloves and start toward the field, Ian turns to me and says quietly, "Masterful, Scottie, just masterful. I hope you're going to tell Liza Eastwick everything you just told Clinton Willey."

"I'll try."

"Because I'll be frank: If it doesn't look like we're going to get our permits to tap the Chittenden and build some new trails down Republic next year, I'm not about to go out on a limb for people like Joel this November."

. . .

MIRANDA HAS PRESERVED her wings, and floats among Laura's flower garden in the moonlight. A border of small lavender ageratum. Pink and orange zinnias. Neon yellow snapdragons and marigolds. Dozens and dozens of sky-blue irises.

In the soft and misty light of this moon, the fact that each flower hangs limp, each petal has withered, can be ignored. The moon hides the fact that each flower is dying, weightless without water, drooping—somehow—nonetheless.

Miranda too may be oblivious, at least for the moment, to the notion that she is dancing among the dead. There is no life left in those marigolds. One breeze and the petals will fall off, fly away, blow across the dry and rocky soil that is a far cry from a bed.

The wires that border and shape Miranda's wings sparkle when the moonlight catches them, and the gauze, painted with silver glitter, glistens.

She sings to herself, humming a song I don't know. She raises her arms over her head, and her wings rise above her golden blond hair, two filmy arches of pink that look as if they just might lift her off the ground.

Sometimes, I see only those wings.

I wonder if Miranda believes she is dancing for rain.

She knows that our well still has water, but many wells don't.

She told me today that she and her mother see Michael Terry's big well-drilling trucks wherever they go.

Michael Terry is indeed having the summer of his life.

Fireflies dance with Miranda, stars that flicker as one with the night sky, stepping aside as she sways and spins and glides.

Miranda is grace. She is grace in her small sneakers in Laura's garden, she is grace on her skis or her snowboard on any trail at Powder Peak.

I may have lied today when I described to Clinton Willey the state of the ski industry. My numbers were truthful and accurate, but I'm not sure that my reasoning was. At least not completely.

If I had wanted to be completely honest with Clinton, I might have told him that it is not simply a lack of snow that is driving ski retailers out of business. It is unrealistically high prices. It is overextension. It is technology and gadgets that are out of control: heated boots and double-tipped skis, ski racks that transform themselves into bike racks in the spring, parkas and caps and fashions that change every year.

If I had wanted to tell Clinton the whole truth about Vermont's ski resorts, I might have added that it is not simply the cost of insurance, or the lack of snow, or even the state's strict environmental laws that are causing them quickly to disappear. It is lift tickets that cost forty and fifty dollars a day. It is mountains that are less steep than the West, and trails that are often miles and miles shorter. It is consistently poor management, poor advertising, poor self-promotion.

Am I willing to trade a river forever so that Joel Stebbins can have a job this fall? I sure talk like I am. I sure act like I am. And if I ran into Joel right now at a restaurant or a movie or softball practice, if I were to see on his face the fear that unemployment can cause, how could I not demand that the state trade some trout for a job?

But I didn't tell Clinton Willey tonight about trades. I didn't tell him that Vermont cannot have everything. If he wants to write his senator so that Joel can have that job, then he shouldn't expect to take his children—if he does indeed have any—fishing someday in the Chittenden River. If he wants Vermont to have a ski industry with profitable boot makers and thriving resorts, then he shouldn't plan on deer hunting ten years from now on the undeveloped side of Mount Republic. Because there won't be one.

My small daughter whirls among the impatiens.

And I stand alone in the dark and watch her dance, unwilling to go inside and face the harsh light of my own house.

13

•

From my perch at the kitchen table, I can see Elias Gray's blue and rust pickup rolling slowly up our driveway early Saturday morning, and then coasting to a stop between the barn and the house. The sun, barely over the mountains, reflects off Elias's windshield and the back of his rearview mirror.

"I knew they'd be on time," Miranda says, dropping her spoon into her cereal bowl, and running to the foot of the stairs. It is not quite six thirty.

"Mom, they're here!" she yells up to the second floor.

"Thank you, sweetheart," Laura yells back from our bedroom.

"Are you coming?"

"Sure am."

Miranda races past me to the back door, rolling her eyes briefly as she reminds me, "I told Mom they'd be here on time." She pushes open the screen door, and leans against the metal frame, half in and half out of the house.

Patience jumps out of the passenger side of the truck, while Elias carefully lowers himself down from the driver's side. Elias is wearing his khaki-colored overalls, and Patience is wearing plaid Bermuda shorts with a striped T-shirt.

"Hi, Aunt Patience, hi, Mr. Gray!"

Patience hoists Miranda into the air and swings her once, kissing her on the forehead as she puts her down. "Morning, Miranda. What are you doing up this early on a Saturday?"

"Mom said I could pick out the candles."

"The colors?" Elias asks.

"Yup."

"Dowse for the ones that'll sell best," Patience says, not wholly serious. Patience and Elias are here to pick up the cases of candles that Laura is donating to this morning's church rummage sale. The rummage sale occurs every year on the second Saturday in July, a small part of the town's annual Old Home Week Celebration: a week that begins with the Fourth of July parade and fireworks, and continues with a variety of events such as the rescue squad's potluck supper, the volunteer firemen's chicken barbecue, and the church rummage sale. Other than Christmas and Easter, the most well-attended church service of the year will occur tomorrow, when anywhere from twenty-five to fifty former members of the congregation who have returned to Landaff to see friends and family will return also to church.

"You two must want some coffee. It's fresh," I tell them.

"Nope, we got three more stops to make before eight o'clock. We said we'd be at the church by eight with the last of the merchandise," Patience says. "So we should keep moving."

"I hope we're your first stop."

"Oh, we've already picked up some goodies from the Moodys and the Woolfs. Laura awake yet?"

Before I can answer, we all hear footsteps on the stairway.

"Yup, she's awake," Miranda says.

Laura strolls into the kitchen, her feet and legs bare up to her tan hiking shorts, wearing a faded blue T-shirt that says, "Dowsing is Sense-sational." She bought the shirt years and years ago at the annual dowsing convention.

"How's the 'Stolen Goods Committee'?" she asks her sister and Elias.

"It's already been a full and rich day," Patience says. "But just between us, I think we'll probably do a heck of a lot better with your candles than with Cynthia Woolf's macaroni jewelry."

Elias shrugs. "Giannine says we always sell a few pieces. And it's easier to just pick the stuff up and put it out on the table than it is to tell Cynthia we don't want it."

Laura fixes one of the shoulder straps on Elias's overalls, which at some point became twisted. "Michael Terry's drilling a well today, isn't he, Elias?"

"Yup."

"And you dowsed the spot, didn't you?"

"You're supposed to be a dowser," he tells my wife, "not some gypsy mystic."

"No mysticism. You just look a little tired today, Elias, that's all. And Giannine told Patience and me years ago that you don't sleep a wink the night before a well's drilled that you dowsed."

Elias nods that she is correct: He didn't sleep much last night. "I was up at the Langtons' on Wednesday. And Terry's got his rig up there today."

"I'm in the wrong business," Patience says, shaking her head. "I shouldn't be finding wells, I should be drilling 'em."

Miranda pushes open the screen door. "I'll go pick out the candles," she says, and then adds, "Aunt Patience said I should dowse them!"

"Just pick out the colors you like, sweetheart," Laura tells her. "I'm sure your aunt was just kidding about the dowsing."

"But I could do it."

"We got no doubts about that," Elias says, hunching over a tiny bit to meet my daughter's eyes. "But you got to treat your talent with respect. You've got a very special gift, and the one who gave it to you doesn't want to see it used on just anything."

Patience looks at her sneakers, no doubt feeling chastised.

"Isn't the rummage sale important?"

"Course it is. But you know what?"

"What?"

"Whether you pick out your mother's pink candles or the evergreen ones won't make a difference. I promise you, we'll sell 'em all either way."

. . .

IT SPRINKLES SUNDAY morning, periodic raindrops that fall for a few minutes before eight, and then again in the ten or fifteen minutes before church starts. It is enough rain to blacken asphalt roads, briefly, and moisten the highest tips of grass. But it is nowhere near enough rain to salvage what's left of the corn, replenish the wells that are low, or in any way slacken the thirst of a state that has forgotten how high its streams and rivers once were.

In church, it is possible for short moments to forget the drought, to forget the red plastic rain barrels that pose as lawn ornaments throughout the county, dotting yards and fields like tombstones. People are in Landaff today who haven't been back in town in years, in some cases sitting in almost the same pews in which they sat many Sunday services ago: elderly people who retired to small apartments and trailers on Florida's gulf coast; college students who now come to church once a year; and the small clusters of "summer people" from Boston and New York City, sitting together, who descend upon Landaff every June, July, and August.

During this morning's service, people in the congregation stand and recall stories of the church and the town that they want to see live on in the community's tradition of verbal myth and oral history. They stand and acknowledge people who once lived in Landaff and have now returned for a visit, and they stand and remember people from Landaff who have now died, and who they believe must not be forgotten. People like Darcy Floyd.

"Darcy," says Anna Avery, standing in her spot in the choir, conjuring an image of the man for much of the church with the simple mention of his name, "meant an awful lot to Landaff. He didn't just raise the money we needed for this organ, and he didn't just run the roads with the town plow for maybe forty winters. He was . . . the conscience of our public debates."

There is a small ripple of loving laughter among the senior citizens in the church who remember Darcy Floyd. Whenever there was an apparently unanimous vote in a town meeting, Darcy would vote no, even when he agreed wholeheartedly with the town. "There's always somebody who doesn't agree with the masses," Darcy insisted, "and that fellow deserves some representation too. Even if it's meaningless. Even if that fellow's an idiot."

One of the church deacons asks us all to recall Prue Minton, the woman who—until she died on March 11 of this year—was the oldest member of the congregation. She died at the age of 101, leaving behind ninety-six direct, living descendants.

Laura nods in awe: there are villages in Vermont that aren't that big.

. . .

OUR RECEPTIONIST'S FAMILY showers with the drain closed, so that they are able to save the water. They then use that water to flush their toilet.

Warren Birch had a new well drilled last week. Five hundred and twelve feet.

An associate in our firm, a fellow who recently purchased an expensive new car, has been known to drive as far as Concord, New Hampshire, to find a car wash that is open.

And Duane Hurley, the third partner in our firm, says that

he and his wife now save the water in which they boil pasta or potatoes or peas, and then use it to douse the potted plants on their porch.

"Flowers love carbohydrates," Duane insists. "They love carbohydrates and starch."

14

After I order a club soda and Liza Eastwick asks the waiter for "the tallest, coldest, most iced-down glass of cranberry juice you can find," the head of the local environmental commission turns to me and says, "I'm only here out of the goodness of my heart. I really shouldn't be talking to you at all."

"I understand."

"And I wouldn't have come if my mind wasn't already made up."

"Is it?"

"You betcha. So, that point noted: Is this going to be a Scottie Winston soft-sell lunch or a Scottie Winston hard-sell lunch?"

"Which will be more effective?"

"Too early to tell," she says, unfolding her napkin and dropping it into her lap like an open parachute. Her tremendous mane of red hair is still wet, and it crosses my mind that the woman enjoyed a quick swim in what's left of the Lamoille River on her way to St. Johnsbury this morning. "Reedy McClure asked me to say hello."

"Gee, that was nice of him. I haven't spoken to Reedy in the longest time. Since yesterday morning, as a matter of fact. Right after church."

"He called me about an hour ago."

"And he'll call you again this afternoon."

"Nope. He thinks he's coming by my house tomorrow afternoon. Tuesday. I told him he can't, not on the day of the vote. That's going too far."

"You've probably heard a lot from the Copper Project."

"I've heard a lot from everybody. All of us on the Commission have." She pauses briefly, shaking her head. "And the thing is, it's all wasted energy. No offense, Scottie, but it's all wasted breath."

"In that case, why are you taking the time to see me now?"

"Catch up on alumni gossip, see who you've heard from in our class. Enjoy a free lunch."

"Liza Eastwick doesn't waste time on free lunches."

"In the last two weeks, I have been asked to discuss this issue more times than I care to admit. I may as well get something to eat once in a while."

The waiter returns with our drinks, and for the first time I glance at the restaurant's menu. "Who have you seen?" I ask.

She rubs her eyes, thinking. "Let's see. I've met with representatives from the Copper Project. I've met with the governor. I've met with Peter DuBois. I've met with at least six or seven state senators, and—as you know—I've met with two young guns from your firm."

"We call them associates."

"And I made up my mind weeks ago."

"What about the rest of the committee?"

"They did too. Environmental politics is like every other kind of politics. Everyone makes a lot of noise, and no one changes anyone's mind."

The restaurant, a training site for the small culinary institute in St. Johnsbury, is staffed largely by students in their early twenties, eager young people who hover by the tables hoping to help. Liza chose this restaurant for the simple reason that it is unlikely she will be seen having lunch with me here. We make the waiter inordinately happy when we tell him that we would like the most complicated special on the menu—whatever that is.

"As long as it's vegetarian," Liza adds quickly.

"Does that mean no fish?" the waiter asks nervously.

"That's correct. No fish."

The waiter smiles, relieved, and rushes back to the kitchen with his news that there are a pair of enthusiastic guinea pigs at the table in the corner.

"Okay, you've made your decision: Will Powder Peak receive its permit?"

"I'm only one vote."

I nod. Rightly or wrongly, this strikes me as an admission that she will vote in favor of the Powder Peak expansion. I press for confirmation.

"You understand the importance of Powder Peak to our economy?"

"More or less. But I'm only one part of the equation."

"The Copper Project won't last forever. No grassroots organization does. I know that right now Reedy's itching to leave Vermont and head for British Columbia. He won't, not with his wedding in September. But we both know there will be other oil spills."

"Well, Reedy's only one of many opponents, most of whom have no plans to leave."

"Governor Webster isn't an opponent."

"But Governor Webster won't be an ally either, at least until you receive your federal impact statement from the Forest Service."

"We'll have that by August. And I expect it to be favorable."

"Doesn't matter. We vote tomorrow night. Besides, the Vermont Natural Resources Council is against your project—"

"It's not my project."

Liza continues as if I never interrupted her. "Some state senators are against the project. Look at Reedy."

"Reedy's a fanatic," I tell her, smiling.

"So are you. Just a different kind."

"Not really. I just happen to care more about people than fish," I respond reflexively, trying to ignore the image that forms in my mind of my daughter whirling at night among the impatiens. "I just care about people having jobs. I just care about people having property taxes they can afford to pay."

"Very commendable, Scottie Winston. As I've always said, you're a role model for us all."

I push on, despite my best intentions to avoid polemics, despite my vows to myself to be truthful. "Sarcasm aside, Liza, you cannot dispute the fact that Vermont needs Powder Peak. And without the permits to make snow and expand the resort, someday the state may not have it."

She pats the top of her head, wondering, perhaps, if her hair is still wet. "I probably understand the economic arguments for Powder Peak better than my two illustrious associates. But even I'm not going to give Powder Peak carte blanche to trash either Mount Republic or the Chittenden River."

"It is not in the resort's interest to 'trash' its highest mountain or one of the state's key rivers. Obviously they don't want to do anything that harms either the mountain or the river. You know that," I tell her.

Liza sighs. "There are ten environmental criteria to Act 250," she says, referring to the state's development control law, a law instituted for the sole purpose of preventing Vermont from becoming a land of condominiums and ski chalets. "Powder Peak's project meets about half of them. I think the best you can hope for is a permit with conditions."

"What kinds of conditions?"

From nowhere the waiter appears and places a basket of bread in the middle of our table. Another young woman whisks our water glasses away, refills them, and almost instantly returns them to their exact spots on the tablecloth.

"You guys want to withdraw something like three hundred and seventy-five million gallons of water a season from the Chittenden, right?"

" 'Us guys' don't, but the resort does. Yes."

"Uh-huh. And the storage pond is supposed to hold about forty million gallons of water. I don't think we can approve a project that large. Not with water this scarce, and the Chittenden River as low as it is."

"The drought won't last forever."

"No, but it may leave scars on the river that will."

"What about the new trails?"

"Aren't they contingent upon snowmaking?"

"Most are. Not all."

"Personally, the new parking spaces don't worry me. Three and a half miles of underground water pipes don't worry me. Cutting down miles of forest for new trails on Mount Republic, however . . . that does worry me. So does putting up one hundred and fifty high-voltage utility poles, and putting in one of those new high-speed gondolas."

I reach for the bread and break off two slices. She shakes her head that she doesn't want one, and I drop both on my plate.

"How many conditions are we talking about here?"

"I don't know yet."

"Okay. Will the permit be thinner than the Montpelier phone book, or fatter than the Manhattan phone book?"

"I grew up in Maine. I've never seen the Manhattan phone book."

"Small children sit on it so they can reach the dinner table."

"Well." She thinks for a moment, smiling for the first time in what seems like a long time. "Personally, I think it'll be closer to Montpelier."

"That's helpful. Any chance we can get it as thin, say, as the Landaff Church directory?"

"Not likely."

"What would it take to get it that thin?"

The waiter appears behind Liza, walking in slow motion so that he doesn't drop our lunch. Liza looks over her shoulder at him briefly, and then turns back to me. "Let me ask you a question: What would honestly happen if the permit were denied?"

The waiter carefully places before each of us a plate with small clusters of immaculately shaped food. Grilled tofu with a spicy horseradish sauce. A coleslaw made with endive and pecans. Something that looks like a potato pancake, but I know is in actuality something much more glamorous.

"Honestly," I repeat.

I have been telling people for over a month now that if Powder Peak does not receive its permits, if it is not allowed to make snow and build new trails, it will be unable to compete with either the western ski resorts or the largest eastern resorts. It will, in all likelihood, go out of business. I have suggested so much today at lunch. It probably wouldn't go out of business this year, I have implied, and probably not next. But eventually it would. Consistently I have argued that without new trails and new snow, the resort will someday go belly-up, taking with it jobs and tax revenue the state desperately needs.

This is what I have told people, this is what I have been telling them for months.

"Looks good, doesn't it?" I ask, nodding down at the food before us.

"Enjoy your meal," the waiter says, grinning.

"We will."

"You're not answering my question," Liza says.

I nod. I reach for my fork. If Powder Peak's permits were denied, some bank somewhere would lose a loan that it wanted to make to fund Powder Peak's expansion. Fifteen million dollars, a pretty good-sized loan. The resort's short-term profits would probably be a little better, long-term a little worse. The resort would not create any new jobs on the mountain, or in the service industry around it. But do I honestly believe that the resort would go out of business without the proposed project?

I don't think even Ian Rawls and Goddard Healy really believe that.

"Off the record?" I ask.

"Off the record."

I open my mouth and start to speak, prepared to say the word *nothing*—the one word that I haven't uttered in the context of Powder Peak in years. I open my mouth with every intention of answering honestly, of telling Liza Eastwick, *Nothing would happen. In the greater scheme of things, not a damn thing would happen if Powder Peak's permit requests were denied.*

But I am unable to say that one word, or to speak the sentences that I had planned. Instead I tell Liza, staring at the red halo that is her hair, "The economic strength of this area would be crippled for a very, very long time."

And I am off and running. Again.

• • •

"GOOD MORNING, IAN," I say into the speakerphone on my desk Wednesday morning.

"Pick up the goddamn phone, will you?"

I lift up the receiver. "Good morning, Ian."

"That's better. Have you heard anything?"

"About the Commission's vote last night?"

"Do you really think there could be anything else on my mind today?"

"No," I answer, "I haven't heard anything. But I don't think I will. The Commission will contact you first, not me."

"I assumed that. It's just that it's almost nine o'clock, and no one's told me anything. So I thought maybe someone had spoken to you."

"It's eight thirty-five, Ian. It's not almost nine o'clock."

"It feels like it's almost nine o'clock. Goddard has already called twice. He called me at my home last night about midnight, and he called here about ten minutes ago."

"It's five thirty in the morning in San Francisco!"

"That's Goddard. Have you read today's paper?"

"I was just about to skim through it. Is Powder Peak in it?"

I hear the sound of rustling newspaper over the telephone, the sound of Ian turning the pages in his office at the resort. "Go to page two of the front section. The national news wire."

I lift my coffee cup up off the *Sentinel* and turn to the first inside page. In the middle of two columns of short news briefs is one with the subhead "Eco-Terrorists Strike California Resort":

> TAHOE CITY, CA—Vandals damaged a golf course and ski trail early Tuesday morning at Mystic Mountain, a four-season resort owned by the San Francisco–based Schuss Limited. According to Jason Belmont, resort general manager, the vandals destroyed four greens and three fairways with a chemical defoliant, spelling out the words "Screw Schuss!" on one green, and "Animal Rights Now!" on another.
>
> In addition, the resort says, the vandals left a note

> claiming that they had ruined the cable for a high-speed chairlift now under construction, by dousing it with a solvent that weakens metal.
>
> Although there are no suspects, the resort says that a number of former employees and environmental action groups will be investigated.

"I suppose that's why Goddard called last night."

"You bet."

"Well, I wouldn't worry about that sort of thing happening at Powder Peak," I tell Ian, genuinely unconcerned.

"Why? Because Reedy McClure is about to become your brother-in-law? Well, I got news for you. Reedy is only one nut among many. Did you read about those crazies over in Maine last April?"

"The ones in the animal costumes?"

"Yes!"

"Yes," I tell him, recalling the photograph I saw of two or three dozen people dressed up as bears and beavers and moose, protesting before the entrance to some paper mill. "I read about them. And frankly, it won't be the end of the world if a few people in beaver suits do stand around Powder Peak for a day or two this fall."

"Those people didn't just stand around! They destroyed hundreds of thousands of dollars of logging equipment! They poured some sort of red dye on the employees of the mill, and told them it was animal blood! Animal blood, for God's sake!"

"Ian, relax. This is Vermont."

"I understand that," he says, and then stops speaking abruptly.

"Go on."

"My secretary just put a note on my desk," he explains, his voice low and frightened. "Liza Eastwick is holding for me on the other line."

"Not the district coordinator?"

"Nope. Liza herself."

"Well, put me on hold and take the call. And remember: Liza may tell you that you have the permit, but there are some conditions. If she says that, don't panic. It's still good news. Realistically, it's the best news you can expect. Be appreciative and grateful and then get off the phone."

"Uh-huh."

"Ready?"

"No. Shit."

A second later the line becomes silent as he puts me on hold, and I sit back in my chair to wait.

• • •

DAYDREAMING, I CONCOCT a conversation with Reedy McClure:

"Reedy? Would you ever dress up like a beaver and pour acid on the cables for a chairlift at Powder Peak?"

"Not likely. I'd never dress up like a beaver—I'm vehemently opposed to fashion fur."

"But it's possible?"

"Well, that would depend."

"On?"

"On whether I found a faux fur or fake fur that looked real."

"Suppose that you did."

"Still. I probably wouldn't."

"Because that would be criminal activity and you're not a criminal?"

"No. Because I just bought my season pass at the Alpine Den's annual preseason sales bonanza. A yearlong lift ticket at fifty percent off the regular price!"

I hope in my daydreams I don't give Reedy McClure too much credit.

. . .

"WE GOT IT."

The three words emerge from the speaker on my desk, and cut through the silence of my office.

"We got it!" Ian says again, this time a little louder.

Instantly the words conjure for me images of yellow backhoes now brown with dirt, digging trenches and storage ponds and deep holes for utility poles. I can see skidders dragging trees from the forest, giant Lincoln Logs the size of tall Vermont buildings, and helicopters dropping pylons into the ground, dozens of them covering the mountain with a man-made windstorm that sends deer and squirrels and rabbits running.

And the words conjure also for me relief. I feel my shoulders relax and sag as I reach for the telephone, and my heart stops beating from wherever it was inside my ears. Although I don't yet know the details, I don't yet know the stipulations, from the sound of Ian's voice I can assume that we won.

I can assume that I won.

Yes, there will be appeals. I am sure of that. But for the moment, there is only victory.

"Congratulations," I tell Ian. "Nice work."

"Damn right," he says happily, the thought of eco-terrorism suddenly the furthest thing from his mind.

"Did Liza give you any specifics?"

"The full permit will be issued next week, but she's going to send me a summary this afternoon."

"So there are conditions."

"Yup. But Liza said they're pretty reasonable: how big our storage pond can be, what's defined as a connecting path, what's an honest-to-God ski trail. That sort of thing."

"Did you talk about the Chittenden River?"

"It sounds like there will be a cap on the number of gallons we can tap each winter. It will depend on the river's depth and water flow. But we should be okay."

"Did Liza say anything else?"

"She asked me to tell you something. It's weird, but she said you'd understand."

"Yes?"

"She said you'd be happy to know that you might mistake the permit for the Landaff Church directory."

15

•

"The thing I don't understand," Reedy McClure says to me over lunch Thursday, "is how the Commission could be so cavalier about the water flow. You shouldn't be allowed to tap the Chittenden River. You just shouldn't."

"You just shouldn't," I repeat, imitating the petulant tone of his voice.

"That's not funny," he says, sipping his coffee. He slams his mug down onto the diner's Formica countertop so hard that some of the coffee spills over the lip.

"I'll stop."

"That's your problem, Scottie. You just don't take this stuff seriously. It's all just . . . it's all just a game to you."

"Not true."

"It is. None of this stuff is more important to you than whether your stupid softball team is winning, or whether you're able to master some new ski trail on some new mountain."

"It's not just a game to me. Honest."

"Then what is it? Do you honestly believe that horseshit you tell people about jobs and tax bases?"

I smile. "It's not just a game to me. It's a job. That's what it really is. It's a job. It's mortgage money. It's Miranda's college tuition. It's—"

"It's dirty money!"

"Dirt is brown. Money is green."

He sits back against the leather-like Naugahyde couch, and spreads out his arms. "You don't believe that."

"That it's just a job? I probably don't. But I also don't have a trust fund that allows me the luxury of what you'd define as proper political activism. We can't all afford to be righteous and politically correct."

"That was an asshole thing to say."

"Well, you put me into an asshole corner."

The sun reflects off the thousand thin sheets of metal and aluminum that comprise the slimline diner: salt shakers and napkin dispensers, the walls along the booths and over the grills, jukeboxes and knives and forks and spoons, the edges of counters and cash registers and the clips that hold menus.

"Can I assume you're going to appeal the decision to the state Environmental Board?" I ask.

"Sure can."

"Too bad. I was hoping you'd realize it was a lost cause."

"It's not a lost cause! Why do you say that?"

"How often does the Environmental Board reverse a decision of one of its commissions? It's rare, and it's not going to happen this time."

He shrugs. "There's still money in the Copper Project coffers, and there's still time on my hands. I'll keep plugging. You should know I also plan on turning up my efforts with the people at the U.S. Forest Service. You still need their permission."

"Yup."

After a long pause in which each of us assesses our separate wounds, he continues, "I'm serious. I just don't understand why you do what you do. You talk about Miranda's college education like you care about her future, but all—"

"Lighten up, Reedy. You know I care about Miranda's future."

"Then how can you help them destroy a river? How can you help them destroy a mountain?"

"Look: No one is going to tap the Chittenden if the water flow falls too far. When the river can't support snowmaking, it won't be used to make snow. If—"

"It can't support snowmaking right now!"

"Then maybe it's time the river disappeared into a goddamn swamp!" I tell Reedy, able but unwilling to keep my voice even. "Isn't that the 'natural' process?"

"You're such a whore!"

"A whore? Because I help create jobs? Because I help keep people's property taxes down? Damn it, Reedy, don't try and make me feel guilty. There's nothing wrong with what I do for a living. Nothing!"

"You're about to kill a beautiful river and the most perfectly shaped mountain in Vermont."

"I don't have to listen to this."

"Sure, close your ears and your eyes. Why not? Go ahead and kill a river to pay for your big house on the hill—"

"You are no one to talk about big houses on hills—"

"Go ahead and ruin a mountain to pay for your vacations in Key West, your ski weekends—"

"This state needs people like me!" I tell Reedy, standing up. "That's a fact!" He starts to speak but I shake my head no, I won't listen. I then reach into my wallet and throw five dollars of dirty money on the table, and leave him alone in the diner.

• • •

YEARS AGO, THE Landaff Volunteer Fire Company was mustered by a loud siren that blared from speakers at the top of the firehouse. That siren always sounded to me like the desperate or angry howl from some monstrous, prehistoric bird. As loud as it was, however, the siren was a far from perfect system: About half the fire company did not live within hearing distance of the speakers, especially in the winter when windows are sealed shut in Vermont, and winds come off the mountains that can drown out the cries of even the largest flying reptiles.

Today, we have an infinitely better system: Most of the twenty-two members of the Landaff Volunteer Fire Company live with radio pagers attached to their belts. When they're needed, when there's a fire, the firefighters are alerted by a small tone, followed by a series of coded instructions from whoever happens to be that day's radio dispatcher. They might be in the middle of church, they might be at a local committee meeting, they might be at work, but it is not uncommon to see a firefighter stand up and say simply, "I just toned out," and then leave abruptly.

The money to purchase the Landaff Volunteer Fire Company's impressive beeper system came from Elias Gray's dowsing donations, one more example of the critical role that water can play in fighting fire.

Last night, Laura and I saw or heard a dozen cars and pickups race down the street to the firehouse, honking their horns when cars wouldn't pull off the road to let them pass. It was about ten o'clock. Within minutes we then heard the sound of Landaff's two fire engines roaring in the opposite direction, their sirens screaming, and we heard the pathetic rumble of the fire company's pumper, the giant silver sausage that carries their water.

And I thought nothing of it. I assumed there was another small fire at the edge of the national forest.

As Laura and I curled up together in bed, and she told me that she had a bad feeling about something, I thought nothing of that too. I kissed Laura on her forehead and said not to worry.

And in the middle of the night when Miranda had a nightmare and crawled into bed beside Laura, I certainly did not think about the fire engines that had sped past our house about ten.

Even when the phone rang at six thirty this morning, a time the phone never rings, I did not think about the fire engines. I don't know what I thought. But I did stop shaving. I wandered to the top of the stairs, my razor in one hand and a towel in the other, and I tried to hear Laura in the kitchen. Miranda, who was in her room getting ready for a small day hike with friends, joined me at the top of the stairs, hugging to her chest her small half-filled knapsack.

When Miranda could not hear what Laura was saying, if she was saying anything, Miranda looked up at me and asked, "Is everything okay?"

And I knew instantly that it wasn't, although I still had no idea why everything was no longer okay, I still had no idea what had happened. I still had not recalled the fire engines.

"I don't know, sweetheart," I said to Miranda. "Let's go see."

Miranda walked past me downstairs, as I remembered that my face was half covered with shaving cream. So I returned to the bathroom to rinse the remains of the lather off my face, although it was clearly a halfhearted effort: Laura and Miranda both told me later that I appeared in the kitchen a minute behind Miranda wearing only a pair of pajama bottoms, my face still sporting a white foamy beard.

There I put my hand on Miranda's shoulder, and together we watched Laura pace between the screen door and the counter with the coffeemaker, the phone pressed flat against her ear. She was already dressed in her hiking shorts, and I was struck—as I am often—by the beauty of her legs.

Laura looked up at us once and shook her head, and we both saw she was crying. And while I knew in that instant that someone had died, I still made no connection with the fire engines.

Names and faces flashed through my mind as I sat in a chair by the kitchen table, and hoisted Miranda onto my lap. I feared that Laura's mother, Anna, had died, or one of her two aunts. I imagined for a brief second that a traffic accident had taken the life of a cousin, a neighbor, a friend.

I feared for a split second for Patience.

I started to mouth the words *what happened* or *who* to Laura, but I could see that the phone call was winding down. And so I sat and waited in silence, and watched Miranda as she stared off into space. Scared.

When Laura hung up the phone she took a deep breath, and the moment she started to speak I thought finally of the fire engines. I recalled hearing them race past our house once, and I realized for the first time that I hadn't heard them return. And I knew somehow even then, at six thirty in the morning, that the trucks and the pumper and the firefighters had still not returned. If I were to have visited the firehouse at that moment, I would have seen a dozen cars and pickups still sitting in the parking lot beside the three wide garage doors.

Whoever had died had died in a fire. Or, perhaps, fighting that fire.

Whoever had died had died sometime in the night, perhaps at that moment when Laura had had her bad feeling. Perhaps it had been when Miranda had crawled into our bed.

It is ironic, but when I understood on some level that someone had died in a fire, I envisioned a house fire instead of a forest fire. I forgot completely my conclusion from the night before that the Landaff Volunteer Fire Company had raced off to battle a campfire that had run amok. I envisioned instead Gertrude and Jeanette Scutter's old place in flames, I thought of poor Archer Moody's farmhouse going up in smoke.

No, my instincts from the night before had been correct. It had been a forest fire, one of the many small blazes that have tormented Vermont as the drought has continued through July. It had been started, apparently, by dry lightning.

That was Patience on the phone, Laura said.

She told Laura that this blaze had been especially close to the edge of the forest, on land that had been in the Gray family for almost two centuries. The fire was out now, or at least under control, thanks to the efforts—*mutual aid* is the official term—of neighboring volunteer companies from Plainfield and Bartlett and West Gardner.

But the fire had taken with it a couple of acres of forest, as well as one structure: the magnificent sugarhouse that Elias had designed for his grandson. They might have saved the sugarhouse, but the wooden bridge that led to it had collapsed when one of the pumpers from Plainfield had attempted to cross it (fortunately, it was the last vehicle to arrive at the scene). Evidently, the bridge had collapsed in slow motion, giving way a little bit at a time, as the pumper sank into the stream that had once been a river, and then rolled onto its side like some mammoth dead jungle animal.

That was why the fire trucks weren't back yet. They were all trapped on the far side of the ditch.

And there had been a fatality. It may have been smoke inhalation, it may have been a heart attack or a stroke or perhaps even despair. At six thirty, Patience did not know the details.

But the old man whom Patience Avery had loved above all else, Elias Gray, had died in the middle of the night, as he had stood beside close to forty firefighters, women and men one-quarter and one-third his age, and watched the woods that he loved and the sugarhouse he had built burn to the ground.

16

•

The Plainfield pumper sits on its side on a slab of concrete, half in and half out of the stream, the rusted metal supports of the bridge squashed beneath it. One of the cables, a thick braid of rusted metal, shattered the pumper's windshield when it snapped.

"A wrecker's on the way," someone says to me from behind. Evidently, Laura and I have been staring.

I turn around and nod at the fellow, a young Landaff firefighter whose name I cannot recall.

"What somebody thinks a wrecker can do with that mess down there is beyond me," he continues. "But anyway, a wrecker's on the way."

On the near side of the stream, the side on which I have parked, there is a virtual used car lot of state and private automobiles and trucks: all the vehicles that arrived on the scene after the old bridge collapsed under the weight of the Plainfield pumper. Between the cars that belong to friends, the state police, the experts from the medical examiner's office, and the state's Fire Prevention Division, there are probably twenty-five vehicles parked on the street side of the collapsed bridge.

There is even an ambulance, with an oxygen tank set up on the ground beside it. According to Chester Woolf, Cynthia Woolf's husband and the chief of the Landaff Volunteer Fire Company, this is the very same ambulance that took away Elias Gray's body over six hours ago. It returned about four in the morning.

Already the sun is high in the sky, although it's not yet seven thirty in the morning, and it feels to me too hot to be a Vermont sun.

"It doesn't look that bad from here," Laura says quietly, referring to the area where the fire occurred.

"No, it doesn't," I agree. Just past a bend in the dirt road, however, perhaps a hundred yards up the hill from what's left of the bridge, I can see that the tips of a long line of spruce have been singed. The sugarhouse wasn't far from those trees.

At some point in the night or the early morning, the state police strung a line of bright orange tape around the wreckage of the pumper. It may have been the two officers standing now beside the long, wide pieces of plywood that span the stream at the bottom of the ditch. Most people could probably jump across that stream without much difficulty.

"Was anybody hurt?" I ask the firefighter, motioning toward the pumper.

"One guy bruised his shoulder. Another guy got a mean-looking cut on his forehead. But nothin' major. They were lucky."

"Let's hurry," Laura says, looking up the hill toward the forest. "I'm worried about Patience up there."

. . .

MOST OF THE firefighters haven't yet bothered to strip off their bunker pants or boots, but they have tossed their long yellow jackets unceremoniously into piles beside their trucks. Although all the hoses have been retrieved and rewound, there are at least a half-dozen air packs still scattered around the remains of the sugarhouse, and three or four now ash-black axes.

Some of the men are naked from the waist up, as they chew on the donuts and sip the orange juice being handed out in tall paper cups. I gather none of the firefighters have slept.

"I was just eatin' smoke," a Landaff fellow named Barton Lutz says to an older firefighter. "It was worse than bein' caught upstairs in a house fire."

Landaff's pumper and the seven fire engines belonging to the companies that fought the blaze last night are lined up bumper to bumper along the dirt road, as if preparing for a vehicular conga line or parade. Until a temporary bridge is constructed, however, they can't go very far.

"It looks like a friggin' battlefield," Lutz continues, wiping a strand of black hair that keeps falling across his face.

The older firefighter steps on a small pile of ashes that is still smoldering and shakes his head in disagreement. "Nope. I've seen battlefields. This just looks like a forest fire was here. And if it hadn't brought down Elias's sugarhouse—and old Elias—I'd say it wasn't even much of a forest fire. 'Specially compared to what they get out West."

Evidently, the flames never exploded into the sort of firestorm that instantly engulfs whole sections of forests, or leaps between treetops in seconds. There was no wind last night. Nevertheless, the woods here have become a small world of tall black toothpicks—toothpicks that almost crumble at the touch. There are no leaves, no shade to block out the sun, and our shoes sink into ash wherever we walk.

The orange tape that I saw being wrapped around the pumper already guards the remains of the sugarhouse. The metal evaporator, now blackened by flame and filled with enough water to fill a wading pool, is all that is recognizable.

Sitting on the hood of one of the trapped fire engines, his raincoat draped across his lap, is Elias's thirty-year-old grandson, Anson. His T-shirt too has been blackened by smoke, and he is still wearing his fire-resistant pants and boots. Every so often he stares at a small piece of paper in his hands, then folds it in half and in half again, and rubs his eyes.

The sweet smell of burnt wood is everywhere, an almost hauntingly pleasant aroma that I equate usually with woodstoves and fireplaces.

From now on, it will remind me of Elias Gray, and I put my arm around Laura's shoulders, and pull her against my chest for a long moment.

"I was sure Patience would still be here," she says finally, her voice almost numb. "I was sure she would have stayed until we got here."

Never has Laura felt so small in my arms, her body so fragile. I kiss her once on the forehead, whispering, "She probably went to Reedy's."

"Maybe," she murmurs.

"Let me see if anyone knows where she went," I suggest, holding her close for one more moment. I am almost afraid to release her, as if she'll melt into the ashes as soon as I do.

"You'll be okay?" I ask.

"I guess," she says, pulling slowly away from me, sighing. "We should also say something to Anson. It looks like no one else wants to."

. . .

ANSON RUNS THE back of his arm across his forehead, replacing the sweat that had been there with a black smudge of soot.

"I'm sorry," he says, apologizing for a yawn, and then twists his head away from us when a second one overtakes him. "I guess I'm beat."

"No, we're sorry," I tell him. "We're so sorry about Elias. About your grandfather."

Anson nods. "I suppose there are a lot of ways to go when you're his age. But I wouldn't have expected this one. Nope. I surely would not have."

He slides off the front of the truck, and before he can open his mouth to say a word Laura wraps her arms around him. Through Elias, she views Anson as a distant cousin of sorts.

"I'm a mess," he says awkwardly, looking over her shoulder at me. "You're gonna get your clothes filthy doin' that."

Like much of Landaff, Anson too works for the mountain, Powder Peak, in the winter. Some days he grooms snow, some days he runs a lift. He has, on occasion, fixed the tables in the snack bar and repaired the railings outside the restaurants. Essentially, he does—as Elias often said—"whatever needs doin'."

This is true at Powder Peak, this is true on the hundreds of acres and dozens of outbuildings that comprise the Gray property.

As Laura pulls away, she asks, "Were you with him?" The front of her shirt and her shoulder, where she touched Anson, are black with ash.

"Yup. I was. I went with him in the ambulance, and came back here when the ambulance did. Wasn't nothing anyone could do at the hospital."

"How's Giannine?" I ask.

"Okay. Not great. But at her age, I guess, you expect this. Not this way, maybe. But she was ready."

"Is she home now?"

"She's with Dad and Mom," he says, referring to his own father and mother. "There's where most everybody is right now. They're all over at Mom and Dad's place."

"I'm glad," I add, shuffling my feet. "I'm glad she isn't alone now."

He shakes his head. "Nah. No chance of that."

"And yourself?" I ask. "How are you doing?"

"I'm just beat."

"Really?"

He shrugs. "Sure."

"Did Elias . . . How did Elias die?" Laura asks softly.

Anson looks down at a long thin burn mark on his arm, and gently runs a finger along it. "He went fast, if that's what you're worried about. He just passed out." He starts walking toward the wide ring of orange tape that surrounds the evaporator, and motions for us to follow him.

"The fire began right around here," he says, pointing at the spruce that bordered the sugarhouse on the south side. "The chief said it probably didn't spread to the sugarhouse till it had been burnin' awhile. It probably got here a little after we were all tonin' out."

On the ground of the forest is one of the metal hinges that once held the huge doors of the sugarhouse in place. Anson picks it up, scrapes some of the ash away from one side with a fingernail, and then throws it into the pool of water in the evaporator.

"Grandpa got here 'bout the same time we all did, a few minutes before the roof went. One minute he was lookin' at it all in disbelief, the next minute he was fallin' against one of the trucks."

Behind us somebody shouts that the wrecker has arrived, and many of the firefighters race down the hill to see if the pumper can indeed be liberated by Timmy Hinesman's tow truck. Anson remains in place, watching the ripples he has caused wash against the steel walls of the evaporator.

"Grandpa died right here. I tried CPR, the rescue people tried CPR. But I think he was gone in an instant. Poof. Not a bad way to go, I guess. I jus' wish the last thing he seen wasn't—"

he says, waving his arms across the black dirt where once the sugarhouse had stood.

"Wasn't the sugarhouse going up in smoke," I offer, trying to finish his sentence for him.

"Ahh, sugarhouses come, sugarhouses go. He musta built a half-dozen of 'em in his life. I meant the woods. Grandpa loved this forest. I jus' wish he hadn't died seein' it on fire."

"You guys wanna join us?" someone shouts at the three of us. "They're about to start hitchin' up the pumper!"

I watch Anson for a response, planning to follow his lead as a courtesy. "I'll be there in a minute," he calls back. He reaches into his pants pocket and removes the piece of paper he has folded into a tiny square. It has been folded so many times that it may be thicker than a small pile of change.

"Wanna see somethin'?" he asks, unfolding the paper.

He starts to hand the paper to me, and then realizes it would be more polite to show it first to Laura.

"You ever hear of that place?" he asks Laura, evidently referring to the name at the top of the paper. I look over her shoulder and can see the words *Neiman Marcus*.

"It's a department store," she answers. "A pretty snazzy one."

She passes me the note, and as soon as I take it in my hands I understand what it is. It's a purchase order for maple syrup from the store's gourmet foods buyer in Boston.

"An order that big," Anson says, a half smile on his face, "I wasn't even sure I'd be able to deliver. We woulda needed one heck of a run."

"You would have made it," Laura says.

"That's what Grandpa said. Man, what an order." He crinkles the paper into a small ball, and tosses it into the ashes on the far side of the orange tape.

"Why did you do that?" Laura asks, stepping into the ashes

to retrieve the purchase order. "You still have plenty of time to build another sugarhouse!" She picks up the paper and brushes off the black residue.

"I don't know."

She flattens the order against her bare thigh, despite the fact the paper is filthy.

"Take it," Laura commands, handing the paper back to Anson. "Take it! I don't mean to sound angry, but I don't want to see you give up."

Anson nods, and looks down at his feet. "I know."

Down the hill we can hear the sound of the chains and hooks being attached to the pumper. "Anson, come on!" one of the firefighters yells. "You guys got to see this!"

"Have you seen Patience?" I ask Anson, as together the three of us start down the dirt road.

"Yup, she was here. She went somewhere with Reedy. I guess either his home or hers."

"How was she doing?" I ask.

"I don't know," he says, rubbing the back of his neck. "Patience can be pretty hard to read. My sense is she was either doin' real well, and was just sort of pensive about it all. Or . . ."

"Or?"

"Or she just shut down. Boom, all systems off. She musta been here fifteen minutes, and in that time I don't think she said one word."

"That doesn't sound like my sister-in-law."

"Sure doesn't. I mean, I grew up with Patience babysittin' me, and I got to tell you, I didn't think she could go five minutes without talkin'."

Around the bend in the woods Timmy Hinesman starts his engine, and the wrecker begins attempting to yank the Plainfield pumper out of the ditch that once held Elias Gray's brook.

17

•

There is a phantom trail on Mount Republic called Ten-Hook Brook. It is one of many designed by Ian Rawls's grandfather, a pioneer in the ski industry, back in the early 1930s. He named the trail for the stream that ran near it, and for the number hook he would use when he would fish the waters at the base of the mountain.

The trail was abandoned in 1948, when the tramway was built on the other side of the mountain, and it can no longer be seen from the air.

Some of Ian's childhood friends and their parents still ski Ten-Hook Brook at least once every season. It's a tradition of sorts, and usually one day between Christmas and New Year's, they will leave the immaculately groomed slopes of the new Powder Peak and ski the phantom trail instead. After the first run of the day, they toast to themselves, and to Ian's grandfather, with homemade blueberry brandy.

Then they toast to Mount Republic, which to this day remains the least developed of the three mountains that comprise Powder Peak.

The members of the group maintain the trail themselves,

pulling up the periodic spruce that falls in the way in the spring, and cutting back whatever small bushes grow tall enough to peek through the snow. But the trail has nevertheless grown thin, and in some points the treetops cover the path like a tunnel.

Until Ian was named general manager, he joined his friends on their annual homage to an earlier era in the ski industry. Now, however, he must disavow any knowledge of the trail's continued existence, and post signs in the area that insist no one trespass. Three years ago, he even fenced off parts of Ten-Hook Brook.

The insurance company demanded it.

Moreover, he has consistently refused to tell me the names of his renegade friends who still ski the phantom trail on Mount Republic. He says he's afraid I would join them.

• • •

I HAD EXPECTED to find Patience in the arms of Reedy McClure, but I should have known better. Reedy sits on the porch beside Patience, but it is into Anna Avery's arms that Patience has folded herself. Mother and daughter sit together on the wicker couch that Patience purchased years ago, at the auction held when the old Tuckerman Lodge went bankrupt.

Her dogs—Cocoa the Lab, and two of the ugliest mutts that I've ever seen in my life—lie on the porch in the shade. The mutts, two puppies from the same litter that Patience rescued on the same day, are brown and white and look something like pigs. Even their tails are piglike, even their eyes. But, like Cocoa, they are unfailingly sweet and loving, and they worship the smell of Patience's sneakers and shoes. They are named Astral and Aura.

Although Patience's house sits squarely in the center of Landaff, with houses on either side and across the street, from her back porch she has an unobstructed view of Powder Peak. That means, ironically, that she has a magnificent view of the ski trails the resort has carved into the sides of some of its mountains.

In the winter, the trails look like wide, white rivers—not white with foam and waves, but white as if they were actual rivers of paint. In the summer, on days like today, they look as if a giant took a monstrous jackknife and gouged out whole strips of the mountain face. It looks raw, painful.

Laura sits at the edge of one of the wicker chairs surrounding the couch, and leans in toward her sister and mother.

Anna smiles at Laura, and says, "Your sister here just never thought Elias would die."

Patience turns toward her mother and glares at her. "Mother!" she hisses. "How can you say that?"

Still smiling, Anna pats her older daughter's shoulder. "Because it's true."

"I knew he was going to die. I gather I'm not allowed to be sad in my own house?"

Reedy glances over at me, and in the brief moment when our eyes meet, we each try to gauge the depth of the anger that has remained from yesterday's lunch. He stands up and wanders to the column beside me, evidently assuming—incorrectly—that Elias's death has softened me.

"Your mother-in-law has been trying to get a rise out of Patience for about fifteen minutes now," he whispers, his conspiratorial tone his attempt at a truce.

"I think she just got one."

"How are you doing?" Reedy asks me.

"Oh, I'm pretty blown away," I admit. "Hell, what Mrs. Avery just said made sense to me. I didn't think Elias would ever die either."

"I'm kind of surprised by Patience," Reedy continues, as if yesterday's fight had never happened. "I always expected when this day came she would fly into overdrive. I expected her to choreograph the most impressive funeral Landaff has ever seen."

"She still might."

"Doubtful. She was okay until we went to the woods. But ever since then, she has been almost catatonic," Reedy says. He stares at me for a moment, then glances down at his watch. "I'm sorry about yesterday," he adds.

My instinct is to tell him he should be, and leave it at that. If we weren't standing right now on Patience's back porch, I probably would. But we are at my sister-in-law's house, and this is the man she plans to marry. Moreover, I cannot escape the fact that the closest person my wife and my sister-in-law had to a father for most of their lives has just died. Reedy's and my fight may continue, but I can't allow it to drone on right here.

"Me too," I mumble, with little conviction.

"I was probably a little heavy-handed."

I look over at Laura, unwilling to meet Reedy's eyes. "Don't worry about it. So was I."

"We should stop by Giannine's this afternoon," Anna says to her daughters.

"Can I get you more tea, Mrs. Avery?" Reedy asks.

"That would be nice."

"Get me some too," Patience demands, pointing at her teacup.

"That's two rises," I tell Reedy. "Take heart."

"Years ago," Anna begins, speaking to no one in particular, "four or five years after Mr. Avery died, Elias came by our house with a truckload of wood. Patience was with me. She was about nine. Laura, I'm not sure where you were. Brownies or something. It was spring, and he was bringing a couple cords by so it wouldn't be green come September. Anyway, Elias was distracted. Very distracted. He said he had just met Robert Frost."

Patience folds her arms back across her chest, and looks at her mother angrily. She knows well the story her mother is about to tell, as do Laura and I. Only Reedy has never heard it. It is the sort of anecdote that I imagine Patience loves to hear over and over, but because she figures prominently in it, she must feign disgust for our benefit.

"He said Robert Frost was driving around Vermont, looking for a new place to settle. He was living at the time over in Ripton. Well, as anyone with any sense might, Frost fell in love with Elias's land, his view. He thought it was just the spot, and living there would be just the thing. Just the thing. So he offered to buy the farm. On the spot. He told Elias to name his price, and he'd be more than happy to meet it."

"Did Elias know who he was talking to?" Reedy asks.

"Yes, he did. He knew exactly who he was talking to. And he told Frost that his farm wasn't for sale. So Frost repeated the offer: Name your price, he said. And Elias said it wasn't for sale at any price. He said he was happy right where he was."

"Did Frost get angry?"

"Oh, no. He told Elias, 'About time I found someone who's actually happy with his lot in this world.' He said that if Elias couldn't put a price on the land, then no one should buy it. But by the time he got to our house with the wood, he was having second thoughts."

Patience snorts, and Cocoa looks up at the sound. "Elias would never have sold his land, not for all the money in the world," she says. She glances down at Cocoa, as the dog rests her snout on the edge of the wicker couch.

Ignoring her older daughter, Anna continues, "Elias said there were a lot of things he could have done with that money. He said there were a lot of people in his family—children and grandchildren, then—who could have used it. He said there were a lot of groups in town that could have used a little help. The Volunteer Fire Company. The Rescue Squad. But he had said no. He had stood on his porch like a stubborn old fool, he said, and said no.

"And that's when Patience spoke up. She had been sitting on

one of the front steps listening to everything Elias had said, but she hadn't said a word up to that point. So then she spoke up. She said to Elias, 'I bet if you sold that land, you wouldn't be able to dowse anymore.' "

Reedy chuckles. "You said that to Elias?"

"She says I did," Patience answers, motioning over her shoulder toward her mother.

"She sure did," Anna continues. "So Elias asked her, why was that? Why wouldn't he be able to dowse if he sold his land? And Patience here told him, 'If you started selling your land every time someone came to your front door, the ground wouldn't trust you anymore.' "

Reedy wanders over to Patience and Anna, and gently strokes Patience's hair. "You know something?" he asks her.

"I thought you were going to get me some tea," she says, looking away.

"You know something?" he asks again. "You were one hell of a weird kid."

. . .

MIRANDA SOBS AND sobs, her face buried deep in her pillow.

Just when Laura and I are convinced beyond doubt that no tears remain, that her body will no longer withstand one more onslaught of sadness, she will curl further into her blanket and press her face deeper into her pillow and she will wail.

When we left Miranda at home this morning with the Scutter twins, she had seemed fine. Otherwise, we would not have left her. She was saddened by Elias's death, but she was accepting it with a maturity that struck both Laura and me as extraordinary, a maturity well beyond her years.

When we returned early this afternoon, however, Jeanette Scutter told us that midmorning Miranda had begun to rearrange the furniture in her bedroom. She had left the garden where she had been playing, and gone inside the house. She had gone upstairs to her bedroom, closed her door, and begun pushing her bed and her bureau and her toy chest all over the room. At least that's what it sounded like to Jeanette. So Jeanette went upstairs to check on our daughter, and she saw that her suspicions were correct: Miranda had indeed rearranged all her furniture.

And then, when Miranda saw Jeanette in the doorway, she abruptly burst into tears, tears that have flowed almost uninterrupted ever since.

Laura rubs Miranda's back softly, and occasionally squeezes one of her shoulders. "Shhhh," she whispers, "shhhhh."

But it is not solely for Elias that my daughter is crying, these are not tears spilled only for a once-ancient dowser. These are, I believe, tears shed also for trees now gone, for land that is scorched, and for rivers and brooks and streams that are dry. They are tears brought on by the drought, tears from a fear—a fear that I am unable to convince her is unfounded—that nature somehow is changing. Moreover, my daughter's tears are tears of mistrust, tears that I know are directed at Laura and me.

"You said it wouldn't matter if we lost some trees!" she has yelled at us twice. "You said it wouldn't matter!"

After each of these outbursts Laura looked over at me and tried to smile, but the words hung in my daughter's bedroom like smoke. For weeks we have been telling Miranda that she had nothing to fear, that she had no reason to be afraid.

A forest fire wouldn't be a big deal, we have told her, nothing's going to happen to the trees. It's all part of nature, I remember telling her one morning over breakfast, Vermont has plenty of trees.

Now, however, the trees among which she dowsed the spot for Anson Gray's holding tanks are gone. All gone. Where there once was a beautiful new sugarhouse is instead a wide, long ashtray, bordered by neon orange tape.

Wells continue to dry up as the springs that feed them disappear. There will be but one sickly cutting of hay this entire summer, the corn crop will be sorry, and the back-door gardens that cover the state will yield little bounty.

And, of course, Elias Gray is dead.

All of this frightens our daughter, it frightens her more than it would most little girls.

"You said everything would be all right!" she cries again, indicting her mother and me for misleading her. "You said everything would be all right!"

"Shhhh," Laura coos. "It will. Everything will be all right."

There are clouds to the west, there is rain in Chicago, Detroit, and St. Louis. I can't believe this system too will break up before it reaches us here in Vermont.

"Miranda," I begin, my voice little more than a whisper, "would you like to go for a ride on a chairlift? I don't think we can go tonight, but Monday maybe?"

One of Miranda's favorite summer treats is an after-dinner ride on one of the Powder Peak chairlifts. Technically, only the tramway is open for rides for summer tourists, and the tram only runs until five in the afternoon. But Ian Rawls occasionally has a repair crew working at the resort as late as five thirty to eight thirty at night, testing the chairlifts and tuning up the machinery. Consequently, if I call Ian ahead of time I can usually commandeer a ride for the Winston family at dusk.

"Wouldn't that be nice, sweetie?" Laura asks Miranda. "A ride on the chairlift?"

Miranda continues to cry into her pillow, but the sobs may be softer.

"I want it to rain," she says to us through her sniffles. "That's all I want. I just want it to rain."

18

•

There are generations of Grays in the Landaff cemetery. Lying flat amid the hydrangea in that part of the cemetery are a full half acre of Elias's cousins and siblings and grandparents. He will be buried beside his older brother and sister-in-law, in a plot reserved for him and—someday—Giannine. He will be buried about ten yards from the boy who would someday have grown into his uncle Willis.

Willis has, perhaps, the longest epitaph of any of the Grays in Landaff. This may be because he had the shortest life. But his epitaph is long, and the light Barre granite of his headstone is illustrated with a carved horse's hoof and a pair of angel's wings:

> Here rest the dashed hopes
> Of Willis Thetford Gray's loving parents.
> A youngest son,
> Born September 25, 1869,
> He died July 19, 1877,
> Aged seven years, ten months.

It was a horse's kick
Which smashed his skull and brain.
He lived 18 days, sick,
In agony and pain,
Until finally he left us.

We think not of the seventy years
Willis lost,
But we thank the Lord instead
For the seven precious years
That he had.

Elias's epitaph has far fewer words, and will include simply his name and age. But before he died, the American Society of Dowsers, the Landaff Fire Company, and our town's Rescue Squad purchased for Elias a tombstone with a small rendering of a pair of hands grasping the ends of a dowser's Y rod.

. . .

THERE ARE A lot of words to the conditions that come with Powder Peak's expansion permits, enough to—as Liza Eastwick said—fill the pages of the Landaff Church directory. But as I examine the conditions carefully Saturday afternoon, sitting in the dry brown grass of our backyard, they really can be distilled to three key issues.

Essentially, the resort can tap the Chittenden River to make snow, as long as the river's water flow does not fall below three-quarters of one cubic foot per second. Powder Peak had requested approval to use the river even if the water flow fell below that speed. Nevertheless, this condition shouldn't prevent the resort from expanding its snowmaking capabilities, and guaranteeing snow throughout the season on virtually every trail on Mount Republic.

Assuming, of course, that Vermont gets some rain in the next year. Right now, the Chittenden River's water flow is just about three-quarters of a cubic foot per second, and slowing fast.

Although the permit for the new trail network on the westernmost edge of Moosehead was denied because it would skirt too close to a wildlife habitat, the wide top-to-bottom trail and high-speed gondola that the resort had designed for the center of Moosehead were approved—as were all the new trails and connecting paths on Mount Republic. The Commission also approved the additional parking spaces.

Probably the most complex issue for Powder Peak is the holding pond for the snowmaking system. The Commission not only denied the resort's request to build the storage pond near the base of Mount Chittenden, it insisted as well that the twelve hundred acres surrounding the proposed site remain a pristine, untouched forest area. While Powder Peak can certainly find another location for the pond—and, I'm sure, will—the engineers told Ian yesterday that building the pond anywhere else could increase the cost of the new snowmaking system by close to four hundred thousand dollars.

Finally, the Commission stipulated that all approvals become null and void if the U.S. Forest Service rules against the expansion, and none of the improvements may begin until the state's Environmental Board reviews the inevitable Copper Project appeal.

The bottom line? This is excellent news for the resort: The new gondola will be up and running this season, and the new snowmaking system will be in place by next fall.

• • •

THE SCREEN DOOR slams shut on the porch. When I turn around I see Laura walking rapidly toward me, her arms wrapped tightly around her chest. I put down the ski resort's permit papers as she approaches.

"My sister's a lunatic," she says, stopping to stand over me, her voice clipped.

I look up at her. "I know."

"No. I mean she's really a lunatic," Laura continues, her tone void of humor. "Really and truly a lunatic. She has completely lost her mind. It's official."

The grass is so dry that it hurts the palms of my hands when I lean back against it. The blades are sharp, parched, unbending. They inflict what feel like small paper cuts, invisible but no less painful, before snapping beneath my weight.

"What did she do?"

Laura shakes her head, disgusted. "She wants me and Miranda to help her divert the noxious rays beneath Elias's grave site."

"Was she kidding?"

"No!"

"Then you're right. She's certifiable."

Laura sits down beside me, seething. There is no humor for her in Patience's madness, not when that madness may affect our daughter.

"What . . . what makes her think there are noxious rays there?"

"She went out there this morning, just to see what the spot was like. She said the place didn't feel right to her, so she dowsed it."

"And there were noxious rays there."

"Right. She said it was a real hot spot."

Overhead are a half-dozen inconsequential clouds—white, puffy, wholly ineffectual. They are the remains of yet another storm system from the west that dissipated before it arrived in Vermont. Laura and I notice them simultaneously, looking up when we hear the sound of a passenger jet miles above us.

"Does it matter?" I ask.

"That it's a hot spot? Personally, I don't think so."

"But Patience thinks so."

"She doesn't want him buried there tomorrow, pure and simple, unless the hot spot is cooled down."

"Why can't she do it herself?"

"She says it's huge—the hot spot—and very, very powerful."

Laura curls her knees up to her chest, and rests her forehead upon them. Her shoulders are bare, and there are small drops of sweat on each.

"I just don't get it. I don't mean to sound cold, but Elias is dead. Even if noxious rays exist—"

"They do," Laura says sharply, without looking up. "That's not the issue."

"Fine, they exist," I continue. "But what difference will they make to Elias now? The man's already dead."

"She's worried about his soul."

"Oh, for God's sake."

"I agree."

"She just gets fucking stranger and crazier every year. Do you realize that?"

I hear her sigh. "Uh-huh. I do."

"I gather you said no."

"Of course. She wanted me and Miranda to meet her at the cemetery right now, so the rays could be diverted before the funeral tomorrow. But I told her no. I told her absolutely not."

"And what did she say?"

Laura looks up and rubs the bridge of her nose. "She got mad."

"She's already mad. She's crazy."

"She got angry. She said I don't care about Elias."

"She knows that's not true."

"She said I would be stifling my daughter."

"That's just crazy."

"I know that! You don't have to keep saying it."

"I certainly don't think you stifle Miranda. I certainly don't think we stifle her."

"Even if we did, I told Patience I would rather we stifled Miranda than frightened her. Especially right now. I will not have my nine-year-old daughter dowsing hot spots in a cemetery. It's that simple."

"So what's she going to do?"

"Patience? Who knows. But she won't sit still anymore. All that energy she stored up doing nothing the last two days has got to go somewhere."

"She'll probably go to the cemetery."

"Fine, that's just fine. Just so long as she goes there alone."

. . .

"SCOTTIE? SCOTTIE! WAKE up!"

Laura is kneeling beside me on the bed when I open my eyes, her legs on top of the sheets. Her hair is an unbrushed mane that falls about my face as she leans over me, staring, wild-eyed. It is Sunday morning.

"What time is it?"

"Miranda's gone!" she says, taking both of my shoulders in her hands and squeezing them.

"What?"

"Miranda's gone! Get up!" she insists, sitting back on her legs.

The sun is high and the light pours through the east window in our bedroom. The floor, a plane of gray-painted hardwoods, looks almost translucent.

I roll out of bed, asking as I rise, "What do you mean she's gone?"

"She just went somewhere with Patience! I heard a car engine start, and when I went to the window I saw the two of them driving away."

"Oh, for Christ's sake. They've gone to the cemetery."

"Yes!"

I sit back down on the edge of the bed, and glance at the clock on the dresser. It is not quite eight thirty.

"You made it sound like she was kidnapped or something."

"She was kidnapped!"

I reach for my pillow, and drop it into my lap. "Going a mile and a half up the road to the cemetery with your aunt doesn't count as a kidnapping."

"I'm furious! I told Patience no, and she took Miranda anyway!"

"Well, what do you want us to do?" I continue. "Do you want us to follow them to the cemetery? Do you want to confront Patience in front of Miranda?"

"I just don't want Patience doing this! I don't want my daughter searching for evil emanations in a graveyard. Not now!"

"I don't either. But I don't think it would do Miranda any good to fight with Patience in front of her."

"We've got to stop them!"

I lean my elbows into the pillow, and rest my head in my hands. Rarely is Laura as upset as she is now.

"Scottie, we've got to stop them! Come on!"

I take a deep breath, trying to wake myself up to deal with Patience—with Patience, with Laura, with Miranda—rationally. "This isn't about Miranda dowsing in the graveyard," I hear myself saying, aware as the words escape my mouth that at eight thirty on a Sunday morning I am about to say exactly the wrong thing. "This is about your sister ignoring you, and taking Miranda there anyway."

"So what!"

"So we've let our daughter do things that are a hell of a lot weirder. My God, your sister conducts her damn 'dowsing school' in our own yard on Saturday—"

"You make it sound like it's our fault!" Laura argues, cutting me off.

"Well, on some level it probably is—"

"It's not! There's nothing wrong with dowsing, if . . ."

"If . . ."

"If you don't start dowsing graveyards!"

"Fine."

"Fine," Laura says, glaring at me. "I'll go alone."

As she starts to roll off the bed, I reach for her arm and her hand. "You're angry. I'm angry. Maybe it's the heat."

"This has nothing to do with the weather," she says, trying to keep her voice even.

"Heat does strange things to people," I continue. "I imagine droughts do too."

She tries to leave once again, and so I climb over the bed until I am beside her. I hold her with both arms.

"It's not the drought," she says.

"Then maybe it's Elias's death," I tell Laura, an insight that strikes me as ludicrously obvious as soon as I say it. Of course, it's Elias's death. That's why Patience is at the cemetery with my nine-year-old daughter right this second, that's why my wife is trying to escape from our bed and chase them. "Patience and you cared for him, you loved—"

"Let me go," she says, her voice so filled with anger that she sounds close to tears.

"No," I insist, trying to muster reasons to keep her. "I don't think you should go to the cemetery. What Patience did was wrong, but—"

"I want to go!"

"But if you go there now you'll only make it worse. You'll confuse Miranda."

"Patience is already doing one hell of a good job of that!" She looks over at the clock, and then back at me. "Church begins in a little over an hour. If I don't bring them in by then, the whole congregation will see them out there!"

"The congregation won't think anything of it. They expect this sort of thing from your sister."

"But Miranda!"

"This isn't about 'what the neighbors think.' You know that. It's about Patience ignoring you."

"I am just furious," she says again, but her tone has begun to soften from rage to resignation.

"I know you are."

"I could kill her."

"Probably."

Her body relaxes, falls against mine, and she rests her head on my shoulder. "I could kill her. I really could."

I nod my head so that she can feel the motion, a tacit but physical peace offering. "Me too," I add. "And when we can get her alone, maybe we will."

. . .

PATIENCE MAY BE insane, but she isn't stupid. She has the common sense not to return Miranda to our home before church.

Consequently, when Laura and I leave for the nine forty-five service, it is clear to us both that we may not be able to speak with Patience for hours. First there is church, which will last until eleven o'clock. Then there is Sunday school, where Laura is substituting today for Susan Gray, one of Elias's granddaughters. And then there is Elias's funeral, with the memorial service at the church scheduled to begin at twelve thirty.

"I'll get her right after Sunday school," Laura says, staring out the window of the truck. She is wearing this morning a black cocktail dress, an odd choice for one of today's Sunday school teachers. It is not particularly revealing, in that its sleeves reach to her wrists and the skirt falls almost to her knees. But it is tight and slinky and there is something seductive about the way its neck curves just below her collarbone.

Unfortunately, it is already almost ninety degrees outside, and this was the only thing black and cotton in Laura's closet, the only dress that she felt she could wear to Elias's funeral. It is, in fact, the only summer dress that she owns that isn't determinedly bright and cheerful. Consequently, we both agreed that none of the six- and-seven-year-olds in her class this morning would be unduly scarred or confused by the sight of a Sunday school teacher in black.

As we drive past the cemetery, we see no signs of Miranda or Patience.

"She must have succeeded," Laura says, referring to her sister.

"Think so?" There is a large pile of dirt next to the hole in the ground where Elias's body will be laid. It is a shady spot surrounded by a pair of hydrangea bushes and a wrought iron bench, now rusted to a shade of red that will match the brightest maples come September.

"She'd still be there if she hadn't." From the corner of my eye I can see her look away from Elias's burial plot, and wipe her eyes with the back of her hand.

The church parking lot is already filled, so I coast to a stop in one of the vacant spaces beside the town clerk's office. As I climb out of the truck I wipe the sweat from my forehead one last time.

. . .

MIRANDA IS ALREADY seated in our pew when we arrive, pretending to skim a hymnal, but turning to scan the back of the room for us every few seconds. She knows she did something wrong.

Laura scoots into the pew first, sitting beside her daughter. Before she or Miranda can say a word to each other, Jeanette Scutter turns around in the pew in front of us and says to Laura, "Musta been one late party. You musta gotten in pretty late if you didn't have time to change before comin' to church."

"Do you like it?" Laura asks, referring to her dress.

Jeanette shrugs. "It's cotton. I don't iron anymore."

Without opening her mouth, Miranda hands her mother the program for this morning's service, and then looks down at her shoes. They're caked with dry dirt, no doubt from Elias's grave site.

I lean across Laura, whispering to my daughter, "After church, we'll talk." I know I should not be annoyed with Miranda, I know I should be directing whatever fury there is inside me now at my sister-in-law. But the sight of that dirt, and what that dirt must be doing to Laura, angers me.

Miranda flips the pages in the hymnal, and doesn't look up.

"Did you hear your father?" Laura asks.

She nods just the tiniest bit.

As the choir begins to file into the church Laura asks Miranda, "Where's your aunt?"

Miranda shakes her head that she doesn't know.

"Did you lose your vocal cords on the way to church this morning?" I ask sternly.

"Scottie," Laura says, "that tone isn't necessary."

After a short moment, Miranda murmurs, "No."

"All right then. Your mother asked you a question. Why don't you try answering her this time with actual words."

Both Scutter twins turn around now, surprised by the sound of my voice. Ignoring them, I stare at Miranda.

"I don't know," she says quietly.

"You don't know what?" I ask her.

"I don't know where Aunt Patience is."

"Thank you," I say, leaning back in the pew.

"You know something?" Gertrude Scutter asks Jeanette.

"What?"

"I got a feeling today's gonna last forever."

• • •

AS WE SING our final hymn and the end of the service approaches, I realize that Laura, Miranda, and I will each leave in a different direction. Laura and Miranda are expected downstairs—Laura as a teacher in the classroom for first-, second-, and third-graders, and Miranda as a student in the room reserved for the fourth through sixth grades. There is nowhere I need to be between now and the funeral, so I decide I will probably head home.

The moment Reverend Taylor completes the benediction and the congregation begins to move, Miranda flies past Laura and me.

"Bye, Mom, bye, Dad," she babbles, once she has escaped the pew and is standing in the aisle. "See you later."

Laura takes hold of her shoulder and bends toward her. "It's your aunt who's in the doghouse," she says, "not you. What you did was wrong, and we'll talk about that later. But don't let your father's or my tone frighten you: It's Aunt Patience who's in trouble."

She nods, but the moment Laura loosens her grip she takes off up the aisle.

Laura then turns to me and whispers, "If you see Patience in the next hour, you still have my permission to kill her. An hour in church didn't make me any more forgiving."

"Really?"

"Absolutely. And feel free to take your time about it."

I squeeze her hand and start toward the back of the sanctuary.

• • •

THE INSIDE OF the truck feels like the inside of a toaster oven that has been on overnight. I pry myself free of my sports jacket, and toss it onto the passenger side of the cab.

I start the engine and switch on the radio, and it crosses my mind that I might have time between now and the funeral to put the second coat of paint on the porch chairs Laura brought home the other day. It would be a nice surprise for her.

As I round the wide bend that circles the front of the cemetery, I see Patience's car parked beside the line of sugar maples at the entrance. I consider driving on, and letting Laura deal with her sister later today. But Miranda is as much my daughter as she is Laura's; moreover, there is an undeniable feeling of protectiveness inside me, a feeling that Laura has somehow been slighted. Undermined by her sister. I too coast to a stop beside the sugar maples.

Patience is sitting, arms crossed, on the wrought iron bench before Elias's grave. She's wearing white tennis shorts, a pair that I believe belong to Reedy.

She says nothing to me as I approach, stomping flat a patch of dead brown grass between us. She doesn't even look up from the hole in the ground into which Elias will be placed for eternity in less than two hours. I stand before her for a long moment, saying nothing, unsure how to begin. Patience has no fear of silence, and I know would be content to sit here and stare for hours without saying a single word to me. Silence, for Patience, is an extremely potent and unnerving weapon.

"You should have listened to your sister," I begin, forcing the confrontation that I know is inevitable.

There are two elaborate rows of steel bars and pulleys spanning the burial plot, with a pair of canvas straps between them. Elias's casket will be rested on those straps, and then lowered gently into the ground.

"You should have listened to your sister," I tell her again when she ignores me, as I sit beside her on the bench. The hydrangeas, which will become a bright pink in the fall, are still dirty white puffs that cause the branches to droop. And like virtually every other plant in northern Vermont, they too have been affected by the drought, and the petals on each flower look dry, transparent, and sickly.

She looks over at me, angry at me for sitting beside her. This has been her bench, probably since church began over an hour ago.

"Don't you have someplace you have to be?" she asks.

"Nope. Don't you think you ought to change for the funeral?"

She turns away from me, disgusted. "There's time."

"Where's Reedy?"

"Home. He had the decency to give me some space this morning. Unlike some other people in this town."

"I'd be happy to leave you alone, if you'd leave my daughter alone."

"Whose daughter?"

"Laura's and my daughter. Your sister's and my daughter."

I hadn't noticed it before, but leaning against one of the legs of the bench are a half-dozen chrome L rods.

"You two don't know what you have," she says.

"No, I think we do. We have a lovely nine-year-old daughter, who happens to have a lunatic for an aunt." I smile as I say the word *lunatic*, hoping to cushion the remark.

"You two are stifling her," she continues, ignoring my comment.

"Oh, come on, Patience. Do you really think it's healthy for a nine-year-old girl to wander through a graveyard looking for evil spirits?"

"We were not looking for evil spirits. You know that." She shakes her head. "I would have expected this kind of behavior from you, but not from Laura."

"We're in complete agreement on this one."

"It's like that time when I was Miranda's age, and the governor himself asked me to find his son. Can you imagine what would have happened if my mother had prevented me from trying? Can you imagine?"

"You were eleven. Miranda is nine."

"I had just turned eleven, and Miranda will soon turn ten. The parallel is . . . perfect."

One of Michael Terry's flatbeds rumbles by, the drills and towers and hydraulic pumps glistening in the sun.

"The parallel is far from perfect. Speaking as an attorney—not an irate father—I can tell you that it's far from perfect. You were safe at home in your kitchen—"

"Miranda was safe with her aunt, on a beautiful morning in July!"

"You were helping to find a missing person, an inherently good—"

"Miranda was helping to look out for a man's soul! Where's the damn harm in that!"

"You crossed the line, Patience! You went from the slightly peculiar to the downright weird! We're talking about . . . we're talking about witchcraft, for God's sake!"

"We are not! This has nothing to do with witchcraft!"

"Do you think a nine-year-old knows that? Do you think a nine-year-old knows the difference between an evil spirit and something you call a 'hot spot'? Do you honestly believe she knows the difference between your 'noxious rays' and ghosts or goblins?"

"They are not 'my' noxious rays."

"Fine. Anyone's noxious rays."

"Noxious rays are real. Hot spots are real."

"You're missing the point."

"Some are the man-made toxins and poisons we put into the world. Chemicals. Carcinogens. Dumps," she says, hissing out the *s* in *dumps*. "Nuclear radiation. Electromagnetic radiation. Natural radiation—"

"What are you saying, there's a nuclear waste dump right over there?" I ask facetiously, pointing at Elias's burial plot. "And you and my nine-year-old daughter made it go away with your coat hangers? Poof, no more waste dump. God, you're good, Patience, you are really good."

She sighs. "The source of the emissions right here was a geopathogenic zone. Perfectly natural, in this case. Probably caused by—"

"Satan," I offer.

"Probably caused by intersecting water veins. Or a geologic fault. Or—less likely, but possible—decaying natural gas. It doesn't really matter. What mattered to me was diverting the emissions, because they were concentrated in a narrow band right underneath Elias's tombstone."

My first instinct is to tell Patience sarcastically that I'm sure Elias's corpse will rest easier now. Less chance of sickness, better appetite. It'll even sleep better. But I restrain myself. As angry as I am with Patience, I can't bring myself to hurt her by verbalizing those two words, *Elias's corpse*.

"And you just had to have Miranda's help," I say instead, trying to focus on what is for me the real issue: taking my daughter against her mother's and my wishes.

"The emissions were projecting negative, unwholesome energy into Elias Gray's eternal resting place. They had to be diverted, and I wasn't succeeding on my own yesterday afternoon. At least not to my satisfaction."

"And your satisfaction is everything in this world, isn't it?"

"How dare you make me sound selfish!" she says, her voice breaking just the slightest bit. "This isn't about me, this is about Elias Gray's soul!"

"No, it's actually about my daughter. A little girl who's scared to death right now that half the state is about to burn down—"

"Then you should be grateful to me for taking her mind off it!" she says, jumping to her feet and grabbing the pile of L rods in both of her hands, the wires dangling in every direction.

"Oh, please, Patience. This stunt was many things, but therapy for my daughter wasn't one of them."

"Your daughter—my sister's daughter—made this spot right here a little nicer! That's what this 'stunt' was all about. It made this spot of earth a better place. Maybe for Elias, maybe not. But certainly for me and Laura and Miranda and everyone else in this town who comes here to visit him from now on! So maybe in that regard this is about Miranda—but only in that regard."

She holds the L rods before me, continuing, "If you could have seen that little girl at work. If you could have seen her . . ."

I rub the back of my head where a dull ache has begun.

"It was Miranda who diluted the rays, not me. It was Miranda who used these very rods to disperse them. You should have seen her. In five, maybe ten minutes, she had the rods in the ground exactly where she wanted 'em, and she had the rays spread over a nice, wide area."

"I'm sure she was wonderful. That's not my point."

"She was wonderful!" Patience insists, as small tears begin to form in her eyes. She looks down at the L rods as she says, "She was using 'em like lightning rods, Scottie, only backwards! They were working just like lightning rods, picking the rays right out of the ground, and . . ."

She shakes her head as the tears start to fall faster, and her voice becomes lost in her sniffles. I stand up and start toward her, but reflexively she turns away. "I won't let you stifle Miranda," she says, crying. "She has too much potential. She's too strong."

I put my hands on her shoulders and hold her. "We won't," I tell her, not quite sure what I'm saying, not quite sure what I mean. "We won't."

Slowly she turns to face me, her body relaxing against mine, its strength lost in her sobs. "Oh, God," she cries, "I'll miss Elias so. You don't realize. I'll just miss him so much."

19

•

Even at Elias's burial in the cemetery, where no fewer than one hundred and fifty of us stand in a wide and deep semicircle around the casket, suspended over a hole in the ground as if part of a magic trick, we pray for rain. This morning we prayed for rain at the regular nine forty-five service, and the children prayed in Sunday school; we prayed again at the memorial service for Elias in the church, and now, underneath a largely cloudless blue sky, as a congregation we petition the heavens above us once more to open up.

Reverend Taylor, our minister, is a man my age who looks ten years younger. Inner peace, people tell me. After the first of what I assume will be three or four different scriptural readings, he turns to Anna Avery, and motions for her to speak. Laura reaches for my hand discreetly, entwining her small fingers in mine. Miranda, standing on the other side of Laura, notices the gesture, and instinctively, nervously, leans against her mother.

With dignity and assurance, with just a trace of sadness in her voice, Anna says, "Elias taught me—Elias taught many of us—to pray before dowsing. He often began with something called the Dowser's Prayer. It's short, but—for Elias—every word in it had a good deal of meaning. It was written by Josefa Rivera."

She pauses for a brief moment, glancing once at Elias's casket, before continuing simply, "This is it, the Dowser's Prayer: 'Lord, Guide my hands, enhance my sensitivity, and bless my purpose, that I may be an instrument of Your power and glory in locating what is searched for.' "

She steps back from the minister, and then looks over at her older daughter, still wearing Reedy's white tennis shorts, her face buried deep in Reedy's arms and chest, and says, "May Elias find now all the peace that there is in heaven."

. . .

ON MONDAY, IAN Rawls and I have lunch together in Barre, in a diner that offers a special every Monday of pea soup, tater tots, and a grilled cheese sandwich. I go there for the tater tots, Ian for the pea soup. Even in July. Barre is a town just south of Montpelier that grew up around some of Vermont's deepest, richest, most abundant granite quarries—hence the name of our softball team, the Quarry Men. And while most of those quarries are no longer active, and many Barre residents now drive to Montpelier and even Burlington to work, the city itself still feels like a mining town, surrounded as it is by tombstone factories on one side, and the quarries themselves on another.

Consequently, Barre is a great place for diners.

"Goddard's taking an earlier plane on Wednesday," Ian says, "so he should be in town by six thirty or seven. Are you and Laura free for dinner?"

"Maybe."

"You'll ask her?"

"Oh, I know we don't have other plans," I tell him, smiling.

"Okay: What will it take to get you to the restaurant Wednesday night?"

"A sunset ride on the chairlift tonight. For Miranda and me."

"Not Laura?"

"I doubt it. Divine Lights of Vermont has a huge order from a department store in Montreal. So I would guess tonight it will just be Miranda and me."

"You drive a hard bargain, Scottie."

I skewer a tater tot with a tin fork. "I'm one hell of a mean lawyer."

. . .

I WONDER HOW much Miranda understands her powers, especially now, the day after her aunt absconded with her to the cemetery. Although she is only nine, I cannot believe the fact that her teacher brought her to Elias's grave Sunday morning to accomplish what she herself felt incapable of doing was lost on her. The pupil became, essentially, the teacher; dowsing was no longer an issue of potential for Miranda, but became instead one of practice.

Since yesterday morning, when she diverted the hot spot Patience said ran underneath Elias's tombstone, she has not said one word about forest fires or the drought. Not a single word. She has expressed no concerns, asked for no reassurances. Whether it is because she has concluded that her mother's and my comforting words were made meaningless by the fire that killed Elias and destroyed his sugarhouse, or whether she has a new faith in nature as a result of her apparent dowsing success, I do not know.

I know only that Patience, for all the wrong reasons, may have been right about her escapade with my daughter: It just may have taken her mind off her worst fears.

Miranda is especially quiet tonight as we ride a slow-motion chairlift to the top of Mount Republic. She rests her chin on the safety bar, staring straight up the mountain, as the sun bounces off her little-girl yellow hair: hair that is thin, transparent, weightless, and soft.

There is no sound on the mountain but the low hum from the motors that steadily pull the chairs upward. Although there is an occasional breeze, each is insignificant, silent. On the seat between Miranda and me is a small red ice chest I have filled with frozen Peacesicles, a miniature picnic of sorts for the top of the mountain or the ride home in the truck.

I touch Miranda's shoulder, and point at the area of thick wood to our left. "In there," I tell her, "will be one of the new trails. Good and long. Really wide in some places."

She turns to face me and raises an eyebrow suspiciously. "Will they let snowboards in?"

"I don't know."

"They better." She looks back at the base lodge, which any moment will disappear from view. "Is this where the gondola will be?"

"No. The gondola will be on Moosehead."

She twists forward in the chair, holding on tight to the armrest on her side, and lowers her head back onto the safety bar.

I ask her, "Doesn't that hurt? Don't the vibrations feel weird on your chin?"

"Nope."

The chairlift glides over a lengthy spot on the mountain where mogul fields form every winter, then an open space that stretches for hundreds and hundreds of yards where two trails intersect.

"Peacesicles at the summit?" I ask Miranda.

"Okay."

We fly over a ravine it's impossible to ski, the ski trails themselves veering off to our right and our left, then a thick patch of evergreens, so close to our feet that it almost appears we could reach down and touch the highest branches. Any second now the peak of Mount Republic will come into view—the wide, flat summit that is recognizable in profile by almost every Vermonter by the age of six or seven—and then the tips of the White Mountains to the east.

Some of the leaves on the mountain have already begun to turn. Republic, which offers a magic display of color every fall, will this year become a kaleidoscope of reds and yellows and greens in August.

I motion toward the evergreens. "I love to look at those trees in the winter," I tell my daughter. "Sometimes, there's so much ice on them they look like they're made of crystal. They look like they're made of glass."

"I like it when the snowballs sit on the branches," Miranda says.

"Me too," I agree, reminded of the cat we once had named Snowball. She died two years ago.

"Someday, I'd like another cat," she continues, the word *snowball* resonating for her too with memories.

"You know I'm allergic to them."

"I'd keep it downstairs."

I nod. "I know you would. Maybe for your birthday."

The chairlift lurches a tiny bit, as if there were a burr on one of the wire cables that caught for a moment in the pulleys at the summit, and Miranda's head bounces once on the safety bar.

"Ouch!"

"Bite your tongue?" I ask.

"The inside of my cheek," she says, disgusted with herself.

I reach over and rub her back softly, as the lift settles down and we float to the top of the mountain.

. . .

"MINDY WOOLF ONCE ate four Peacesicles in a row," Miranda tells me as we begin our descent down the mountain. She still holds the wooden ice cream stick in one hand, occasionally bouncing it off her lower lip like a tongue depressor.

"Carob?"

"Nope. She hates carob. Rainforest Bridge Mix."

"Gross."

She rolls her eyes and shakes her head in disgust. "Tell me about it."

We watch the sun fall below the mountains to our west, disappearing into the horizon as if it were sinking aflame underwater. Red sky at night, sailor's delight . . .

"It's supposed to rain tomorrow afternoon," I tell Miranda, as much to reassure myself as her. And then, afraid I have gotten her hopes up, I add, "At least that's what the weather forecasters are saying. And we know how often they're right."

"Not very."

Certainly that has been true this summer. At least a half-dozen times that I can recall we have been told that rain is imminent. And then, those few days or nights that storm systems actually visited Vermont, all they left behind were short bursts of inconsequential sprinkles. I wish I could convince myself that this time will be different.

I rest my elbow on the ice chest, and close my eyes. I try to clear my mind of the image of the meteorologists on the six and eleven o'clock television news, folding their arms across their chests as they apologize for the lack of rain. As if they were responsible. I try not to think of Ian Rawls, telling me with a straight face today over lunch that a small group of Powder Peak employees had approached him last week, concerned that the drought was a sign meant for them: Perhaps, they had told their managing director, the expansion and all it involved—tapping the Chittenden, cutting down acres of trees on Mount Republic—really was going to damage the local aquatic and forest environments.

Ian admitted to me that he had been spooked. And I admitted to him that his story spooked me. It is not so much that either of us is superstitious, or believes for a second that the drought is an event meant solely for us, for the resort, for the industry; rather, it is the idea that the drought may actually be an indication of great climatic changes over which we at one Vermont ski resort have little control that we both find disturbing.

Miranda's small hand grabs my elbow, her thumb and her fingers digging through my shirt and squeezing my arm. I open my eyes to see her staring out toward the forest, the woods where someday soon will be the beginning of a new network of trails.

"What?" I ask, and she shushes me, bringing a finger from her other hand to her lips.

Blinking, I follow her eyes, trying to see what she sees.

"What?" I ask again, whispering so softly that I can barely hear the word myself.

With the finger that only a second before had silenced me she points, raising her arm slowly as she straightens her finger. "There," she murmurs.

At first they look like house cats, three of them, one that is huge and two that are smaller. Kittens. Except even those two smaller animals are each as big as a good-sized dog. Perhaps a full-grown springer spaniel. Their fur is the color of wheat.

"Look," Miranda says, her voice tiny but filled with wonder. "A mom. And her babies."

The babies—the cubs—are covered with spots the color of pinecones, and there is a series of black bars along their tails.

As the chairlift continues toward the animals, sliding on cables at least twenty-five feet off the ground, the mother cat looks up at us, studying us for a brief moment. Her tail rises into the air, her ears go back, and she bares for us her teeth: Even at this distance, I can see her bottom fangs—sharp, white obelisks that look almost as long as my fingers.

"Catamounts," Miranda says, drawing her arm back inside the chairlift. "Right here."

The mother turns toward her cubs, nudging them with her mouth. When she turns, her full size becomes clear. She must weigh seventy-five, perhaps one hundred pounds. The cubs finally notice us, and become excited, jumping upon each other's backs and swatting each other with paws the size of my daughter's fists. One of the two animals tries to roar or hiss at us, but the sound that comes out is little more than a squeal.

"Have you ever seen one?" Miranda asks me.

I shake my head no, never. "Hardly anyone has," I mumble.

The mother starts to race toward the cliffs above the ravine, away from Miranda's and my chair, the cubs following close on the big cat's heels. As they pick up speed they disappear into the evergreens, and then, only seconds later, emerge on one of the boulders that ring the steep-sided hollow. From that rock they can watch us at our level, but at a safe distance. They must have covered one hundred and fifty wooded yards in about fifteen seconds.

"They're beautiful," Miranda says, unwilling to turn away from the family, receding further and further behind us. "I think they're the prettiest things I've ever seen."

Lulled by the white noise around me, mesmerized by the wildcats on the rocks, I nod. Although my daughter cannot see the gesture, I know she's aware I agree.

20

Catamount. The word, I have been told, is French for mountain cat. Cat of the mountain.

A mountain lion. That's what a catamount is. It is northern New England's wildcat. Our bobcat. Our panther, our cougar, our leopard, our lynx. No one is quite sure how many remain in northern Vermont, but the general feeling among naturalists is that there are either few or none. There are three or four sightings reported every year in the Green Mountains, always by people without cameras (like Miranda and me), or by people who are unable to photograph the elusive animals before they disappear from view.

Consequently, most people believe that development has driven the animals north into Canada and west into the Adirondack Mountains, despite the signs that hunters sometimes find in the woods: a tree used as a scratching post, with gashes four or five feet up on its trunk; a round track or a paw print that is four inches long; a stride that measures easily two feet.

Despite these signs, despite the occasional sightings, most people believe that catamounts no longer live in Vermont.

And until last night, I was one of those people.

No longer. Now, even as I drive the winding hill up to the Powder Peak base lodge, and the executive offices in its west wing, I find myself glancing out the truck's side windows, half expecting to see a catamount staring at me from atop a boulder or fallen tree. The road twists and turns through deep wood, climbing up through the mountains that form the resort. There is little traffic on this road in July: If there are catamounts awake right now in any one spot in Vermont, I would not be surprised to find that spot here.

. . .

IAN RAWLS SITS behind a circular table, facing a wall of windows that stares up at Moosehead—the three-peaked mountain that once must have looked vaguely like a moose's long head and wide antlers to the person who named it.

"Must be pretty important to get you up here before nine o'clock in the morning," Ian says, today's *Sentinel* buried underneath the wax paper from a bakery donut, and two empty paper cups browned by coffee. "I didn't see any crisis in the newspaper. Did you hear something from Reedy McClure? About his group's appeal, maybe?"

"No. Nothing like that."

"Then what?" he asks, his voice suddenly nervous.

"There are catamounts up there," I tell him, and motion with my eyes up at the mountains. "On Mount Republic."

He reaches for one of the paper cups, and when he sees that it's empty, he grabs the other. "What is this," he asks, trying to smile, "some sort of asinine joke? If it is, I don't get it. I must have missed the punch line."

"No joke."

With the empty cup in his hands he stands, and wanders out of his office. He then puts his head back in the doorway. "You want some coffee?"

"No, thanks. I'm fine."

He nods. "I'll be right back."

There is not a soul on Moosehead, at least on the part I can see from Ian's office. It's hard to believe that on any given Saturday or Sunday afternoon in January there might be five or six hundred people in view.

When Ian returns he has refilled his paper cup, and he takes a long sip. He sighs. "Catamounts, huh."

"Catamounts, right."

"How do you know? Who told you?"

"No one. I saw them myself."

He rubs his chin, thinking. "Them."

"Three of them. Miranda and I were riding the lift last night, over on Republic, and we saw three of them. A mother and two cubs. They were at the edge of the ravine, not far from the top of the mountain."

"Where the new trail network starts?"

"Well, where it's supposed to start. Right now there are only evergreens there."

He sits back in his chair, and then allows himself to slump down into it. "Are you absolutely positive that what you saw wasn't a fox? Maybe some deer?"

"I'm positive. I know a catamount when I see one."

"I gather you've seen a lot of them?" he snaps at me, irritation creeping into his voice for the first time.

"No. But I can tell the difference between a mountain lion and a deer, for God's sake."

He takes a deep breath. "Who have you told?"

"Laura."

"Your friend, Reedy?"

"No."

"Your sister-in-law?"

"No."

"Did you get a picture?"

"No."

"Okay," he mumbles. "Okay. There's no proof."

"What the heck does that mean?"

Ignoring my question, he continues, "Have you spoken to Miranda?"

"About?"

"About keeping this . . . quiet."

"Oh, I see where this is going," I tell Ian, trying to keep my tone light. "Laura and Miranda are able to raise one eyebrow at a time. At times like this, I wish I could too."

"You're avoiding my question."

"Because it's a stupid question, Ian. I'm not going to muzzle my daughter. I'm not going to muzzle my wife."

"You don't even know you saw a catamount! There's no proof!"

"I know what I saw. My daughter knows what she saw. There are catamounts on Mount Republic. That's a fact we have to deal with."

"If word gets out—"

"Word will get out. That's why I'm here," I explain, cutting him off. Keeping my voice as even and reasonable as I possibly can, I continue, "We need to manage the flow of information. We need to make the appropriate development decisions, and then take charge of the communications process ourselves."

"Why are you doing this to me? Why are you doing this to yourself?"

I push the door shut. "First of all, if Miranda and I saw the catamounts, other people might too."

"No one has yet."

"They might. And even if no one else does, ever, Scott and Miranda Winston know they're there. You can't cover that up, it just won't happen."

Pushing against the sides of his chair with his elbows, Ian sits forward and leans over his table. "Well, we could—and I don't like the words *cover up*—keep this issue quiet. But it doesn't sound like we'd get much cooperation."

"No, you wouldn't."

"So what are you proposing?"

"We move the new trail system to a different mountain, and explain our reasoning. We—one of your attorneys and his daughter—saw three catamounts, and now Powder Peak wants to do the right thing. I know it wouldn't be easy, but it would be great public relations for the resort."

"Miranda's probably telling all her little friends right now that she saw the animals, isn't she?"

The power lines just outside Ian's windows sway like jump ropes in the breeze. "No. I explained to her that she should keep this a secret. For now."

"Oh, I see. A short-term muzzle."

I shake my head. "I'm not proud of that."

"You've got one weird and twisted set of ethics, Scottie. That's probably why Goddard likes you so."

"I told Miranda that until the people at Powder Peak know what we saw, she shouldn't tell anyone."

He tilts his head back and finishes his coffee, and then looks up at Moosehead. "My grandfather founded this mountain," he says. "I know you know that. But I find it amazing. He built the son of a bitch. He cut down trees himself. Can you imagine? He carried axes and saws up the mountain, and he cut down trees himself. Probably thousands of them in his life. Some of them went into this building in 1932. When my own father was only five years old."

He takes a long tube of blueprints that is resting against the wall, and begins to bounce it distractedly against the tabletop. "My grandfather designed the first thirteen trails this resort ever had," he continues, his voice low. "Heavenly Rest. Deer Canyon. Ten-Hook Brook. He was an honest-to-God pioneer."

"He was. You're right."

"I'm right," he says. "I'm right. So how dare you tell me I'm taking this all wrong?"

"Because you are."

"How dare you suggest we move the new trail system to a different mountain? Is it your money?"

"This isn't about—"

"It sure as fuck is. Move the trail system to a different mountain. Which one, Scottie boy, Killington? Stratton? Sugarbush? What about Aspen? Why don't we just move the whole son-of-a-bitch system to Aspen?"

"There are three mountains at Powder Peak."

"Gee. I must have forgotten."

"The resort's goal was to add new trails. Not, specifically, new trails on Republic."

He drops the tube back onto the floor, and rolls it with his foot against the wall. "For over eight months engineers studied this place, figuring out just where the new system should go. They looked at every hill. Every tree. Every fucking animal turd they came across. And you know what?"

"I know what you're going to say—"

"There is no other spot for this system!"

"You're wrong. I've seen that report. You could—"

"I could have a whole new system designed, you're right, a smaller network, a less interesting one. No, Scottie, the fact is this: The area we've chosen on Mount Republic is not only the most cost-efficient spot for expansion, it's also the best. It's the best in terms of terrain, it's the best in terms of aesthetics, it's the best in terms of the skiing experience. It's that simple."

I take a deep breath. "We're friends, as well as business associates, right?"

"Right now, I sure as hell hope so. Because you've got a goddamn gun in your hands, and I don't think you have the slightest fucking—"

"Ian, give me a minute here."

"No, you give me a minute," he says, his voice made almost unrecognizable by anger. "Shit, I'll buy that minute. After all, I pay you by the hour, don't I? Hell, I'll buy another goddamn hour."

"Would you relax?"

"Move the new trail system. Give me a fucking break. Do you have any idea how much that would cost? Any idea?"

"Of course I do."

"New engineering studies, new plans, new site work. Beginning the state's hellish permit process all over again. God, those hearings, the paperwork." He pauses and looks into my eyes. "The legal fees."

"The legal fees would be the least—"

Disgusted, he ignores me, continuing, "Not to mention the loss of time. That loss would be incalculable. Moving the system would cost us a season, one whole season. That means the new trails wouldn't be up and running until two years from now. Two years! Frankly, I don't know if Powder Peak can afford that. I don't know if Schuss would stand for it. I don't think they could stand for it."

"The legal fees would not have to be a factor. If you were to reconsider the plan to build trails on Republic, I could certainly minimize—"

"Minimize? Do you know what this resort has paid your firm this year alone? And it's only July." He swivels his chair to face the computer on the credenza behind his desk, and starts opening different files on the screen.

"Ian, you don't need to check that. I know exactly what Powder Peak has paid, and what it owes."

"I'll bet you do."

As his fingers slam into the letters on the keyboard, I stand up to leave.

"Where are you going?"

"To my office. I'll call you later to see if you've gotten your sanity back."

"I'll have the payables up in just a minute."

I salute him sarcastically from his door, but he doesn't look back from his computer.

21

•

You're an optimist," I tell Laura Tuesday afternoon, as she enters my office. She is holding an umbrella, a bright blue and orange golf umbrella that is wide enough to shelter Laura, Miranda, and me together when it is open.

"No, it's going to rain today," she says, her voice light.

"I didn't know you were coming into Montpelier this afternoon."

She holds up a bank deposit slip for the Divine Lights of Vermont with at least a half-dozen checks paper-clipped behind it. "I wasn't. But these came in the mail, and I figured I'd go by the bank."

"Good figuring."

"How did things go this morning?" she asks.

"Bad. They probably couldn't have gone worse."

"What do you think they'll do?"

"I don't know."

"Well, they can't build the new trails on Mount Republic now. Do they understand that?"

"I hope so. But I doubt it."

"Do they understand you won't help them if they do?"

I pause, thinking about her question. "I understand no such thing. Why should they?"

"Scottie!"

"Laura, please. Let's not discuss this now."

"I didn't think there was anything we needed to discuss. I can't imagine there's anything more you need to say to Miranda," she then adds, a reference to the fact I have asked our daughter to keep the catamounts a secret. For now.

"There isn't."

She nods, and begins to chew one of her nails. She had had this habit when we were in college, but she had stopped before Miranda was born. I noticed the habit had returned on Saturday, the day Patience first asked if we would allow our daughter to dowse a grave site. We were getting into bed that evening, and I saw Laura gnawing at one of her nails. At the time, I attributed it primarily to the stress from Elias's death, and the fact the funeral was the next day. Patience's request of our daughter, I assumed, was in actuality merely the catalyst.

"Patience called this morning," she continues, removing her pinky from her mouth to speak. "She wanted Miranda. Again."

It was late Sunday afternoon, when I finally had a chance to tell Laura in detail about my encounter with Patience in the cemetery, that I realized her sudden nail-biting had more to do with Miranda than with Elias.

I try to smile. I hope we're through arguing. "What now?"

"The Mitchells need a new well drilled. And they asked Patience to dowse the spot."

"And?"

"And Patience wanted Miranda to do it."

I sit back against the windowsill, and look out at the gold dome of the statehouse. The dome shines when it's sunny, it glistens when it rains. On a day like today, the sky a flat sheet of gray, it looks dull, as if the gold came from crayons.

"You know, I really do think the world's losing its mind this summer," I tell Laura. "I really do. Saturday I only figured it was Patience. And this morning I only figured it was Ian. But you know something? It's probably everybody."

She shrugs. "As you said yourself, maybe it's the heat."

"Maybe." The governor and two younger assistants start across the statehouse lawn. "What was Patience's reason this time?"

"For wanting Miranda?"

"Right. For wanting Miranda."

"She doesn't feel well. She said she feels out of sorts from the funeral. She feels out of sync."

"Can't dowse when you're out of sync, huh?"

"Nope."

"Can't you do it?"

"I said I'd be happy to."

"But Patience wants her niece."

"She thinks it's time," Laura says, abruptly ripping a cuticle off her thumb with her teeth.

"It's time?"

"Time to start allowing Miranda to use her talents. Regularly. She thinks the Mitchells' well would be a real confidence-builder."

"What did you say?"

"I said fine." She laughs, one small, nervous chuckle. "I don't mind her dowsing for water, you know that."

"Is she with Patience now?"

"Yes. They left about an hour ago. You don't mind, do you?"

"Well, as a matter of fact, I do. I wish we had talked about it first."

"I'm not letting Miranda accept any money," Laura explains. "As far as she's concerned, she should be honored that she's even allowed to do this."

"I'm sure she is."

"You sound angry."

"I know I do. And I know I shouldn't be. It isn't that big a deal."

"Right. She's dowsing a well. That's all."

There is a small smudge of blood along Laura's thumb.

"Can I ask you a question?"

"Sure."

"If none of this is a big deal, how come you're tearing apart your nails and fingers?"

She wraps a piece of tissue around her thumb, and raises her eyebrows in mock innocence. "This?"

"That."

She looks up at the ceiling, and then down at the carpet. Reedy left a permanent stain there earlier this summer when he dragged his feet across it.

"It's not the dowsing itself," she begins slowly. "On one level, it wasn't even the dowsing at Elias's grave that upset me."

"That was pretty weird."

"I agree. And I'm still very angry at Patience for what she did. But . . . but it's not just the dowsing. It's what the dowsing means," she says, pushing her hair back behind her ears.

"Patience will never come between you and Miranda. You know that," I reassure Laura.

"Probably."

"Is there more to it?"

"I think so. I think it's the idea that our little girl's growing up," she says, finally meeting my eyes. "That's what this dowsing is all about. Miranda's growing up, and that's very sad for me. I didn't think it would be, but it is. Miranda's growing up."

Outside a raindrop blows against the windowpane, and then one falls onto the windshield of the car parked on the street below my office. Within seconds the rain begins in earnest.

"See?" Laura says, forcing a grin onto a face that—like mine—is about to turn forty. "I told you it would rain."

. . .

IF THE SUMMER is wet, a good rain in July can turn our dirt driveway into a river of mud that will suck tires down into it, and yank cars with rear-wheel drive into the grass on either side.

In this summer, one of the driest on record, today's rain must have bounced off the rock-hard ground and run off into the grass, because our driveway Tuesday night is as firm as ever. It looks and feels under the truck's wheels as if, in fact, it never rained.

Reedy's beaten-up Volvo is parked between the barn and our house. As I coast to a stop beside it I can see Reedy, Patience, and Laura just inside the barn, leaning against the cartons Laura plans on shipping tomorrow. There is a transparent rainbow off to the west, a welcome sight any summer but this one. Today's rain may have kept some of the county's lower wells in business for another few days or even a week, but it will not have a significant impact on the drought. For that we would need days and days of steady rain.

Patience is holding in her hands four candles from the Divine Lights of Vermont, blue with a white ribbon around them.

"You made it home early," Laura says, glancing at her watch. "It's not even five o'clock."

I squeeze her shoulders as she automatically offers me her cheek to kiss—a habit of marriage. "Tomorrow's going to be a long day," I tell her. "I figured I'd get out of there while I could." I turn to my sister-in-law and Reedy. "Evening, Reedy, evening, Patience. What brings you two by?"

Although Reedy and I have seen each other twice since I stormed out of the restaurant last Thursday, once at Patience's house Friday morning and again at Elias's funeral on Sunday, it is clear to us both that the wounds from that fight have not really healed. We may have said we were sorry as we stood together on Patience's porch, but my apology, at least, was insincere. The fact is I wasn't sorry, and I only feigned civility for the benefit of Laura and Patience and their mother.

If there was any doubt that my anger had not diminished, two days later I consciously and completely ignored Reedy at Elias's funeral. We saw each other, but I made sure that our eyes never met.

Patience holds up the candles for me. "We're having dinner at the Atwoods'. Hostess gift."

"How's life up at the mountain?" Reedy asks me.

"Couldn't be better."

"Your daughter dowsed her first well today," Patience says, aware of the awkward tension between her fiancé and me.

"So I gather."

Patience shakes her head. "I can tell, you are just bursting with pride," she says sarcastically.

"I'm very proud of her."

"Three hundred and nineteen feet, seven gallons per minute," Reedy adds, forcing a smile as he speaks. "Patience told me the details."

"Where is she now?"

"With Mindy Woolf," Laura says. "She should be home any minute."

Reedy runs two fingers over the coarse grain of the wood on the barn door. "You got a minute?" he asks me.

I shrug. "Sure." For a brief second it crosses my mind that he knows about the catamounts, that Miranda may have slipped and told her aunt about the animals while up at the Mitchells'. But the thought almost instantly passes. If Miranda had slipped—an absolutely understandable and forgivable transgression—Reedy would be far less pleasant and agreeable.

He waves an arm across our backyard. "Then walk with me,

my son," he says, trying to make a joke of the fact that he wants to speak to me alone.

. . .

REEDY AND I stroll toward the vegetable garden, and the perfectly straight rows of small sickly corn. Like friendships between most men, Reedy's and mine revolves largely around our work. We talk mostly about business, rarely raising issues that might force us to reveal emotions more pronounced than irony, anger, or satisfaction. We might skirt select, softer subjects—my feelings for Laura, his involvement with Patience—but we approach them tentatively, and usually retreat before either of us has exposed more than we'd like.

"Did you file your appeal yet with the state Environmental Board?" I ask Reedy, trying to find something to say.

"Nope."

"I didn't think so. I figured I would have heard." I bend over to examine the bean plants, surprised to discover that there are actually drops of moisture on the leaves. I would have thought they would have evaporated by now, or been absorbed.

"Will you be filing this week?" I continue.

"Probably not."

There are spotted bugs I've never seen before climbing among the eggplants. "Well, I have to assume you are going to appeal. I can't imagine you're already prepared to throw in the towel."

He chuckles, a laugh that sounds strange and forced. "Oh, no. I think this one is far from over."

"Good. I'd hate to think you were going to give it to me," I tell him, as I stand up and wander toward the carrots. "Can I ask when?"

"A few weeks."

At the end of our driveway Cynthia Woolf's car is approaching. "A few weeks?"

"We've got thirty days."

I nod, understanding his plan. "And you're going to wait until the last possible moment."

"That's right," he says, pushing around some of the dirt at the edge of our garden with the toe of his hiking boot. "I have enormous faith in this drought. I really do. The way I figure it, the longer we wait, the lower the river. The lower the river, the worse the aquatic environment."

"And the better your chances of winning the appeal."

"Right. I'll probably wait until August eleventh to file, which means the hearing won't occur until sometime in September—at the earliest."

I pull up some of the weeds surrounding the carrots' green tops. There aren't many weeds this year, perhaps the only good thing about droughts. Even weeds suffer. "It's probably a good strategy," I admit. "If I were a betting man, I think I'd bet on this drought lasting a while longer."

"You know, I didn't suggest we walk out here to talk about Powder Peak," Reedy says. Then, quickly, he adds, "I think next spring Patience and I'll have a garden."

"Averys are excellent gardeners."

"I would expect that."

Miranda climbs out of the backseat of the Woolfs' car and runs to her mother and her aunt, then waves good-bye to her friend.

I ask Reedy, "How go the wedding plans?"

"Fine. I'm pretty sure the invitations will be ready Thursday or Friday. We'll spend Saturday or Sunday afternoon addressing them."

"Sounds like an exciting weekend."

"I said Saturday *or* Sunday. I don't expect this to be a weekend-long project. God, I hope it isn't."

"What's the final count?"

"One hundred and forty."

"How many dowsers?"

He smiles. "One hundred and forty."

Miranda glances over at us, and it looks as if she wants to run over and join us. Her mother says something to her, however, and she races inside the house instead.

"I want to talk about the other day," Reedy says suddenly. "That's what I want to talk about."

"What about it?"

" 'What about it?' " he says, imitating me. "Listen to you. You sound like you have no idea what I'm talking about."

"Look, Reedy, I said I was sorry. What more am I supposed to do?"

"And I said I was sorry too. That's not the point."

I sigh. "As long as you and your group are opposing—"

"I've opposed your projects before. There's something different about this one."

"The word *rape* maybe?"

"Is that what this is all about? The fact I got carried away when I named the group? Well, if that's all it is, I'm sorry about that too. I really am."

"Yeah, there is something different about this one," I agree. An image of the three catamounts atop the ravine, magnificent wheat-colored mountain lions, flashes briefly before me, but that wasn't what I meant when I concurred with Reedy.

"I think it's the drought," I continue. "The heat. We're not used to it."

"Or we're scared."

"Scared?"

"Yes, scared," he repeats patiently. "Frightened. There's something unnerving about it all. It's like the weather and the environment are conspiring against us. It feels that way, doesn't it?"

I envision my little girl dowsing for underground springs

by this very garden, and crying at night over forest fires. I have sat this summer in hearings in which experts babbled on about global warming and wind currents, and I have sat around conference tables and been nonplussed by the sound of running tap water in the next room.

"Come on, Scottie, admit it."

On some instinctive, atavistic level, Reedy is probably right. This drought feels more serious than most, it feels more significant than others I've lived through. And it has felt this way for a month. But when I think about the drought rationally, I am able to push those fears from my mind, reminding myself that droughts come and go; that they don't last forever; and that there are explanations for diminished snowfall far less frightening than global warming.

Besides, it rained today. Not a lot. But it did rain. There are drops on the bean plants to prove it.

"The drought's an annoyance," I tell him. "But it's not all that frightening."

He shakes his head, smirking. "Not all *that* frightening, or not *at all* frightening?"

"Shouldn't you and Patience be leaving for Burlington?"

"Just a teeny bit frightened, Scottie? Just a teeny-weeny bit?" he says, holding his index finger and thumb perhaps one inch apart.

"If I say yes," I ask, trying hard not to smile, "are you out of here?"

"Like the rain. I'll be gone like the rain."

"Then, fine. There have been moments this summer when the drought has seemed a little bit scary to me. How was that?"

He punches me lightly on my shoulder. "You are a big man, Scottie Winston. You aren't one-half the macho asshole you pretend to be."

"I'll take that as a sincere and well-intentioned compliment."

As we start back toward the barn, he continues, "We have to try not to take all this stuff so seriously." He looks straight ahead as he speaks, as if staring at Patience and Laura. "We have to try not to let it become personal."

"The expansion," I add.

"Right, the expansion. After all, we've known each other an awful lot longer than you've worked for Powder Peak. Besides, resorts come and go."

"Oh, I hope not," I tell Reedy, shaking my head. "I sure hope not."

. . .

IN THE HEAT of this summer, Miranda sleeps most nights in one of her mother's T-shirts. Her light is already off when I wander upstairs to tuck her in, and she has pulled one sheet up to her elbows.

Nevertheless, in the moonlight that pours through the screen window I can see that tonight Miranda has chosen to wear instead a white Quarry Men jersey from two seasons past, before we decided to change our colors to neon yellow and red.

Her eyes are shut. Without sitting on the side of the bed, I reach over and pull the sheet up to her chin.

"I'm awake," she says.

"You fooled me."

She rolls over and opens her eyes. "I tried falling asleep, but I couldn't."

The room is warm, but the air is dry. I sit beside her on the edge of her bed. "Well, you had a big day."

She reaches over for a small stuffed dinosaur, a pink triceratops, and bounces it by its middle horn off her chest. "I was nervous."

"When you were dowsing the Mitchells' well?"

"Yup. Aunt Patience told Mrs. Mitchell to go inside and

clean out a closet or something, but I knew she was watching me from the window."

"I hear you did a great job."

"Once I started, it was easy. The vein was really big."

"It was easy for you. It wouldn't have been easy for most people."

She rests the dinosaur on her forehead. Then, lowering her voice into a conspiratorial whisper, she asks, "Did you tell Mr. Rawls about the catamounts?"

I whisper back, "Yes. And we don't have to whisper."

"It's not a secret anymore?"

One of the sheer curtains in her window is moved just the tiniest bit by a breeze.

"Because I can't wait to tell people," she continues. "About a hundred times today I started to tell Mindy, but I always had to stop myself."

"Think you're going to burst, huh?" I ask.

"Yup."

"Well, I am too. So's your mom."

"So I can tell people?"

"Can you wait one more day?"

She rolls the pink dinosaur onto the pillow beside her, and opens her mouth in astonishment. "One more day!"

I nod. "Your mom and I are having dinner tomorrow night with Mr. Healy. He's the man who's president of Powder Peak." I keep my voice light, serene, despite the disgust I am feeling inside: I may be the only father in the world who would insist his daughter keep a catamount sighting a secret. "And once we tell him, then you can tell the whole world that you saw a catamount."

She holds three fingers up before her. "Three! You can't forget the cubs."

"Right. Three."

"Okay," she says. "Let's see. Tomorrow night is Wednesday. So Thursday I can tell people."

"Yup."

"Because I think I'm going crazy, keeping this inside me. Sometimes, I just can't believe it. We saw catamounts, Daddy! Practically no one else in Vermont can say that."

"I know."

"Weren't they pretty?"

"They sure were."

She takes a deep breath, as a small frown begins to form. Suddenly, she looks almost gloomy.

"What's the matter, sweetheart? What are you thinking about?"

She turns toward the window. "The catamounts."

It is possible that Miranda has realized that we saw the animals in an area of the mountain that the resort plans to clear for ski trails, but I am fairly sure that's not her concern. I don't believe she has made that connection, at least not yet. I believe instead this is about a more pronounced fear of hers.

"Why the scowl?" I ask.

"The woods."

"That's their home," I murmur. "The woods. That's where they live."

"I know."

"Then what?"

"The woods are so dry," she says, a tremor in her voice that could grow with each word. "And there have been so many forest fires this summer . . ."

I brush her bangs away from her forehead, hoping that whatever breezes are left in the night will somehow cool my little girl's face.

22

•

El Niño. Spanish for "the boy" or "the child." Often, the Christ child.

There is a weather pattern called *El Niño* that begins off the coast of Peru. It is called *El Niño* because it often affects that South American country just before Christmas.

El Niño occurs when a tremendous current of warm water abruptly displaces a patch of cold in the Pacific Ocean. It happens every four or five years. The result, aside from warmer Peruvian coastal waters, is a huge weather system of warm moist air that can affect much of the globe as it moves east. It can nudge the jet stream further north into Canada. It can cause heavy rains from California to Texas. It can warm up the mythically cold winters of northern Vermont.

Last winter, we blamed *El Niño* for the limited snowfall we had here in Vermont, watching in envy as the snowstorms we felt we deserved were pulled further north into Quebec. When the temperature would hover in the high thirties for days at a time, making it impossible to make snow, we nodded knowingly and said to each other, "*El Niño.*"

Now, in the midst of the drought, we are finding new reasons to point fingers at *El Niño*. It is probably more important than ever for us to find a meteorological rationale for days and days in a row without rain.

. . .

LATE WEDNESDAY MORNING Ian Rawls phones to tell me that he isn't bringing his wife to dinner, and he recommends that Laura steer clear as well.

"Boys' night out, Ian?" I ask facetiously.

"I told Goddard about this catamount thing, and the three of us need to talk," he says, his voice flat.

"Ah, the catamount thing."

"Are you going to be reasonable about this?"

"Yes, absolutely."

"Thank God," Ian says, evidently taking my use of the word *reason* more seriously than I meant it.

"Seven thirty?" I ask, the time I assume we will meet for dinner.

"Make it eight o'clock. In case his plane's delayed."

I scribble the time on a piece of paper, and before I can confirm the restaurant, he adds, "I closed the tramway today to tourists."

"I'm sure that pleased the Chamber of Commerce to no end."

"No sense in asking for trouble."

"Guess not."

"Besides, these days we get it whether we ask for it or not."

. . .

BECAUSE I AM not meeting Ian and Goddard until eight o'clock, I go home after work Wednesday afternoon. I leave the office just before five thirty, anticipating an hour and a half when I can sit on the porch and think. An hour and a half in which I can try and understand my options.

For a brief moment I can feel a smile form on my face at the thought, but the smile passes quickly. Options. The word implies there are alternatives. It implies I have choices, one of which may be better than another.

Ahead of me is a compact car held together by duct tape, and ahead of that car is a minivan. The minivan climbs the winding road east of Montpelier at twenty-five miles an hour. I honk the horn, one gentle beep.

I have no idea which of my choices is better. There may be moral differences, but even there I may be deluding myself, even there I may be reducing the issues to the sorts of Birkenstock politics that sound great at rallies but often make little real sense.

There is no passing on this stretch of road, and there won't be for miles. I could pass the two cars illegally, of course.

Are you alive in there? I ask the minivan's driver in my mind. *Are you awake?*

On the one hand, I can let Miranda tell whoever she wants about the catamounts. Let the cats out of the bag, so to speak. The two of us could tell the world that we saw catamounts on Mount Republic, a mountain that is beautiful and magic and happened to have had the bad luck to have risen toward the sky in the middle of a ski resort. And then we could let nature take its course. I could let nature take its course. I could try and help Powder Peak manage the fallout.

No, that's not likely. I certainly wouldn't be working with Powder Peak once we started telling people about the animals we saw on the mountain. They probably wouldn't let me near the place.

I tap the horn again, trying to give the minivan a wake-up call. Trying, perhaps, to convince the little car before me to pass the van illegally, so that I'll have only one car to race past on a winding road with two yellow lines.

I want to get home. I want to be home.

Or, I could instruct Miranda that she and I must never, ever tell anyone what we saw on the mountain. Give her some reason, some excuse. And while it is clear to me that my nine-year-old daughter will not be taking this secret with her to her grave, if she can keep it inside her for a few more months, the permitting process will be behind us.

I hold my thumb down on the horn for three or four seconds. *Drive, please,* I hear myself murmuring in disgust in my head. *Please put your fucking foot on the fucking accelerator and press the fucking pedal down. Please.*

The fallout from that decision? Just how angry would people like Patience and Reedy become? Just how long would it take people to forgive me? I hate to think. I probably won't live that long.

But it would allow our firm to retain Powder Peak as a client. It would allow us to maintain our position and reputation with corporate Vermont. And it would allow me continued access to the sorts of clients who can pay what is—by Vermont standards—an astonishing hourly rate for my services.

The minivan slows to a crawl. Twenty miles an hour. Then fifteen. Whoever is driving is punishing me for honking.

I look down the road into the oncoming lane. There is a small straightaway here, enough length to pass two cars if one of them is creeping along at fifteen miles an hour. Unfortunately, there is a dump truck lumbering our way from the opposite direction.

Son of a bitch. Son of a fucking bitch.

. . .

"WHAT DO YOU think you're going to tell them?" Laura asks, watering the petunias on the porch.

"I don't know." I want a beer, but I don't dare. Not yet. I sip club soda instead, and sit unsatisfied in one of the chairs facing west. I can't believe I'd looked forward to this in the truck.

"You must have some idea."

"One would think so."

There are six baskets and pots with flowers at this end of the porch alone. There may be another half-dozen on the other side. Laura has already filled the copper watering can twice.

Without looking up from the petunias she says, "This isn't just another rate hike for some utility. You know that, don't you? This isn't about just one more trail at one more ski resort."

She saw I was irritable when I came home. She knows I am irritable now. "Why are you doing this?" I ask her.

She stands up. "Because I want to know what you're going to say to those people."

"Those people," I remind her, "have names. We've known Ian Rawls for a very long time. Good God, you went to high school with the man."

She places the watering can down onto a porch table as if it were a piece of antique china, setting it soundlessly in place. "Fine. I want to know what you're going to tell Ian. And Goddard."

"If I had the slightest idea, I'd tell you."

"I hope you don't expect Miranda to keep quiet forever."

"I hope it doesn't come to that."

Three croquet balls sit in the grass, the yellow one dusty gold in the sunlight.

"And if it does?"

My immediate reaction is to tell her that if it comes to the point where I have to take sides with my daughter against them, then her candle company will have to become more than a hobby. My first reaction is to tell Laura that she would have to start taking her business seriously, because I would no longer have clients like Powder Peak, and we would probably need the income. But I am able to keep the thought to myself.

"If it does?" she asks again.

I finish my club soda in one long swallow, the carbonation burning the back of my throat. "Laura, stop! Okay? Just stop."

Stop is a harsh word, it's not a word either of us uses often. At least with each other. At least with that tone. Instantly Laura's eyes widen, and then for a very long second remain that way. Her cheeks become taut as she considers how to respond. And then, abruptly, she turns and leaves me alone on the porch, letting the screen door slam behind her.

. . .

ONE OF THE ways that Powder Peak has tried to survive is by evolving from a winter resort into a four-season resort. Four years ago they built the golf course and sixteen new tennis courts, and they changed the name of the more casual of the resort's two restaurants from Moguls to Peak Eats.

Despite the drought, the summer tourism business hasn't been half-bad this year. After all, people visiting the state these days can be assured of dramatically more sun than rain.

By eight o'clock in the evening, however, a family restaurant like Peak Eats is largely empty—which may actually be the reason that Ian chose it. There's a much older couple finishing their iced tea at a table facing the wide western windows, and a family with two little boys, each eight or nine years old, seated near the salad bar. One of the boys, the taller and thinner of the two, has been up to the salad bar at least four times since we arrived, each time piling onto his plate a slightly larger pile of macaroni salad.

"Save room for supper," his mother keeps telling him, to which the boy's father replies, "He's a growing boy. He'll eat plenty."

Goddard twists the loaf of bread at our table in his hands, as if he were wringing a small animal's neck, and tears the baguette in half. He leans back into his chair and stretches his legs out before him, taking up as much space with his body as he possibly can.

"I still have that article about catamounts," Goddard says. "The one I saw in the magazine the last time I was out here."

"You saved it?" I ask.

"Information. Most important thing you can have when you run a business. Information. I save a lot of stuff that doesn't seem to have a whole lot of value at the time. But sometimes it pays off." He spreads a huge dollop of whipped butter onto his bread.

"I think you and your daughter saw a feral cat," he says abruptly. "I read a little book about them on the airplane today, probably in that hour we spent flying between Colorado and Iowa. Know what a feral cat is?"

Ian says he doesn't, so I sit quietly.

"It's a house cat gone wild. A domestic cat that, for whatever the reasons, takes off into the woods. They can be fierce, and they can look big."

I consider correcting Goddard: A feral cat can never look that big. A house cat can never look like it might weigh seventy-five to one hundred pounds. Instead I keep the thought to myself.

"You were moving, you saw them at dusk," Ian says to me. "I'll bet when those animals fluff their fur, they look much, much bigger."

I wish they were feral cats. I wish I could convince my daughter they were feral cats: *Miranda, we didn't really see catamounts, we were mistaken. We just saw somebody's house cats that now live in the wild.*

"I know what we saw," I tell them. "We saw catamounts. And nothing can change that."

Goddard chews his bread without looking at Ian or me, staring instead into the empty fireplace. Finally he asks, "How many people in Vermont think they see catamounts every year? Not photograph them. I know that hasn't happened in a century. Just see them, like you and your little girl."

"My guess is there are probably three or four sightings every year," I answer. "Reported sightings."

"Not very many."

"Nope. Not very many. But there aren't very many sightings of bears either," I add quickly. "And we know they're out there."

Goddard is wearing a short-sleeve sport shirt. Despite his age, the muscles on his arms are still long packed tubes, and they stand out on his forearms as if he were a tennis pro thirty years younger. No one meeting him for the first time would ever doubt that Goddard was once an Olympic athlete.

"Ian says your solution to our problem here is to go public with the news, and move the new trail network to another mountain. That true?"

"It is."

He shakes his head slowly. "Pretty lame, my boy."

"I'm open to other suggestions," I tell him. Although Ian and I have removed our jackets and loosened our ties, we still look like weaklings compared to Healy.

"It's dated, Scottie, it's yesterday's newspaper." He brings his legs back under his chair and sits forward, folding his hands on the table. "Even in the northwest—even in the very heart of spotted owl central—our liberal president is letting loggers cut one point two billion feet of timber a year on federal lands. One point two billion! And you know why? Jobs. That's what this is all about. Jobs. Pure and simple."

I take a long swallow of beer, preparing my response. Before I can speak, however, Goddard continues as if he never even stopped for air.

"I love animals, I really do. When I saw the picture of the eastern catamount in that magazine last month, I felt a chill. I really did. But as much as I love animals, I love people more."

"Are you still dating Tanya?" I ask. "That woman from Greenpeace?"

He shakes his head. "Not really. Hell, not at all."

"That's too bad." I had hoped I would have an ally in Tanya.

"Some assholes torched some greens at the golf course out at Mystic earlier this month, and tried sabotaging a chairlift we're building. I'm pretty sure her older brother was involved," he says.

"I'm sorry."

"Not as sorry as I am. I was a horny old man who used his balls for his brains. I was used. And now I'm paying the price."

Ian signals to the waitress that she should bring us another round of drinks.

"Scottie, I wish to God this wasn't a choice between three animals and hundreds and hundreds of people," Goddard insists. "Because I do love animals. But that's the choice you're asking this resort to make. We can either kill the expansion and look out for these animals—let's work on the assumption you really are right about what you saw—or we can proceed, even though we'll be clearing the land where those critters might live. It's a choice: You can either offer people the three to five hundred jobs you yourself have talked about all summer, or you can offer them the existence of three cats."

"There's more to it than that," Ian says. "The expansion doesn't simply mean new jobs. It also prevents the loss of existing jobs. I'm not sure how viable Powder Peak will be in a decade without the expansion."

Goddard nods in agreement with Ian, as his eyes wander toward the waitress, an attractive young woman with blond hair the color of Miranda's.

"I guess I'm not as convinced as the two of you that this is an either-or proposition," I tell them, trying to keep my voice light.

"Scottie, we've been through this and through this!" Ian snaps.

"The engineers went over every possible inch of every mountain we have, and Mount Republic is the best spot there is."

I spread my arms, palms up. "So we use the second-best spot."

Goddard allows himself a small laugh. "Use the second-best spot. Where might that be, Scottie? In the wildlife habitat? On the cliffs up top of Mount Chittenden? How about those twelve hundred acres on Chittenden your friend Liza Eastwick said we can't touch anymore? Right there?"

"Powder Peak has a lot of land. Somewhere, there's a spot to build—"

"There probably is," Goddard says, leaning over to face me as he cuts me off. "And I'm sure if we were willing to fund another million dollars in engineering work and planning studies and legal fees, we could find that spot. I'm sure if we were willing to go through the permit process all over again, give up another year or two of our lives, we could find that spot. But that's just not realistic in this economic climate. I've seen a lot of this industry disappear over the last decade, and I've seen a lot of it fall to its knees. Well, I'm not about to let that happen to any Schuss property."

"Our permits already cut us off at the knees!" Ian adds, abruptly forgetting his initial relief and happiness when Liza called him a week ago today.

As the busboy refills our water glasses, the waitress returns to our table. "Would you like to order, or would you gentlemen like some more time?" she asks.

"Give us five more minutes," Goddard says to her.

The older couple stands up to leave, pausing for a moment before the western picture windows, savoring the echo of a red sunset that remains in the distant sky.

"We've done most of the talking here, Scottie," Goddard tells me, smiling. "You must feel like a trapped animal yourself."

"Sure do," I admit. It crosses my mind that although Ian and I have never been particularly close, we have been friends now for over a decade.

"Want to tell us where your head's at? Right now?" Goddard asks.

But if anyone were to walk into the restaurant at this moment and glance at our table, they would find it hard to believe that Ian and I are friends. Were friends, perhaps. He sits with his arms folded across his chest, occasionally shaking his head the tiniest bit back and forth, his eyes two thin slits. His lips move when he sighs, frustrated.

"I'm not sure," I hear myself mumbling in Goddard's direction. My voice sounds pathetic to me, but a mumble is all I can muster as I stand at the edge of the cliff. One step forward and I'm over the precipice; one step back and I will have begun the retreat that will keep me safe, my firm secure, my professional future intact.

"Well, you've got a lot to digest."

I wonder what I look like to him. To Goddard. I do indeed feel like a trapped animal, but it's not because I'm scared. At least I hope it isn't. Nothing Ian or Goddard has said is particularly frightening, none of it has surprised me. I've seen this cliff approaching since Miranda told Laura about the catamounts Monday night, and I heard the excitement in her voice. I sit up straight in my chair when I realize I've been slouching.

"There's really nothing I can do," I tell them, intentionally vague.

"I tend to agree," Goddard says. "But I'm not exactly sure we're on the same wavelength. Are we?" he asks hopefully.

I am silent for a long moment, and Ian takes that silence for agreement. "I think we are," he says knowingly, conspiratorially, to Goddard.

Suddenly I am overwhelmed with the desire to go home, to

get away from here as fast as I can. I think it was the sound of Ian's voice, the way he looked at Goddard with satisfaction. Suddenly, I know I won't stay for dinner. A part of my life is about to come to an end, relationships that have helped define my life for a decade. Who I am. How people see me. How I see myself. And postponing that with a dinner I don't really want, with people who without question will hate me in the morning, seems to me now a ridiculous waste of time. Of words. Of emotional capital.

I smile at them, hoping they can't tell that I'm shaking, and I wonder how much money is left in my wallet. It's a small detail, but I find myself hoping there's a five-dollar bill in there I can toss on the table when I stand up to go. Like the time I left Reedy in the diner.

"There's really nothing I can do," I repeat. "I'm not going to tell my daughter she can't tell anyone what she saw."

Goddard rubs his chin. "She's eight years old. That probably isn't the end of the world. It's not as if she's president of the Nature Conservancy."

"It may not be the end of world, Goddard," Ian hisses, for once in his life a step ahead of his boss, "but it will quickly become one major pain in the ass. His daughter will tell her aunt, who will tell Reedy McClure. And he probably *will* tell the Nature Conservancy."

"She's nine," I correct Goddard. "And pretty soon she'll be ten."

"Word will get around," Ian continues. "Within days, it will be all over this state that our lead lobbyist and his little girl saw three catamounts running around smack in the middle of our proposed trail network."

"Is that true, Scottie? In your opinion, is that what's about to happen?"

I reach for my wallet inside my sports jacket, still hanging over the back of my chair, and stand up. "Yes, I think so. I think

Ian has a pretty good handle on what's about to happen," I tell Goddard.

Inside my wallet are four ones and a receipt for my dry cleaning. I leave the money on the place mat before me, and drape my jacket over my arm.

"I'm going to call it a night and head home," I tell the two of them, trembling, dizzy from something—standing, maybe, but probably not. No, I know it's not from standing. "I don't think you guys need me here to figure out your next steps."

• • •

EARLY THURSDAY MORNING, well before anyone else arrives at the office, I examine the firm's financial statements, and try to assess the damage from the night before.

The Powder Peak Ski Resort this year was projected to represent approximately twenty percent of our firm's billings. In a typical year, a year in which the resort isn't battling for expansion permits, it represents about five percent. The Vermont Ski Areas Consortium, a loose affiliation of the state's nineteen ski areas, accounts for about ten percent of our firm's business. That revenue, along with our Powder Peak business, will now disappear.

Birch, Winston, and Hurley has twelve employees, including its three partners. I doubt we will have nine other employees a month from now.

Who will be the first person Miranda tells today? Mindy Woolf? Her aunt Patience? An entire troop of Landaff Brownies? I chose last night not to ask her who she thought she would play with today. I don't want to know. As I tucked Miranda in bed for the night, I told her to tell anyone that she wants everything that she wants, and I said those words, somehow, with a smile on my face.

I have no plans to tell Reedy myself what my daughter and I saw. I'll let him hear it through the grapevine. Besides, I feel I owe it to my partners, to Duane and Warren, to tell them first. Especially after the damage I have wrought to our practice.

The sun, still low in the east, warms my hands through the glass windows of my office, and I wander into the hallway to turn on the firm's air-conditioning. The low rumble that precedes the first jets of cool air has become for me yet one more sound I will associate always with drought, one more sound that—viscerally, unreasonably, instinctively—now has the power to frighten me.

Last night Laura said she was proud of me. I thanked her, but I also corrected her. Ethics and principles really had very little to do with my decision. Make no mistake about it, I told Laura: I do not hope to be a great man or a fine man. I simply do not want to be a terrible father.

Had I seen the catamounts alone, I wonder in my heart if she or anyone else in the world would ever have known.

23

On a Wednesday evening early in August, exactly fifteen days from the last day that it rained in northern Vermont, Patience sits on the steps of our back porch and asks me to give her away at her wedding next month. She stares out at the yard where Miranda and Laura are playing croquet, twirling her jade pendulum between her thumb and forefinger.

"I'm flattered," I tell her.

"Don't be. There aren't many men in my life."

"Not a lot of choices, huh?"

"Few and none."

Giggling, Miranda sends her mother's red croquet ball between a pair of Colorado spruce we planted the spring before last. The trees, about five feet tall now, look pretty wilted these days. Their branches droop as if covered with invisible snow, and they never did turn their almost transparent blue this summer.

"Well, how can I refuse such a polite request?"

"You can't," she says, not looking at me.

"Then I will be happy to."

"Thank you," she says, nodding.

Laura runs her fingers lightly over a row of needles on one of the young trees, unable to hide her concern.

"You're welcome. But I have to admit, Patience, for the life of me I don't understand your fixation on tradition. I just don't understand why you feel someone—some man—has to give you away."

"It's not tradition. It's ritual."

"Oh. That explains everything."

Laura taps her ball back into play with one hit. The ball splits the two trees, and rolls to within eight or ten feet of her next wicket. Patience and I both applaud.

"I never told you this," Patience says, "and I don't know why I'm about to now. I'm probably going soft."

"Not a chance."

"I hope not. But I want you to know: I think you did a good thing last month. A lot of people in your shoes would have kept their mouths shut if they saw a couple of catamounts."

"It didn't do a hell of a lot of good."

"I disagree. Powder Peak's getting hurt bad in the press these days. They look even worse than usual."

"They don't care, they're not about to change their plans. They'll begin cutting down trees for the new trails the minute Reedy's appeal is behind them. That mountain will become—as Goddard Healy would say—logger heaven."

"Don't they have to hear from the Forest Service?"

"They did. They got their permit this afternoon."

"Aren't there any conditions, isn't there something that will slow 'em down at least?"

I shrug. "I don't know the details, I just know what I hear from people like Roger Noonan, down at the paper. Ask John Bussey. He's their new attorney."

"Bussey? That little twerp I used to babysit?"

"The one and the same."

"What a little shit he was. He used to threaten to tell his parents I beat him if I didn't let him do whatever the hell he wanted. Eight-year-old kid, I'm about fourteen, and he's screaming 'Don't hit me!' the second I remind him it's bedtime and he should turn off the television. What a prick that child was."

"Is. He still is a prick. But he'll do a good job for the resort."

While Miranda lines up her next shot, Laura looks at the maple trees beside the barn, so dry this summer that their leaves already are turning, and some have even begun to fall. Unaware that we're watching, she holds her mallet against her side with her elbow, and chews at whatever's left of the nail on her pinky.

• • •

SOFTBALL STOPPED BEING fun the day I left Goddard and Ian alone at Peak Eats.

Ian Rawls and his brother, Clark, grew colder than Lake Champlain block ice, and spoke to me solely in the context of the game: when Clark was calling me off a pop-up, or when Ian was coaching third and wanted me to tag up on a fly ball to center. Otherwise, they never even said hi.

The tension among the three of us was apparent to the rest of the Quarry Men, but there was no one on the team willing to mediate our dispute. As long as Scottie Winston and the Rawls brothers weren't actively punching each other, no one was about to step in and try to patch things up.

Moreover, it was not as if my teammates—most of whom were native Vermonters who had lived all of their lives within twenty-five miles of Barre or Montpelier—viewed my stand as particularly heroic or noble. As far as Hugo Scutter, one of the engineers involved with the expansion, was concerned, I was jeopardizing his job. His twin aunts told me exactly that. And I could tell that Joel Stebbins, who had been laid off by a Montpelier ski company after six years, suddenly saw in me the sort of self-righteous, smug, and moneyed liberalism that comes from Manhattan, and vacations once or twice a year in his mountains. His hills. His woods. The fact that I had lived in Landaff for close to twenty years, married to one of the local Avery girls, held no weight. I was, abruptly, an outsider.

My friendship with Reedy McClure became a source of suspicion. Although I had no intention of joining the Copper Project, a point I made clear to both Rawls brothers and the partners in my firm, no one was dissuaded from the opinion that I had suddenly lost my mind. I tried explaining to Ian on two separate occasions that I felt it would be unethical for me to take all the proprietary knowledge I had gained over my years with Powder Peak, and use it to work for the resort's opponents. That just wasn't going to happen. My decision to tell people I saw catamounts when they asked, to allow my daughter to tell every reporter and writer who called, was not part of some calculated, invidious plan to undermine the resort's expansion. It—everything from sighting to revelation—just happened.

Nevertheless, when we played our last game the first day of August, when we lost to a team from Norwich by three runs and were eliminated from state play-off contention, I was glad the season was over. I put my old wooden Hillerich & Bradsby in the hall closet for the winter, not giving a damn if the noxious rays beneath it poisoned the bat for eternity.

. . .

"I JUST GUESS we'll have to find a new mountain to ski," Reedy says Thursday afternoon, as we walk together down Montpelier's Main Street. "I've never thought of myself as the type who skis Stowe, but what the hell? People change, right?"

"Sure do. But don't feel you have to move on my account."

"Seems to me, they screwed you pretty bad."

"Not true. They simply fired my law firm. I gave them no choice."

I loosen my tie, deciding I probably won't return to the office today. It's not quite four o'clock, but without Powder Peak, my days have become very short. If we don't have significant new lobbying business lined up for the next legislative session, we will have to let one of our associates go, as well as one secretary. This too is a ramification of my decision.

Reedy opens the door to the health food supermarket, and motions for me to go first. Compared to the air outside, the store feels like a refrigerator.

"We're going to win that appeal next month, Scottie, so I would have to be an idiot to ski at Powder Peak. Ian Rawls would probably have me killed."

"An accident on a chairlift?"

"Probably. You know, the safety bar would break, and I'd somehow fall to my death."

"Yeah, you have to watch out for that stuff."

"Or some paid assassin on a snowboard would slam into me. Make me a quadriplegic for life."

I nod my head in agreement. "We used to do that sort of thing a lot."

We stroll toward the refrigerator case, stopping before the rows of Tofu Pups, Not Dogs, and Phony Baloney.

"How do you eat that stuff?" I ask, waving my hand over the meat substitutes.

"You get used to it. If I'm willing to spend a good part of my life scrubbing oil off animals so they live, it doesn't make much sense to eat the poor things when I'm done."

"Oh, God, don't tell me they're now putting penguin meat into hot dogs!"

He drops an eight-pack of Tofu Pups into his wire basket.

"We're barbecuing tonight. Katherine Whiting's coming over—Patience and Laura's friend."

"Ah, the dowsing doctor from Montpelier. Patience sometimes threatens to have her dowse my gene maps. Tell me how I'm going to die."

Reedy starts toward the aisle marked Fiber. "She's a very fine physician, you know."

"I'm sure she is. Is the barbecue at your house or Patience's?"

"Patience's. Actually, we're hoping Katherine and her husband will be willing to rent the place."

"I thought Patience was going to sell it? Bring her dogs and move up to the McClure compound?"

"We're definitely going to live at my house. We've decided that. But Patience doesn't want to sell her home right now."

I smile at him. "I gather that would represent just too much commitment?"

"It has nothing to do with commitment. It has to do with real estate values. She doesn't want to sell until the market bounces back."

In the midst of the natural bran cereals, special bran beverages, and bags and bags of all-natural carob and bran cookies are two kinds of Bran Buns—one for meat substitute hot dogs, and one for meat substitute hamburgers. Reedy reaches for one of the packages, and drops the buns in his basket.

"I got a phone call today from Rosamond Donahue at the *Sentinel*," he says. "Seems your buddies at the resort have hired some naturalists from Colorado to see if there really are catamounts up on Mount Republic. Did you know that?"

Without looking at Reedy, I shake my head no. I try to feign disinterest, but the idea that I'm now getting my news about Powder Peak from Reedy McClure galls me. Suddenly, I really have become an outsider: I am outside of Powder Peak, I am outside of the ski industry, I am—for all I know—now outside of whatever development decisions are made both by state officials and Vermont's business community.

"Yeah," Reedy continues, "they're bringing in a couple of experts on mountain lions. Two guys. They're going to spend some time on the mountain, and see if there's any evidence at all of the animals."

We walk toward the store's rows of organic vegetables, most of which were probably trucked in from the south. "Why did the paper call you?"

"The appeal. They wanted to know what the Copper Project thought of all this."

"And? What did the Copper Project decide?"

"I told Rosamond that I thought if Powder Peak really gave a damn about the mountain and the area, they wouldn't plan on draining what's left of the Chittenden River."

"When do the trackers arrive?"

"Tonight. The resort's flying them right in. They're going to start work tomorrow," Reedy says, filling his basket with ears of corn.

"You know why Ian's moving so quickly, don't you?" I ask.

"I assume it's because of next month's appeal."

"Right. They're hoping there won't be any proof of the animals, and they can have those findings recorded in the prehearing testimony."

Reedy laughs. "Hoping? I'm sure they're positive there won't be! This is all a sleazy public relations ploy because a pretty little nine-year-old girl named Miranda Avery-Winston and her dad have been all over the news the last two weeks, talking about the animals they saw on Mount Republic. It makes the resort look good right now, and even better at the hearing when Ian or Bussey stands up and says, 'We don't know what those Winston folk saw on that chairlift, but they weren't catamounts.' "

"Ian doesn't have much of a spine, but he wouldn't lie," I tell Reedy. "If the trackers find something, Ian won't cover it up."

"It won't matter anyway. The Chittenden River is practically a puddle right now. I told you, I had great faith in this drought, and it hasn't let me down. Unless it rains for the next forty days, there is just no way in hell the Environmental Board will let the permits stand."

"Because of the drought."

"Right. Because of the drought."

We wander up the store toward the cash registers, Reedy walking with a sudden rush of enthusiasm. After he has unloaded his basket before a pregnant young woman in a tie-dyed housecoat and bandanna, after he has paid for his groceries and we are back outside in this summer's absurd August heat, I try to remind Reedy that it's not that simple.

"The Board can do a lot of things. Even if they agree with you—"

"Not me. My experts. My 'experts on the aquatic environment.' "

"Even if the Board agrees with your experts that the water flow is too slow to touch, that doesn't mean they'll completely reverse Liza's decision. There's a lot of middle ground."

He switches his bag of groceries from one arm to another, pushing corn silk from the top of the bag out of his eyes.

"Such as?" he asks.

"They might agree with you that the resort shouldn't proceed with a snowmaking plan that involves the Chittenden River, but still allow it to clear away half of Mount Republic for new ski trails."

"Maybe."

"No maybes about it. The fact the Chittenden River is low won't affect the construction of those new trails on the mountain. Not one bit. You don't need a fast river to chop down a tree."

"That depresses you, doesn't it? I can hear it in your voice."

Sweat is already beginning to show along the side of Reedy's shirt, along the spot where he had been holding the grocery bag. I can feel my own shirt sticking to my back and shoulders underneath my sports jacket. "A bit. The sort of things that would cause the Board to rule against the new trail system are those catamounts. And if you're right about the trackers Powder Peak's bringing in, there won't be any evidence that they're out there."

"Which they are."

"Right. I saw them. Miranda saw them."

He stops walking and turns to me. "Are you going to testify?"

"Of course not."

"You should. You and Miranda both should."

"It wouldn't be right. I know too much about Powder Peak. I worked for them for too many years."

He shakes his head. "No way, that's no excuse. If you want to be so damn ethical about all this, then limit your testimony to the catamounts. Don't say one word about any other part of the expansion, but tell the Board what you saw."

I climb out of my jacket, and then pull my handkerchief out of an inside breast pocket. I wipe my forehead.

"Our testimony would hold much less weight than two naturalists'."

"It would be better than no testimony."

"And it certainly wouldn't endear me to my partners. Or our other clients."

"I don't imagine they're real wild about you right now anyway."

"Probably not."

"Will you think about it?"

I sigh, and rub the back of my neck. A vision of my nine-year-old daughter in a huge leather chair before a wide mahogany table passes before me. She looks very small. I can see clearly the members of the Environmental Board in one of the old statehouse conference rooms, a row of adults asking Miranda to describe over and over what she saw.

"I'll think about it," I agree. The fact is, Miranda has been fine with the press the last two weeks, she has actually enjoyed all the attention. She probably wouldn't mind testifying; it probably wouldn't be traumatic for her at all.

"You'll think about it seriously?" Reedy continues. "You're not just patronizing me?"

It would be harder for me to sit before the Environmental Board and undermine Powder Peak's expansion plans than it would for Miranda. For almost all of my life in Vermont I have represented one set of issues, an agenda of growth and development and jobs. I have been powerful, I have been an insider. Now, because my daughter and I happened to see three animals from a chairlift, because I have let myself become spooked by a drought, I have been thrown onto the other side of the fence, I have been tossed—metaphorically, literally—onto the other, undeveloped side of the mountain.

I take a deep breath and clear my throat. "No, I'm not patronizing you," I tell Reedy, trying to find courage in words. "I'll talk to Laura about it tonight."

24

My daughter makes a great sound bite. Over the past two weeks, she has provided Vermont's television and radio stations with excellent three-second quotes. The sorts of quotes that distill a story down to its essence, the sorts of quotes that people can remember and talk about the next day at the garage, the general store, or on Church Street in Burlington.

"I don't think there's an animal anywhere as pretty as a catamount."

"Was I scared? No, those poor things should be scared of us!"

"I can go anywhere to go snowboarding. They can't go just anywhere to live."

She has been on one of the TV stations, the CBS affiliate, twice since we saw the animals, and the Sunday living section of the *Burlington Free Press* ran a fifteen-hundred-word story about Miranda that began on the section's front page. One of the two photographs of Miranda was taken in the Mitchells' yard. In it she is holding her Y rod, smiling proudly beside the knee-high blue cap for the well that she dowsed.

Most of the media were originally drawn to the story because of me, because of my involvement with the ski resort. The first coverage, forty-five seconds on the NBC affiliate's eleven o'clock news and a seven-inch short on the *Sentinel* business page, focused on the fact that Powder Peak's—and the ski industry's—chief lobbyist was jeopardizing a fifteen-million-dollar expansion project by claiming to have seen catamounts at the resort. As the story unfolded, however, it grew into both a business and a lifestyle story, with most newspapers in the state covering it in their money and living sections. Reporters discovered quickly that Miranda is a personable, pretty, and articulate little girl, a child with absolutely no fear of the camera. Often positioned opposite angry adult men like Ian Rawls or John Bussey, she looks and sounds very good. (As Roger Noonan said, "She's a chip off the old block. That chip just fell a little to the left of where you expected it.")

Consequently, I have purposely fallen as far into the background as possible. Laura has been present for most of the media's interviews with our daughter, not me: Miranda's story rings true without her father's nodding corroboration, it is decidedly more powerful without my hovering involvement.

. . .

SUNDAY MORNING, AS Laura, Miranda, and I are climbing into the truck to drive home after church, Elias Gray's grandson, Anson, yells at us from across the church's front yard.

"It's too pretty a day to go racin' outta here!" he hollers, walking briskly across the grass toward us.

The sun is high and bright, but the first cool harbinger of fall blew into Vermont from Canada Friday night, and the temperature today won't climb above seventy. Laura and Miranda are actually wearing sweaters for the first time since, I believe, early May.

"That's exactly why we are racing home," I tell Anson when

he reaches the truck. "It's too nice a day not to fix the clapboards on the barn."

Miranda leans out the window on the passenger side of the truck, watching as her parents greet Anson.

"How's your grandmother doing this morning?" Laura asks, lightly patting his back. "I didn't see her in church today."

"No, she didn't feel like havin' one of us drive her in. But she's doin' okay. Not great, but okay," he answers, looking down at his work boots. "She said to tell you she liked the blueberry pie you brung her Friday a whole lot. She really appreciated your stoppin' by to visit," he adds.

Laura shrugs. "How about you? How are you doing?"

"I'm good," he says, smiling. "Fact is, I'm here to ask a favor."

"Name it," Laura says.

He looks up at Miranda tapping her arm aimlessly against the outside of the passenger door of the truck. "I been readin' 'bout you, Miranda," he says. "I just guess you're ready to do some more dowsin'."

Suddenly he turns back to Laura and me, afraid that he has overstepped his bounds. He pulls at his ear nervously, and says to us both softly, "If it's all right with you, that is."

"What do you have in mind?" Laura asks.

Miranda pushes open the truck door and jumps down.

"Yeah, what do you have in mind?" Miranda giggles, echoing her mother.

Laura glares at Miranda and clears her throat, chastening her daughter. Miranda has received a lot of attention the past two weeks, and Laura has worked hard to convey to the child the subtle difference between confidence and arrogance.

Anson becomes flustered, and starts waving randomly at other parishioners as they wander from the church to their homes or their cars. "Howdy, Gertrude!" he screams at one of the Scutter twins, somehow aware of which one she is. "Barton, where did you get that flashy tie? Boston?" he yells at Barton Lutz, a friend of his from the fire company. It's as if Anson is afraid that he has gotten Miranda in trouble, or he's embarrassed because he's not sure whether he should be speaking to mother or daughter.

"Want me to wait in the truck?" Miranda asks quietly.

"No, you don't have to," Laura says, her voice even. "Go ahead, Anson, what's up?" she continues.

He rubs his hands together, trying to compose himself. Finally he says, "We're building a new sugarhouse. We've picked a spot on the other side of the hill from the one that burned, and we think it's just right."

Laura rests her hand gently on the top of Miranda's head, and tussles her hair a bit. "And you want this one to dowse the area," she says.

"Yup. If you . . . if she . . . wouldn't mind."

Underneath her mother's hand, Miranda shakes her head no, she wouldn't mind at all. Laura looks down at her daughter. "I gather you're willing to help Mr. Gray?"

"Uh-huh!"

"Do you want her to dowse the spot for the house, or the spot for the holding tanks?" Laura asks.

"Well, I was thinkin' both," he says, folding his arms across his chest, and toying with a button on the pocket of his blue flannel shirt. "And, if it's okay," he adds nervously, a long pause between almost every word, "I was wonderin' if she could see if the spot feels, well, fireproof."

I watch Miranda's reaction to the word *fire*, her response to Anson's reference to the blaze that killed his grandfather. She gazes up at the man in sympathy, unblinking, holding her stare until he becomes aware she is looking at him, and turns away.

"I'm mighty glad this awful heat finally broke," he says in

nobody's direction, speaking off toward the walls of the church. "First Sunday in a month I haven't been stuck to the back of the damn pew."

• • •

MONDAY MORNING, WARREN Birch squares off the edges of the spreadsheets as if they were playing cards the size of place mats, and rests his hands on the pile. The spreadsheets summarize the firm's billings and our projected revenue.

"We," he begins, referring to our firm, "won't stop bleeding until we get a new client, or we eliminate two positions. I've looked at the projections for all of our clients, and I don't see sufficient work in the pipeline to compensate for the loss of Powder Peak."

"Or the loss of the Vermont Ski Areas Consortium," Duane Hurley adds, staring out the window of our conference room at the statehouse. Duane was a state senator from Bennington for close to a decade before joining Warren and me the year before last.

"And personally, I don't see any new clients falling into our laps in the next few months, not with the legislature recessed until January," Warren continues.

"How long do you think we can continue before we should start letting people go?" Duane asks.

Warren pushes the spreadsheets across the table to him. "See for yourself. The simple fact is, we don't have enough billable hours in this firm right now to keep twelve people on staff. My opinion is that we can wait until the end of the year, if we're willing to freeze all salaries."

Duane chuckles. "A year from September—thirteen months from now—I'll have three kids in college at the same time."

Warren shrugs. "Or, we can let some people go, and keep the raise and bonus structure intact."

"Well, you know where I stand," Duane says. "We're not a charity. We don't employ people out of the goodness of our hearts. If we don't have the billable hours, keeping people around is only postponing the inevitable. And it's postponing it at the expense of the people we're keeping on board."

I look at my watch. As the three of us talk, Laura and Miranda are probably on their way to the spot Anson Gray has chosen for the new sugarhouse. Anson had told them he was working second shift at the printing plant today, and so they had agreed they would meet at the end of the Grays' road around ten o'clock this morning.

"You've been very quiet, Scottie," Warren says. "I know you've spent some time with the finances. What do you think?"

Reedy will file his appeal with the state Environmental Board this week. Prehearing testimony will follow next week, with people like Miranda and me, people like Reedy's environmental experts and the resort's paid naturalists, offering our depositions to lawyers in private. It is ironic, but I will be providing my testimony to Reedy's Copper Project attorney, an environmental activist he has brought in from Boston.

The actual hearing before the Environmental Board will probably be conducted the first or second week in September, and it will be held in public. It will, I imagine, be held in one of the rooms on the third floor of the statehouse, in one of the huge conference rooms that faces away from the parking lot. I hate those conference rooms. They're big, but they're dark and damp, and there's never any sun.

"I know some of our clients have been disturbed by my position," I answer. "Companies like Glisten Skis. Well, I believe they may have reason to get even angrier in the next month." An image of Miranda dowsing among the ashes of the old sugarhouse crosses my mind, and I quickly blink it away. Anson described for me the location he has in mind, and I believe it's at least a mile from the old spot. I doubt Miranda will be anywhere near that particular patch of forest that burned.

"What now?" Duane moans. "I suppose you and your daughter saw a fucking Chinese panda by New England Power's hydroelectric plant?"

"Miranda was asked if she would testify at the hearing before the Environmental Board. I expect her prehearing deposition will be next week."

There is a long moment of silence as my partners digest the information. Finally Duane breaks the stillness in the room.

"Damn it, Scottie!" he begins. "Are you fucking suicidal, or just stupid? Are you trying to run this firm out of business, or is that just a happy coincidence?"

Ignoring Duane, Warren says, "Who asked her?"

"Reedy McClure. With my permission."

"I guess you said yes," Warren says.

"Damn it to hell," Duane says. "Damn it to fucking hell!"

"She doesn't understand exactly what testifying will involve," I continue, "but she's happy to tell the Board about the catamounts."

"Can't they just read the newspapers?" Duane asks.

"They could, but I'm not about to stifle my daughter. That's what this whole thing is about. I'm not about to teach my daughter that she has to keep her mouth shut because she saw some animals that are nearly extinct in Vermont."

"You know what I think?" Duane asks, his voice low. "I think this has more to do with you than Miranda."

"You think so?"

"I do," he says, nodding his head yes. "I really do. You've reduced this situation to some overly simplistic version of right and wrong. And you know why? Because you're suddenly feeling like a guilty shit for the two decades you've spent defending power plants and ski resorts and condominium developers. Well, your *mea culpas* are going to cost, buddy. They're going to cost you and your family one hell of a lot of money, and that's fine. But what isn't fine, is that they're going to cost me one hell of a lot of money. They're going to cost Warren one hell of a lot of money. They're going to cost some of the people who work here their jobs. And that's not fine. That's not fine at all. That is just fucking inconsiderate. And fucking stupid."

When Duane is finished, I hear myself saying in a voice that sounds faintly hoarse, "There's something else."

Neither man will look at me as they wait for me to continue. When they remain quiet, I tell them, "At that hearing, I will be testifying along with Miranda."

. . .

AT THE WEDDING ceremony of Patience Avery and Reedy McClure, there will be two rings. There will be a thirty-nine-year-old man giving away a forty-two-year-old bride. The bride, a woman embarking upon her third marriage, will not wear white. She will wear instead what she refers to as an aura-blue dress. Not an auroral-blue dress, she has explained to me, an aura-blue dress: It is a blue that represents positive human auras, positive human energy fields. It is a blue that reflects human atmospheres, not celestial ones.

To me, it is simply the blue of the shallow Gulf waters off the coasts of Key West.

There will be no groomsmen opposite the half-dozen mothers and daughters whom Patience has recruited to form her own metaphoric phalanx, although under duress Reedy agreed to ask his brother to stand beside him at the altar, serving as something vaguely akin to a best man.

Patience and Reedy will be married in the small Congregational church in the center of Landaff, in a ceremony that is close enough to something Christian that Reverend Taylor will perform it, but sufficiently esoteric, new age, and quasi-druid that it will draw a fair number of dowsers away from the annual convention's "Earth Energies" field trip to a sacred site. Angel Source Brandy, the former JoAnn Pomerleau Brandy, will lay down a labyrinth in white lime in the commons across the street from the Landaff church, and then around the church itself. The church will be in its center.

The bridal party, led by an extremely earnest nine-year-old girl, will enter the labyrinth about one hundred yards from the church. That group, seven women, three men, and Miranda, will then proceed to walk the labyrinth through the dead grass in the heart of the commons, around the church parking lot, behind the church's new addition, and then through the wide front doors. We—I, specifically—have been instructed by Patience to walk the labyrinth with "appropriate gravity and dignity," which I have interpreted to mean no disco.

For Patience and Angel and many of the dowsers who will be in attendance, the labyrinth represents balance and harmony. The labyrinth that Angel will design for the wedding of Patience Avery and Reedy McClure will, Angel has boasted, serve as an initiation chamber of sorts for the bride and the groom, initiating them into their roles as flesh-and-blood bonds between heaven and earth, and among the energies of the human psyche.

I asked Patience what we in the bridal party should do if we become lost in the labyrinth, and she said that wouldn't happen, that I was confusing a labyrinth with a maze. While the purpose of a maze was to torment, disorient, and entrap all who entered it, a labyrinth was usually built to help channel positive earth energies into those who walked it, to help one literally and figuratively find one's way. The pathways of an Angel Source Brandy labyrinth, Patience reassured me, would lead me inexorably to its center.

Patience has also reassured Laura that if she stops biting her fingernails right now, a full month before the wedding, there will be sufficient time for her nails to recover.

. . .

THE PHONE RINGS Tuesday night after dinner, while Laura and Miranda are at Patience's house, helping the blushing bride to refine the reception menu. Miranda has promised me that she will fight hard for a bridge mix of Cap'n Crunch and Cocoa Puffs. I answer the phone in the kitchen, the one nearest the back porch where I was dozing, listening to the Boston Red Sox take one of their early leads that they inevitably lose.

"Hi, Scottie, this is Rosamond Donahue at the *Sentinel.* I'm on deadline, and I want to ask you a question. We heard from Powder Peak—"

"Hold on, Rosamond. You don't want to be speaking to me. You should be speaking to John Bussey or Ian Rawls. Our firm no longer represents—"

"I know that, just listen. Powder Peak faxed us a news release today that said the naturalists they brought in found no signs of catamounts on Mount Republic. They spent four full days nosing around the mountain, especially the area where you and your daughter claim to have seen the animals, and the resort says there isn't one bit of evidence that mountain lions live anywhere near Powder Peak."

"Gee. Imagine that. What a surprise."

"Is that your response?"

"Can I think about my response and call you back?"

"No. I'm on deadline."

"Five minutes?"

She groans, exasperated. "Fine. Call me back in five minutes."

I thank her and return to the porch. If I am smart, if I want truly to do all that I can to minimize the aggravation I cause my partners and our firm's clients, I will take my phone off the hook and fail to call Rosamond back. I will let her run the story with either no comment from me, or the simple statement that I was surprised.

But I also don't want to allow Powder Peak to get in the only word on this story.

I decide I will phone Reedy McClure. This was his fight from the beginning. I'm sure he'll be as happy to scream now for a family of cats as he has been for Chittenden River fish.

• • •

IT IS AN odd sensation for me to read or hear news about Powder Peak that I did not anticipate, plant, or at the very least respond to. I am conditioned to reading the *Sentinel* and the *Free Press* largely to discover how they have translated the information we—the resort—have given them, to see how the Rosamond Donahues of the press have used the charts or the facts or the opinions we have spun for their benefit.

Wednesday morning, I read Rosamond's story about the naturalists' findings, while sipping my coffee at my office. Reedy told me last night what he thought he had told the reporter, but it is still jarring to read his remarks and see Ian Rawls's comments on the front page of the newspaper. It is the lead Vermont story, running along the bottom right column of the page under the headline "Resort Finds No Sign of Endangered Animals."

> BARTLETT, VT—The mystery of the Powder Peak catamounts may have moved a step closer to resolution yesterday, when two naturalists whose expertise is mountain lions said they found no evidence of the animals on Mount Republic.
>
> The findings were reported by Ian Rawls, managing director of the Powder Peak Ski Resort.

The investigation was triggered when Scott Winston, 39, a lobbyist who worked for the resort until recently, and his 9-year-old daughter claimed they had seen three of the endangered animals while riding a chairlift in July.

"I think the operative word here is relief. The last thing any of us wanted to do was pursue an expansion project that might affect the environment adversely," Rawls said.

Powder Peak hopes to begin $15 million worth of improvements to the resort sometime next month, when it breaks ground for what spokespeople have said will be the world's fastest gondola.

The planned improvements also include a new snowmaking system, an expanded base lodge, and a new network of trails, all of which are scheduled for construction next spring and summer.

The resort's building and land-use permits will, however, in all likelihood be appealed by the Copper Project, a local environmental group opposed to the expansion project.

That expansion was further complicated when Winston and his daughter said they saw the catamounts in an area targeted for clearing.

The naturalists, Carl Macomber and Jason Richardson, faculty members at Colorado State University, spent four days searching for proof of the animals, especially within a three-mile radius of the reported sighting.

Macomber, the author of two books about mountain lions as well as numerous articles, said the fact that they saw no evidence of the animals on Mount Republic does not definitively mean there are none there.

"Mountain lions roam a wide area, and we confined our study to a very small area. Just because we didn't see any signs of them doesn't categorically prove there are no catamounts on that mountain," Macomber said.

"I must admit, my opinion is that there aren't any [catamounts] up there, and there probably haven't been for decades," Macomber added.

The naturalists looked for catamount tracks, scat (excrement), claw marks, fur, signs of kills, and evidence of a den. Macomber said they discovered none of these signs.

Reedy McClure, a state senator from Washington County and the leader of the Copper Project, disputed the two professors' findings.

"I find it ludicrous that two guys have the nerve to claim there are no catamounts on Mount Republic, after spending a grand total of four days up there," Senator McClure said.

"Is there a connection between the fact these guys are being paid by the resort, and the fact their findings support the resort's plans? I'd say so," he continued.

Macomber and Richardson have been retained by Schuss Limited, the owner of Powder Peak as well as two ski resorts in the West. Rawls would not say how much Schuss was paying the professors.

Rawls said the naturalists will testify if the Copper Project appeals the resort's permits.

Scott Winston, whose lobbying firm, Birch, Winston, and Hurley, was fired by Powder Peak less than a week after he and his daughter told people they had seen catamounts at the resort, said simply that he was surprised by the two naturalists' findings.

Releasing the news that the naturalists found no signs of the catamounts for today's press was a sound strategy, it is exactly what I would have recommended. It will give the Environmental Board time to digest the findings, to begin to accept them as gospel.

. . .

I AM CAUGHT like a deer by some car's headlights Thursday night.

I step to the side quickly, nearly walking into the side of another automobile in the Scoop Shop parking lot just outside of Montpelier, trying to see who is there. Even before my eyes can focus, however, whoever it is leans out the driver's-side window of the car and yells to me in a voice I know well, "It's official! You hear? Your buddy filed his appeal today."

"That you, Roger?" I realize I am holding in my hand a bag with two pints of ice cream, and I am holding it up as if it were a lantern.

"You betcha." Roger Noonan turns off the lights and climbs out of the car. "At about four twenty-eight this afternoon, about two minutes before the State shuts itself down for the day, the Copper Project formally filed its appeal. They waited until just about the very last minute of the very last day."

Even in the dark, even at night, I can see that Roger is bemused.

"I hear you're planning to testify," he continues. "Can I have Rosamond give you a call tonight?"

"Since when does Rosamond need my permission to call me?"

He shrugs. "Course she doesn't. Just thought I'd be civil."

"If I thought it would stop her from calling me, I'd tell you no. As it is, I'll tell you I probably won't comment. I might not even answer the phone."

He raises his eyebrows and frowns. "Scottie Winston, just when did you become an uncooperative paranoid? Just when did you become afraid of the First Amendment?"

I point at the bag in my hands. "I have two pints in here, Roger. You want to know the meaning of fear? Fear is not returning to Landaff soon with this ice cream intact. Fear is letting a perfectly good pint of Green Mountain Chocolate turn into cold swamp water." I smile. "Sorry, Roger. I have to run."

. . .

MIRANDA MASHES DOWN the ice cream in her dish with the back of her spoon, and then licks the back of it.

"Will it be like a courtroom? Will it be like TV?" she asks her mother and me, as we savor our ice cream in the family room. There is a small hint of nervousness in Miranda's voice.

Laura pushes shut the glass door to the porch, keeping outside the slight August chill in the air. She smiles at her daughter, and then looks at me. "It won't be that scary, will it?"

I stretch my legs underneath the coffee table. "I hope it won't be scary at all, sweetheart," I tell Miranda. "Next week should be cake."

"Next week is the part in your office?" she asks. She looks down at the ice cream in her dish, and then proceeds to stir it quickly into soup. I lied when I told Roger that my family dislikes chocolate swamp water. Miranda, at least, believes that is indeed the proper way to eat ice cream.

"Maybe. It will either be in my office, or a fellow named John Bussey's office. He's a lawyer—like me. And his office is right in Montpelier too."

Laura shakes her head. "John Bussey is not a lawyer like you."

Miranda spoons some of the soup into her mouth, leaving a small splotch on her chin. It makes her look even younger to me than nine. Younger, certainly, than almost ten.

"Your daddy and I will be with you," Laura tells her. "We'll be right beside you the whole time."

"You're going to tell them about the catamounts too, right?" she asks.

"Yup."

Laura places her empty dish on the table beside her. "How many people will be there?" she asks me. "Just a couple, right?"

"Absolutely. There will be the star witness here," I begin, gesturing toward Miranda. "There will be the star witness's parents. That makes three. There will be John Bussey, the man who works for Powder Peak these days, and the attorney Reedy has been using from Boston. I think her name is Dawn. That's five. And I'd expect a clerk or administrative assistant from John's firm. How many is that? Six?"

Miranda nods. "Yup. Six."

The phone rings, and Laura stands up. "I'll get it," she says.

"Don't bother," I tell her quickly. "It's just the *Sentinel*."

The phone rings again, and Miranda looks first at her mother, and then at me, concerned. "How come you don't want to answer the phone?"

"Because we'd rather talk to you," I tell her, smiling.

Miranda puts her ice cream dish down beside her mother's, and watches as her mother sits back down beside her.

"What about the trial? The thing you said would happen in September?" Miranda asks, as the phone is caught by the answering machine.

Laura wraps her arm around Miranda's small shoulder. "There's no trial, sweetheart. It's just a . . . a hearing."

"What's the difference?"

"A hearing is a lot less scary," I tell my daughter, on at least one level lying. That hearing could be every bit as frightening to a child as a trial. "There's no judge in a black robe, and there's no jury. There's just a group of adults who want to hear your story."

"How big a group?"

"Nine people."

"What if they just read the newspapers?" she wonders, almost the very same question Duane Hurley asked me. "I must have been in most of them." There is no arrogance or vanity in her statement. She is simply probing for excuses not to testify.

"They want to hear it directly from you. They want to hear it in your words, not some reporter's."

"Other than those nine people, will there be anyone else at the . . . the hearing?"

Miranda has asked a good question. If an adult had asked it I would probably answer, *There will be as many people as will fit in the room.* Environmental Board hearings are open to the public, and this one has the potential to draw hundreds and hundreds of people, every single one of them with a stake in the decision.

"What do you think," Laura asks me, her voice filled with hope, "a couple dozen, maybe?"

"That's hard to say," I admit to my wife and my daughter. "I'd say we should see how next week goes, and then we'll take it from there."

"We saw Anson Gray today," Laura tells me, trying to change the subject. "He couldn't be happier with the place Miranda chose for the sugarhouse. He and some friends are going to start work on it tomorrow."

25

I sit back in my chair at the end of the day, another week, another Friday behind me.

This morning, Warren Birch was asked to have lunch with Governor Webster next week. He is one of a dozen lobbyists and resort presidents whom she asked to join her to discuss the ski industry in Vermont. I was not invited, a fact that surprised me, but probably no one else.

This afternoon, Peter DuBois, the governor's administration secretary, asked Duane Hurley to join the governor's emergency task force on the drought. The task force, which includes agricultural experts, state senators, and select businesspeople, will hold its first meeting next Tuesday.

I doubt I would know now that Duane had been asked to join the task force if the two of us hadn't wandered into our firm's lobby at the same moment a few hours ago.

I spent part of today examining a list of new business prospects. It included three of Powder Peak's primary competitors, as well as Vermont's seven largest consumer product companies. All of them will need a significant lobbying presence when the legislature convenes next January.

A month ago, I believe, all the resorts and companies on the list would have been flattered to hear from me. No longer. I doubt that today they would even have taken my calls. A lobbyist with no clout, no connections, no inside information is not particularly valuable.

Of course, that assumes that I even wanted to approach these companies in the first place. And I realized as I stared at the list today and envisioned each company—its products, its philosophy, its senior management—that I really didn't give a damn if these people wanted to talk to me or not. Because I didn't want to talk to them. I didn't want to work for them.

One by one, I turned the question marks I had scribbled by each company into an X, my symbol to myself not to call them. I have no idea where my billable hours will come from, but I am sure that I do not want them to come from companies that pump dioxin into Lake Champlain or clear-cut whole forests for condominiums.

I wish I knew whether my born-again environmentalism was the result of a deep and real philosophic conversion, or a product of a childish oversensitivity. My fear is that I have become sensitive. My feelings have been hurt by people like Ian Rawls and Peter DuBois. I have been snubbed by people I thought were my friends. Suddenly, because my little girl and I saw three rare and beautiful animals, I am an institutional pariah. No one in Vermont phoned me today, and I phoned no one.

The only call I received was from Massachusetts: It was from the Copper Project attorney, a woman with a thick Boston accent named Dawn Ciandella. Dawn will arrive in Montpelier next week to meet Miranda and me, along with her other witnesses.

At four thirty, when I decide to go home for the weekend, the only thing I have accomplished all day is that I have laid off a junior associate. Duane and Warren agreed that we shouldn't postpone the inevitable. And because our financial fortunes have changed because of me, I alone told Alice LeBlanc that two weeks from today would be her last day at our firm.

. . .

"I THINK OUR well's about to go."

Laura says the words evenly, as we stroll up our driveway Friday night. We can see the light on in the den, where Miranda is watching a video.

I imagine if I were not married to a dowser, I would probably ask her how she knows. I might wonder if the tap water looked brown or rust-colored today, whether the pump in the basement had sounded as if it were straining. But because I am married to a dowser, because I am married to a woman with the Avery gene, I simply nod.

"Gone for good?" I ask. "Or gone until we get some rain?"

"We should probably get on Michael Terry's calendar."

I sigh. "Gone for good."

"I think so."

"How long do we have?"

"There's no rain in the forecast. So I'd say a week, maybe."

The Vermont sky is magnificent tonight, a black umbrella dotted with diamonds.

"Have you dowsed a new vein?"

"No. I thought I might let Miranda do that tomorrow. It might make our need for a new well less frightening to her."

"That's a nice idea," I agree. I am unable to resist, however, one small jab: "After all, just because our entire life is falling apart, there's no need to be frightened."

Laura is wearing a cardigan sweater that I bought her this past Christmas in Boston. "Our life is not falling apart," she says.

"Okay. Just my career."

"You're being ridiculous. You know you're doing the right thing."

"Sure, I do," I tell her, wrapping my arm around her shoulder, savoring the feel of the cashmere. "If worse comes to worst, we'll live off your candles. We'll live on candles and cake."

. . .

"YOU'LL LIKE DAWN," Reedy says to me Saturday afternoon. "She's like you. She's slick as ice, and just as hard."

The sails on the boats on Lake Champlain, bright yellows and reds and one that is purple and green, almost in unison whip over the small boats below them as the wind changes. The boats are racing south to Burlington, passing by the spot we have chosen for a picnic on a beach perhaps five miles north of the city.

No one is allowed to swim in Lake Champlain today. People are allowed to boat on the lake, but no one may swim or ride their sailboards upon it until it rains. Until it rains a lot. The water level is seventy-nine feet at the marker by the city boathouse, ten feet below normal for this time of year. Consequently, the discharge from Burlington's antiquated sewage system represents too great a portion of the lake, the percentage of coliform bacillus in the water is too high for people to swim without becoming ill.

Although we knew we would be unable to swim, Laura, Miranda, and I decided to come to the lake for a picnic today anyway—as did many Vermonters. The beach itself is crowded this morning, especially since no one is allowed in the water.

When Patience heard we were going to Lake Champlain, she asked if she and Reedy could join us. Of course, we said, that would be fine. None of us have gotten to the lake this entire summer, and I know I have felt a desperate need to sit beside one of the closest things we have in northern Vermont to a body of water where you can't see the entire shore from one spot.

"Slick as ice," I repeat. "Can I assume that's a compliment?"

Reedy nods. "Sure can. I don't want my doctors to be particularly slippery, but my lawyers? You bet."

Down at the edge of the water, Laura and Miranda are carving something into the sand. It looks like they've built a series of small ducts and gullies to collect the murky lake water, and are using it as some sort of moat.

They are both still wearing their sneakers.

"When she called," I tell Reedy, referring to his attorney, "we only spoke for about five minutes. But she sounded competent."

"Competent? She's a barracuda. About twenty-eight, twenty-nine years old. The kind of person who you just know has worked her butt off every second of her life to get where she is."

Patience rolls onto her stomach, and lowers the straps of her bathing suit off her shoulders. Speaking away from her fiancé, she grumbles, "I don't see any reason to describe an especially hardworking woman in the context of her bottom."

Reedy pats the back of her thighs good-naturedly. "I would have said Dawn worked her butt off if she were a man too. Honest."

"Is she pretty?" Patience asks. I can tell that the woman's age hit a nerve with my sister-in-law. It did, on some level, with me too.

"I won't lie to you, Patience. She is."

Patience turns her head to us, and raises an eyebrow angrily. Speaking very slowly, she asks, "Just how pretty, Mr. McClure?"

I stand up and brush the sand off my legs. "I'm going to go see how the construction project is going down at the shore. Either of you want to join me?"

"I will," Reedy says. "Come on with us," he says to Patience.

"I want to know how pretty this woman is whose butt you seem to have become obsessed with," my sister-in-law says firmly, and so alone I start down to the water.

. . .

SUNDAY AFTERNOON MIRANDA walks across our yard with her Y rod before her, its tip aimed up at the sky, whispering to herself short questions. Small August breezes blow her bangs into her eyes, but most of the time she doesn't seem to notice.

Most of the time her eyes are closed.

Her mother walks a few steps behind her, occasionally reminding her of a question or two she should be asking. They are probably questions of depth, questions of potability.

This morning, the water pump in our basement began to strain. When I turned on the kitchen sink for a glass of water, the pump came on and hummed for at least thirty seconds. It reminded me of the sound the truck makes when I try starting it in January, after a night when the temperature has fallen far below zero.

As Miranda wanders into our croquet court, she stops just inside one edge of the wickets. The tip of the Y rod abruptly swings down, aiming almost straight into the ground. She opens her eyes and raises the rod back into the air. Laura kneels beside her and places one hand on Miranda's shoulder. She whispers something into her small ear, and Miranda nods. She asks something else, and my daughter giggles.

If the spot for our new well will indeed be where Miranda is standing, there will be no more croquet this year. Deep trenches will be cut through that area of our yard, as if we expect an invasion by some unhappy neighbor. And next year it will mean finding a new place for the croquet court, because at that spot there will be a well cap extending about eighteen inches aboveground.

I stand up and walk toward the dowsers until I can hear what they're saying. Miranda smiles at me, her face full of accomplishment and pride.

"How deep?" I ask. It has crossed my mind that because my

daughter is smiling, the vein is fairly close to the surface. I remind myself that the water table is low, and I should not get my hopes up. I doubt that Miranda understands the vast difference in cost between a deep well and a shallow one. Her pride may be founded simply upon finding a rich vein that is filled with good water. In all likelihood, the well will be deep, and it will be expensive.

Moreover, given the fact that my testimony could jeopardize Powder Peak's expansion, it could cost Michael Terry a major contract with the resort. We, the Winston family, could pay dearly for this well.

"Two hundred and twenty-five feet!" Miranda says. "Maybe two hundred and thirty."

Two hundred and twenty-five feet is much shallower than I expected; it is barely half as deep as the vein Patience found for the Scutters. It is almost too good to be true.

"Really?" I ask, looking to Laura for confirmation.

Laura nods her head. She believes that her daughter is correct.

"Well, that's something," I murmur.

Miranda swings her Y rod at my legs, gently hitting my knees. "Daddy, what did you expect?"

"I expected a much deeper well."

She rolls her eyes at me, a little girl's way of chastising her father for his skepticism. She is right to do so. As Patience has said to me any number of times, any number of ways, there may be no dowser in the world with the gifts of Miranda.

26

Miranda sits between her mother and me on one side of a long table in the conference room of Fletcher, McCoy, Bussey, and Brown. The conference room feels more like a dining room to me than a business office. The overhead fixture has so many small lights in it that it looks like a chandelier, and the table is an immaculately preserved antique.

"There were three of them," Miranda says, answering Dawn Ciandella's question. "I think it was a mom and two cubs."

Dawn nods at Miranda, acknowledging that she has provided the correct answer.

Reedy was right about Dawn. I don't believe she is as merciless a barracuda as he does, but it is clear that she has always been driven. In my mind's eye, I can see her struggling as a teenager to find a way out of some old mill town in central Massachusetts. Ware or Worcester or Lowell. I can imagine her working as a teenager at a Friendly Ice Cream parlor, wearing an institutional beige uniform that she despises. Clearly Dawn is determined, disciplined, and methodic.

"How big were the catamounts?" she asks Miranda.

"They were bigger than a big dog. At least the biggest one

was. It was taller than Mindy Woolf's sheepdog, and maybe even a little bit longer," she answers, using the comparison we came up with last night.

John Bussey takes off his jacket and folds it over the back of his chair. He smiles at Miranda as he does this, and I can't help but feel that he is trying to distract her.

"And the two smaller ones? Can you remember how big they were?"

"Of course I can!" Miranda says, reinforcing for John Bussey her faith in her recollection. "They were half as big."

"Half as big?" Dawn repeats. Although our hearing next month before the state's Environmental Board will resemble a courtroom trial, there will be many differences. At that hearing, and in this morning's prehearing deposition, attorneys are allowed significant latitude when it comes to leading a witness.

"About as big as a regular dog," Miranda answers.

"Your father said the two smaller animals were each the size of a springer spaniel. Do you—"

John slashes at the air before his face with his hand. "Come on, Dawn, that's enough. Give us all a break here."

Ignoring him, she continues, "Do you think the smaller animals were the size of springer spaniels?"

"Yup."

Immediately John asks, "Miranda, when was the last time you saw a springer spaniel?"

"Don't answer that, Miranda," Dawn tells my daughter, more firmly than I would have liked. She then turns to John and says, "I must insist you keep your mouth . . . closed. You know as well as I do you'll have your chance to question her statement."

"And you know you're going too far!" John says, trying to mitigate his anger with a small chuckle. "You're not just asking the questions, you're answering them, for God's sake!"

"That's not for you to decide," Dawn argues.

"Miranda, have you ever seen a springer spaniel?" John asks, plowing ahead. "Do you know how much one weighs, how big they are?"

Although I am supposed to remain silent, I hear myself saying reflexively, "John, you're completely out of line."

"Fine," he says, pleased to see Dawn turning an angry gaze in my direction. "That springer comparison won't stand up at the hearing."

"Then leave it be," I tell him.

"I'm doing you all a favor!"

"You're bullying a nine-year-old girl!"

"Ten, in six weeks," Miranda says, correcting me.

All the adults turn toward Miranda. "I have a birthday next month."

After a long pause in which we all catch our breath, Dawn says, "Can we get on with this?" and John nods, sitting back in his chair to fiddle with his eyeglasses.

. . .

WHEN I COME home from the office late Tuesday afternoon, one of Michael Terry's platforms is parked in the middle of the yard, a path of lawn and field and driveway chewed up behind it. The drill, a diamond-tipped rotary monster with four stories of scaffolding around it, sits like a small skyscraper under construction in my own backyard.

The croquet court is destroyed.

Laura wanders over to the barn to greet me as I climb out of the truck.

"How far did they get?" I ask.

"About one hundred and ten feet today. They'll probably reach the vein tomorrow."

She brushes some loose, flaky dirt off one of the carrots she has just picked, and offers it to me. There is dried blood along the cuticles of most of her fingers.

"You did quite a job on your hands today," I tell her, taking the carrot. "Did you do that during the deposition?"

"I don't know when I did it," she says, shrugging. "Did Roger Noonan get ahold of you?"

I find myself flinching. "No."

"He called here a half hour ago. I said you were still at the office."

"Well, clearly we just missed each other," I answer, unable to restrain the anger creeping into my voice. "Did he say what he wanted?"

"No. Well, yes. Sort of."

I stop walking and glance once again at the huge rig on our property, and the way our yard has been ruined. "Sort of?" I repeat, afraid that I understand instantly when Laura attacked her nails.

"There's going to be some stuff in the *Sentinel* tomorrow about the appeal. Maybe in the *Burlington Free Press* as well."

I sigh. "Do I need to call Roger back?"

"Yes. He wants to talk to you because he views you as a friend." She takes back the carrot in my hands. "I need to clean that better. Wait till we're inside."

. . .

ROGER NOONAN'S OFFICE sits in a back corner of the *Sentinel* newsroom, its two interior walls made of glass. He has positioned his desk so that the two exterior windows are behind him, and his view instead is the three dozen reporters and editors who write and design each issue.

The *Sentinel* is a morning paper, meaning that the newsroom is still crowded when I arrive there Tuesday night. As I approach

Roger's office, I find myself having to nod at a fair number of Roger's staff. People like Rosamond Donahue. Or the *Sentinel*'s city editor, Noel Holmes. I have been a source of information—and, to be fair, propaganda—to Noel for a decade.

Roger's door is open, and he waves me inside.

"Fine," he is saying to someone on the phone, "continue the bridge story on the inside. No one gives a damn about bridges anyway unless they collapse."

He hangs up the phone and sits back in his chair. "Howdy, Scottie. You want something to drink? Coffee? A Coke? A beer?"

"I want to see the cartoon."

"Yup, I know you do. Sit down."

Reluctantly, I take one of the two chairs across from his desk. As he begins digging through the piles of papers and books, I feel a wave of nausea cross my stomach, stronger—by far—than the ones I felt when I spoke to Roger on the phone before dinner, and when I started my truck to drive here. I take a series of small breaths, trying to relax.

"You plan to hyperventilate on me?" Roger asks.

"No."

"Good. I'd probably give myself a heart attack if I ever had to give somebody CPR."

I glance over my shoulder at his staff, and catch Rosamond Donahue staring in at the two of us. She is probably appalled that Roger is sharing with me Chuck Pierson's cartoon before it appears in tomorrow's paper.

"Aha! Eureka!" he says, as he discovers a sheet of paper underneath the phone book. "Here it is."

He flips the paper across his desk, a copy of the cartoon the local artist has submitted to the editorial page as commentary. Three witches, complete with black robes and long, pointed hats, are stirring a tremendous cauldron. The words "Copper

Project" are written across their chests. One of the witches looks like Reedy McClure, and one of them has a passing resemblance to me. The third witch is a child, a girl, although Pierson made sure that she looks nothing at all like Miranda. She could be anybody's daughter.

The witches are stirring their concoction with Y-shaped divining rods, and on a rock behind them sit three catamounts. In the midst of the boiling waters in the cauldron is a graphic of Vermont, a mountain, and the word *jobs*. The witches are singing a parody of a famous couplet from Macbeth:

> *"Double, double toil and trouble;*
> *It takes just one cat to burst Vermont's bubble!"*

"You're really going to run this?" I ask. "It's shit."

"Well, it's not Danziger. But I think it's clever."

"You know that Ian Rawls and John Bussey probably commissioned Pierson to draw this."

"Come on, Scottie. Half the letters to the editor in this world are ghostwritten by special interests. Your firm alone probably has someone cranking out every fifth or sixth letter we get."

"Not true. We—"

He waves me off. "I just want you to know, I wouldn't have agreed to run this if the little girl looked like Miranda."

"She'll know it's her."

"Maybe. But she is news."

He stands up and wanders to the table in the corner. There is a coffeemaker on it with a pot half-filled. "You sure you don't want some coffee?"

"I'm positive."

He fills his cup, and says, "I probably shouldn't tell you this either, but we've been friends a long time. So I will."

I wait for the next blow, while he returns to his desk. "I have it on good authority that Ian Rawls will have an opinion piece in tomorrow's *Free Press* about the importance of the expansion."

"Swell."

"And I've been told I'll be getting an editorial from one of those Colorado naturalists Schuss brought in. It'll be here tomorrow or the day after, so I can run it in Sunday's paper."

Involuntarily I find myself glancing down again and again at the drawing in my hands. "I gather you think somebody should start responding?"

"Hell, that's up to your friends with the Copper Project. I know you personally can't do a whole lot, not if you want to keep a few clients around to pay your mortgage."

"Then what? Why are you telling me this?"

With his hand he wipes away a drop of black coffee that sits like a bug on his desk blotter. "I just thought you should know it's beginning. The Powder Peak counterattack. It's beginning, and nothing's going to be sacred. Not you, not your family. And it won't stop for one second until the hearing next month is over, and they've done everything they can to win."

. . .

EVERY MONTH THERE is a mortgage payment. There is a phone bill, a gas bill, and one for electricity.

"What would happen if she didn't testify? What would happen if neither of you testified?" Laura asks that night in bed, her face half-buried in her pillow.

"I doubt the world would come to an end," I answer. In my mind, I try and calculate what we pay each month on our two American Express cards, and the four separate Visas and MasterCards between us. As far as I know, we always pay the total balance on each card each month. Even without interest charges, however, the balances must be significant.

"No. I don't think it would either."

There is car insurance and home insurance. There is all the money we send to Mobil and Exxon and Texaco each month.

"A year from now, this whole thing will probably be forgotten," she continues.

There are the miscellaneous expenses that always crop up. Cords of wood each May. Repairs to the slate roof in October. Expanding the baseboard heating into the bedroom beside Miranda's in March.

This month, there will be the new well.

"That's not true," I tell Laura. "A year from now, a lot of the construction will be in full swing. And that's when people's emotions will be most . . . heated. Two years from now, maybe, people will have forgotten about it. Maybe."

There is the money we save every month for Miranda's college tuition, for our own eventual retirement.

"Maybe," she repeats. "But you doubt it."

"Yup."

"When did it all get so personal?" Laura asks.

It is Laura who pays all those bills each month, it is Laura who writes the actual checks. It is Laura who knows which money is in bank CDs, and which is in municipal bonds. It dawns on me that I have no idea how much money is in our checking account right now.

"It has always been personal," I tell her. "We're just used to being on the other side."

Sometimes, Laura has the accountant who looks over the books for the Divine Lights of Vermont look at how we are managing our own money. I gather I shouldn't be worried.

But lately I have been.

This is one more ramification, apparently, of being on the other side. The side that isn't invited to lunch with the governor, or asked to join high-profile state task forces on droughts. The side that offends the only businesses in Vermont with the money to pay for lawyers and lobbyists who cost over one hundred dollars an hour.

"You never risked hurting a child," Laura says, referring to the cartoon that will be in tomorrow's newspaper.

"No, I never did," I murmur, as I roll over and rest my hand on her shoulder, rubbing it gently. The cotton of her nightgown feels thin as gauze under my fingers.

"You never used the likes of a Chuck Pierson."

"Oh, I don't know about that. We may have."

"Really?"

"Really."

She sighs once, a sigh that is loud and long and perhaps slightly bitter.

"You're all unbelievable," she says, disgusted. She then burrows her face further into her pillow, mumbling, "You. Reedy. Powder Peak. You are all completely unbelievable."

27

•

As the days grew shorter in August, Miranda filled a scrapbook with newspaper articles about the catamounts that she and I saw, and about catamounts in general. The newspapers were filled with stories about the rare animals, and at least a dozen different people came forward to claim that they too had spotted catamounts in Vermont. Most of these people were kooks, and one of them would turn out to be legally blind with an astigmatism so bad that she could barely fit a house key into a lock.

One of them, however, a sometime sheep farmer and sometime English professor at Middlebury College, was so measured, even, and coherent in his story that Dawn Ciandella decided that he should testify at the hearing.

Miranda began her scrapbook with the very first articles about our sighting, the ones that were published in July. By Labor Day weekend, the scrapbook must have had thirty stories in it, each one cut carefully from the pages of the *Montpelier Sentinel*, the *Burlington Free Press*, and the small weeklies scattered throughout the state. The stringer for *The Boston Globe* garnered two clips from our sighting, both of which suggested strongly that the reporter believed the animals we saw were indeed mountain lions.

Miranda evidenced no desire to censor the stories about our sighting, and save for posterity only those ones that took our side. She saved all of them, even the cartoon that Chuck Pierson drew for the *Sentinel.*

While Laura and I worried occasionally about what school would be like for Miranda when she returned there the Tuesday after Labor Day, the fifth, our fears never lasted for more than a moment or two. Unless we were dramatically misreading our daughter, unless she were keeping inside herself her embarrassment, her trepidation, or her doubts, she wasn't disturbed by the publicity. She actually seemed to enjoy the attention.

Only when a brush fire grew into a forest fire in the Northeast Kingdom near Newport, and raced over and through seven separate hunting cabins, did Miranda's interest in catamounts wane. For two days at the end of August she wandered with her L rods throughout our yard and the yards of our neighbors, finding the underground veins that she needed, I imagine, to reassure herself that an environmental Armageddon was not upon us.

It was during those two days that Laura and I worried most about our daughter. Schoolchildren can be much meaner than newspaper cartoonists and editorial writers. Especially ten-year-olds. It crossed our minds that if some child picked up on Miranda's fear of the drought, or her fear of fire, Miranda would become easy prey in the classroom for abuse.

Fortunately, so many other events were penciled into the calendar on our kitchen wall for the week after Labor Day that the start of school seemed almost inconsequential. The formal appeal before the State Environmental Board was scheduled for the Thursday of that week, the seventh, followed the next day by the beginning of the wedding weekend of Patience Avery and

Reedy McClure. There would be a rehearsal dinner that Friday night at the McClure family compound, and the wedding itself at one o'clock the next day.

And for any Avery dowser who happened to have a spare morning or afternoon, the annual convention of the American Society of Dowsers would be occurring that entire weekend in Danville, a small village about twenty minutes away. Over two thousand dowsers from around the country and around the world had registered this year, most to learn or teach or share, but some—a good thirty or forty, according to Reedy—for the sole purpose of witnessing the third marriage of the Master Dowser of Landaff.

. . .

AT THE REHEARSAL dinner for Patience Avery and Reedy McClure, the bridesmaids will be giving the couple a very special gift: the results of the blood dowsing Dr. Katherine Whiting performed, a full blood map and blood report that will tell them with far greater certainty than palmistry what sort of life will stretch out before them.

"You let them take your blood?" I ask Reedy, unsure exactly who I mean by *them*. My sister-in-law's friends, perhaps. Perhaps something more generally paranoid, something general like dowsers. I know I don't mean my wife and my daughter, although I realize they will be standing right beside Katherine Whiting when the gift is presented and explained after dinner at one end of the McClures' long, wide dining room.

"Sure," Reedy says, shrugging. "What the hell? She said she'd throw in the test the state requires for a marriage license."

On the morning of their wedding, there will be a special nondenominational sunrise ceremony for dowsers of all religions and spiritual proclivities. It will be held on one of the small hills in the McClure compound. Patience expects at least half the people who have been invited to the wedding to attend the sunrise ceremony, as well as some crashers who simply want to hear radio personality and psychic Sas Santoli in person.

"Your parents are turning over in their graves," I warn Reedy. "I can't envision your father savoring the image of five or six dozen dowsers trampling through his meadows, and waving around a bunch of divining rods."

"I don't see any harm," Reedy says, shaking his head. "Patience promised me they'd replace all the divots."

. . .

AT THE WEDDING ceremony, Patience will be wearing pearls worn by Reedy's mother at her wedding, and at his grandmother's wedding before that. It's a tradition.

In return, Reedy will carry in his pants pocket the calcite crystal that Patience brought back years before from a dowsing assignment in New Mexico. Sharpened to a fine, triangular point and mounted on a pure silver chain, the crystal balances energy fields, elicits positive human auras, and—carried by a male in a front pants pocket—eliminates snotty comments from the mouths of nonbelievers. So Patience says.

. . .

THE SKI INDUSTRY is a nonunion industry, but it is nevertheless a tightly knit club. Environmentalists, however, are an equally supportive and clubby bunch.

Consequently, the first Thursday in September, the day of the Copper Project appeal, the wide front lawn of the statehouse is packed with pickets and people. If there had been four hundred and fifty people at the hearing before the District Five Environmental Commission the last night of June, there may be twice that many this morning at the statehouse. Perhaps there are an even thousand.

Automatically Laura and I both reach for one of Miranda's hands, so that our daughter is sheltered between us as we walk through the group to the steps of the statehouse. Dawn Ciandella cuts ahead of us to ensure that no one tries to stand in our way, walking briskly with one hand just over her head to keep the sun out of her eyes.

"Are Reedy and Patience already inside?" Laura asks me softly, staring straight ahead.

"Maybe. Reedy had to pick up his 'aquatic expert' at his hotel in Burlington this morning, and escort him here. Seems he had a bad experience at one of these events in the Southwest. Someone threw a dead fish at him."

I can feel Miranda tighten her fingers in mine, pressing my wedding band against my skin. Lined up on both sides of the walkway, surrounding us, are reporters and legislators, and the hundreds of foot soldiers recruited by both sides. I recognize Phil Robinson, director of the Vermont Natural Resources Council, standing at the top of the statehouse steps, as if he were waiting for us.

Phil and I have never gotten along, we have never been on the same side of any issue. Until now. Phil's face is tan but the top of his bald head is a pasty white, as if he has lived outside this summer underneath a small hat.

He smiles at the four of us as we approach him.

"Doesn't anybody work in this state anymore?" Dawn asks him quietly, almost whispering. The two of them spent most of yesterday together with Reedy McClure and his Copper Project appeal committee, rehearsing witnesses and preparing their cross-examinations.

"I thought you'd be pleased with the turnout," he says, his voice defensive. "I know we made an impression with the Environmental Board."

She shakes her head. "Well, you sure got out the vote."

Phil kneels before my daughter as if he were an uncle. "And how are you today, Miranda?"

On some level Miranda understands that this man and her father are not usually friends. Consequently, she has remained reserved and distant from him. "Okay," she says simply, looking back once at the crowd behind her.

"Going to give those people a piece of your mind?"

"Phil!" Simultaneously Laura and Dawn chastise him, together turning the man's name into something that sounds like an obscenity.

He stands up and looks back and forth between the two women, forcing an apologetic smile onto his face.

"Ease off," Dawn adds, sharing a glance with Laura. "Okay?"

He nods.

"Let's go inside," he says. "I wanted to catch you before we started because they've moved the room for the hearing."

"Who are 'they'?" I ask.

"The Environmental Board. They want to allow as many people as possible into the hearing, so they've moved it from the Aiken Conference Room to the cafeteria."

Dawn chuckles. "The cafeteria? We're meeting in a cafeteria?"

"The Aiken Room only seats about fifty people," Phil explains to our attorney. "The cafeteria seats a couple hundred."

"Oh good," Dawn says. "I'd hate to think our friends on the lawn can't join us inside."

"Me too," Phil agrees, oblivious to Dawn Ciandella's sarcasm.

. . .

I KNOW THE statehouse cafeteria well. When the Vermont legislature is in session, from January through the first days of May, I often have breakfast there, meeting with the senators and representatives from Vermont's counties and towns, asking them in detail about their children and grandchildren, their lives from

June to December. I rarely talk business at breakfast, but the hours I spend there are worthwhile. It is at those breakfasts that I become friends with legislators, wearing down their resistance for when it is time to press hard on a bill, when my clients absolutely must have their votes.

The room is clean, modern, but surprisingly dark. Although one wall has a picture window, it faces the woods behind the statehouse and actually gets very little sun. The remaining three walls face the interior of the building.

The Environmental Board, nine volunteers appointed by Governor Webster and her predecessor, have had all but six of the cafeteria tables removed. Of those six, four have been lined up end to end at the front of the cafeteria, creating what amounts to one long judicial bench behind which the Board will sit. The remaining two tables have been placed opposite it: One of those tables will be for our witnesses, and one will be for Powder Peak's.

All of the cafeteria's straight-back chairs have been lined up in rows facing the front end of the room, as if this were an auditorium and the metal warming trays and heat lights were the stage.

There are dozens of small groups of two, three, and four people already chatting idly throughout the room, but no members from the Environmental Board or the Powder Peak defense team have arrived yet. Nor is Reedy McClure anywhere in the cafeteria.

"Where do we sit?" Dawn asks, but I am unsure whether she is directing her question at me or Phil Robinson.

"We should be in the first row, by the windows," Phil answers, motioning for us to follow him across the room. When he raises his arm, I notice the time on his watch. Quarter past eight. The hearing is still fifteen minutes away.

"Fine," Dawn says. "Scottie, why don't you and your family take the three seats closest to the windows?"

There is some noise, some activity, near the open doors at the back of the cafeteria, and Patience marches into the room carrying an attaché case in each hand, and pressing a third one against her ribs with her elbow. Her hair looks as if she has been asleep for a month, and her dress—something dated and blue that may once have belonged to her mother—needs desperately to be ironed. She is shaking her head in disgust as she stomps through the room toward us, and no one dares stand in her way.

"What the hell do you people think I am, a bellhop?" she asks me.

"Us people?" I ask in return.

"You and Reedy and your environmental wackos! We get to Montpelier, there's not a parking space within eleven hundred miles, and so Reedy and Dr. Strangelove give me these briefcases to haul into the statehouse! I swear, they've got bricks in 'em!"

Laura quickly takes the attaché from Patience that her sister is balancing under her arm. Although I was enjoying the image of Patience Avery as a pack mule, I reach for the other two she is holding.

"Where are they?" I ask. "Reedy and the professor?"

"I told you, trying to find a damn parking space! Don't you listen to a word I say? Ever? They should be here by this afternoon."

Trying to pacify my sister-in-law, Phil Robinson gently touches her elbow and starts to guide her toward the front row of seats by the window. "Why don't you sit down," he says, his voice affected but serene.

"Don't patronize me, Phil," she snaps, whipping her elbow away from him. "And don't think for one moment we're going to sit in those seats by the window. By two thirty it'll be so damn dark on that side we won't be able to read our damn notes. No way. I want seats on the side of the room opposite the windows, because that's where all of the overhead lights are."

Phil takes a deep breath and nods. He manages to smile and croaks out the word, "Fine."

. . .

ALTHOUGH THERE ARE nine members on the Environmental Board, only a quorum of five is necessary at any one hearing. Given the economic significance of this particular hearing, however, and the media attention it has received because of the catamounts, all nine members of the Board file into the cafeteria at exactly eight thirty.

Mitch Valine, the Board chairman, nods briefly at me and then at Ian Rawls, seated in one of the chairs in the first row on the opposite side of the cafeteria. Mitch reaches for his wooden gavel, and smiles at the room.

"I do this," he says, referring to the time he spends as chairman of the Environmental Board, "because they let me have a gavel. Real wood, too."

Virtually everyone in the audience chuckles, including Reedy and me. It is not that either Mitch's joke or his delivery is particularly good, but everyone appreciates the idea behind it: alleviating some of the tension in the room. Exclusive of the witnesses that Powder Peak and the Copper Project have lined up, there are approximately three hundred and fifty people squeezed—seated or standing—into the cafeteria, including at least a dozen reporters. One of the maintenance workers told me that another six or seven hundred people are scattered in rooms throughout the statehouse, watching the hearing on closed-circuit television.

Mitch slams the gavel down once on the table. "Oyez, oyez, attention. This hearing is now formally in session." He allows himself another grin, and adds, "I love that part. Oyez."

Mitch Valine has always struck me as an odd person to have joined the Environmental Board, but absolutely perfect once he was on it. Somewhere in his midthirties, he was sent to Vermont five years ago from Philadelphia by a cellular phone company to open the Vermont market. He has, as far as I can tell, no hidden agendas, and unlike the other eight members of the Board, he is neither a committed environmentalist nor a strong proponent of business growth.

Miranda sits between Laura and me, the three of us in the chairs closest to the wall. Patience surprised us all by expressing an interest in sitting beside Reedy in the front row during the proceedings, although Laura has whispered to me that it was not so much a longing to stand by her man in public, as it was a desire to prevent anyone in attendance from mistaking Dawn Ciandella for Reedy's woman.

The remainder of the Copper Project's side of the first two rows has been taken up by the witnesses that Reedy and Dawn have chosen, a series of economists, environmental experts, and representatives from the Vermont Natural Resources Council, the state Sierra Club, and VPIRG, the decidedly leftist Vermont Public Interest Research Group.

In the first two rows opposite us is the team John Bussey and Ian Rawls have assembled, a combination of people whom I know well, people I worked with for years, but now will not even look in my direction: Powder Peak's own environmentalists, hydrologists, economists, and engineers, as well as the two Colorado naturalists who insist there is no reason to believe there are catamounts left anywhere near Mount Republic.

Not one of these people will glare at me, not one of them will even glance my way. I am, in their eyes, not just a lunatic, I am ungrateful. I am a traitor of sorts, a turncoat to the cause.

And, on some level, I can understand their anger. They have convinced themselves, rightly or wrongly, that Powder Peak's future depends entirely upon their expansion. If the Environmental Board fails to uphold the permits that Liza Eastwick's district commission granted the resort; if the Board rules against tapping the Chittenden River because the water has—for the moment—stopped flowing; if the Board rules against cutting huge swaths through the mountain's forests because a father and daughter claimed to have seen three mountain lions there, then Powder Peak may, in their eyes, someday soon cease to exist.

28

•

Mitch has called today's hearing a "quasi-judicial tribunal," and he is running it in what he would probably describe as a quasi-judicial fashion. First the Copper Project will present its appeal, as if we were the prosecution, and then Powder Peak will present its defense. If the morning proceeds as we expect, I will testify around eleven thirty, and Miranda will tell her story just before lunch.

"What is the flow of the Chittenden River right now, Doctor?" Dawn Ciandella asks Dr. Jackson Bazemchuk, as she leans against a column by the picture windows, folding her arms across her chest.

Bazemchuk, a professor at the University of Miami, has achieved national recognition over the past two decades for his efforts to protect the Everglades. According to Reedy, however, he knows he is losing his battle, and over the last two days has been prone to almost incomprehensible outbursts. He worries Reedy.

Bazemchuk looks as if he has lived at least forty or fifty years in Florida: His skin is a deep and probably permanent tan, and his face and hands and neck are covered with small scars where cancerous growths evidently have been removed. He speaks with a deep Southern accent, and adds emphasis to his pronouncements by twirling in his fingers the tufts of snow-white hair that dot his forehead like bad topiary.

I can understand why Patience called him Dr. Strangelove.

"In the area that the resort wants to tap, the river's flow is about a quarter of a foot per second," he answers, shaking his head.

"What about other parts of the river?"

"Please!" he says, touching one of the shrubs on his head. "Parts of that river don't even exist anymore! Parts of it have dried up completely!"

"As you know," Dawn continues, "one of the principal conditions of the resort's permit is that Powder Peak may not tap the Chittenden if the river falls below three-quarters of one cubic foot per second. It already has. As a result of the drought, the Chittenden has plummeted to one-quarter of one cubic foot per second. Legally, the resort couldn't tap the river this season even if it had its snowmaking system in place. It just couldn't do it.

"Now, based on your examination of the Chittenden River, do you believe that the resort should be allowed to tap the river if—next year—the flow returns to three-quarters of a foot per second?"

Some people will not be coached. Some people will not be led. Perhaps forgetting the fact that Dawn is consciously leading him on, or perhaps because of it, Dr. Bazemchuk taps the sides of his head with the index finger on each of his hands, and says, "Are you crazy? Is everyone in this state as stupid as everybody in Florida? No one should touch that river! Not this year, not next year! It's going to take years for that river to recover from this drought, years! Let that river fall too far and you'll screw up your entire ecosystem! You'll screw up your plant life, you'll screw up your insect life, and then you'll screw up your marine life! That's just in the first year or two. Just wait till you get up the food chain to mammals."

Dawn tries to smile, but it is clear that Bazemchuk has unnerved her with his outburst. After taking a deep breath, she asks, "In your opinion, how strong should the flow be before the ski resort should be allowed to tap it to make snow?"

"My opinion? At least one full cubic foot per second."

"Thank you, Doctor Bazemchuk," Dawn says, returning to her seat.

Mitch Valine motions toward John Bussey. "John," he says, "you're up. Any questions for the doctor?"

"Sure have," he says, buttoning his suit jacket as he stands, a mannerism that I am sure he picked up from courtroom dramas on television.

"Dr. Bazemchuk, your discipline is . . . water. Correct?"

"Natural aquatic environments, yes indeed."

"I'd wager there isn't anyone in this country who knows more about the Everglades than you do."

"Nope, there isn't. Or rain forests."

"What about northern rivers and waterways? How many of those have you studied?"

"Many."

"Many," John repeats, glancing down at a paper in his hand. "This is the Jackson Bazemchuk bibliography. I count here thirty-seven separate papers, articles, and books about water. Does that sound right?"

"It does."

"Well, I don't see here one piece of writing about any river further north than, oh, New Orleans. Ever written about one north of New Orleans?"

"No. But I certainly understand different aquatic environments."

"Ever skied?"

Dawn instantly shoots to her feet. “Objection. That’s not relevant.”

Mitch smiles. “Dawn, we don’t exactly have formal objections here. But I think your principle’s right. John, whether the man skis or not doesn’t make a difference.”

John nods, and turns toward the witness. “How many miles of fishable waterways are there in Vermont?”

“I haven’t the foggiest idea. But that doesn’t—”

“That does indeed matter,” John says, cutting him off. “There are forty-eight hundred miles of them. Forty-eight hundred. How much of that area do you think Powder Peak’s proposed withdrawal will affect?”

He shrugs. “I don’t know the exact amount, but—”

“Try a mile and a half. One more question. How many snowmaking water withdrawal studies have you conducted in your career?”

I lean close to Reedy. “Why him?” I whisper, referring to Bazemchuk. “He’s killing you.”

Without turning to me, Reedy says softly, “He’s supposed to be the best. He really is.”

“That depends on what you mean by a study,” Bazemchuk answers. “As you said yourself, I haven’t published anything on the subject just yet.”

“I’ll rephrase that. How many times have you visited an area where there’s a ski resort that plans to make snow, and studied the ramifications?”

Bazemchuk takes a deep breath and reaches for one of the thicker shrubs at the back of his head, and then hisses, “You are a shortsighted young man, and I won’t play this game with you. If you want to destroy a river, go right ahead. But you will destroy it. Mark my word, you will—”

Mitch pounds his gavel, and then rolls his eyes in mock astonishment at the echo.

"I'm going to have to ask you to answer the question," Mitch says. "I know this isn't a courtroom, but you will recall that you are under oath."

"You people," Bazemchuk says. "I thought it was the Florida sun that fried people's brains and made them stupid. But clearly it's something more deeply rooted inside us all than that. Fine. The answer is two."

"Two? You've studied water withdrawal at exactly two ski resorts?"

"Yes."

"Thank you," John says. "I think we're all through here."

. . .

". . . and do you swear to tell the whole truth, and nothing but the truth, so help you God?"

"I do," Russ Budbill answers from the seat at the table just vacated by Dr. Bazemchuk, his right hand raised.

"Thank you," Mitch says. "Consider yourself sworn in."

Dawn's plan had been to present our two environmental experts first thing in the morning: first one of national prominence, and then one with less renown but perhaps greater local credibility. The plan was to have Bazemchuk discredit the water withdrawal generally, and then Russ Budbill of Bartlett, Vermont, attack it specifically. In theory, Bazemchuk was going to overwhelm the Board with his brilliance, taking the pressure off Budbill.

That didn't happen. As a result, Reedy and Dawn must be hoping now for unprecedented rhetoric and eloquence from Budbill. Budbill, a wiry fellow in his midthirties, is not an impressive speaker.

"I'm a hydrologist," he says to Dawn, answering her question, "an aquatic engineer."

"Do you work for Powder Peak?"

"Not now. But . . . I have in the past."

"Tell us about that."

His eyes dart between the Environmental Board and the hundreds of spectators watching him, dark little marbles of fear.

"Okay. Two . . . no, three years ago, I studied the Gardner River, to see if they could use it as a source for man-made snow. That was when they wanted to increase the snow coverage on Moosehead."

"What did you decide?"

"I decided it could support snowmaking."

"How did you come to that conclusion?"

"We used a computer program that was designed by the U.S. Fish and Wildlife Service. It's the one used by most aquatic engineers. Anyway, it figures out the impact on a river of different water withdrawal levels. On the fish and plants and insect life."

"What did the resort do with your study?"

"They used it. It was part of the reason the District Five Commission gave them their permits a couple years back, and you can ski right now on so darn much of Moosehead."

"In other words, Powder Peak is using the Gardner River to make snow, because in your judgment it was ecologically safe to tap that river."

"That's right."

"But you don't work for Powder Peak anymore, correct?"

"Correct."

"How come?"

"They didn't like my last set of findings," he says.

John Bussey stands up. "Mitch, that statement is only Mr. Budbill's opinion."

"I understand," Mitch says.

"Would you tell us about those findings?" Dawn asks.

He nods. "Last September, about a year ago, they asked me to study the Chittenden River. They wanted to do some pretty major expansion—much more than adding snow to a half-dozen trails on Moosehead—and they were looking at the Chittenden as the source."

"What did you tell them?"

"I told them not to use it. I used the same methodology on the Chittenden that I used on the Gardner, and I told them that they shouldn't let the flow fall below one cubic foot per second. Anything less than that would affect the river."

"What did Powder Peak do?"

"Got themselves another hydrologist," he says, smirking.

Reedy gives me a small nudge, and when I turn to him, he is nodding his head almost imperceptibly. We shouldn't have worried about Budbill, that nod says, he's doing just fine.

• • •

OVER THE NEXT hour and a half, Dawn Ciandella parades before the Environmental Board an impressive series of witnesses. There is a naturalist with the Vermont Natural Resources Council, a woman who not only expresses her concern with the idea of using the Chittenden River to make snow, she explains why the proposed storage pond should not be placed near the base of Mount Chittenden. There is the professor from Middlebury College who—along with his wife—claims to have seen catamounts recently in Vermont, as well as an expert from the state Sierra Club, who presents what he describes as "significant and reasonable evidence of the existence of catamounts in Vermont."

And then there are the economists, two of them, one a professor from the University of Vermont and one a member of VPIRG. Both of them insist that there will be no economic cataclysm if Powder Peak's permits are overturned.

Besides, the economist from VPIRG insists, Vermonters deserve better than the "degrading, minimum-wage table scraps the ski industry tosses us."

• • •

FINALLY IT IS Miranda's and my turn. I will go first, with Miranda right behind me. By design, my daughter will be the last witness we present, and the last witness the Environmental Board will see before the lunch break. It is already quarter to twelve. Dawn is going to try and get me on and off the stand in ten minutes so we can get to Miranda.

• • •

"HOW LONG DID they remain on the rocks?" Dawn asks me, referring to the catamounts.

"They were still there when the chairlift started down the final stretch of the mountain," I answer.

"How long were you able to see them?"

"Perhaps forty-five seconds. Perhaps a minute."

Laura is holding Miranda's hand. She probably has been holding it off and on all morning.

"And you are absolutely sure that what you saw were mountain lions? There is no doubt in your mind?"

"There is no doubt in my mind at all. We saw three catamounts, and we saw them for what seemed like a very long time."

Dawn stands still for a moment, allowing my final words to sink in with the Environmental Board. Finally she thanks me and sits down.

Mitch Valine looks up at John Bussey. "John, your cross," he says simply.

When I had been in my seat in the front row, I had certainly been aware of the size of the crowd in the cafeteria. But my back had been to the group, and as I had followed the testimony of each of the witnesses throughout the morning, I had lost track of the number of people in attendance. Or the cameras for the closed-circuit broadcast. Sitting now at one of the two single tables at the front of the room, however, I am reminded of the size of the audience.

As John Bussey stands, as John Bussey buttons his coat and approaches, I feel almost vulnerable. I know if I were in his situation, I would attack me mercilessly. After all, the next witness is a little girl, and he will win no friends attacking her.

"How long have you lived in Vermont?" John begins.

"Almost twenty years."

"How long did you work for Powder Peak?"

"At least five years. Maybe six."

"Six years," he repeats. "Did you spend a lot of time at the resort?"

"In my judgment, I did."

"Do you think you know the mountains that comprise Powder Peak pretty well?"

I fold my hands on the table, stalling. This is a deceptively savvy question, one that presents me with a no-win situation. If I answer yes, John will then wonder why it was that I never saw a catamount there in all those years; if I answer no, he will use that as a reason to outline for the Board all the evidence that suggests there are no longer mountain lions in the area.

I nod my head. "I think so."

"If someone had asked you on July seventeenth—the day before you and your daughter took your ride on the chairlift—if there were catamounts on Mount Republic, what would you have said?"

There is a small length of chain, perhaps two inches, dangling over one of Patience Avery's thumbs. She is holding one of her crystals in the palm of that hand.

"Remember," John adds, a small dagger for fun, "you're under oath."

"I would have said I doubted it."

"Before July eighteenth," he continues, "had you ever seen a catamount?"

"No."

"You had never seen one at Powder Peak?"

"No."

"Had anyone ever seen one at Powder Peak during the six years you worked with the resort?"

"That I don't know."

He turns to the Environmental Board and rolls his eyes, and then turns toward the audience and rolls them again. "Had you ever heard of a sighting?"

"No."

"Thank you." He picks up a clipboard from his chair, and glances at the top sheet. "How old are you, Scottie?"

"Thirty-nine."

"You'll turn forty this fall, right?"

"Right."

"Do you wear glasses?"

"Nope."

"Think you see pretty well?"

"I do."

"When was the last time you went to an eye doctor?"

The reporters from the *Burlington Free Press* and the Associated Press are scribbling madly, trying to catch every word of our exchange.

"Three years ago."

"Three years. You're about to turn forty, and you haven't been to an eye doctor since your midthirties." He carefully returns his clipboard to his seat, allowing his words to settle.

"Do you know the percentage of people your age who wear eyeglasses?" he asks.

"No."

"Eighty-nine percent. Almost nine out of every ten people in their forties wear eyeglasses or contact lenses. Think you're that lucky tenth man who doesn't need them?"

I glance over at Dawn, trying to will her to her feet. In my head, however, I know it would be useless for her to try and object. If I were representing Powder Peak, I too would question my eyesight; moreover, if I were Mitch Valine, I would allow this line of questioning.

"I think so," I tell John. "My eyesight has always been excellent."

"Even at five hundred and thirty feet?"

"Five hundred and thirty feet?"

"Five hundred and thirty feet. That's the distance between the rocks where you think you saw some animal, and the chairlift."

I shake my head. "That was the second sighting, John. There—"

"Oh, now there were two sightings? You saw catamounts twice?"

"No, of course not—"

"Of course not? Of course not? Is your story *that* improbable?"

"No, John, what I'm saying—"

"What are you saying?"

Dawn finally stands: "This is badgering. John is asking questions, and he's not letting the witness answer them."

Mitch rolls his gavel across the table without thinking about the noise it will make, and says to John in a friendly tone, "Slow down, could you? We've got all day."

John nods, asking me more evenly, "Is your eyesight that good that you could tell exactly what you saw at five hundred and thirty feet?"

I take a deep breath, gathering my thoughts. "When we first saw the catamounts, they were much closer. When we first saw them, they weren't up on the cliff. They were at the edge of the woods. The evergreens. I'd guess at one point we were within forty or fifty yards of them."

"Fifty yards. One hundred and fifty feet."

"Or forty yards. One hundred and twenty feet."

"This was before these . . . supposed . . . animals saw you, disappeared into the woods, and suddenly reappeared at the rocks five hundred and thirty feet away—five hundred and thirty feet away at best. As the chairlift moved, they were even further away, you realize."

There is nothing I have to answer here, so I sit impassively. Finally he asks, "And you think you saw this something while the chairlift was moving, right?"

"Right."

"And you think you saw this something at eight thirty at night?"

"Right."

"Do you know what time the sun set on July eighteenth this year?"

"Sure do, John. It set at eight seventeen. We checked that too."

Facing the Environmental Board for emphasis, he continues, "We will certainly agree with you on that. The sun did indeed set at about quarter past eight that night . . . almost fifteen minutes before you think you saw something. So let me ask you this, Scottie: Are your almost forty-year-old eyes that good that you know exactly what you saw from a moving chairlift a full fifteen minutes after the sun has gone down?"

"It's still very light out at eight thirty in the middle of July. Yes, technically the sun had set, but it was still light out."

"It was nighttime!"

"No, it wasn't, John. It was barely twilight. It was barely dusk—"

"Fine. It was twilight. That's a terrible time to see—"

"That's John's opinion only," Dawn says, interrupting. "Neither of these men is an optometrist, and neither should be allowed to offer an opinion on whether twilight is a terrible or a terrific time to see."

Mitch looks at both of us, and then at Dawn. "Both these fellows play a little softball. So do I. And I think we would all agree that unless a field has lights, you call the game at twilight. Is that true, Scottie?"

Although these hearings are, at best, only vaguely judicial, I can see that Dawn Ciandella from Boston is appalled at the chairman's idea of using twilight softball for a legal precedent. Before she opens her mouth and says something that might antagonize any member of the Board, I answer Mitch's question, as ludicrous as it might be.

"Twilight is a vague concept, and yes, you might call a game at twilight. But I assure you, Mitch, I have never, ever seen a game called in the middle of July at eight thirty at night."

Laura moves one of her fingers toward her mouth, but catches herself. Her hand partly raised, she uses it instead to brush Miranda's bangs from her eyes.

Mitch nods and turns to John. "Are you done?" he asks him. "Do you have any more questions?"

He rubs his shoulder. "No more questions."

"Fine. In that case, let's break for lunch."

Dawn raises her hand, and Mitch turns to her.

"We would like to bring forth our last witness."

"It's almost twelve thirty," Mitch says.

Dawn walks past me to the Board's long table. Speaking softly she says to the chairman, "Our last witness is Miranda, a little girl. I don't think it's fair to make her wait another hour to speak."

"Is she nervous?" Mitch asks.

"She's nine years old," Dawn says, evading the question.

"Fine. Let's do it," he agrees. He then motions for John Bussey to join him. "Go easy on her, John," he says, speaking as much for my benefit as John's, "even if she is Scottie's kid."

. . .

MIRANDA'S FEET DANGLE at least six inches above the floor, and they sway like a pair of her aunt's pendulums. Occasionally she sits forward as far as she can in the chair, and stretches her legs and her feet so that she can anchor herself for brief moments by the tips of her black patent leather shoes.

"Do you have a cat, Miranda?" John asks my daughter.

"No."

"Have you ever had one?"

"Oh, sure. Snowball. But she died a couple years ago."

"How many years ago?"

"I was in second grade. So two years."

"Do you miss Snowball? Do you miss her a lot?"

This is a personal question for Miranda, and she answers with some reserve. "I guess I do."

"Do you want a new cat?"

"Well, my dad's allergic to them," she answers. "But I still might get one for my birthday," she continues, her voice brightening at the idea as she looks in her mother's and my direction.

When Snowball died, I had hoped my daughter would lose interest in cats. Lately, however, it has become clear to Laura and me that she hasn't. Consequently, for Miranda's birthday later this month we have promised her a new cat.

Beside me, Laura scribbles a note.

John asks, "Do you think a lot about cats, Miranda?"

"I don't know."

Laura turns the note toward me: *Is he trying to show she made up the catamounts?*

"Maybe," I whisper.

"Were you thinking about getting a cat the night you and your dad took that ride on the chairlift?"

"I could have been."

"Did you and your dad talk about getting a cat that night?"

"I think we did."

He nods and smiles at my daughter. "Do you know what a feral cat is?"

Miranda shakes her head that she doesn't.

"A feral cat is sort of like the kind of cat I'll bet Snowball was," John explains. "You know, a regular old cat."

Miranda quickly raises her hand as if she were in school.

"Do you need to ask something, Miranda?" Mitch Valine asks her.

She drops her arm to her side and says, "Snowball wasn't exactly a regular old cat. See, Snowball could fetch things, just like a dog, and she'd come when you called her."

"My mistake," John says. "All I meant was that feral cats look sort of like the kinds of cats your friends must have. Except for one thing: They live in the wild. And do you know what they have to do to live in the wild?"

Miranda follows John with her eyes as he paces, but she doesn't answer his question.

"They have to make themselves look as big as they possibly can," John says. "So, sometimes, they fluff up their fur so they look huge. Huge!"

I sit back in my chair and sigh. Any moment now, John will plant the final seeds of doubt in the minds of the Environmental Board, by convincing my daughter to admit that there was at least some small chance that what we saw were feral cats.

"Could Snowball fluff herself up a bit?" John continues. "In the winter, maybe, when it was cold outside?"

Miranda nods and smiles. "She sure could."

"I'll bet. Now those animals you and your father saw that night at Powder Peak, those cats. Were you close enough to pet them?"

"No way!"

John nods. "Now you understand that when things are far away, sometimes it's hard to see exactly what they are, right?"

"Boy, not this time, Mr. Bussey."

"That wasn't my question, Miranda," John says, a hint of disapproval in his voice. "I'll repeat the question: Sometimes, it's hard to see things exactly right when they're real far away. Isn't that true?"

"But, Mr. Bussey, I know—"

"Miranda?" he says, drawing out the length of my daughter's name.

"John, I think she understands the intent of your question," Mitch says, interrupting. "Go ahead, Miranda. What do you want to say?"

She takes a deep breath. "Mr. Bussey, I know the animals were far away, but they weren't so far away that I couldn't see what they were! Snowball was never, ever that big! The catamounts me and my dad saw were much bigger," she says, pulling her hands from the table and spreading her arms as wide as she can. "Even the babies were bigger than Snowball. And the mom? Ho-boy, she was big. She must have been taller than Mindy's sheep—"

"Mindy who?" Mitch asks.

"Mindy Woolf. She's got this sheepdog named Merlin. Anyway, the mom—the catamount mom—was taller than Merlin. And Merlin's the biggest dog I've ever seen!"

"Thank you, Miranda," John says, his voice even.

Shaking her head back and forth, my daughter continues, "I'm not kidding, Mr. Bussey, I'll bet you've never seen anything like it! And the mother catamount, she wasn't just big, she was beautiful. No offense to Mindy, but she was a lot prettier than Merlin. And a lot faster too, I'll bet."

The Powder Peak attorney glances once at Ian Rawls, his client, staring out the window at nothing. John then turns to Mitch Valine. "No more questions, Mitch," he says. "Let's go get something to eat."

. . .

"YOU WERE SENSATIONAL, Miranda Avery-Winston!" Patience coos at her niece at the vegetarian cafeteria a few blocks away from the statehouse.

Miranda pushes her falafel burger around on her plate with her fork, and tries to smile. "Will the people at the ski resort change their minds now?"

"About cutting down the trees where we saw the catamounts?"

"Uh-huh."

Laura looks at me as she massages her daughter's back. "Well, there's a chance now, sweetheart. And that's more than there was a couple of days ago."

"What else can we do?" she asks.

Before Laura or I can respond, Patience smiles and answers, "You did everything—and more—that anyone could do to beat that little shi—"

"Easy, Patience," I tell my sister-in-law, cutting her off.

"You did everything you could to beat the pants off John Bussey, King Twerp," she continues.

I can tell that Miranda isn't satisfied with her aunt's conclusion. "I hope so," she says simply.

The afternoon session is scheduled to begin in fifteen minutes, so I begin to pile my family's plates onto my tray. "Do you plan to eat that, or just build a falafel mountain?" I ask Miranda.

"Finished."

Laura joins me with a tray full of plates and glasses, and together we bring them to a special return window on one side of the cafeteria.

"Honestly," Laura says, "do you think there is a chance to win?"

"There's some. A lot will depend on how well the Powder Peak witnesses do. And how well Dawn's cross goes. She and Reedy are practicing right now. But it has become one of those 'battle of the experts' kind of hearings. 'Our experts are bigger than your experts.' 'My dad's experts can beat up your dad's experts.' "

"What if we lose?"

"We? Must we be the Copper Project?"

"Scottie, come on."

"I mean that," I tell her, trying to keep my voice low. "Hasn't this been hard enough? Hasn't everything I've . . . I've given up been enough?"

"This isn't about what you've given up."

"It sure as hell is."

"Scottie—"

"At least it should be. For you, for Reedy. I've given up a career that—"

"For your daughter," Laura snaps at me, angry. "You're not doing this for Reedy McClure, and you're not doing this for me. So don't you dare try and make me feel guilty."

I shake my head. "Let's face it: If Miranda and I hadn't seen those stupid animals last July, Miranda would be in school right now, you'd be running your business, and I'd be where I'm supposed to be. Where I like to be."

"Where do you like to be? Drying up rivers?"

"And creating jobs."

Laura presses her tongue against the inside of her cheek, and takes a deep breath. People at nearby tables in the restaurant have begun to stare. "But you did see the catamounts," she says. "We've been through this and through this. Wondering where you'd be right now if you hadn't seen them is like some scientist wondering where he'd be if he hadn't discovered that some invention of his that he thought helped people actually caused cancer."

"I wish the stakes were that high. I'd feel better about all this."

"In some ways, they are. You've said yourself you're doing this because of the drought, because something has changed in Vermont. You've said yourself you're doing this because you saw the catamounts with Miranda—"

"And if I'd seen them alone?"

"I hope you'd be doing exactly the same thing."

"We'll never know. But I doubt it," I tell her, saying those words for no other reason than to be argumentative. To be hurtful.

"I don't. It's not like you've spent the last twenty years of your life doing what you do because you feel so damn strong about defending high utility rates or high phone bills." She shakes her head. "You just like to be where the power is!"

Patience glances in our direction, motioning with a nod of her head that we should hurry up.

"I do like to be where the power is. I'm not shy about admitting that. And do you know why? It's not ego. It's pragmatism. It's because in Vermont, the only people who can pay hundreds of dollars an hour for my services are the people in power. So you're right, I do like to be where the power is."

"Well, maybe that's changing. Maybe you've moved to the right side just in time."

"Nothing's going to change," I tell her slowly. "As long as people who insist on wearing sandals in November represent things like the Chittenden River or the trees on Mount Republic, nothing's going to change."

Annoyed with me, Laura says, "You haven't answered my

question. Who has the better experts? What do you think will happen this afternoon?"

I sigh. "My prediction? Powder Peak's experts won't be able to defend tapping the Chittenden. And they might not be able to defend building the holding pond where it's currently planned. But they will make your daughter and your husband—at least your husband—look like raving idiots."

Laura wipes her hands one more time with the napkin.

"And what will all that mean?" she asks. "They won't be able to use the Chittenden to make snow, but they will be able to build the trails where you saw the catamounts?"

"Yup. They'll rip down so many trees that a squirrel won't find shade—much less a mountain lion."

Ignoring the melodrama in my response, Laura says, "That will upset Miranda, you realize."

"I realize that. But the overall decision will probably satisfy most of the maniacs in the Copper Project. And while it won't thrill Powder Peak, the Board will have thrown the resort a pretty good-sized bone. No, my love," I continue, unable to mask the irritation in my voice, "the only two complete losers in this whole fiasco are your husband and your daughter."

. . .

THROUGHOUT THE AFTERNOON, my allies for years explain Powder Peak's desperate need to make snow, and Vermont's desperate need for Powder Peak. Evidently, John Bussey plans to make the economic arguments for expansion first, and then wrap up with his environmental defense.

"Those are the numbers," says Claude Cousino, the director of Vermont's Agency of Economic Development. "If Powder Peak gets to build those new trails and make some new snow, we believe it will create somewhere around four hundred jobs in this area."

Kimberly McDonnell, an economics professor at Lyndon State College, explains with sardonic glee, "The formula is simple. Vermont needs between six and seven hundred million dollars in tax revenue every year. It can get it from places like Powder Peak, or it can get it from private citizens via property taxes. But it will get it, because that's what it takes to run this state."

And Sara Chesmen, head of the Vermont Ski Areas Consortium, tells the Board in a voice that is even and assured, "Vermont mountains don't get anywhere near the same snowfall as our competitors out West, and skiers have figured that out. Every year, more and more of them head west to Colorado or Utah. In my opinion, if the Vermont ski industry is not allowed to make snow, it will eventually cease to exist. At least at its current size."

"How many ski resorts were there in Vermont twenty or twenty-five years ago?" John asks her, using what has always been one of my favorite questions.

"Well, as recently as 1971 there were eighty-one."

"How many are there now?"

"Nineteen. That's how sick the Vermont ski industry is. We've lost three-quarters of our ski resorts in a couple of decades, and now people are willing to throw away one of the remaining industry jewels. I cannot stress strongly enough how important it is to allow Powder Peak to expand."

. . .

IT HAD CROSSED my mind that John Bussey might end the day with Ian Rawls, expecting the resort's managing director to make an impassioned and eloquent plea for expansion. It would not have been my strategy, however, because I have worked with Ian for years, and I know that while he is a solid and capable manager, he is a mediocre public speaker.

John must have known this too. Immediately after the short recess, he brings Ian to the front of the room to testify. That means Powder Peak will end the hearing with a hydrologist from the Department of Fish and Wildlife, followed by one or both of the trackers from the University of Colorado.

"If we don't have snowmaking, we don't open," Ian says at one point.

"Snowmaking today is every bit as important as chairlifts were twenty-five years ago," he adds. "Can you imagine a ski resort without chairlifts? Of course not. Well, that's how important snowmaking is now in Vermont."

Dawn wanders over toward the table behind which Ian is sitting. "How many trails at Powder Peak currently have snowmaking?"

"Forty-eight."

"How many would have snow if you were able to complete your planned expansion?"

He sits back in his seat, and then, when he realizes he is slouching, he slides forward. "Well, if we'd gotten everything we wanted . . . needed . . . if we had gotten the full approvals, we would be able to make snow on fifty-nine trails."

"What do you mean, 'if we had gotten everything we needed'?"

"We think we should be able to use the Chittenden even if the river's running at one-half of a cubic foot per second. But our permit only allows us to use the river if it remains at three-quarters of a cubic foot per second."

"Meaning?"

"Meaning we probably can't expand snowmaking to fifty-nine trails."

"How many trails can you add to the system at three-quarters of a cubic foot per second?"

"Our engineering studies show we can probably add another eight trails."

"Giving you fifty-six?"

"Yes . . . right."

Dawn begins to circle Ian, wandering around his table in a wide arc. "You've said that your resort cannot survive without your new permits."

"I've said that, sort of. Yes. Sort of."

"So your resort's entire survival depends upon being able to make snow on eight more trails? Is that right?"

"Well, that's mislead—"

"You're claiming that Powder Peak's entire survival depends upon increasing snowmaking coverage from forty-eight out of seventy-one trails to fifty-six out of seventy-one trails," she continues, repeating the sort of thing I said with a straight face almost all summer. "You're saying that if Powder Peak is not allowed to increase its snowmaking coverage from sixty-seven percent to seventy-nine percent it will go out of business. Is that accurate?"

He slumps forward a tiny bit, his upper body beginning to sag.

"What I said was . . . was . . . what I meant was we need snowmaking."

"You've got snowmaking!" Dawn says, laughing. "You've got snowmaking on two-thirds of your resort!"

Ian looks toward Mitch Valine, pleading to be excused with his eyes, but Mitch merely looks down at his notes.

"Well, we need more," Ian says finally, speaking to no one in particular.

If I were Dawn, I would now move on. She has hurt Ian about as much as she can on this issue, without either alienating the Board or risking the sort of desperate, but occasionally successful, counterattack of which a wounded animal is capable. It's clear, however, that she is not yet ready to end this line of questioning, and I find myself almost trying to will her ahead.

"How much more, Mr. Rawls? One hundred percent coverage? Will that satisfy you?"

"It's not that simple."

"No? Your plan isn't simply to tap the river until there's nothing—"

"Our plan is to keep Powder Peak profitable and to keep people employed," Ian says, rallying.

Instinctively I look away when I hear Dawn asking, "Eight trails will do all that?" I know Ian well, and I know she has now given him too much room.

"We wouldn't spend fifteen million dollars for snow on eight new trails, or on eleven new trails," he says, his voice becoming angry. "Yes, the new system will allow us to add snowmaking to another ten percent of the mountain, but it will also allow us to make snow on a lot of other trails a lot more profitably. A lot more competitively. And those eight trails you keep talking about are indeed an important part of the resort. Maybe they only represent another ten percent of the mountain, but they're half—one-half, Ms. Ciandella—of our beginner runs. We have to get new skiers to survive, and that means having beginner trails with snow all season long."

Dawn watches him for a long second, gathering her thoughts. Instantly Ian fills the void, continuing, "And don't forget, the snowmaking is only one part of the whole expansion. There's the gondola, there are new lifts, and there are all those new trails on Mount Republic. That's part of the fifteen-million-dollar price tag too. That's what we need to survive."

Across the aisle from us John Bussey tries hard not to smile. Beside me, Laura chews on her nails and Reedy looks down at his shoes.

. . .

"IT'S A TRADE-OFF, we understand that," Bolton McKenna admits to Dawn under oath. "I'll be the first to admit that we're letting the river fall a little lower than I'd normally like."

McKenna, a hydrologist with Vermont's Department of Fish and Wildlife, signed the permits that allow the resort to use the Chittenden River to make snow, even if the water flow slows dramatically.

"Then why did you do it? Jobs?"

He shrugs. "I guess. Sometimes you have to make compromises."

"Do you understand that your permit is in direct opposition to the guidelines established by the United States Fish and Wildlife Service?"

He shakes his head. "No, it's not. It may be opposed to the computer model, but it doesn't oppose any rules. It doesn't violate anything. All rivers are different. I don't see any reason to use a computer model as gospel."

"We're not dealing with just any computer model here. We're talking about the computer model that every single ski area in the state of Vermont uses. Except, evidently, Powder Peak."

Bolton McKenna stares at Dawn, but says nothing.

"This morning," she continues, "two other aquatic experts testified that it is absolutely incomprehensible—incomprehensible—that Powder Peak should be allowed to tap the Chittenden at the level you and the District Five Commission have allowed. And yet you call it merely a compromise."

"I could probably find you two experts who would agree with me," Bolton says.

Ignoring him, Dawn asks, "Now, the Chittenden River was studied well before the severity of this drought became clear, right?"

"That's right."

"You read the Powder Peak hydrologist's report four months

ago, and you signed the permits two months ago. Has the drought changed your mind?"

"About?"

"About the hydrologist's findings?"

"I'll stand by 'em."

"You honestly do not believe that this drought will leave scars on the Chittenden River?"

"I didn't say that," Bolton answers quickly. "I just said that I stand by my permit."

"Does that mean this drought could be inflicting long-term damage on the Chittenden River?"

Behind me, the rows of people who have been fidgeting, stretching their legs, disappearing with increasing frequency to the water fountains and bathrooms scattered throughout the statehouse, stop moving.

"Let me ask you the question more plainly," Dawn continues. "Has this drought hurt the river?"

He rubs the bridge of his nose with two fingers. "It may have."

"Is that a yes?"

"Yeah. I guess it is."

"If you yourself were asked right now to examine the Chittenden River, would you authorize water withdrawals for snowmaking once the flow is back up to three-quarters of a cubic foot per second?"

He sighs, frustrated. "No."

"Why not?"

"Because the river's low."

"Do you mean that it has been hurt?"

"Yes."

Dawn watches Bolton for a long moment, hoping the silence will force him to elaborate on his answer. Finally: "Yes. It has been hurt."

"The river, you mean."

"Yes."

Dawn nods, satisfied.

. . .

"THERE WERE ABSOLUTELY no tracks that could have belonged to a catamount. There were no prints of sufficient size, and no prints of sufficient gait," Professor Carl Macomber of Colorado State University tells John Bussey. The sun is now well below the mountains west of Montpelier, and the room has grown dark. It's after six o'clock. Fortunately, Macomber is the last witness.

"Gait?"

"Stride," the professor explains. "There were no prints made by an animal with a stride long enough to have been a catamount."

John lets the answer settle before continuing. Then: "In that case, Professor, what do you believe the Winstons saw?"

Macomber takes a deep breath. "I will speculate on what they saw," he says, "but please remember that I really am merely speculating."

"That's fine," John reassures him. "Could the Winstons have seen feral cats?"

"They could have. They could even have seen fisher cats, but I think that possibility is rather remote."

"But they—the animals—could have been fisher cats," John continues quickly, trying to get the professor back on track.

"Yes, sure." Macomber is probably my age, but his hair is grayer and his skin more wrinkled. Perhaps because I envision him wandering around out West in the sun, trailing mountain lions through Colorado and Wyoming, he looks to me a bit like a cowboy.

"Basically, the Winstons could have seen any one of a dozen different kinds of wildlife," John adds.

"Basically."

"Except catamounts. What they saw was not, in your opinion, a family of catamounts."

Macomber shakes his head no, and smiles in a way that looks condescending to me. It probably wasn't, but it felt that way. "That's correct. I doubt very, very much that what they saw were catamounts."

. . .

DAWN WARNED REEDY that there would be little she could do during the cross-examination, other than argue that just because Macomber did not see any evidence of catamounts on Mount Republic did not mean there were none there. The Copper Project's catamount "expert," a researcher with the state Sierra Club, had already argued that catamounts still roamed Vermont. Her hope now, Dawn said, was that Macomber would be sufficiently open-minded to allow room for dissent.

"How long is a fisher cat?" she asks him.

"Twenty to twenty-five inches. About two feet."

"How about a feral cat?"

"Feral cats are just ordinary house cats that have returned to the wild. So they're a little smaller than fisher cats."

"How about catamounts? How long are they—the kind of mountain lion found here in Vermont?"

He rests his chin in his hands, weighing his response. "If there were mountain lions in Vermont, I'd estimate they would be about four feet long."

"Twice as big as a fisher cat?"

"At least twice as long. But, overall, four or five times as big. And that's an important distinction."

"I agree. Given the difference in size between a fisher cat and a catamount, how likely is it that two people—two—could mistake a fisher cat for a catamount?"

"If you're referring specifically to the Winstons, I would have to say it's possible. They saw the animals at night—"

"They saw the animals at eight thirty in July."

"In my experience, the light that's left that time of the day can play tricks on anyone. It certainly has on me."

"You spent four days in Vermont. How long do you spend, on average, tracking mountain lions out West?"

"Significantly longer."

"What is significantly longer? One more day? Two? A week?"

"Professor Richardson, an associate of mine at the university, and I have been known to track mountain lions for months."

"Months. And yet after only four days in Vermont, you're willing to rule out completely the possibility that any mountain lions remain in the state?"

"I don't rule out the possibility completely. I simply said that, in my opinion, it is not very likely."

"After four days."

"Ms. Ciandella," he begins, as if speaking to a stubborn student, "when we track a mountain lion for months, we're not tracking it in a vacuum. We don't wander aimlessly through the Rocky Mountains, hoping we will stumble upon it. It isn't like that. We follow evidence. We look for signs. Claw marks that are fifty or sixty inches high on a tree trunk. Indications that an appropriate kill has occurred. We find and follow a trail."

"Did you hear the testimony from the Sierra Club this morning?"

"I did."

"The state Sierra Club believes catamounts might still live in Vermont. Is that organization, and all the evidence it has amassed, absolutely wrong?"

"All I can do is give you my views. I can't speak for the Sierra—"

"That's what I want. Your views. Based on your four days on Mount Republic, is the expert from the Sierra Club completely mistaken? Is there absolutely no possibility—none—that catamounts remain in Vermont?"

"No."

"In other words, it is possible?"

"Yes."

"And if catamounts still live in the Green Mountains, isn't it also possible that Scottie and Miranda Winston saw some?"

"Yes, it's possible. But—"

"Thank you. That will be—"

"But it isn't likely," Macomber continues, turning to face Mitch Valine and the Environmental Board. "In my opinion, whatever the Winstons saw were not mountain lions."

29

The sun has been high and bright all Friday morning, and the weather report doesn't predict much change tomorrow. A few high clouds, little more. We may get some rain late Sunday night or Monday morning, but by then Patience and Reedy's wedding will be behind them, and the two will be far from Vermont. No one but Reedy knows exactly where the pair will be: Reedy has claimed that he is taking Patience with him to the coast of British Columbia, where an oil tanker ran aground in July, and the cleanup crews have barely begun to make a dent in the spill. Patience says that he wouldn't dare do such a thing, and is taking them to Scotland instead, where together they will savor and study the country's mythic cairns: the piles of stones that may have been pushed together by an ancient people. The cairns are considered by some—such as the faculty of the Green Mountain School of Earth Science—to have extensive spiritual properties.

And then there is Miranda's guess. "Wonderland," she suggested, meaning, I have to assume, Disneyland.

A little before noon, our receptionist tells me, "Senator McClure is here. He wants to know if you have a minute."

I sit back in my chair and smile. Do I have a minute.

"Oh, I think I can squeeze him in," I answer. "Send him back."

• • •

"SHOULDN'T YOU BE home, doing whatever it is you're supposed to be doing for the rehearsal dinner tonight?" I ask him, as he sits down opposite my desk.

"We're ready. Or we'll be ready. I'm not worried. I know it's supposed to be my show, but the bridesmaids seem to have taken over."

"So I gather. Still . . ."

"I know, my parents would never have approved of half the stuff that will probably go on. At the day of reckoning, however, I'll be pretty darn pleased with myself if my worst sin was letting an army of new agers trample what was once my mother's garden, or paint some runes on my father's stone wall."

"You realize, don't you, that you took your life in your hands coming to this office?"

"Not really. I called first, and made sure that your partners had both gone to lunch."

"Cowardly. But smart."

He looks down at the carpet, and recognizes instantly the stain he once left there with his boots. He points at it with his finger. "Did I do that?"

"Sure did."

"Good Lord, I did that months ago! Don't you guys ever clean your carpets?"

"It never came out."

He shakes his head. "I'm sorry."

"It's a carpet. Don't worry."

He sits forward in his chair, and says softly, "I saw an empty office. Did I do that too?"

"No, I did. At least literally."

"I guess I should be sorry for that also."

Perhaps because this is his wedding weekend, I decide to be charitable and let him off the hook. "Not at all. Did you come by for lunch?" I ask.

"No. I really should get back to the homestead, you're right. But I have some news."

"Your appeal? It's not possible. It's going to take the Board at least two or three weeks to write up their decision."

"Well, yes and no." He stands up and pushes the door shut with the tips of his fingers, and then sits on the radiator by the window. "This is all very secret still. The Board expects the news will be leaked to the *Sentinel* soon enough, but I was still asked to keep the decision quiet."

"So you came right here to spill your soul."

"Right. Mitch Valine called."

"Mitch Valine called you?"

"He called me and Ian. Some of the other Board members convinced him that the Copper Project and Powder Peak deserved to have a sense of their decision as soon as possible."

"Because you're about to disappear for two weeks?"

"That may have been part of it. But it's also in Powder Peak's interest to know quickly."

Outside my window and across the street, a small breeze blows some of the leaves off the maple trees on the statehouse lawn. It's still early September, but with a dry summer, the leaves will go fast.

"And? You're smiling. You must have won."

"You? It still isn't we? Why can't you bring yourself to say that?"

"We?"

"Yes!"

I sigh. "I can."

He picks up one of the photographs of Laura, a picture of her taken at the top of Moosehead the March before last. Spring skiing. One of those days when the temperature is forty degrees, but the sun feels even warmer as it bounces off the snow. As I recall, Laura and I skied that afternoon until five thirty. We were the last two people down the mountain that day.

"Then say it," Reedy continues.

"All right. We. How was that?"

"Adequate. No more."

"Okay, here's a wedding present: Did *we* win?"

He grins, replacing the frame on the radiator, angling it so that the glass doesn't reflect the sun and I can see my wife right now from my desk. "Yes, sort of. I'm seventy-five percent happy."

I nod, waiting for Reedy to continue.

"We won our appeal on what was for me the biggest issue. The Chittenden River. Mitch says the Board is going to overturn the approvals Liza's commission granted the resort. Powder Peak won't be allowed to use the Chittenden to make snow until the river has recovered."

That day in the March before last, Laura and I went straight from the mountain to one of the slope-side condominiums that wasn't rented that week, and slipped nude into the soothing bubbles of its Jacuzzi.

"That could be years," I tell Reedy, something he already knows.

"Yup."

When we finally climbed from the Jacuzzi, our muscles were Jell-O, and we were unwilling to remain on our feet and walk the twenty or thirty feet to the bedroom. We made love on the carpet on the living room floor, with the drapes to the sliding doors open so we could watch the snow that glowed under the moon.

"What about the new trails?"

"That's the other twenty-five percent," Reedy says.

"The Board is going to uphold the commission on that one?"

He nods his head yes. "Yup. They can start clearing trees on Republic as soon as the decision is official, and dropping pylons for the gondola on Moosehead."

When Laura and I finally returned home, Miranda was watching television with Gertrude Scutter. I remember standing for a moment in the front hallway of our house, watching my daughter as she emerged from the den in her nightgown, and Laura as she tossed her ski parka into the closet, and thinking to myself that there wasn't a luckier man in the world.

"Well. That's it then, isn't it?" I can feel Reedy watching me, preparing for my reaction. I look back at him, and wonder what he sees in my eyes. "So much for the catamounts. So much for Mount Republic."

"I'm sorry."

"Me too. It really was a beautiful mountain, wasn't it?"

"You make it sound like it's going to disappear."

"Oh, I know it's not. And I know at night it will look the same. When there's a moon. But not during the day. During the day you'll be able to see all the trails. Those big, wide cuts. When there's no snow on the ground, they look like they must hurt the mountain. Physically."

"God almighty, is this Scottie Winston talking? Listen to you, you sound like me!"

"Ironic, isn't it?"

"It is indeed."

"I spent a good part of last night apologizing to Laura. I've been sort of . . . I've been a prick to her lately."

He looks out the window at the statehouse, unsure what to do with my confession. When he turns back to me, he does what most men—certainly what I—would do. He turns my admission into a bad joke.

"You're a lawyer. What does she expect?"

"She expects better. She deserves better."

He nods. "So what's next?" he asks awkwardly, trying to change the subject. "What will Powder Peak do now?"

"If I know Goddard," I answer, "he's going to push to have at least some of the trails up and open this season—by Washington's Birthday, maybe. He needs that water a hell of a lot more than he needs those trails, but he'll take anything he can get at this point."

"The hills are alive with the sound of chain saws," Reedy says, trying to lighten the point. He then adds, "I guess we knew that part of the appeal was a long shot."

"I guess."

"If it were my decision, I would have ruled in favor of the little girl and the lobbyist. I mean that, being as objective as I possibly can."

"Which is being, of course, completely biased."

Outside my window the noon siren wails.

"You know what's too bad?" I ask Reedy.

He says nothing, waiting.

"Miranda has turned out to be the real loser in this whole process. She'll be really and truly saddened by that decision. She'll be as saddened by it as any kid her age can be."

"It was a rough summer for her."

"You bet. I don't think she went two days in a row without bringing up Elias, or the catamounts."

"Or forest fires, I'd imagine."

There are two photos of Miranda on my desk, one of which was taken earlier this summer, when she grew into a butterfly for the Fourth of July. "And I agreed to let her testify. I just can't believe it. I must have been out of my mind. I must have been out of my fucking mind."

"Well. Don't get mad at yourself. Get mad at me. It was my idea."

"No, I'm not mad at you. On some level, I'm not even angry with myself. Not really. I'm just disappointed. I'm disappointed for Miranda," I tell him, shaking my head as I speak. "I just can't believe what kind of summer she had. The poor kid, she even lost her croquet court. Can you believe it? She had to trade her croquet court so we could have water to flush the damn toilets!"

Reedy tries to smile at the reference, and says, "I wouldn't worry about Miranda. She's a resilient kid. She'll bounce back."

"I know that. But that doesn't make it any easier for her right now."

"And she may have had some disappointments, but you saved her from the big one."

"Which is?"

He rolls his eyes. "You're such an asshole, sometimes. I mean you! Her father. She knows the sacrifice you made. She knows it now, and she'll know it forever. Scottie, she'll appreciate what you did as long as she lives."

30

I chose Las Vegas for the same reason Mother Teresa chose Calcutta," Carpe Tiller tells me Friday night before dinner. "You go where you're needed."

"You can't imagine the negative energy in that place," she then adds. Probably unconsciously, she has wedged the toe of her boot underneath one of the slates on Reedy's patio.

I ask, "Your dad's a private eye, right?"

"The best."

"Is he a dowser?"

"He could be if he wanted to be," she says, finally removing her sunglasses. Her eyes are the closest thing to a neon green I have ever seen on a living creature. They have to be contact lenses with a cosmetic tint.

"Good energies?" I ask, trying to sound serious as I sip my beer.

"He is extremely open to the intuition we all have. Unfortunately, he carries a gun."

"Yup. I'll bet a gun wrecks a psychic connection every time."

She raises an eyebrow. Without even a trace of a smile on her lips, she says, "I will never understand what a person of Laura's qualities sees in a person like you."

Normalcy, I think to myself, but I keep that thought inside me.

. . .

IN THE KITCHEN, Laura winks at me as she glides between the caterers, two students in their final year at Vermont's culinary institute.

"Don't be concerned when some of the people need to be reassured that there's no meat in the pâté," she says to them. "That's just how some of these people are. They're the type who need to ask."

One of the students, a fellow barely half my age, asks, "Should we tell them that none of the food was irradiated?"

"Sure," Laura says, "feel free to tell them that." She tastes one of the stuffed mushrooms on a serving tray, and smiles approvingly. "One more thing," she continues. "You'll see a few people dangling pendulums over their food before they eat it."

"Are they that religious?" the student caterer asks, impressed.

"No, they're that pecul—" Laura says, before catching herself midsentence. "They're just dowsing it," she says instead, "to see if their bodies need whatever vitamins are in the food right then."

. . .

A QUARTET PLAYS classical music at the edge of the patio, by the doors that open into the living room. Behind them, inside the house, I see Miranda looking at a photo album on the couch. Reedy is sitting beside her.

I slide behind the violinist into the living room, and look over their shoulders at the pictures. I then kiss my daughter on the top of her head, and squeeze her shoulder gently. Each time

I have seen her today, I have either kissed her or hugged her. I have asked her twice if she knows how much her mother and I love her.

Evidently, she does: With the flexibility and strength of a child about to turn ten, she told me *of course* the second time that I asked, and then shook her head in mock irritation.

"That's a manatee," Reedy is telling her, nodding at me as I hover behind them. "I met him in Florida. On the Gulf of Mexico."

"What happened to him?" she asks.

"He got sick on some polluted water. He and a lot of his buddies. A soap company accidentally pumped some detergent into the water."

"Did you save him?"

"I helped save him. I certainly didn't do it all by myself."

"Are they all that big?" Miranda asks.

"Oh, they're big. But they're also very smart."

Miranda looks up at Reedy. "Big things can be smart, you know."

"You're right."

"Look at elephants," she says. "They're very smart."

I tap Reedy's shoulder. "The only pictures in that book are the animals that made it, right? The ones that survived?"

"Scottie, my man, of course! This is a happy occasion!"

Wide-eyed, Miranda asks, "Do you mean you keep pictures of animals that died?" I can't tell by her voice if Miranda believes that such a concept is horrifying, or if it's extremely cool in a twisted, almost-ten-year-old sort of way.

Reedy finishes the wine in his glass in one long swallow. "Another time," he says. "Another time."

. . .

PATIENCE STANDS AT the edge of the lawn, having some sort of conversation about logistics with Angel Source Brandy of Danville.

"Hello, Scottie," Angel says. For a moment I believe she is offering me her hand to shake, but that handshake becomes a hug. "No handshakes for me, only hugs," she explains. "I'm a hugger."

"Watch it," Patience says to her bridesmaid, "Scottie's the type who can get real uptight with affection."

"How are you, Angel?" I ask, ignoring my sister-in-law.

She smiles broadly. "I'm great."

"Good."

"But you're not," she continues, her smile widening even further.

"Oh, I'm fine."

"No you're not. But I won't pry."

"Thank you."

"You're welcome," she says, exposing in her grin two rows of perfect white teeth. "Patience and I were just discussing the labyrinth I've designed for the ceremony tomorrow. Have you ever walked the labyrinth, Scottie?"

"No, but I used to be a pretty good slalom skier."

She tilts her head, as if the joke might make more sense to her if she sees my face at a forty-five-degree angle. The smile never leaves her lips.

"Bad joke," I admit.

"There's no such thing as a bad joke, Scottie Winston," Angel says. "Some simply have more apparent meanings."

"I'll remember that."

"You'll like the labyrinth, I can tell," she continues. "It will do you a universe of good right now."

"I'm looking forward to it."

She shakes her head. "No you're not," she tells me, her voice one endlessly happy lilt. "But you will."

• • •

"THE SUMMER MAY be over," Reedy says, loosening his tie after dinner, and sitting back against the stone steps that lead down to the patio, "but our appeals don't have to be."

"Appeals? What are we supposed to appeal? The fact the Board thinks my daughter and I are insane?"

There is no moon tonight, but the sky is filled with stars. There is a fall chill in the air, and the rustle of leaves in the grass. The glass doors between the living room and the patio are open, and sounds drift outside to us as the caterers clean up in the kitchen.

"I've decided they shouldn't be allowed to build those new trails on Mount Republic. Not with those animals there," Reedy continues. "If you could have seen your face today in your office . . ."

"You saw on my face whatever you wanted to see."

"I saw disappointment."

"Of course you did. But it's still over."

He shakes his head. "There has to be someone who can overrule the Board." He pulls his tie through his collar, and then rolls it into a ball the size of my coffee mug. "I'm a state senator. That must mean I have some clout."

In the living room, Laura and Patience are laughing at something that Angel has said. I believe all the other guests have gone home. "No, you know as well as I do: There's no one left to appeal to."

"Then couldn't we cut some sort of deal with them? With Powder Peak? You used to always be cutting deals with people."

"You make me sound like a used-car salesman."

"You know what I mean. Isn't there some sort of deal we could offer the resort?"

"You mean to save the catamounts?"

"Right."

A shooting star crosses the sky. It's too bad that Miranda is asleep in one of the bedrooms upstairs. Miranda loves shooting stars. "A deal implies that we have something to offer Powder Peak. Something they might want. Any suggestions?"

"Well, you tell me. You know those people. What do they want?"

"They want their permits to make snow."

"Well, they can't have that."

"Then they want water. They want it to rain. They want it to rain so much that the Chittenden River returns to the way it used to be."

He snaps his necktie into the air like a bullwhip. "They wouldn't take a couple thousand candles from the Divine Lights of Vermont?"

"I doubt it. They want to make snow. That's it. That's what they want. That's what they need. Snow." I press the palms of my hands against the stone, and push myself to my feet. It's late, and suddenly I'm very tired. Reedy remains where he is, staring off at the wide field that is his lawn. Tomorrow morning, it will be trampled by sandals.

"There's some ice caked to the insides of my freezer," he mumbles. "They can have that."

I shake my head no, although he can't see me. "They'd never do it," I tell him. "They'd never trade anything of value for frozen granular."

. . .

LAURA AND I undress each other on the couch in our library. We begin slowly, necking, and for long moments she slides her tongue back and forth over my lips. In my head is the music from the rehearsal dinner, strings now as erotic as moans. When she raises her arms over her head and allows me to pull off her dress, however, we both begin to move with more urgency: I unclasp her bra at the same instant that she reaches for the zipper to my pants, and within seconds, it seems, our clothes are scattered around us on the floor.

She starts to lean me back against the wide pillows that frame the walls of the couch, her hands rubbing circles along my chest and my stomach, but I take her fingers in mine and hold them together as if she were praying, and kiss each of their tips. I pull her onto the couch beside me, massaging her thighs.

"The towel," she murmurs, opening her eyes for a brief second. I nod, remembering, and brush my lips over hers, savoring the lingering, licorice-like taste of sambuca. I then slip the fresh bath towel beneath her hips, raised, and kneel on the carpet before her, running my tongue slowly along the insides of her legs.

"I love you," I tell her, looking up into her eyes, grateful for the smile that graces her face. "I will love you forever."

. . .

LAURA'S BREATHING IS soft, her body still. Her hair has fallen across her eyes and onto the pillow. She, like me, fell instantly asleep when we went to bed three short hours ago. I am not sure what woke me now. I recall no dream, the house is soundless.

I consider stretching my legs and rolling over, but I fear if I move I will wake Laura.

In less than two hours, the dowsers will arrive at Reedy's home for their nondenominational sunrise service. The sun will rise, and the dowsers will share their new age faiths and fellowships. Reedy will stand among them, smiling, the congenial host. Ironically, Patience will not be with him. She does not want Reedy to see her on their wedding day until the ceremony. Ritual. Tradition. Superstition.

Our room is without light and shadow. I close my eyes, I try not to think. But images of my summer pass through my mind, as well as my fantasies of my tomorrow. My today. We are already four hours into the wedding day of Patience Avery and Reedy McClure. The ceremony itself is only a workday away, only nine hours. I wonder what the dowsers will do between the sunrise service at Reedy's and the ceremony at the Landaff church. Perhaps they can find the town water.

"Water is the most important thing in the world," Angel Source Brandy told me last night. She said that she almost took the name Water solely, instead of Angel Source. But then she had a vision that showed her the origins of water, its cosmic formation in the beginning: a beginning before time, before Genesis.

"In the beginning God created the heavens and the earth. The earth was without form and void, and darkness was upon the face of the deep; and the Spirit of God was moving over the face of the waters." There was water, she pointed out to me, before there was light and before there was day. She would therefore be doing water a greater justice, she explained, paying water a greater honor, if she were to take the name *source* instead. Angel Source. Because that is indeed what water is: the source and origin and informing factor of all that there is. There is nothing alive without water.

And that, she said, is why a drought is so frightening. And that is why she became a dowser. Water is everything, and—someday, if we are not careful—it will become more precious than gold. Always at least a half smile on her face, but becoming more animated as she spoke, Angel Source Brandy reminded me that already we buy water in bottles, paying premium prices for that which we once took for granted. That which was meant to be free. That which is the source of all life.

At Powder Peak, we used to call snowfall white gold. Water made snow, and that was our most precious resource: either the natural flakes that fell from the sky or the unnatural flakes that we made ourselves with our snow guns. Without snow, after all, there was no skiing. There was no business.

I sit up in bed, and brush the hair away from Laura's eyes. I kiss her softly on her cheek, and then brush my lips over hers. I purr her name into her ear, trying to wake her as gently as I can, but to wake her nonetheless. I take a deep breath to try and calm my excitement. If Reedy wants to deal—if Reedy and I together want to deal—we may have in our hands after all the one thing that Powder Peak really wants, the one thing Powder Peak really needs: the water it must have to make snow.

31

It's three o'clock, Winston. In the morning. Three fucking o'clock in the morning."

"Not here," I say, my voice chipper. "Here in Vermont, it's six a.m. The sun is rising, and it's going to be a beautiful day. Just grand."

"What do you want?" Goddard asks me. "If it's help licking your wounds, you've called the wrong man."

"Now, Goddard, you don't want to burn any bridges. As I used to counsel you and Ian, you always want to make friends with your adversaries. Right after you win. Vermont is too small a state to let people hold grudges." I glance out my kitchen window. The sun is beginning to peer over the trees; the service on Reedy's lawn is probably in full swing, with one-hundred-plus crystal dowsers hugging, singing, and sharing more intimate confessions than they might in a twelve-step group.

"If you're calling to apologize, three o'clock is a stupid time to do it. Especially on a Saturday."

"In all the years that we worked together, did I ever demonstrate the kind of stupidity that would lead me to wake you up just to say I was sorry?"

"You seem to have gotten stupid in your old age."

"Nope, Goddard. *Sorry* isn't in the lexicon. Not on a beautiful day like today."

His voice low and angry, he says, "Tell me why you're calling. I want to go back to sleep."

"Okay, I'll get right to the point. Which would you rather have for Powder Peak: the permits to build a few new trails on Republic, or the permits to use the Chittenden to make snow?"

"Don't be an ass."

"Simple question."

"You know the answer to that."

"You'd rather make snow, right?"

"Of course."

"Then I have a deal for you, Goddard Healy," I tell him, trying to imitate the voice of a television game show host. "I think we have something worth talking about."

. . .

ANGEL SOURCE BRANDY stands on the top step of the Landaff town hall, a Georgian brick box that sits across the commons from the church, with the sun high overhead. Reedy stands on her left and Patience on her right, while the rest of the bridal party is lined up on the steps below them, forming an arc—or, to use Patience's description, a phalanx. Because I will give Patience away during the actual ceremony inside the church, I too get to walk the labyrinth: a series of squiggles and circles that Angel has drawn in white lime on the grass between here and the front doors of the church. In theory, there is a pattern to the labyrinth, and if I were to look down at Angel's work from the top of the church steeple, I would see an oval, with paths inside it that are shaped vaguely like a chalice.

"At the Cathedral of Chartres," Angel says, a smile of almost unbearable happiness on her face, "the labyrinth occupies almost the entire width of the nave." She shakes her head in blissful astonishment.

The design of Patience's wedding dress is fairly conventional, and would probably be perfect for a bride half her age. It is a floor-length gown with a train that must be fifteen yards long, sleeves that puff at the shoulders, and a bodice of flowery lace. What makes the dress unique, however, is that Patience has dyed it a deep and dark blue, the color that was dowsed and chosen by bridesmaid Sas Santoli. Evidently, blue represents both balance and power, and it emits a positive atmosphere the size of a football stadium.

". . . and so I believe that the translation of that name for the labyrinth was the 'path to Jerusalem.' When people walked the labyrinth at Chartres in the thirteenth century, they were walking a metaphoric path to God."

The bridesmaids are wearing white, because their support of the marriage is pure and vestal and chaste. Unsullied. Much to Laura's chagrin, each dress is identical, a midcalf sack without adornment. They have sleeves, but might otherwise be mistaken for grocery bags with holes cut for a head and two arms. Patience vehemently denies it was her intention to create the single ugliest bridesmaid dress in the history of marriage—she says she was merely after simplicity—but this was the result. There can be no question in the mind of anyone attending this wedding: The bride is the star of this show.

". . . our path here, the bridal party's path, is a path to kindness. And serenity. For those of us supporting their bond, it is a path to love. For Patience and Reedy, it is a path to passion," Angel says, raising an eyebrow mischievously at the word *passion*.

Reedy tugs at the edge of the sleeve of his jacket, pulling it down closer to his wrist. He is wearing the sort of navy-blue business suit that is perfect for the first marriage of a man about forty. Unfortunately, he probably hasn't worn this suit in close to ten years, a decade in which both his shoulders and his stomach have broadened.

". . . and so it was during the hanging times that we lost our heritage. It was during the hanging times that we stopped dancing in moonlight, and moving intuitively over the power centers of the earth."

Two older dowsers, men much closer to Elias Gray's age than to mine, flinch at the words *hanging times*. Angel is one of a growing number of new age dowsers who believe that many of the women New Englanders hanged as witches three centuries ago were actually practicing dowsers: not water dowsers (or, ironically, water witches), but forerunners of many of today's intangible target dowsers, the breed that dowses for auras and vitamins, noxious rays and radon gas, and the pollutants and pesticides that may lurk in our foods. The two older dowsers, men who probably knew Patience through Elias, exchange brief but appalled glances.

"It wasn't hard to design this labyrinth. It wasn't hard to find a power center here in Landaff. All of you from Landaff have probably suspected all along that this town is filled—filled!—with sacred sites and power centers. Is it any coincidence that so many wonderful dowsers come from right here? Just look at the people assembled for this ceremony. Look at our bride, Patience. Look at her maid of honor, her sister Laura. And Laura's daughter, Miranda, I am told, may have the greatest gift of all."

Laura smiles down at our daughter, who preens just the tiniest bit at the compliment.

"And let us not forget that the master dowser Elias Gray was born in Landaff, he lived his entire life in Landaff, and he died here in Landaff. There may have been no dowser, ever, who helped as many people as Elias Gray, who lived as fine a life of service."

Automatically, almost everybody nods in agreement. Angel lets her pause grow into a short moment of silence and remembrance, in which we all may recall our own special memories of the old man.

"Let us begin," Angel says finally, the joy that seems almost always to envelop the woman returning to her voice. "Let us begin our short journey. And let Patience and Reedy begin their long one."

. . .

REVEREND RUSSELL TAYLOR believes in dowsing for water. Electrical currents is his explanation for the phenomenon. He believed in Elias Gray's powers, and—when they dowse for drinking water at the site itself—he has faith in the powers of all the Avery women.

He is, however, merely tolerant when Patience or her friends start dowsing for the imperceptible. He explained to Patience and Reedy when they were planning the ceremony together that he would allow "some dowsing mumbo jumbo" into the service because he loved them and he respected their opinions, but he himself did not intend to start dangling pendulums all over the sanctuary.

Consequently, that responsibility fell to Carpe Tiller. Before the service began, with her ruby pendulum she dowsed exactly where close friends and family should sit—which pews should be reserved for the Averys and which for the cousins, aunts, and uncles of Reedy McClure. She pinpointed the locations of the positive ley lines under the ground, and carefully dowsed the inside of the church for noxious rays, evil emanations, and something she called malevolent attachments.

Happily, there were none.

. . .

"WHAT I HAVE found most reassuring about your love," Reverend Taylor says to the bride and the groom, "is that it is a love I have seen grow over time. It is a love I have seen mature and age like a magnificent wine."

Taylor is the sort of man who talks a lot about fine patinas. The metaphors may have great appeal for Anna Avery's generation, but I doubt that Patience, at forty-two, was thrilled to hear her and her fiancé's love compared to old wine. She and Reedy are facing the minister, however, so if she allowed herself a small look of disgust, I was unable to see it.

"But it is a love that has also retained the enthusiasm and ebullience of youth," he continues, more aware of Patience's sensibilities than I had realized.

Of the six bridesmaids, Miranda's posture is best. She is standing at rigid attention, head high and shoulders squared, an earnest smile upon her face. The white grocery bag doesn't look as bad on her as it does on the adult women: On Miranda, it looks merely like the bloomers students might wear to gym at an old-fashioned girls' school.

"And that is no small accomplishment. A love that somehow manages to combine both the boundless enthusiasm of youth with the . . . patience . . . of age, is something rare."

The congregation smiles at his use of the word *patience*, and some of us allow ourselves a small laugh.

Laura glances at the couple, and then looks toward me. We were married in this church seventeen and one-half years ago, we stood exactly where Patience and Reedy stand now. Twice before Laura has stood as well in her current spot, beside her older sister as Patience's maid—matron, technically—of honor. She knows this ritual by heart, and she allows herself a moment to look into my eyes: Unconcerned with whatever anyone in the congregation may think who should notice, she winks.

There will never by anything matronly about Laura Avery.

• • •

THE BRIDE AND groom race briskly down the aisle, as something that sounds like trumpets blares from our church's small organ. The pair are followed with somewhat more dignity by Laura and Reedy's brother, arm in arm, and then by the remaining bridesmaids.

Anna Avery in turn takes my elbow, and together we follow the bridal party outside into the sunlight, and toward one of the three waiting Lincoln Continentals ("Limousines look stupid in Vermont," Patience explained) that were planning originally to take us to the reception at the hotel in Montpelier.

"Is everything all set?" Reedy asks me, as if he were oblivious to the fact he just got married. Patience is already seated in the lead automobile.

The driver opens the back door of the car for Anna. "Congratulations, Mr. McClure," I tell Reedy as I shake his hand, "and welcome to the Avery family."

"I'll take that as a yes. I'll assume we're all set."

"Yes. We're all ready."

"Has Ian told his people to let us onto the mountain?"

"Grudgingly. But we'll have whatever access we need."

"And you've told the drivers?"

"Sure have."

He nods his head, murmuring, "Good, very good."

Behind us Patience bangs her fist on the inside of the rear window of the Continental, and gestures for Reedy to get in the car that very second.

32

•

And so it begins. In spirit an incantation, in practice a diversion. The ultimate test for a dowser.

I stand about one hundred yards up the hill at the base of the mountain, in a wide patch of cleared land where a half-dozen trails converge in the winter. The hill feels steeper to me now than it does in February or March, when I ski down it after a run from the summit; then, this part of the mountain feels almost flat. It is the runway on which I slowly coast to a stop. Now, at moments, I feel almost as if I am falling forward.

Below me, on the flats at the foot of the mountain, the dowsers amble, trancelike, across the grass. Five women and a little girl in white, and one woman in something she calls aura blue. They are all using Y rods, even Carpe Tiller, who says that normally she prefers L rods. In the interests of harmony and convergence, however, she has agreed this one time to work as part of the team with a Y.

Reedy has left me to assist Russ Budbill, the hydrologist who recommended against tapping the Chittenden River. The two of them are now a half mile downriver, by a spot in the riverbed where the shallow waters barely look like they're moving.

There is something like a method to the efforts of the women on the flats. They are searching for power centers, sites where two or even three underground springs intersect. Three women have begun on one side of an invisible square, and three others on the adjacent side, hundreds and hundreds of yards away. The two groups of women are walking toward the center of that square, moving with small, slow, and infrequent steps. Eventually, the women will meet one another in the center of the box.

It's a good thing that Patience and Reedy have rented Montpelier's Hotel Havington for the entire day. At the pace the dowsers are moving, I doubt the bridal party will arrive at the reception much before four.

And then there is Miranda. Whenever the six adult women find a spot where veins intersect, she will dowse that spot's true potential for diversion. Can a vein be moved? Can it be used to feed the Chittenden River? In her bright red knapsack are perhaps a dozen of the wooden vegetable stakes that she and her mother use each year to mark the garden. Today she is using them to mark instead those power centers with potential.

The evergreens that border the ski slope wave in a small breeze. Ever since we emerged from the church in Landaff, the sun has been disappearing with increasing frequency behind clouds: puffy cumulus clouds that rise like whipped egg whites—like white sea foam—into high, dark blue skies.

There is, however, no rain forecast for today, and I have no reason to believe that these clouds will grow into thunderheads of hope, that they will darken from cumulus into cumulonimbus. I reach for one of the crowbars beside me, one of the six that Reedy and I managed to track down this morning, and hold it disinterestedly in my hands like a baseball bat.

Laura stops walking, and Miranda races across the grass

toward her and plants a vegetable stake into the ground. Her mother said nothing, and I hadn't even realized that Miranda was watching her.

By now, the guests must have arrived at the reception. Most of them are probably finishing their first drink, savoring their first watercress sandwich. Most of them—since most of them are dowsers—are probably toasting with great earnestness to our success.

In addition to a half-dozen crowbars, I have carried a sledgehammer with me to the ski slope, a twenty-five-pound monster that I had to borrow from a builder who lives near us.

I swing the crowbar through the air once more, and then toss it back onto the pile with the others. The sound of iron upon iron echoes across the mountain like a gong, and the women look up at me, annoyed. I have disturbed their concentration. Until the crowbar crashed onto the pile, I hadn't realized how quiet the hills had become. How still.

. . .

FOR POWDER PEAK to increase its snowmaking capabilities, the Chittenden River must rise. Water must again race through the bed in which it winds, water must flow at a pace and a depth that will allow what the experts call—coldly, in my mind—the aquatic environment to return to normal. There must be a healthy ecosystem of trout and mosquitoes, of walleyes and flies. The water must again rush at a pace of one full cubic foot per second.

The deal I have, to use Reedy's word, *cut* with Powder Peak is really very simple. If the Chittenden River's water flow can be restored to normal, which will in turn allow the resort to draw water from it to make snow, then Powder Peak will clear no more land on Mount Republic. Any new trails the resort builds will be on either the eastern side of Moosehead or Mount Chittenden, the areas of the resort furthest away from the National Forest, the wildlife habitat, and whatever catamounts remain in the area.

How the Chittenden is restored is irrelevant, as long as the method is legal and the river remains viable for snowmaking for thirty consecutive days. The fact that I am counting on a group of dowsers to pump up the water flow by diverting underground springs into the river is my business. Goddard said he didn't give a damn if I wanted to spend all afternoon jumping up and down on the mountain, doing a new age rain dance with people in tie-dyed nightshirts.

From the corner of my eye I see Miranda pushing a vegetable stake into the grass in a spot dowsed by her aunt Patience. As Patience and Carpe and Angel continue past her, Miranda holds her own Y rod directly over the stake in the ground, its point raised almost straight toward the sky, and begins whispering to herself the key questions.

Reedy has less faith than I do that Goddard Healy will keep his word to me if the dowsers do indeed succeed. But that is because Reedy hasn't worked with Goddard for over half a decade. I have. And in all those years, in all the business deals we have been involved in together, I have never seen Goddard go back on his word. He has always been a tough negotiator, but he has also, as far as I know, never lied.

The two groups of dowsers are within perhaps twenty-five yards of each other, as they each approach the center of their invisible box. Unfortunately, there are only two stakes in the ground. Given Patience and Laura's confidence this morning, I would have expected the ground to look like a slalom course by now.

Overhead, clouds continue to roll in, until, almost abruptly, there are no shadows left on the grass. It is possible these are the clouds due here late tomorrow or Monday, the clouds that are supposed to tease us with inconsequential sprinkles for perhaps half a day.

Angel stops walking and looks up, her face registering surprise at the suddenly overcast skies. She may have been so deep in concentration that she was unaware of the approaching clouds. After a moment she resumes her methodic shuffle, however, her feet never leaving the ground.

. . .

WHEN THE DOWSERS have completed their survey, they have found three power centers. The six women surround Miranda while she stands over the third and final stake, dowsing its potential to salvage the Chittenden River. I stand up, brush some dry dirt off my suit pants, and start down the hill with the crowbars. I'll have to return for the sledgehammer.

"So? Success?" I ask the group generally, not directing my question at any one of the dowsers. They are all watching Miranda intently, as she stands over the small piece of wood, trembling slightly.

Of the six women, only Angel is smiling. When it is evident that no one else plans on answering my question, she whispers to me, "As far as power centers go, these are not very impressive."

It has never seriously crossed my mind that these women will not succeed. Since the middle of last night when I first had the idea, I have been firmly convinced that between my wife and my daughter, between my sister-in-law and her friends, there will be sufficient dowsing prowess to divert all the water we want into the Chittenden.

. . .

A HALF MILE downriver, Reedy and Russ Budbill are waiting patiently, hoping to be able to gauge an increase in the water flow. In my vision last night, I imagined that the dowsers would be able to divert so much water into the river that before our very eyes the water level would begin to climb. It would begin to run over the tops of the dry stones in the riverbed, it would begin to inch its way up the bank, covering the exposed roots of trees, the dirt that has become almost the color of sand. In my mind's eye, I saw it rising faster than runoff from the mountains after the first big thaw, I saw it climbing faster than the Winooski River rose that day in 1992 when ice jammed up the river in March, and the water flooded over the banks and into the state capital.

I wonder now if my vision of water rising in the Chittenden riverbed was all just a dream. I wonder if I have set myself and my daughter up for yet one more defeat. In a summer with loss, perhaps there is no recovery in fall. Fall, after all, is no season for healing.

I place the sledgehammer on the ground silently, laying it in the grass a few feet from the crowbars. The Y rod in Miranda's hands twitches, and then twists abruptly toward the ground. She asks it a question, and it responds. The sky above her—the sky above all of us—has steadily darkened. If the drizzle does arrive a day or two early, Patience and her bridesmaids might wind up doused at the reception—an irony that might be funny if this weren't Patience's wedding day.

Finally Miranda backs away from the last vegetable stake, and drops her Y rod to her side. She looks breathless and tired, and that part of me that loves her as desperately as any father can love his daughter wants to go to her and hold her and tell her what a fine job she has done, but now she can relax.

Somehow I restrain the impulse, somehow I remain still where I am. I watch as Laura kneels on the grass before her, and takes Miranda's free hand in hers. "How many veins intersect here?" she asks.

"Three. It's a better spot than the others," Miranda says, waving her Y rod in the general direction of the other two stakes.

"Are the veins strong?"

She shrugs noncommittally, unimpressed by what she has learned here.

"Do they currently feed into the Chittenden River?"

Miranda shakes her head no. "But they could."

"What about the veins at the other centers? Can we move them too?"

"I think so."

Laura stands up. "All right then. Let's see what happens." She then picks up one of the six crowbars and forces it into the ground as if it were a giant building nail.

. . .

I DON'T KNOW if Reedy and Russ Budbill can hear the sound of Patience Avery slamming the sledgehammer onto the top of the crowbar, banging it into the ground. I hope that they can, if only as a signal that the process has begun.

Laura, again kneeling, holds the crowbar steady with both hands. Drops of sweat have begun to form along Patience's forehead, where only an hour before she was wearing a veil. Every time she hoists the sledgehammer back up over her head, the shoulders of her wedding gown fold together like an accordion, and then on her downswing stretch further than they were ever designed to. Any moment, those shoulders might tear.

"Are you sure you don't want me to do that?" I ask for the third time.

Patience has insisted on wielding the sledgehammer because she is a dowser and I am not. If Miranda were older and stronger, she would probably have Miranda swinging the hammer right now.

Patience rests the sledgehammer by her side for a moment, and takes in a great swallow of air. "Was I speaking English when I said I was positive?" she answers, irritated with both my request and my persistence.

"He was only asking to be nice," Laura says sternly to her sister, defending me. "The fact is, this is hard work."

"And you do look ridiculous," I add undiplomatically, a reflex in self-defense.

Patience watches me for a long moment. "Fine," she says simply, about as close as she ever comes to a truce. An apology.

A raindrop falls onto my hand, and I stare up into the sky. As I do, I feel a second drop splash onto my forehead, and then almost instantly a third.

"Let's wrap this up, Patience," Laura says. "We need to get you to your reception."

. . .

THE CLOUDS BURST. Patience swings the sledgehammer down onto the third crowbar above the third power center for the last time, just as the skies are uncorked. It is as if the final wrought iron bang is the signal for the seams of the woolpack above us to be ripped open, and ablution to fall.

No, not fall. This rain doesn't fall. This is not the "gentle rain" of Archer Moody's prayers. This is a rain that showers upon us in sheets, a rain that flows down from the clouds in waves, a river begun in the sky, a teeming stream that I know in my heart was formed in the heavens. The rain descends in literal curtains, shielding for whole seconds at a time the people standing beside each of us.

"It's raining!" Angel Source Brandy screams happily, twirling amid drapes of water. "It's raining!"

It is indeed. It is a downpour. But although it is not the gentle rain prayed for by Archer Moody, nor is it the punishing rain of a monsoon or a hurricane. It is a good rain, a windless rain, a rain without gale, a storm without gusts. It is the rain that is not due for days, but the rain we have needed for months. And I know now it will continue raining for days, I know it with the confidence of a life lived among the fantastic, a life lived among the astonishing, the wonderful, the unexpected, the bizarre.

Laura rises slowly to her feet and stares up into the tidal wave, smiling, as her eye makeup begins to run down her cheeks and neck, dripping in splotches of blue onto her snow-white dress. "Where did this come from?" she asks, yelling to be heard over the torrent. "Where did this come from?"

It is a question asked rhetorically, a question asked because while we all think that we know the answer . . . none of us, not even Laura or Patience or Miranda, is prepared just yet to verbalize it.

Katherine Whiting, a respected and dignified physician, is transformed before my eyes into Katie, a girl/woman hopping in place in the grass, her arms raised over her head in victory and success.

"You know the answer to that better than me!" Katie screams hysterically at my wife. "You know, you know, you know!"

Laura stands still for a brief moment, then nods her head that she does. In one swift flurry of motion she turns to our daughter and takes both of Miranda's hands in hers, giggling, and mother and daughter start to spin, jumping and dancing amid balneal waters of hope. Patience looks at them, and then at her bridesmaids, and then—with a wide-eyed smile of astonishment on her face—she too starts to laugh.

The water surges through grass and dirt into the earth, it fills underground veins and cavities and springs. Manna. The drops pelt our faces and hands, the rain soaks almost instantly through our clothes, moistening, refreshing, soothing our skin. Holy water. Drenched, Carpe Tiller and Sas Santoli fall together into each other's arms, twins clad in white, a mirror, squeezing each other and pounding each other's back.

"Believe it, Scottie Winston!" Patience commands me, shouting over the tempest, her voice euphoric.

"I do!"

"Believe!"

"I do!" I shout back, as rainwater courses through my hair and down my spine, as it fills my shoes and overflows the cuffs on my pants. But I believe not just in the power of these women, each an enchantress, a wizard, a magician, a witch; I believe also that the rain falling now will continue falling for days. It will slow, once it has rewarded these women—these women and me, these women and Reedy McClure—for our faith, but it will continue. It will continue to rain until the Chittenden River flows as it was meant to, it will continue to rain until the springs deep below us are strong and healthy and powerful, until those springs are able to sustain the Chittenden River for . . . ever.

This too is my faith.

From the woods just beyond the base lodge, Reedy and Russ Budbill start running up the hill, splashing whole puddles of water into the air with every step.

"The river! Scottie, you won't believe it!" Reedy is screaming, smiling. "You won't believe it!"

I shake my head that he is wrong. "I sure will!" I scream back, unsure for one moment whether the water running down the sides of my face is rainfall or tears, but never for one second caring. "I sure will!" I scream again as loud as I can, yelling louder than I've ever yelled in my life, yelling as I spread wide my arms and stare up into the sky.

"I . . . will!"

Part Three

33

Neither my father nor I ever saw catamounts again.

We looked for them. We looked for them all the time, we looked for them everywhere that we went. But we never saw one again, and as the years grew into decades our memories likewise grew dim—as did our conviction that the creature we had seen was without question the catamount.

Once, we—my father, my mother, and I—returned to Powder Peak, and we visited the area on Mount Republic where we had seen the animals. It was in the summer, a year after the resort had reopened the tramway to tourists, and people could again hike freely throughout the mountains. My father had started his new practice by then, one he would run for twenty-plus years without any partners (it was, he would say, just him and his shingle).

We wandered all the way to the top of the mountain, and we hiked deep into the evergreens, following the path we assumed the catamounts had taken. We even had a picnic on the rocks where another small family—in our wanting eyes, a mother and two cubs—may have watched my father and me disappear on a chairlift down the mountain.

Goddard Healy kept his word to my father, and to this day no ski trails wind into those woods. I don't believe Ian Rawls ever forgave my father for his stand, but I think his old law partners and many of his old friends did. At least they acted that way when they ran into him on the streets of Montpelier, or at the county fairs and parades that pepper a Vermont summer.

My mother refuses to move in with my family these days, just as her mother refused always to move in with her. She lives still in the house that she and my father bought in Landaff soon after they were married, although the place has begun to look pretty tired.

Unlike my mother and my grandmother, I actually married a local boy. My father said it spoke volumes about Vermont, and perhaps something about our abilities as a people to heal and forgive and to love, but I married the son of the man who cross-examined me one day years ago in the statehouse cafeteria. I married John Bussey's son Parker (a name that means, ironically, "guardian of the park" in Middle English).

My father never learned to dowse in his life, but I think that he could have if he had wanted to. He died a believer. When he would watch his granddaughter dowse—dowsing with more assurance than me, more success than my mother—he would shake his head and smile. "Natural selection," he used to say. "We're breeding a generation of extrasensory giants."

He never took credit for his role in that evolution, attributing it all to an Avery dowsing gene. But there is no doubt in my mind that what makes my children as fine and wonderful as they are—what makes them kind, what gives them faith—is attributable as well to the heart they received from my father.